Alexis Wright is a member of the Waanyi nation of the southern highlands of the Gulf of Carpentaria. Her books include *Grog War*, a study of alcohol abuse in the outback town of Tennant Creek, and the novel *Plains of Promise*, which was shortlisted for the Commonwealth Prize, the *Age* Book of the Year Award and the NSW Premier's Award for Fiction.

Carpentaria has won the 2007 Miles Franklin Literary Award, the Australian Literature Society Gold Medal, the Victorian Premier's Award for Fiction, the Queensland Premier's Award for Fiction and the ABIA Literary Fiction Book of the Year.

ALEXIS WRIGHT

Carpentaria

GIRAMONDO

FIRST PUBLISHED 2006
FOR THE WRITING & SOCIETY RESEARCH GROUP
AT THE UNIVERSITY OF WESTERN SYDNEY
BY THE GIRAMONDO PUBLISHING COMPANY
PO BOX 752 ARTARMON NSW 1570 AUSTRALIA
WWW.GIRAMONDOPUBLISHING.COM

DESIGNED BY HARRY WILLIAMSON
TYPESET BY ANDREW DAVIES
IN 10/17 PT BASKERVILLE
PRINTED AND BOUND BY MCPHERSON'S PRINTING GROUP
DISTRIBUTED IN AUSTRALIA BY TOWER BOOKS

NATIONAL LIBRARY OF AUSTRALIA
CATALOGUING-IN-PUBLICATION DATA:

WRIGHT, ALEXIS, 1950– .
CARPENTARIA.

B FORMAT EDITION 2007

ISBN 978 1 920882 31 0

I. TITLE.

A823.3

FOR TOLY

Inspired by all of the beauty that comes
from having an ancient homeland that is
deeply loved by those who guard it, and
especially by my countrymen, Murrandoo
Yanner and Clarence Waldon.

The first words got polluted
Like river water in the morning
Flowing with the dirt
Of blurbs and the front pages.
My only drink is meaning from the deep brain,
What the birds and the grass and the stones drink.
Let everything flow
Up to the four elements,
Up to water and earth and fire and air.

Seamus Heaney, 'The First Words'

CONTENTS

Chapter 1
From time immemorial

A NATION CHANTS, *BUT WE KNOW YOUR STORY ALREADY.*

THE BELLS PEAL EVERYWHERE.

CHURCH BELLS CALLING THE FAITHFUL TO THE TABERNACLE WHERE THE GATES OF HEAVEN WILL OPEN, BUT NOT FOR THE WICKED. CALLING INNOCENT LITTLE BLACK GIRLS FROM A DISTANT COMMUNITY WHERE THE WHITE DOVE BEARING AN OLIVE BRANCH NEVER LANDS. LITTLE GIRLS WHO COME BACK HOME AFTER CHURCH ON SUNDAY, WHO LOOK AROUND THEMSELVES AT THE HUMAN FALLOUT AND ANNOUNCE MATTER-OF-FACTLY, *ARMAGEDDON BEGINS HERE.*

....

The ancestral serpent, a creature larger than storm clouds, came down from the stars, laden with its own creative enormity. It moved graciously – if you had been watching with the eyes of a bird hovering in the sky far above the ground. Looking down at the serpent's wet body, glistening from the ancient sunlight, long before man was a creature who could contemplate the next moment in time. It came down those billions of years ago, to crawl on its heavy belly, all around the wet clay soils in the Gulf of Carpentaria.

Picture the creative serpent, scoring deep into – scouring down through – the slippery underground of the mudflats, leaving in its wake the thunder of tunnels collapsing to form deep sunken valleys. The sea water following in the serpent's wake, swarming in a frenzy of tidal waves, soon changed colour from ocean blue to the yellow of mud. The water filled the swirling tracks to form the mighty bending rivers spread across the vast plains of the Gulf country. The serpent travelled over the marine plains, over the salt flats, through the salt dunes, past the mangrove forests and crawled inland. Then it went back to the sea. And it came out at another spot along the coastline and crawled inland and back again. When it finished creating the many rivers in its wake, it created one last river, no larger or smaller than the others, a river which offers no apologies for its discontent with people who do not know it. This is where the giant serpent continues to live deep down under the ground in a vast network of limestone aquifers. They say its being is porous; it permeates everything. It is all around in the atmosphere and is attached to the lives of the river people like skin.

This tidal river snake of flowing mud takes in breaths of a size that is difficult to comprehend. Imagine the serpent's breathing rhythms as the tide flows inland, edging towards the spring waters nestled deeply in the gorges of an ancient limestone plateau covered with rattling grasses dried yellow from the prevailing winds. Then with the outward breath, the tide turns and the serpent flows back to its own circulating mass of shallow waters in the giant water basin in a crook of the mainland whose sides separate it from the open sea.

To catch this breath in the river you need the patience of one who can spend days doing nothing. If you wait under the rivergum where those up-to-no-good Mission-bred kids accidentally hanged Cry-baby Sally, the tip of the dead branch points to where you will see how the serpent's breath fights its way through in a tunnel of wind, creating ripples that shimmer silver, similar to the scales of a small, nocturnal serpent, thrashing in anger whenever the light hits its slippery translucent body, making it writhe and wrench to escape back into its natural environment of darkness.

The inside knowledge about this river and coastal region is the Aboriginal Law handed down through the ages since time began. Otherwise, how would one know where to look for the hidden underwater courses in the vast flooding mud plains, full of serpents and fish in the monsoon season? Can someone who did not grow up in a place that is sometimes under water, sometimes bone-dry, know when the trade winds blowing off the southern and northern hemispheres will merge in summer? Know the moment of climatic change better than they know themselves? Who fishes in the yellow-coloured monsoonal runoff from the drainages, with sheets of deep water pouring into the wide rivers swollen over their banks, filling vast plains with floodwaters? The cyclones linger and regroup, the rain never stops pouring, but the fat fish are abundant.

It takes a particular kind of knowledge to go with the river, whatever its mood. It is about there being no difference between you and the movement of water as it seasonally shifts its tracks according to its own mood. A river that spurns human endeavour in one dramatic gesture, jilting a lover who has never really been known, as it did to the frontier town built on its banks in the hectic heyday of colonial vigour. A town intended to serve as a port for the shipping trade for the hinterland of Northern Australia.

In one moment, during a Wet season early in the last century, the town lost its harbour waters when the river simply decided to change course, to bypass it by several kilometres. Just like that. Now the waterless port survives with more or less nothing to do. Its citizens continue to engage in a dialogue with themselves passed down the generations, on why the town should continue to exist. They stayed on to safeguard the northern coastline from invasion by the Yellow Peril. A dreadful vision, a long yellow streak marching behind an arrowhead pointing straight for the little town of Desperance. Eventually the heat subsided. When the Yellow Peril did not invade, everyone had a good look around and found a more contemporary reason for existence. It meant the town still had to be vigilant. Duty did not fall on one or two; duty was everybody's business. To keep a good eye out for whenever the moment presented itself, to give voice to a testimonial far beyond personal experience – to comment on the state of their blacks. To do so was regarded as an economic contribution to State rights, then, as an afterthought, to maintaining the decent society of the nation as a whole.

Normal Phantom was an old tribal man, who lived all of his life in the dense Pricklebush scrub on the edge of town. He lived amidst thickets of closely-growing slender plants with barely anything for leaves, that never gave an ant an inch of shelter under a thousand thorny branches. This foreign infestation on the edge of Desperance grew out of an era long before anyone in the Phantom family could remember. They had lived in a human dumping-ground next to the town tip since the day Normal Phantom was born. All choked up, living piled up together in trash humpies made of tin, cloth, and plastic too, salvaged from the rubbish dump. The descendants of the pioneer families, who claimed ownership of the town, said *the Aboriginal was really not part of the town at all.* Sure, they worked the dunny cart in the old days, carted the rubbish and swept the street. *Furthermore*, they said, *the Aboriginal was dumped here by the pastoralists, because they refused to pay the blackfella equal wages, even when it came in. Right on the edge of some-body else's town, didn't they?* Dumped the lot of them without any sign of lock, stock or barrel.

No, the Pricklebush was from the time before the motor car, when goods and chattels came up by camel train until Abdul and Abdullah, the old Afghan brothers, disappeared along the track called the 'lifeline', connecting north to south. After much time had passed the jokes came about Afghans being *shifty dogs*, *dodgy dogs*, *murdering dogs* and *unreliable*. When the cupboards turned bare, the town talk finally turned to the realisation that very likely the camel men were never coming back – then everyone in town assumed they had died. A few of the Christian-minded, trying to capitalise on the gross lack of decency in town, sniffed, *Well! That ought to teach you now, won't it?* But no one else thought so, because by then the grog and the tucker was being freighted up by mail truck, which everyone thought was a more convenient method of road transport by any stretch of the imagination.

One cloud-covered night, the camels finally turned up in Desperance, jingling and a-jangling, their foreign bells swaying around their necks, vespers on such a still night. The residents woke up in childlike fright, sitting straight up in their beds, eyes wide open like zombies, seeing dark figures moving in their pitch-black bedroom, same time reckoning it was ghosts with an Afghan smell, true God, just came straight in, levitating, taking over, helping themselves, walking around people's homes with no *mind youse*, not one shred of good manners whatsoever. Couldn't even knock on the door first before coming into someone's house. That was the trouble with new Australians the town claimed: *Even dead ones had no manners*. Unnaturalised. Really un-Australian. *You shoulda sent out a search party*. What a relief it was for dawn to come and everyone could see for themselves it was just poor old Abdul's and Abdullah's camels.

Over the following days no one thought to capture the animals to retrieve the rotting pack saddles. The townsfolk had a deeply felt aversion to touching the belongings of dark-skinned foreigners – or their animals. So, the camels just wandered around at their own will, covered with sores from the rotting packs of foodstuff: flour, sugar, grain growing sprouts that had died, still strapped over and hanging off their backs until something had to be done. The poor beasts were officially rounded up. The screaming, uncooperative animals didn't comprehend English, or barbarism either. After being hounded for several hours by their pursuers on foot and horseback, and stoned and whipped, the camels were eventually moved out over the claypans and shot. In the archival records written with a thick nib by a heavy-handed municipal clerk it is recorded, *Camels removed*. The first entry of work completed by the Town's Municipal Council.

In the old camel-drivers' camps the seeds of mimosa embedded in camel dung sprouted their hard little shoots in the Wet season. Thousands of seeds spread along every track and gully, flooding with sheetwater from the rain to regenerate in shallow mud pools. The shoots sent down their fat roots to take a steely grip on the clay-pans, holding the land together in a mirage that looked like it might last forever without water. In this mirage the cattle properties prospered on traditional lands taken but never ceded. Today, herds of Brahman-cross cattle leave their tracks crisscrossing the landscape in the dry season, as they search for stubbly patches of bluegrass and grind the top layers of soil to powdered bulldust.

The Pricklebush mob say that Normal Phantom could grab hold of the river in his mind and live with it as his father's fathers did before him. His ancestors were the river people, who were living with the river from before time began. Normal was like ebbing water, he came and went on the flowing waters of the river right out to the sea. He stayed away on the water as long as he pleased. He knew fish, and was on friendly terms with gropers, the giant codfish of the Gulf sea, that swam in schools of fifty or more, on the move right up the river following his boat in for company. The old people say the groper lives for hundreds of years and maybe Normal would too. When he talked about the stars, they said he knew as much about the sky as he did about water. The prickly bush mob said he had always chased the constellations: *We watched him as a little boy running off into the night trying to catch stars.* They were certain he knew the secret of getting there. They thought he must go right up to the stars in the company of groper fish when it stormed at sea, when the sea and the sky became one, because, otherwise, how could he have come back?

'How you do that?' was the question everyone asked.

'The water doesn't worry me,' Normal Phantom answered simply, although he knew that when his mind went for a walk, his body followed.

Everyone in Desperance was used to the sight of Normal's jeep driving north to meet the river's edge. It was the only vehicle he had ever owned. Always, the small tinnie boat, full of dints, a stray bullet hole or two, strapped onto the roof. A vessel purchased with cross-country road transport in mind, much more than water safety.

They say he knew these deep muddy waters better than the big salties: crocs that got tangled up in the nets in the middle of the night. Glassy-eyed monsters that came over the side of his tiny craft looking for action with the big river man. Jaws charging for a winner-takes-all kind of fight in the swamping boat, snapping in full flight, water splashing up into a storm with the swishing, thrash, thrash, thrashing of an angry tail against the side of the boat. People like to remember Normal saying in melancholy fashion (faking a thoroughly modern Americanised impersonation of a Presidential Captain Hook): those snapping jaws meant diddly squat to him. Meanwhile, he moved like a hopping hare, fumbling for what seemed like ages to find the gun. Normal ended hundreds of lives of prehistoric living fossils this way, with his gun pointing all over the place in a turmoil of water and thick leather crankiness, until he made a direct hit between the eyes of the reptile caught in an instant of moonlight.

In this otherwise quietly living population of about three hundred people, no living soul remembered what the port had looked like before. No picture could be put on display in a showcase at the museum of scarce memorabilia, because no one at the time of the heyday thought it was worthwhile to take a photo. But everybody knew that this was Normal's river.

One day, someone in town, whose name is not worth a mention, was languishing around in a laconic stupor following the months of heatwave in the Wet season build-up, waiting for the rain to come. Lying flat-out like a corpse on the bare linoleum floor in the hallway of a house exactly like the one next door. Capturing in a long sigh of appreciation the northern sea breezes that came waltzing straight over twenty-five kilometres of mudflats, whistling their arrival through the front door while, on the way out, slamming the back door open and shut. All of a sudden this someone of no consequence thought of changing the name of the river to Normal. And, in a town where change never came easy, it came to be.

There was a celebration by the local Shire Council. The occasion was the anniversary of the port's first one hundred years. It coincided with a spate of unusual happenings during a short-lived era of Aboriginal domination of the Council. *Harmless coercing of the natives,* the social planners hummed, anxious to make deals happen for the impending mining boom. Meaningful coexistence could now accommodate almost any request whatsoever, including changing a river's name to Normal. During this honeymoon period, those Aboriginal people who took the plunge to be councillors, wisely used their time in public office to pursue scraps of personal gain for their own families living amidst the muck of third-world poverty.

All this was part and parcel of the excitement of Desperance when the first multinational mining company came into the region. Numerous short-lived profiteering schemes were concocted for the locals, in order to serve the big company's own interests as they set about pillaging the region's treasure trove: the publicly touted curve of an underground range embedded with minerals.

The elaborate white linen ceremony, paid for by the mining company, attracted southern politicians who flew in for the day. Most of them were known by the local dignitaries as a bunch of fly-by-nighters. And what's more, as they rolled out the welcome smile, some locals whispered unmentionable insults behind the backs of their very important visitors. Other locals who liked the sound of their own voices attacked the politicians straight out with a diatribe of insults. Yelling out, the crowd picked up bits wafting in the wind gusts: *Youse are always cowering down on the ground. Are youse the runt of the Australian political litter or something? Yah! falling over yaselves to any foreign investor flocking up the steps of Parliament, knocking on the big door, and smelling like money.*

The politicians and mining executives mingled uncomfortably with the crowd, then pushed themselves up against the old hero Normal for a photo opportunity, and got snapped by members of the media circus who had jockeyed for free rides on the official executive jets. Then everything got ruined by a normal sort of dust storm thundering in from the south. A thick wall of red dust mingled with all manner of crunched vegetation and plastic shopping bags gathered up in its path, damaging the cut sandwiches when it came through. The fidget-prone adults panicked, running for cover along with their red and green cordial-stained screaming children.

Then came a violent electrical storm when the rain ruined the day anyway – as the town's sceptics said it would. A taut occasion, despite these dramatic interventions; enough time for the now disposed-of State Premier to complete the ceremony of officially changing the name of the river from that of a long deceased Imperial Queen, to 'Normal's River'. Traditional people gathered up for the event mumbled, *Ngabarn, Ngabarn, Mandagi,* and so did

Normal in a very loud and sour-sounding voice over the loud-speaker in his extremely short thankyou address, although those who knew a fruit salad full of abuse in the local languages knew he was not saying *Thank you! Thank you!* and belly-laughed themselves silly because the river only had one name from the beginning of time. It was called *Wangala*.

It was a funny thing about the river. Anybody and everybody thought they might ride this river like some legendary buck-jumping wild horse called Diesel or Gidgee or Mulga. People were always travelling up to the northern coastline over the rough roads of the Gulf on long weekends. They'd haul up and launch straight over the side into the yellow river: flash fishing boats with sixties country and western names, like *Donna*, *Stella* and *Trixie*. Bright-coloured boats, powered by engines of many horsepowers, bought with top dollar gained from doing stretch shifts two kilometres down underground, hauling up rich ores scraped from the mother load embedded in sequences of rock that looked like the growth rings of a powerful, ancient being.

And on the water they would cast a line here, a line there, over the sides with state of the art fishing tackle, but no knowledge of the way of the river. Nothing was thought about it. There was a considerable number of people living in the region now, with the great influx of mine workers who had nothing to do on their days off. More new mines became established in the region with little regard to anyone's say-so.

After the mining stopped, neither Normal Phantom and his family, nor his family's relations, past or present, rated a mention in the official version of the region's history. There was no tangible evidence of their existence. Even in Uncle Micky's collection of bullet cartridges.

Micky had lived with a metal detector for God knows how long.

He said he had a fever which drove him on because he would never know when he picked up the last piece of evidence – all of those forty-fours, thirty thirtys, three-o-threes, twelve gauges – all kinds of cartridges used in the massacre of the local tribes. He had maps, names of witnesses, details, the lot. A walking encyclopaedia. Now his voice lives on in the great archive of cassettes which he left for the war trials he predicted would happen one day. But no tourists go to Micky's museum. Maybe because it was built in the wrong spot. That's fighting for you. Fighting, fighting all the time for a bit of land and a little bit of recognition.

All the old mines, old mining equipment, old miners, old miners' huts, skeletons of miners in the cupboard, anything to do with mining was packaged in a mishmash of nothing words and marketed on gloss as the ultimate of local tourist attractions. The shiny covers of these tourist brochures celebrating selected historical sites and museums ought to grab you from across the room at airports, hotels and motels, or from the rack of any tourist or travel centre selling the highlights of mining. You can't even hide the stuff because of its iridescence.

But this was not Vaudeville. Wars were fought here. If you had your patch destroyed you'd be screaming too. The serpent's covenant permeates everything, even the little black girls with hair combed back off their faces and bobby-pinned neatly for church, listening quietly to the nation that claims to know everything except the exact date its world will end. Then, almost whispering, they shyly ask if the weather has been forecast correctly today.

If you are someone who visits old cemeteries, wait awhile if you visit the water people. The old Gulf country men and women who took our besieged memories to the grave might just climb out of the mud and tell you the real story of what happened here.

Chapter 2
Angel Day

ONE EVENING IN THE DRIEST GRASSES IN THE WORLD, A CHILD WHO WAS NO STRANGER TO HER PEOPLE, ASKED IF ANYONE COULD FIND HOPE.

THE PEOPLE OF PARABLE AND PROPHECY PONDERED WHAT WAS HOPELESS AND FINALLY DECLARED THEY NO LONGER KNEW WHAT HOPE WAS.

THE CLOCKS, TICK-A-TY TOCK, LOOKED AS THOUGH THEY MIGHT RUN OUT OF TIME. LUCKILY, THE GHOSTS IN THE MEMORIES OF THE OLD FOLK WERE LISTENING, AND SAID ANYONE CAN FIND HOPE IN THE STORIES: THE BIG STORIES AND THE LITTLE ONES IN BETWEEN. SO...

....

Normal Phantom turned away from the glory of the storm clouds lacing the sea, to look in the eye, grab by the horns, all the grey-coloured calamities of a man's life. Behold the sight of welcome home, embedded in the never-ending rattling corrugated-iron shanty fortress, built from the sprinklings of holy water, charms, spirits, lures acquired from packets of hair dye, and discarded materials pinched from the rubbish dump across the road.

This was Number One house. Normal Phantom's house was the first blackfella place built on the edge of Desperance, before the two warring nations, one with, one without land, ended up circling the whole town. The structure of the house was a tribute to far-off monuments representing noteworthy moments of history.

His marriage to Angel Day had climbed the crest of a mountain

of misgiving, and, 'only when she had gone', was he able to understand that the woman had always been a hornet's nest waiting to
be disturbed. After three decades of shared life, such a single,
independent thought was a total revelation to a big man like
Normal Phantom.

The house was a hornet's nest, like Angel Day, and Normal
spoke of it as if it were her. The house had been inadvertently built
on the top of the nest of a snake spirit. He always blamed her for
that. From day one, he knew and always said, 'This house makes
my bones ache.' He told her how he felt something was wrong, how
he could feel something coming from under the ground into his
bones. He only spoke to deaf ears. But he knew whenever he left
the house, he would instantly feel as though he had unshackled
himself from the weight of a sack strapped over his back. Then,
when he came back, he felt as though he had been hypnotised
into thinking that he would never be able to move away from its
field of gravitation again, even if he willed himself from it. Perhaps
some day he would be stuck forever. So what? He should have told
someone who cared.

He knew such a phenomenon existed, because each time he
left, it was harder to pull himself away from the house. 'Move,' he
told her, but if she had heard anything he said, she gave her usual
response to the movement of his lips and in her flattest voice said,
'No way.'

'I was born near lilies so I must see lilies,' she once told him,
calmly pouting towards the waterlilies growing in the swamp at the
back, and once that happened, not even a grappling pick would
have plied another word about the matter from her own sweet lips.

To be fair, Angel Day had looked around for days before
choosing what she called 'her spot', if anyone could be so blatantly
shameless to go around thinking they were so high and mighty,
to just pluck out a spot for themselves in the bush and say, 'This is

mine.' Well! Our Angel did that and got away with it. The spot she chose was amidst a grove of prickly pear thickets, right next to the mosquito-swarming swamp. She said she chose it because it was a private place not seen from the road. Afterwards, still all hot and bothered from searching up and down the countryside for her house site, she parked herself.

The first six children born had sat beside her under the shade of a snappy gum until she erected a more permanent shade with two blankets. This was all she owned, but it was good enough. She told Norm, when he returned from the sea next time and found her there, that she would not move again. He retaliated by not speaking to her for days. While those two fought out their differences, the whole family lived their daily lives under the blankets, six months of cold winds, then heat, followed by rain blowing left, right and centre down on top of them, again and again, until? Until there was peace. Norm did nothing, not a single thing, to help her to build a roof over their heads – as if that would stop Angel Day from doing what she wanted.

He caught bream fish if he felt like it: he did no more, and no less. If there were no fish, he expected her to provide, which she did. The whole of Uptown rallied over that poor Aboriginal woman struggling under a tree with her children, condemning Normal Phantom. If he thought there was going to be an end of it, he was wrong. She, smarter than a snake, plied enough work out of pity to permeate the pure, undiluted quintessential essence of herself into that ground, much as she used magic to erect a home from scraps.

Angel Day always claimed the spot where she forced Norm to continue building their house was the best place they had ever lived, because all she had to do was walk across the road to the rubbish dump, and there she could get anything her heart desired – *for free*. She thought the dump was magnificent, as anyone dirt poor would. The way she talked, you would have thought she was a very rich woman, and it was nothing for her to walk back and forth to the dump two dozen times a day to cart back pieces of sheet iron, jerry cans, bits of car bodies, pieces of rope, logs, plastic, discarded curtains and old clothing. She got the family through the Wet as dry as a bone. Diligently, she undertook the chore of checking for leaks, making alterations, choosing the right bits and pieces from her pile of accumulated junk which she leant, tied or stitched to the original blankets, until she ended up with an igloo made of rubbish.

Norm fretted, saying, Blah! Blah! This and that. Saying that he thought his children had disappeared forever in amongst the piles of old clothes stored inside their dark, dank dwelling. Constantly he called them, 'Come outside,' so he could see them, lest they were tricked by the lurking snake. She never heard a single word. She was busy with blood on her bare hands from extracting nails from rotted timber. The six little children helped her by sizing the nails, bolts and screws. And months passed by.

Norm was still a young man who either wanted to be out at sea fishing, or else riding wild horses on the spinifex-covered high plains, working with the cattle. Away jobs in the stock camps. Oh! Those were hard but fair days that was the truth. Working with cattle, grown men whipped the living Jesus out of other grown men but who cared? He looked at all this newfangled activity of self-sufficiency being built on sheer stubbornness and said to her his final word, 'Let's go back to the river country.' He loved the sound of the clear waters running through petrified forests hidden for millions of years beneath the gently calling sounds of fronds dangling down from the old palms and fruit-giving date trees lining the river. But Angel Day had crossed the bridge. She had no jolly intention of leaving. Look! Can't you see the pile of riches she had accumulated? Was all this for nothing? 'How would I be able to move all of this down there?' she replied.

Goodness! Those were modern days, and Angel Day was a very rich woman, too good now in comparison to the years she had spent living, eating and sleeping...where? in a swag? Oh! Those were the good old days Norm dreamed for. Her fortunes were growing out of hand. She now possessed dozens of Heinz baked bean tins and pickle bottles full of nails, loose screws and bolts. She became a genius in the new ideas of blackfella advancement. Bureaucratic people for the *Aborigines* department said she had 'Go'. She became a prime example of government policies at work and to prove it, they came and took pictures of her with a Pentax camera for a report.

The old Pricklebush people said what Angel Day had was purely magical, it was true, but sorry to say, of no benefit to anyone. This led them to say privately that she had acquired a disease from making her life out of living in other people's rubbish. Who knew what kind of lurgies lurked in white trash? The dump was full of disease. And the Pricklebush said, *If she had any sense, she ought to stay right away from the rubbish dump*. It was of no benefit to anyone if she had magical powers to make her more like the white people.

At the same time, there was no sense in denying the truth staring them in the face because there evidently was some: the great magnanimity given to Angel Day by the haunting spirits residing in the smelly residue, deep down in the gloomy, slime-dripping serpentine caverns of the dump. The ponderous, thinking people among the Pricklebush jumped to her defence, *Who was Normal to say he wanted to live elsewhere, under a log with a bit of rag, worse than a dog?* Angel accused him of chucking rubbish in her face. She said he did not think properly. When she told him he made her stomach sick just by thinking she should go and live like a dog in the bush, he replied: 'You sure it is not the snake keeping warm there? Can't be anything else.' She was not listening, she was a genie counting her nails like a millionaire, drawing the world to her beck and call like a queen, mind you.

Poor old Normal Phantom, he caught a lift and took his soul down to the river country by himself, and when he returned weeks later, she had one basic room erected. 'You can't come back,' she told him, unless he helped her. The old people intrigued, buttoned their lips and whispered: 'She has airs for a woman.' The stand-off was to last one minute with Norm. 'Alright then. You won't see me for five years.' She was not a complacent woman, the old people remarked. His ultimatum was over-the-top, so she claimed. So it was final. He walked back up the road, all the children were crying. She ignored the whole scene and continued working on the nails as though he did not exist.

Normal Phantom kept his promise. He went to sea and stayed away for five full years. When he returned, after the storms, he had his own small fishing boat. He had inherited his father's memory of the sea, and he walked straight up to Angel Day, and told her in the face that he was prepared to hang around. He said there was too much water under the bridge to have to go around fighting his wife all of the time. Why waste his breath? In any case, the spot she had chosen was now just across from the driftwood piles thrown from the sea. She accused him of coming home smelling like a catfish but that didn't stop child number seven being born: Kevin.

Angel was on her way to the rubbish dump palace where her seagull sentinels sat in the thousands on dead foliage, cardboard boxes, rusted iron, slashed tyres, pink plastic purses and cheap whatnot, guarding for nothing a humpteen amount of untold treasure.

It was Angel Day's palace, so she thought. The other Pricklebush women said she thought of herself only, since that dump belonged to everybody. Oh! If that was so. It should be said that sometimes light breezes turned sour as lemons, as they did on that particular day. Back in the bay, where Normal Phantom was working on his boat, was the one place of tranquillity on earth left, where total ignorance reigned. Those idly watching Normal working, while taking little notice of him, scrubbing or something up and down along the side of his sea vessel, would have been mesmerised by the purity of peace and goodwill that belonged to the simple man out in the warming sun, trouser legs rolled up to the knees half covered in tidal mud. A leisurely job scraping the summer-dried fish guts from his paint-weathered boat, his head down to the work, wondering about painting the boat some fancy colours – capillary red, or a kingfisher's azure blue, or sunflower yellow. Oh! The good old days. What a memory. A reminder of the showing-off days when men were men, and the fish were plentiful, and boats never dreamt about the colour of camouflaged grey.

Angel walked on towards the rubbish dump away from the children left asleep in their beds. She wanted to be alone with the seagulls who waited on guard while others followed, flapping quietly in her wake. Occasionally, one would flutter above her head for several moments, emitting small squalls, telling her secrets, reminiscing, reciting little prayers recalled from prior reincarnations, before, and just as suddenly, swinging off into formation again to rendezvous with the flocks following in from behind. After having spent the night roosting in the precinct of low-lying headlands and the swamp marshes of low tide, these large groupings of birds joined the ones already waiting, noisily parcelling out their prized scavenger lots for the day.

The morning jostling at the tip grew more infectious, as increasing numbers of birds squawked and screeched with their beaks open wide at one another, or flew above in threatening circles. Angel walked through it all, as if it was nothing. The mist was still heavy, and she went about her business, tearing apart the piles of rubbish delivered to the dump over the weekend.

The steamed contents smelt high. Her followers gladly tore apart the rotting scraps from the dinner tables of Uptown – *Oh! Yum! Fish and chips, steak and chips, sausages and chips*. Angel paused for a collection of well-used children's storybooks, and sat down on the ground to gather them up into a pile, all of the little picture books, pages flung open halfway through the adventures of Mickey Mouse, Donald Duck, Peter Pan, Cinderella, Alice in Wonderland. She flicked through the books with her thin childlike fingers. The blue-eyed gulls hovering, watched with disdainful interest, over her shoulder. They were just as engrossed as she was with the fantasy lands created in faraway places, of icy winters, cool forests and the paradise land of the rich people. Eventually, she placed the books carefully into the bottom of her sack so they would not become damaged. She had more to do. Ahead of her there were many mysteries to be discovered in the piles of fat green bags.

With the mist lifting, it would soon become too hot. She could already feel the sun piercing down on her head. The humidity was thick in the air. A light frown crossed her face. The crease in between her eyebrows was deepening with the thought of her chaotic life.

She moved on, gracefully climbing through a hill of vegetation which she recognised from somewhere in town. She had seen the council men putting a chainsaw straight through the overgrown oleander hedges that concealed the goings-on in the offices and houses belonging to the Town Council's very important staff. Truckloads of hedge clippings headed to the dump while under the cooling fans the Town Council debated whether to erect a giant something or other in the middle of town. Could it be the world's biggest stubby, or the world's biggest town drunk? The two truths of the matter were abandoned, by their choosing instead to lasso in icons of the sea. Whereas other more fetching images were uttered – *Choose the biggest fibreglass barramundi, or the biggest concrete groper imaginable* – some preferred the steel-spiked wild boar celebrating Abilene, or the biggest lead-framed bull – a brown Brahman, or a fantastic Santa Gertrudis bull with a blazing star in the forehead – which would light up the main road like a beacon at night. Either would distinguish the town. *But what about a miner with a pick?* It was such a hard choice. Angel Day had no idea of the debate since no one spoke to her about the issues of Uptown. She just climbed through the official vegetation, still uptight with confidentiality because it gave away no town secrets to her. But they should have asked people like Angel Day. She often spoke about the absence of God in Desperance and the need for him to make his appearance in Uptown to redeem the cursed with his light.

The branches with olive-green limbs and limp leaves felt cool against her skin, so Angel Day moved on through the lot, just to reach the pile of green bags underneath. When she established a position where she could balance herself inside the branches, she sat there in the shade, concealed from the rest of the world. One by one she opened the bags, checking to see what was worth taking. All there was were sheets of white paper which she thought had probably come from the Council office. She did not read them because she was not interested to waste her time examining the rates and whatnots other people owed to Uptown.

Angel Day might have been surprised if 'official' papers did not intimidate her to the point she could never read them without her heart pounding. Even her fingers felt shaky, just to touch official-dom, as she pored through the refuse. If she had scant interest, just enough to flick through leaf by leaf, even taking a cursory glance at the contents, she may have been fortunate to stumble eventually across correspondence relating to her own family and how their poor state of wellbeing was becoming an issue, for the Council at least. Especially 'the house' the mother built. All the fringe people thought it was such a good house, ingenious in fact, and erected similar makeshift housing for themselves. *Why couldn't they have waited for a government grant?* But pay no neverminds for hooraying Angel Day for economic independence. Mrs Angel Day's dream house was considered an eyesore by Uptown. All of them humpies popping up all over the prickly bush would have to go. Those eyesores could not live next to the dream of the big Santa Gertrudis. Fibreglass, steel-spiked, ironclad monuments preoccupied the Town Councillors, and they were using plenty of ink and paper recording what they had blabbered to each other.

What else was life for except just for coping, nothing else, so why be bothered reading what white paper says only to make it worse? She knew what white persons had to say just by looking at them, particularly the ones who wrote official papers. She called them gammon.

Lost amongst these piles of discarded papers, she was left with a sense of melancholy the more she touched them. Nothing seemed promising for Angel Day and her treasure bag. At least she could sit in a shady nook amongst the dying oleander hedge cuttings. Then, suddenly from out of the rustling papers, she discovered a large black mantelpiece clock with a cracked glass cover. Carefully, she pushed the paper away. The clock had come from the mayor's office. She could not believe her luck, not only that the clock had been thrown away, and she had found it, but the key to wind it was still in the back socket. She wound the clock and smiled. It worked.

Convinced that the Council people had discarded the clock because it was too old-fashioned for the new modern office building, Angel Day now had to choose what she could discard from her potato sack. Decisions, decisions, she mumbled to herself, sorting tins and bottles to make room for the big shiny clock. Then, recovering from the excitement of finding something so valuable at the rubbish tip, she realised the danger it would bring. She peered outside her shelter, scanning around to see who else might be walking about. She asked herself, what if she encountered the Council men who drove the rubbish truck? They would accuse her of stealing the clock and drive straight up to Constable Truthful's office to report her. She considered the likely consequences of sitting around like a stuffed mullet at the police station.

A vision of the Magistrate's face found its way into her little oleander nook. Come back at night he warned. Come back at night and get it. She looked around, considering where to hide the clock, knowing the wild pigs owned the dump at night. She thought of asking Norm to bring her back when he went hunting for the pigs, but she did not feel comfortable with the idea of walking around in the bush with him during the night. Half of the contents had been emptied from the bag for the clock. To leave without it was a betrayal of the future she was already imagining in which the Phantom children would be going to school on time. No one in the Phantom family would be guessing the time anymore from where the sun sat in the sky. In the new sweet life, the Phantom family would be marching off to bed at the correct time, just like the school thought was really desirable, then they would march off to school on time to do their school work.

With the clock in the bag, she was preparing to leave her little world of white paper and decaying foliage, when something else caught her eye. First of all she saw the base of the statue with a handwritten date – 1947. It had to be broken she thought, as she pushed the rubbish away, but found it was not even cracked, as she inspected a statue of the Virgin Mary. The statue looked old and the paint was chipped in places. Angel thought Norm might have some spare paint she could use to repaint the statue, particularly where the lines of gold and silver had disappeared on the cloak. The Virgin Mary was dressed in a white-painted gown and blue cloak. Her right hand was raised, offering a permanent blessing, while her left hand held gold-coloured rosary beads. Angel Day was breathless. 'This is mine,' she whispered, disbelieving the luck of her ordinary morning.

'This is mine,' she repeated her claim loudly to the assembled seagulls waiting around the oleanders. She knew she could not leave this behind either, otherwise someone else would get it, and now she had to carry the statue home, for she knew that with the Virgin Mary in pride of place, nobody would be able to interfere with the power of the blessings it would bestow on her home. 'Luck was going to change for sure, from this moment onwards,' she told the seagulls, because she, Mrs Angel Day, now owned the luck of the white people.

Not only would her family be able to tell the time, and be able to tell other poor outsider people like themselves what the time was, but they would also be prosperous. They would become like the white people who prayed and said they were of the Christian faith. This was the difference between the poor old Pricklebush people and Uptown. This was how white people had become rich by saving up enough money, so they could look down on others, by keeping statues of their holy ones in their homes. Their spiritual ancestors would perform miracles if they saw how hard some people were praying all the time, and for this kind of devotion, reward them with money. Blessed with the prophecy of richness, money befalls them, and that was the reason why they owned all the businesses in town.

The seagulls, lifting off all over the dump, in the mind-bending sounds they made seemed to be singing a hymn, *Glory! Glory, Magnificat*. The atmosphere was haunting, with steam rising from the ground, hovering birds in every direction, and she simply appeared from nowhere, walking out of the oleander. Fugitively, she searched around for potential robbers with her magical brown eyes, checking every angle for movement in the distortion of haphazard, mass waste. She hurried, carrying the statue and the potato sack, eager to escape before the Council men started work in the slow-moving truck. She did not expect to see so many other people from the Pricklebush walking about so early in the morning.

Her movements had startled the otherwise peaceful scene where dozens of others from the Pricklebush had ensconced themselves under cardboard boxes, pieces of corrugated iron, inside forty-four-gallon tar barrels, or broken parts of abandoned water tanks. Suddenly, people appeared from everywhere, poking and pulling everything apart, tilling the dumping ground. Children were playing in the puddles, parents gossiping, others walking about with their bags full up.

Angel Day, queen herself, surveyed their stares and started abusing first. She started it. 'What are you all staring at me for?' Her voice had no problem emptying the contents of other people's lives in the rubbish and calling it nothing. Angel stood her ground. She just started yelling out in a very open manner what she liked, to all and sundry: the same kind of things she called other people all the time around the house.

'Hey! What are you people doing here?' she hollered. 'What's wrong with you people? You people don't belong here. Who said you got any normal rights to be hanging around here? On other people's laaand for? Just taking what you want, hey? What about the traditional owner then?' Her voice radiated like shock waves all over the dump. Well! Most people had heard that argument before. Angel Day was mouthing off again about the poor old traditional owner being bypassed – once again. And this time, it must have been an unlucky day, because they were having naught of it. You could hear all those people sucking in their breath. Angel had no shame causing all of that trouble. She was a hussy, first class, the old ones had heard people whispering about Angel while she went on her way, cursing them for nothing, as though she was the keeper of other people's lives.

Goodness knows so much happened then. It was hard for two eyes to keep up. Those poor people were pretty upset, and Angel had no intuition about other people, none at all. All those grim faces were just glaring at her but she did nothing. After several moments the air broke like dynamite. The air broke clean: *We can't help that, Mrs Who-Does-She-Thinks-She-Is*. This came out of the mouth of someone who had picked up straightaway that business line of hers of *not belonging here*. She called out for everybody to decide who she thinks she is. There was going to be a war, good and proper. Gravelly morning voices sounding like someone was jumping up and down on their lungs shouted back, *She's bloody nobody, that's what*.

Everyone started slinging off about who would want to belong there anyway? The place was a mess. The place was too full of fighting all the time. Everyone was moving forward, screaming at each other. Then they started taunting, throwing sticks and stones at the ones trying to defend the peace. Nobody listened to the other because everyone was either that mad in the head or did not care whether they were defending the peace or not. Each was well and truly sick of it. Sick of Angel Day.

One big woman, dressed in a big white dress: Well! She looked like the white cliffs of Dover, and it was she who did most of the shouting, spitting out incoherent words, on and on, like she was never going to stop. She was yelling through spit, asking who that woman thought she was: *The bloody nobody*. When Angel Day said the woman looked like a fat white pig eating up the traditional owner's country, the woman said she was going to fix Mrs High and Bloody Mighty, once and for all. What happened then was the war started again. Imagine that. Precarious modernity squashed by hostilities dormant for four hundred years, and Angel Day started it up again over an old clock and a statue. Probably all wars start off by a bit of taunting like this.

Everyone began picking up weapons the ancient way, arming themselves with whatever they could lay their hands on. People and children were running around, picking up lumps of wood, iron bars, or else brown beer bottles picked up and broken along the neck. Everywhere, all you could hear was the sound of bottles being smashed. When all the memories of that day had faded away, that sound of glass smashing still haunted everyone.

You see, all the alliances had to be weighed up then and there and on the spot. People who had been getting on well, living side by side for decades, started to recall tribal battles from the ancient past. It was unbelievable, but Angel Day was standing there oblivious, hugging her statue, and telling people to get off her land. There were little black flies swarming all over her face but she took no notice. Nobody had seemed to notice the fly squadrons soaring into the air as though struck by an electrifying volatility; as they swarmed up, they were drawn like magnets to the hot smell of human skin, and thousands buzzed around people's faces.

The old people believed in phenomena as great as this, and said the flies had been drawn up through the centuries to join the battle. They claimed the spirits would never let you forget the past. They drew lines in the dirt, calling people out from the shadows of complacency, *Get it straight where you belong*. People must have felt the chilly spike prodding them to arm, to prepare them to add another chapter in the old war. Otherwise they might have never known how to go to war in the way of the old people. Living in harmony in fringe camps was a policy designed by the invader's governments, and implemented, wherever shacks like Angel Day's swampside residences first began to be called a community. The old people wrote about the history of these wars on rock.

Now, centuries later the poor things had turned up with nothing fancy, not one of them weighed down with the spoils of war to live in the Pricklebush, yet carrying a heavy weight all the same. Angel Day's heart was big and ignorant in those days, but she believed she filled the shoes of Normal's grandfather, who had been the keeper of this land. No one entered these parts without first speaking their business to the keeper, and to her mind, she was it. She welcomed those who walked heavy with the inheritance of antiquity stashed in their bones. Pride swelled up inside her when she saw those with a landscape chiselled deep into their faces and the legacy of ancestral creation loaded into their senses. She guarded those whose fractured spirits cried of rape, murder and the pillage of their traditional lands. Over time, they all became fringe dwellers living next to the rich white man's municipality, all squatting next to Angel Day's lake, on her so-called land, where she reigned like a queen over her dominion. And the domiciated? Well! They ignored her.

It is hard to determine how sides were forged, but when the fighting began, the blood of family ties flew out of the veins of people, and ran on the ground just like normal blood, when face and limbs are cut like ribbons with broken glass, or when the body has been gouged with a piece of iron, or struck on the head over and over with a lump of wood. Angel Day did not fight because she was still hugging onto her statue and encouraging the human explosion to take hold. It was like sinking an anchor. 'What about the traditional owner?' She was still screaming out her esteemed rights. Maybe she did not register the carnage. The woman who looked like the white cliffs of Dover, whom the fighting had carried some distance away, picked up the voice of Angel Day screaming, and looked over at her with a perplexed look, then walked out of the fight, straight back over to where she had originally challenged Angel, and wrestled the statue away from her.

The children, their bodies twisting in and out of the maze of adults at war, were wondering what was going to happen next. They rushed in like frantic butterflies to be next to kinfolk bleeding, or to others falling on the ground and not moving again. Young Will Phantom was running with his brothers and sisters to protect his mother from the big woman whose eyes were protruding, as she wrestled with the statue splashed with blood. The woman acted like she was possessed by a demon, whose body continued to use all of its strength on one thought alone: to secure the statue into a position to slam Angel Day off the face of the earth.

Young Will Phantom thought quickly. He ran home as fast as his ten-year-old legs would carry him, rushed into the kitchen and grabbed the cigarette lighter left lying on the kitchen table, then ran back to the dump. Any stack of papers he could find, he lit. He lit the dry grass around the edge of the dump so there was fire spreading over the claypans in every direction. Black clouds billowed straight through the dump. The smell of burning grass and debris was suffocating, and everywhere people were coughing. Very soon, people could be seen moving through the dense smoke, helping others through the burnt grass and back along the path with smouldering smoke on either side. Nobody spoke as they limped by as fast as they could, passing others, helping to cart injured relations home. Then, when the alarm was rung in town, they scattered.

Seeing the black smoke rising from the dump, everyone started to hear about the big fight going on. They all wished they could have killed Angel Day, walking with her statue and surrounded by her kids, following her home. The fire brigade, already moving slower than a month of Sundays, became bogged on the muddy road to the dump just two minutes out of town.

The Pricklebush around the Phantoms' place was silent when

the policeman arrived to investigate, followed by half of the Uptown Town Council on foot, after they came through the water-logged road. They claimed it was their business to find out what caused the fire. It was a wasted trip at the taxpayer's expense, because nobody living around the swamp had seen a thing. *Maybe, the fire was just some old log smouldering over the weekend and caught alight.* It was a strange thing to say. All the same, the young cop Truthful said he could not help noticing a lot of injured people everywhere he went. He got to asking: 'What happened to you then?' While his entourage waited in anticipation for a different answer. 'Just an accident, sir, no problem.'

'No?'

'No, there is no problem here.'

'What happened then?' he asked, just to show the Council men he was on top of the job.

'Ah! I fall over.'

'How did you fall then?'

'I fall over.'

'Where?'

'Fall over?'

'What?'

Everywhere Truthful asked the question, he received a grand demonstration of hand movements. 'Hmmm! Oh! My. I am feeling no good! No good at all today! If you had any sense you'd run us up to the hospital like a good boy.' Truthful had the woman with what was left of the white dress with him. Angel came straight up to her with outstretched arms, and hugged her, but it was full of hate.

The Council men and women too, following Truthful into every household in the camp, looking on in mock silence, gave knowing looks to one another of a familiar: Nudge-nudge! Wink-wink! *If you please! What's he been up too, jumping over the back fence at night already*? Look at the familiarity if you please. What was the world coming to, when the police force had no power over these people? Acutely embarrassed by his lack of progress, and over-hearing the whispering behind his back, Truthful terminated the sideshow with a demonstration of Brisbane Valley cop briskness by saying he was arresting the first likely suspects to catch his eye. The bemused Council people crowding around, uninvited, huddling to avoid bodily contact with anything inside the Pricklebush home in case they picked up something quite dreadful, and having had an eyeful of poverty chipped at Truthful: *Let's take em and take em, get em off our backs, bloody mongrels are a prime nuisance to everyone anyhow. Send these two little buggers off to a reform school or something. That will show them who's boss of this town.*

It is true that silence has a cloak because it covered all of those little tin humpies all day after the official people went back to minding their own businesses. Normal Phantom sat at his kitchen table glaring at Angel whenever she came into the room. Neither spoke. He knew what had happened. And she was not repentant, not one bit. There was no end of her fussing over her statue, cleaning it, looking at it, examining the cracks and chips, helping herself to the full range of Normal's fish paints, making a pride of place for it in her bedroom. The day slipped into an even quieter night with no lanterns lit. The Pricklebush wore the total darkness of cloud cover.

Once the dawn broke, Normal Phantom stepped out of his house to go down to the boat. It was then he felt the eerie quietness, a stillness he found difficult to place, where even the birds did not sing. And no sign of his bird.

He was expecting retaliation, and he looked around up in the branches of the trees to find his bird. As he surveyed the surroundings, something struck him as being out of place, a surreal quietness: silence had replaced the noise of children's crying, families arguing. The Phantom family was on its own. The other families had moved during the night. In complete and utter silence, they had picked up everything they owned, and moved to the other side of town. That was when the war of the dump caused the division, and people realigned themselves, Eastsider or Westsider, and that was that. The Phantoms lost whatever near and dear or distant relatives they had, except some old people who refused to move. No one else wanted to put up with another minute more of what they called Mrs Angel Day.

The war of the dump burst apart the little world of the Phantoms and their related families. Everyone in the Pricklebush from elder to child, Eastsider to Westsider, injured and uninjured started bringing up their faded memories of the ancient wars, to be renewed with vigour and the hard evidence of all facts. Everyone now knew of someone in their families who had been assigned to make the long pilgrimage over their vast lands which occupied dozens of cattle stations, where they travelled in clapped-out vehicles, near and far within their tribal territories, to seek out their very old senior Law people. The old people were always elusive too, never being where they should be, when their relatives turned up.

'Well! Where's old White Whiskers?'

'He must have gone that-a-way.'

The challenge was to be always on the move, following the old ones travelling their country to at least a thousand sites they knew by memory. It was a test of how good they knew the country before they were able to find old White Whiskers waiting for them. Every family had to know the story of the past. Know, to go about their separate ways, by reclaiming land from fighting long ago.

On the other hand, the townsfolk of Desperance could not make heads or tails out of why they were being sandwiched between Aboriginal people, not only living on either side of them now, but setting up two camps without even saying to anybody what they were doing. All of those families that moved over to the Eastside to get away from the Phantoms, had walked noisily through town in the middle of the night. Everyone had been in a state of high agitation, with loud arguments taking place about the decision to move, *Should've, shouldn't've*, all to the rhythm of cyclone fences being scraped with heavy fighting sticks by some of the youths. People were complaining to each other about the weight of their ragtag belongings, while children zigzagged all over the street with their laughter and cries being heard everywhere. What did it matter to try to hush all the little children since that many dogs in tow, stirred up by the scraping sticks, joined in the racket by running up and down the fences of white people's homes barking their heads off or leaping up and throwing themselves against the tin walls while trying to get over the fences, and equally with the town dogs inside doing the same, trying to get out? None of this racket worried their owners. Nor did the straggle-taggle give one iota to the peace and quiet of the town. Whatever! Nevermind! as if the town with all of its laws and by-laws for inhabitation did not exist. It was as if they could not care less whether the towns-folk, woken up with all the noise, switched on every single light in their houses in the middle of the night, and stood silently in the front yards, gobsmacked, comprehending they were in the middle of a riot.

Word quickly came back to Norm about what they were saying down at the Council. The town was up that quick smart, nice and early in the morning, looking out around their front yards again, as if searching for order, trying to locate some sense of normality, and the main street was normal, as though nothing had ever happened in the night. Everyone of the white skin jumped into their showers and scrubbed themselves hard for this was what high and mighty powerful people did when they felt unclean, before running out the door, where they went straight over to the Council to talk about the uproar.

Everyone was up in arms even before the meeting got started. This was the normal way they talked straight. No, no coloured person was ever going to forget about this incident of lawless carrying-on like they owned the place. A whiff on the gossip grapevine said who was to blame. 'It was bloody Normal Phantom. Wouldn't you believe it. So what then? The man is incapable of handling his wife. What then? Teach him that's what. Well! We will teach him what's what.' That year, Normal Phantom had no chance of winning citizen of the year, nor forever perhaps.

The bell was tolling, ringing non-stop for half an hour, but Normal Phantom never responded to the sound of bells. When no one in the prickly bush camps saw the Phantoms getting involved in Uptown business, they also ignored the bells. The Phantoms only went into town when the bells rang for the sea. Normal said that was the only important reason for ringing the bell, because what happened to the sea affected every single one of them. 'We are the flesh and blood of the sea and we are what the sea brings the land.' This was not a sea matter, so no adult person from the Pricklebush went running to see what they wanted.

Yes, there was plenty of worry. Worry straight for Uptown. The Council had a string of evening meetings so everyone could come along and have their voice heard. It was like living in a democracy. Paranoia was the word that best described what took place inside of the squashed Council chambers. Everyone had a story to tell about some Aboriginals who they saw sitting under a tree thinking about lighting fires. Some Aboriginals were seen pushing up into Uptown itself – abandoned car bodies to live in. You could see Aboriginals living in them behind the fences at the end of their backyards even. Aboriginals were thinking about setting up another camp. The net was not working. What was happening to the net? Wasn't the net supposed to be there for the purposes of protecting the town against encroachment from people who were not like themselves?

'Ya mean coons?' Sanguine-voiced, the local mayor was speaking. A big, beefy, six-two, no-fuss man, who liked to call chalk chalk, or night night. That was his motto. He overshadowed the town with his power.

'Excuse me, Mr Bruiser, Mayor, you don't have to talk like that. We are just saying that they are an eyesore, so what are you going to do about it?'

Stan Bruiser was a straight speaker and was such a popular mayor for Uptown of Desperance, that for ten straight years, he had been voted its citizen of the year. *It was rigged*, some said of the voting box in the Council office. But be what it may, tampering with a ballot box was no great sin when conspiratory theorists worked with no proof. Bruiser, now fifty-six, was a prosperous cattle man, with Elvis combed-back hair and sideburns, dyed the colour of a Santa Gertrudis. He was a hawker by trade until his change of luck due to a foray into the Australian stock market, after he picked up a hint late one night on the radio in the mining-boom seventies. Next day, he piled his last quids in the stock exchange on a tin-pot mining company that struck it rich in Western Australia. So very quick, he was rich.

Good luck to him one supposes, for he cleaned up with his shares and with the spoils, means and wherewithal, he reinvented himself, from somebody driving around the outback's dying towns and Aboriginal camps on pension day, selling the necessities of life for a profit of three to four hundred per cent after costs. A quid to be made. But just how could one uneducated man, a man just like themselves, make so much money in his lifetime? It was unnatural. Anyone could have done it, he joked, if he had been half smart about prices by collecting drought-time cattle properties like lollies, paying unpaid debts.

Bruiser spoke of being the epitome of the self-made man, and the 'self-made 24/7 man' angle was slotted into his utterings to other Desperanians during Australia Day, May Day, Picnic Day, Pioneer Day celebrations where he had the right to speak, right through, down to the demands he made of politicians whose colleagues heard his booming voice on the phone in the hallowed halls of southern parliaments.

The old people in the Pricklebush said the story about the money of hell was different, because Bruiser had unnatural scars that looked like someone had welded an extra skin to his body. They had observed the extra piece of skin that ran from his skull down the left side of his face, along one side of his body, down to his feet and back again, running up the back this time, right up to his skull. Was that unusual? Darn right! Everyone in the Pricklebush thought so. Some of the old ladies were more than curious and yelled out whenever he came down to the Pricklebush camps – 'Hey! How come the devil stitched you up like a pod?' Bruiser was sensitive about his scars and ignored their questions. So they spread the word he was an alien, though wisely no one dared say such a thing to his face. You would have to be nuts to say anything like that to Bruiser.

Bruiser said he had seen everything as far as he was concerned and there was only one motto to life. 'If you can't use it, eat it, or fuck it, then it's no bloody use to you.' It brought the house down as usual. This was how the town would size up the problem of Aboriginal people squatting behind their houses, he explained with a loud clap of his hands, encouraging others to do the same. He said the government should put the Abos to work and he would write a letter to every politician this side of the black stump telling them exactly that. He nutted out how this employment policy would work. He said they would do what he did to make a living. 'Put them to work making keys so they can lock their food up somewhere and not have to share everything they get with their families.' He explained that when he was a hawker the one thing everyone wanted was keys – 'There was real money in keys.' Number two, he explained, 'They should be forced to make bathtubs, like the old tin ones, so they could take regular baths.' And number three, 'They should be sent back to the cattle stations and made to work for nothing, board and keep, that's good enough for them if they aren't interested in making money to get ahead like everyone else.'

Bruiser got a huge round of applause and after a bit of rumbling about the government doing nothing, someone suggested that they needed direct action. Once Bruiser got the meeting stirred up, he went out the back with a few of his cattlemen friends to enjoy the fresh air and partake in some liquid refreshments, to keep them charged up to go back later on, and finish off the meeting. Although how it ended up, they stayed outside making themselves so pickled and pie-eyed, nothing mattered anymore. What was strategy? This left the new town clerk, Libby Valance, a man accused of neither being local nor understanding the region and its values, to chair the throng.

Yet Valance was educated in local government, and had been given the job in the first place because he was considered to be sensible. He addressed the meeting in his fine voice which reached no higher than midway, by saying that it was his Christian duty to take a more civil line of approach in advising what a town could do with its citizens. No way, voices were beseeching, *Why couldn't we just? Bulldoze the crap out of those camps, flatten the lot?* Why not? 'Well! The last time the Council did it,' Valance explained, 'they just started rebuilding, because they had nowhere else to go.' So! The meeting went on. *Make them go, there must be somewhere else they can go, why do they want to come here for anyway?* Those of the Pricklebush mob who had taken up the offer to attend the meeting listened, stunned again by how they had been rendered invisible, while

Valance continued, 'It is because they have a right to be here just like anyone else.' Bruiser, having come back inside, responded with the following salient points on behalf of all indignities: 'Huh! Think they do. Then they should live like everyone else then. Right! Let's go tell 'em.'

A small delegation, made up of representatives from Uptown and the black busybodies who went along to these popular Council meetings, came over one afternoon, to have a word with Norm Phantom. It had never escaped Norm's notice that somehow Uptown had encumbered him with the title with all of its glory – leader of the Aboriginal people. They said they wanted him to get those people who had moved out of Westside, and were now living in abandoned car bodies and their makeshift camps behind people's housing, to start living like white people, if they wanted to live in town.

'Couldn't give a stuff about them,' Norm grunted, still bent over his taxidermy efforts on a giant prawn.

The Uptown prospect, Cilla Mooch, an Aboriginal man learning how to shape himself into a white mould with one of those perpetual traineeship work-for-the-dole programs spread over the length and breadth of Australia in the name of economic development, worked in the Council office. He stood next to Valance, and as it had been predetermined by the Council, was the voice in this delegation. Norm Phantom might reason with someone of his own ilk. Moochie spoke in broken English.

'You know?! That what's what they is saying about you and all. Saying you started all of this town camps stuff springing up here and there for we mob. Saying they got to stop it. Show a bit of respect for the place. Place belonga Desperance Shire Council. Stop the place looking like an infestation of black heads and what have you.'

'You sound like a fuzzy wuzzy, Mooch. Aren't got anything to do with me and talk English,' Norm muttered irritably, still engrossed with the delicate operation on his prawn with a toothpick in one hand and a large magnifying glass in the other. Norm always remembered the prawn. He did not attempt many, but this one was a special creature. Rare, for it only lives in the crystal clear waters away in the gorges of his father's father's country. Unique for its size.

Norm had hoped by saying little, the insignificant white ants would disappear and let him get on with his work. However, too little was too late. It was not to be. 'Whatya doing around here for Moochie?' Full of grace, Angel Day stepped into the fishroom. She said she was nosing around to see what all the talk was about. She had torn herself away from the statue of Mary, which she had now repainted in the colour of her own likeness. She had examined pictures in the children's prayer books and after considering every detail of what needed to be done, she believed she knew how to restore the statue. Every bit of her time and attention had been given in its reconstruction, which had now departed from that of its familiar image, to one who watches over and cares for the claypan people in the Gulf country. Improvisation with Norm's fish colours and textures resulted in a brightly coloured statue of an Aboriginal woman who lived by the sea. The work had taken her several days. She had not even noticed that the other families had left, or believed it was possible when Norm blamed her for their leaving.

'If they gone, then they'll be back,' she had told him flatly, as she did to the delegation who had come from Uptown to confront Norm. She said she thought they would not have the wherewithal to go setting up camp on the other side of town. 'Where's the water? Anyone mind telling me that? No tap? No tap! So how are they going to get water from them mob then?' She looked the delegation over with her cold eyes, waiting for a response, and when no one dared to offer her a peep, she sighed heavily and launched into her attack.

'What you people worried about then? Stupid, you people. You want to think about things if you got any sense. Isn't it, they going to get sick and tired quick smart when they have to keep walking 'bout this other side of town to cart water for themselves?'

The delegation turned their attention away from Normal to Angel Day, who engaged them further in discussion about the water situation for the itinerants, as she called them. Norm could not help but be impressed with her ability to mislead people. The delegation looked at her talking down to them with awe written across its faces. Where did she get it from he wondered? *Itinerants* was not the language of the Pricklebush.

Some people in the delegation began talking about how they had carried the cross of Jesus to protect them. 'We prayed to God to help us today and we carried the big crucifix along to shield ourselves.' Those who wore them around their necks, proved their point by dragging crucifixes out from under their clothing and displaying their crosses to each other, as though the gesture would provide them warmth, and secure them from the wrath of God, which they suspected hovered over Normal Phantom's household. Holy smoke! It was hot. Angel was not amused by the religious posturing Uptown always used to get its own way. Norm watched her run back into the house, listened with the others to her footsteps on the tin floor of the corridor, and suddenly she burst back in the room, brandishing her statue, held up high above her head as she danced around the delegation like a strutting pigeon. It was a transfixing sight. The delegation was shocked by this spectacle of irreverence for their religion, some even recognising the statue, and were about to say: 'I know where that came from,' but were speechless. All eyes followed the Aboriginal Mary, bobbing past them, jumping back and forth. It did not trouble Normal. He tried to concentrate on his work while there was still light left in the day. He knew what Angel was capable of doing, or thought so.

What she had to say was long and hard: 'We are decent people here, my family. We make no trouble for anybody. So why for you want to come down here making trouble for *we* all the time? I tell you how I won't stand for it; I can't even stand you people. I don't want you murdering types around here bothering my family all the time, you hear me? Covering up for someone who even tried to murder me once and other atrocities as well going on. If you mob come back here again, (she paused to think), I'll tell you what I will be doing. I will be pressing that many charges through the legal service for Aborigines for attempted murder, that's what. And while I am at it, I will be suing the town as accomplices to a conspiracy to have my person killed and the persons of my family murdered before they were born, and for damages for the ones who were born. Goodness knows how we can't sleep at night as it is with the worry. I don't know how much money you've all got in the bank, but you will be paying who knows what for damages. It might even cost the whole town. I have already spoken long distance on the phone to my lawyer and he said it might be a pretty good test case. Watertight even, so what do you think about that, hey?' Under heavy cloud cover which brought on a premature nightfall, the Uptown delegation looked at each other through flashes of lightning in the fishroom, and were shocked, like the suspended school of silver fish from the sea, jumping up and down in fright.

Normal remembered feeling that there had been no end to Angel's obsessive behaviour since she laid her hands on the statue. She had even placed it in the bedroom looking onto their bed, so he could not be bothered sleeping there anymore. She had forced him to live in the fishroom, which she now took over, with half the town having a heated argument in there as well. The cockatoo screeched its head off in the storm outside as it flew around, cir-cling the house. Then, to cap it off, the crickets were stirred into wakefulness, and began their choice of music. Ears pricked and prickled to hear the foreign, shrilling sounds of Handel's oratorio in full orchestra. The delegation listened for a short time, and this strange and severe sounding improvisation must have taken the cake, because there was a mad rush to leave via a rubble of disorientation, and rumble, as they raced over the puddles on the corrugated tin-floored corridor.

Normal, forced to become part of the excessiveness of his home, helped the disoriented delegation outside into the storm, where they set off up the muddy road to Uptown, hoping to find their way home in the darkness. Until, that was, lo and behold, Mayor Bruiser turned up wet and blind drunk, and when he got the drift of Angel's argument, he started to kick the air and shout into the kitchen doorway, that he was not going to have a bunch of blacks tell him what to do with the town.

Bruiser could see Angel Day inside, still carrying on about lawyers, and laughed drunkenly, 'Here's a woman who still likes a good poke. Don't you like a good poke Angel?' He started to tease the Christian man Valance, 'Go and ask her if you can have a go.' When she ignored him the mayor started taunting her about the times he chased her on horseback down to the creek until her bony legs gave up. 'Oh! Don't be bashful, you remember me.' Everyone in town knew how he bragged about how he had chased every Aboriginal woman in town at various times, until he ran them into the ground then raped them. He had branded them all, like a bunch of cattle, he gloated.

Angel Day came out of the house with a billycan full of boiling water and threw it at Bruiser's voice in the dark, but missed. She went back into the house and the delegation could hear her stomping around the kitchen, throwing things around, screaming out how she was looking for a sharp knife so that she could slit Bruiser's neck from left to right. What was left of the embarrassed delegation stood around in the rain. Next thing, Norm came

41

flying out of the house threatening the Mayor with his boning knife, screaming, 'I got this to make you shut up, you dog.' With the knife swishing back and forth, Norm backed Bruiser through the mud, out of the yard. Bruiser moved away but kept yelling, 'I'll be back later and I will fucking get you, Norm Phantom.' With that, the deafening sound of squawking seagulls took over the court with a loud crack of thunder, so everyone looked up, and when lightning illuminated the skies, they saw that there were thousands of the seagulls gathered overhead, hovering above the Phantom's house, and right back up the road towards Desperance.

In an era when people were crying for reconciliation, there was fat chance that day. The little delegation started walking back to town, heads bent like wet seagulls in the stormy rain, away from the troubles of the Pricklebush. Every now and again, someone would tell Bruiser to come to his senses because nobody was going to risk their lives in that monstrosity ramshackle deathtrap of a house. So forth and so on, he was pulled along with the little throng, all muddied up to their knees, unable to untangle himself from the glue of their humiliation.

These matters were not helped by Angel Day, even though Normal had pushed her back into the house, for she kept slinging on about conspiracies, and letting her foul mouth go forth like a Cape Canaveral launch, full of the most slanderous truth or half-truth she could muster from every nook and crevice of her brain, and directed to and then from Bruiser downwards, as she bade them farewell. Normal could have slapped her hard across the face. Everyone was egging him to do it: *Go on, go on, you tell her to shut the fuck up*, but instead, for he had calmed down a lot, he forced his hand to hold the boning knife pinned to his side. What a hostess. Angel Day was too much for a mild man the likes of one who only wanted to work on a prawn.

Chapter 3
Elias Smith comes…and goes

Once upon a time, not even so long ago, while voyaging in the blackest of midnights, a strong sea man, who was a wizard of many oceans, had his memory stolen by thieving sea monsters hissing spindrift and spume as they sped away across the tops of stormy waves grown taller than the trees.

The mariner, robbed of fear, his navigation birthright and his good sense, did not call to his God, but cursed the raging sea in the foulest language of his homeland. Unheard by the tempest, an austere cyclone called Leda that came this way from across the seas in a once-in-a-hundred-year storm, the man chased after her black wind to recapture his memories. Like a man possessed, he flew through towering banks of waves whose crests collided and rolled with the spirit clouds of the heavens above. Open-mouthed waves roared with thousands of others in that terrible, deafening nightmare of the troubled sea, and rolled poor old Elias Smith down into the crushing depths of hell before throwing him back up again, flinging him to and fro. And he? Mouth agape, hoarse throat yelling nothing but silence, he kept on chasing the black wind before losing his memory forever.

It was in those precise moments when Elias Smith was fighting hopelessly to save his identity, when his loss became absolute, that another unusual thing happened in this part of the world, that was far away from everything else. Lightning forked up from the sea, springing out of the mouths of sacred underwater locations along a straight line heading many kilometres in a southerly direction, towards the coastline, until the last arm of the white golden fork went straight up the trunk of the lightning tree of an important Dreaming story hereabout. Fortunately for some, unfortunate for others, the tree was growing in the small coastal town of Desperance, tucked away in the Gulf of Carpentaria.

There was nobody alive who could claim to have seen this strange thing happen before, but history was repeating itself, because this was the ancient story of the prodigal coppiced tree standing there, in the middle of town. A tremendous thunderclap exploded above the tree. It came from deep inside the world of those black serpent clouds and even from far away, people said later on, as word filtered back, that they too had listened to the haunting echo of the thunder rolling back to the sea. Finally, when the thunder had faded away, a wind full of sand whistled over the coast from the sea bringing with it the hardest rain ever imagined, and afterwards, all time stopped.

Time stopped tick-tocking, because there was too much moisture in the air and it had interfered with the mechanical workings of dozens of watches and clocks that ended up jiggered, and afterwards, were only fit to be thrown down on the rubbish dump.

In the morning, the drowsy people of the little town of Desperance unbattened the hatches with an enormous sigh of relief, because all they had copped from Leda was a *dry* storm. They had been awoken by the eerie feeling of hearing complete silence for the first time in their homes, and they were out of bed in a flash, long before the cursed town's roosters started to crow. Noticing every clock had stopped ticking the time away, the towns-people flicked on the radio. Everyone listened in silence to the weatherman's voice saying the potentially destructive Leda had passed by the coastline, but she had raged like a madwoman, causing havoc for all the ships in the area, one hundred kilometres away out at sea. Though the town felt the joy of escaping the full force of the cyclone with winds up to 225 kilometres an hour, an uneasy feeling developed. They sensed something else hung heavy in the air. They were suddenly struck with a single idea, a sense of hopeless prognostication that before too long there would be another ominous piece of bad luck, because all bad luck happened in threes – the storm, the clocks, so something else was sure as hell going to happen to them. It was hard to describe how the anxiety intensified through people's bodies after they had awoken to the strange sensation, for everyone quickly collapsed back into slumberous dreams of aching bones, which ripened the next day into change-in-weather influenza.

The static electricity hung in the air, so in the morning, when Uptown people awakened again with woolly mouths and runny eyes, they were completely startled to find that everything they touched gave them a little shock, but this did not stop them from going around touching this and that, like the charged fur of a whining dog, or a startled domestic cat, just to see what would happen. All askew, and sticking out like porcupine needles, were the big, mutton-chop sideburns of every man, black or white, in the entire district, who had unconsciously modelled himself on the image of Elvis Presley.

This strange occurrence of the static electricity was a part of the unsettling state of things even before the soot-stained kettles blew their whistles in all those humid kitchens nestled across the flat lands. Moribund householders sat wondering what in the hell's name was going to happen to them in the end. Even before a single sip of tea from a rose floral china cup, or any old tin pannikin with the scratched initials of the owner's name on the side, or plastic mug, or heavy earthenware cup of fawn and brown, had reached dry lips, bringing some life and sense of propriety back into the bleak faces of all who dwelled safely within this world of Uptown, everyone knew something was amiss.

It was not a funny thing at all for any town that believed itself to be swathed in the providence of good Christian beliefs from the Bible, to be reduced to the basest feelings of primordial insecurity. And what was more unsettling was the spine-chilling realisation that such a mighty town like Desperance might have no power at all, if it came to the crunch. Not a single bird had begun its morning tune, and on top of it all, as daylight came, everyone could see for themselves that the world had turned red. When they looked at their own fair skin, it was another shock to their lives to see their skin was red.

Everyone local by nature ventured out of their houses. They were trying to understand what was happening, for everywhere they looked, they saw trees, the landscape, grass, even the sea water had taken on hues of red. No one had ever witnessed such an abnormal sunrise, struggling through the cover of misty cloud and haze of smoke coming from those fires in the inland bush, further south from Desperance. It was such an extraordinary kind of day. The cloudy-coloured sea was high and brought king tides several kilometres inland. Sea water lapped at the town edge. Waves pounded the flat lands. The broken clocks were compared and it was established that, for unknown reasons, all local time had stopped at precisely eleven minutes past midnight. And the wise around town said, *This was interesting indeed*.

No one remarked about the way the air smelt of putrid salt from the odour of stinking corpses washed off the stagnant floor of the ocean and dumped nilly pilly at their doorsteps. They were only interested in speaking about how lucky they were that the Christmas decorations in town had not been ruined. They regarded it as a very strange miracle to see that all the nativity pieces the Town Council had placed in every front yard for free, could and did survive the galing winds of Leda. She had given the whole town the heebie-jeebies just listening to her whistling her ghostly crying. But the relief was, she had not singled them out.

After a spot check was completed, the damage was regarded as minimal. At least a dozen plastic reindeer statues had been blown down South to kingdom come, while for some unknown reason, the brightly-coloured plastic Santas still sitting upright in sleighs had remained. What was even more noticeable to the drowsy-looking residents was that all the big puffs of cotton-wool snow that had adorned the tops of every fence post in town were hanging limp and sorry-looking. At first glance it looked as though the town had been dragged through a blizzard. However, all said and done, the entire population, the heart of which claimed to be very Christian-oriented, felt fortunate and humbled that the cyclone had not struck the town or any of its residents. They regarded their luck as a late Christmas present, in spite of everything else, from the invisible one called Almighty, and claimed He must have listened to all the feverishly whispered prayers that were said across town throughout the previous night.

But, before the prayers of thanksgiving could be sent to the Almighty for not causing a catastrophe, danger signals struck again. Word of another miracle began spreading like wildfire from the kids running up and down the muddy street with heart-stopping excitement. *What? What?* said the people who never listened. Listen! Please! These little kids! The children, full of natural innocence from the obsessive parental protection that was the most endearing thing about Desperance, were yelling out how Santa's sleigh must have fallen out of the clouds in the storm. Parents yelled: *Come back here you kids!*

One youngster who stopped to speak, said: 'He is coming, so all you people you better come quick and have a look at Santa Claus, because he is walking if you please from the sea, coming straight towards Desperance.' Christmas was too much. High time to be getting over Christmas – it makes parents go mad. Next, a galloping pantomime of people began running through the mud with arms flying, chasing one another, and going after those naughty kids to get them to come back.

The truth was that the town's locals had flocked down, in droves mind you, to watch the stranger who had long white hair and beard, walking in the sea. As they stood together on the foreshore, no one had a clue from what anchorage the mariner might have originally pulled up his anchor and set his sail. This truth was just a mere speck of dust in the minds of Uptown, and the speck was roaming, growing into something else altogether. Uptown being different to everyone else, never let the truth stop a good story from circulating around when there was time to chew the fat.

The chitchatting was like a strong wind along the foreshore. The people of Uptown talked and talked and never cared two flaming hoots if anyone was listening, and there were people listening. There were the old Pricklebush people who kept the chronicles of the land hereabouts since time began. They were talking in lingo about the huddling of the *house flies* they were noticing up along the beach. These old people were saying how paradoxically foolish of Uptown with their airs and fancies to equate this miracle with the beliefs of the original founding people of the seaport of Desperance. You only needed to take one look and you could see yourself that most of them white folk, about twenty or thirty adults and twice the children standing up on the high ground there – a half a foot above the new sea level – were hand-me-down generations who were nothing like a patch of the original stock: *And thank goodness for small mercies*. You could have counted on one hand who amongst Uptown had even been on the sea.

These people are not any good. They don't believe in God, the old people explained, because knowing the seas, even far from the Great Southern Land, they referred to the seafarer as a descendant of English gods.

They don't even remember their own religion.

All the Uptown white folk stood well back from the water's edge because if you could read their thoughts, you would know how frightened they were of sea water. This was how it should be: water could jump right out and suck anyone in the undertow of blackness and a terrible death. Up high then, they gathered, all nodding and gesturing self-righteously to each other in their fashionable proclamations of how they could recognise straightaway any old so-and-so who lived by the sea. You could hear their voices wafting in the wind westward down the beach, saying things like the old sailors would, like – *Even anyone, even every child of the Port, could recognise a sea man when they see one coming.*

On this long, fine morning, they recognised the mariner's harsh golden skin as their own. *Ah! Ah!* and *Ole la la!* exclaimed one, two and three female voices, possibly more, when sighting that shiny skin glowing like torchlight whenever a spot of sunlight escaped through the clouds to beam upon him. *A fine looking skin.* Someone describing this kind of skin said it could only belong to a sea man because for one thing, he was not coloured – not black or yellow for instance.

His hair, long and tatted, was the colour of the antarctic snow. Sometime, long ago, it became bleached from canary yellow in wild winds and seawater salt in his voyages on oceans far and wide. The cantata further proclaimed as though he were a priest: *He cometh soon, a paragon, the quintessential old man of the sea himself.* Some folk thereabout Desperance had already claimed to have seen giant serpents in the sea so the magical appearance of the sea man was calming compared to stories like that. Others said the lost mariner resembled a perfect human pearl amidst his tangles of ornaments.

He was like Jonah with cockle-shells, green seaweed and starfish enmeshed together in a crown of snow. They noticed in his eyes a piercing sea-grey glare of bewilderment. Oh! Well sung the oracle: *I repeat, there is nothing to fear from being a stranger to the Great Southern Land.* They sang praises. *Please put him at ease*, cried all. How ears burned down in the Pricklebush: *So in their dreams*, they murmured.

You got to believe what was true in the homes of Desperanians. A folktale of ancient times elsewhere was stored in treasure chests in the minds of these people. A sea people such as themselves come from so far away to be lost, would forever have all seas in their sights. That was their story.

The young people of the Pricklebush who could see distance, said his hands, hard-skinned, scarred and ready, were exactly the same as those men whose skilled hands customarily dragged nets and hooked lines for a job. It was easily assumed on the high-water mark that the man who later became known as Elias Smith, had come from some distant, mysterious place on the globe, where mourning people wearing dark woollen clothes prayed to weathered statues of the Maria de la Mer, or Maria Candida, Senora de la Spain or Madonna, Blessed Virgin, or Saint Nicholi – many, many countless rosaries for the children of Oceanides lost at sea.

You could tell this man might be equated with the Dreamtime world because when his memory was stolen, the mighty ancestral body of black clouds and gale-force winds had spun away, over and done with, in a matter of a flash. The old people said they knew the time this had happened to Elias Smith because they had been awake all night watching the sea, and seen the whole catastrophe of clouds, waves and wind rolling away, off in another direction. Elias was left floating face down in the watery jaws of the Gulf of Carpentaria, and as luck would have it, he grabbed a polystyrene fruit box with a bit of fruit still left inside to eat. *He floated away on the currents heading our way.*

The old people who refused to go down and join the watch because white people were there, said no one should go about making a major spectacle out of watching a wretched man walking out of the sea, even if he had walked through twenty-five kilometres of tidal flats full at high tide with the shallow mud waters at the height of the Wet season. Rightly! But that was *town*. Uptown kettle pot was different, Pricklebush whinged, wanting to go too.

While the Pricklebush stayed home, the Uptown people swooped in for the arrival of the stranger like it was something to rejoice about. Call it a phobia about not allowing legends to die. Call it flights of fancy that had driven every man, woman and child down onto the high-tide mark to wait patiently, ankle-deep in the mud, totally abandoning all of their daily jobs and duties, just to relive a familiar old story about their origins. Afar, at the same time, up along the foreshore, way back up the beach away from the town where the old people watched what the white people were doing, the Aboriginal people of Westside Pricklebush started to stir too.

Having heard the commotion, the elders climbed out of their damp bedding on the ground where they had slept through the cyclone, to go see where the noise was coming from. *Someone's excited today*, they agreed, while settling down again in the long grass to watch. They always watched the goings-on of Uptown with restrained interest, and shortly afterwards, began their memory revisions. This was a daily task, a memory tribunal, undertaken with relish by the old people for everyone's matter of concern – talking oral history about the sequestrators who owned Uptown. Every now and again, they would cast scathing glances up the road in the direction of the town. But on this day, the ancient owl-face woman, staring up the beach with the others in her company, and who knows what she saw with her eyesight, on behalf of all her people proclaimed sarcastically in a loud disgusted voice, 'Ha! Ha! Look at us. We are the old people, and we knows *you* not even know where you ares from.' The 'we' she was talking about, were her relations, the blackfella mob from Westside of town, belonging to Normal Phantom, the rightful traditional owner.

The Eastside camp was old Joseph Midnight's mob exiled from Westside because they wanted to say that nobody else but they were the real traditional landowners where Desperance had been built. That idea originated from Old Cyclone who was Joseph Midnight's father. They even made up a name for themselves – Wangabiya – and said that their tribe were the real traditional owners, before Norm Phantom's group which they called the tribe of the *Johnny-come-latelies* came to the Gulf. Well! Even though no tribe on earth existed with that name Wangabiya, you had everyone going around claiming to be a Wangabiya. Lost Wangabiya started turning up in the Gulf from all over the place: Brisbane, Sydney and even one came over from Los Angeles saying he was a Wangabiya, and could speak the lost Wangabiya language. It was the hint of big bickies to be had from big mining that did that. It was unfortunate to have to say it, but those Eastside people of old Joseph Midnight were just a lot of nuisance dogs, which was only natural to expect because they were nothing but rubbish.

They lived among a hundred and one pussycats with pigs. This was how the old people on Westside rubbished those people on Eastside who, they claimed, knew nothing about culture if every one of them had been derived from the genes of trash, from Joseph Midnight. They saw his rubbish blood running through the lot of them so-called Wangabiyas. Even all the pigs you see lying around their yards – all called Aunty and Uncle – can never be shot, *Oh! No! You cannot shoot that good pig, he's Uncle*. And living in car bodies and whatnot, which was illegal. All of it was part of Joseph Midnight's extortion racket with the government. This was what he got for agreeing to the mine. The government gave him a lot of money, a thousand dollars, and said, *Go out there and shoot the vacuum cleaners, all of the Hoovers and Electroluxes – all the feral pigs.* Money talks. This was what he got for his Native title rights. Money to shoot all the pigs. He was supposed to exterminate them from the entire Gulf of Carpentaria once and for all but he never did that. He let his useless relatives take all the little baby piglets home for pets and they bred up ten piglets each.

The so-called Wangabiyas over Eastside were also responsible for cane toads, millions of cane toads living in the district to this day. When they heard that the government was paying fifty cents for a cane toad, you could hear them right over Westside talking and talking. They could not stop wishing for the toads to arrive. *Oh! Other people are really lucky they got them frogs.* Well! How do you think the cane toads got into this pristine environment? Joseph Midnight brought them in his port from Townsville, smuggled them in, not that anyone was there to stop him. Now, shine a torch around outside and you will see nothing but a plague of cane toads all over the place. So, this was the type of people they were – unscrupulous, nasty kind of people – even without talking about the land they tried to steal.

What was really offensive to the Westside elders was that those squatter people even had the audacity to open their mouths about somebody's else's land. *They forget they never had any land for a thousand years.* And if you see that there are no little native animals around anymore it was because those people ate them. Ate everything. You would think that would be a good case for a bit of serenity around these parts from those people, when they are living on somebody else's land, and treating it like vacuum cleaners sucking up the wildlife. You would think that, but their loose tongues did not know the meaning of the word serenity.

Over there on Eastside, the thieves talked about nothing all day, and all night long. It was enough to drive people away. These people were so habituated to talking, the drone of their voices drove other people mad, and even some people who had got trapped on Eastside and could not escape because they had no money to buy a ticket out of the place had to be taken away down South on the Flying Doctor's plane, to be put away in a mental institution.

A lot of people wanted to know what Eastside talked about? Well! Nothing much. They just talked about anything that popped into their heads. Mention a word. Mention horse, and they would talk about horses all day long. Mention shopping, and all night long they would talk about shopping. Mention fighting, and they would go out after dinner and half murder someone. Westside old people accused those people of being so full of madness, they said it had to be punishment from the spirits for disgracing the country not rightfully theirs, in any case.

So there it was: fringe camps sandwiching Desperance, and nothing better to do with themselves than to sit about watching white folk of Uptown going about their business. It was hard to imagine something being so ingrained it cannot be scrubbed away like ink stains on the carpet. It was like blood stains. This was exactly what it was like.

So, the 'edge' people, all of the blackfella mob living with quiet breathing in higgily-piggerly, rubbish-dump trash shacks, all popped any old where in the prickly bushes, all along a cobweb of dirt tracks running crooked, left, right and centre outside of town, sat back and watched this spectacle of the snow man taking place on the beach. It was the beginning of the story of the day the spirits of the seas and storms mixed their business, and sent Elias from out of oblivion into Desperance with good reason. This was the story about Elias Smith which was later put alongside the Dreamtime by the keepers of the Law to explain what happened once upon a time with those dry claypans sitting quietly out yonder there for anybody to look at, and wonder about what was happening to the world, and to be happy knowing at least this was paradise on earth, and why would anyone want to live anywhere else.

It is important to say straight up that it was no good at all for Elias coming in from the sea empty-handed like he was, and no good being anywhere with an empty head with even less than ten cents worth of the richness of his own memory anymore. If you put an empty shell in struggle town, or Uptown like the prickly bush mob called it, expect a ton of bad things to happen. His was a lethal combination, he would have been better off being an ant under a leaf if he had zilch left, not even his memory for a bit of a trade.

Little towns belonging to the white folks are like this. You could hear the town struggling to survive, to make good of itself, crying out – *Save me! Save me!* But who listened? This was the old, unanswerable question: how the heck were they going to keep themselves out of the water? And, with no disrespect, it is expedient to say at this point, that such little towns are apt to do one thing right, and this was how a town like Desperance shared a slither of similarity with others. You know, it too sought glory in its own legends. A single, important legendary lore of place developed over a century or two:

> *impossibly hard to reach by land or sea,*
> *it cast a spell on those who came,*
> *planted them like ground rock,*
> *and because there is a measure of love in acts of permanency,*
> *they found it too hard to leave.*

Oh! Fashionable city people, Southern people who like noise would say that somewhere north of the Tropic of Capricorn like Desperance, was just a quiet little town, but if you listened hard enough, you would have heard the silence screaming to be heard. Noise was everywhere, and if there was an original God who had come along with all the white people, who created everything for them, then this place was where he made his music. There could not be a more windy town anywhere in the world of tin flapping, like an orchestra growing louder with age. And they never knew it, or realised, but that music drove those town people half mad. You should watch the wind music for it is the undoer of a man's toil.

The winds. Well! The winds blew over the claypans from other places in the world with no respectful acknowledgment for a town having been built *good and proper* in its path. Over time, the whirly-whirly local winds composed much of the new music for the modern times. The winds squeezed through every crack and hole to loosen sheets of corrugated iron for the salt in the air to rust nails that went pop, until all those old pieces of tin whined, whistled, banged and clapped. Every day, all day and all night sometimes, the town jammed jazz with bits of loose tin slapping around on top of the mud-stained fibro walls to pummel the crumbling, white-ant-ridden, honeycombed timber frames, until one day, only paint held up those buildings.

This indescribable concoction of rhythms escaped into the atmosphere, and was spirited away across the continent to some-where else more fraught with modernity than Desperance. There, wafting into the minds of modern day composers like lights of star-dust, inspiring them to create weird, unfathomable orchestral music which the old people now heard on the radio and recognised as the uncontrollable airs of Desperance. What a fright! They turned the radio off.

The coming of Elias Smith generated an era of self-analysis not seen in the Gulf for a very long time. The truth was you had to think about Uptown more carefully, for those people had more than one legend about how they got to belong to a place. Uptown whitefella mob was full of people claiming they had no origins. They usually met one another on the street with greetings like:

Hey! stranger, where did you come from? They said that they were not strangers because they had originated from nowhere. This was the reason why they contrived the waiting for Elias into an honest act of homage to the comings of their forebears. The occasion revealed through this unusual disembarkation of a person from the sea how people like themselves had also once, turned up, appearing from out of nowhere.

True Desperanians were those blue-eyed, blond, nervy, skinny, freckled types belonging to the old families whose origins in town stretched back several generations, not Johnny-come-latelies – no way. On request, these descendants of the original residents could rattle off from the top of their heads the who's-who in town, and who went six foot down and under in the local cemetery. They could trace back the family line on a sheet of paper or a line drawn with a stick on the ground just to prove they could reach the point of infinity to show they did not exist. *Told ya!* they would say. Their original forebear, a ghostly white man or woman, simply turned up one day, just like Elias. On the scale of things, their history was just a half-flick of the switch of truth – simply a memory no greater than two life spans.

There were other little secrets about Uptown. The town was marked on no map. The Uptown folk had a dogged nature, and through their own sheer perversity had over many decades become unnaturally acclimatised, withstanding the tropical humidity at heatwaves so extreme in summer, their fair skin dripped like a tap. They marvelled open-heartedly at having bred a stoical population of backbone which made them a *cause célèbre*. And what of? The Pricklebush mob took a good look at themselves. The old people gave the little kids whom they had sent into Uptown every day to get educated, a job to do. *Go*, they told the schoolkids, *search through every single line of all those whitefellas' history books*.

The little boys and girls flicked through all the damp pages to find out the secrets of white people. They reported finding not one single heroic deed about Uptown. The old people almost flogged those kids for lying about white people, or laziness, or both. *How could you find nothing?* The little scholars insisted that they were telling the truth. *Alright! What else then?* Not any religious places of worship so steeped in prayer and devotion the ground was too holy to walk on belonged to Uptown. *They got no sanctified ground?* They got no sanctified ground.

Well! It could not be but it was so. Look around and you will see no monuments of brass and gilt, nor any places of high culture and song in Desperance. No Mozart, Beethoven nothing! All this stuff the cheeky little buggers scoffed. *There! There!* Uncrumpling on the ground the pictures they had ripped out of books. Mistakenly, then, Pricklebush thought their educated children had all the knowledge stuffed in their heads about white people and started to believe the town had nothing – no culture, no song, no sacred places. But stop that fantasising! Hold your horses. Why? They were – Wrong! Wrong! The town still shone with *succès d'estime,* just because they had rejected the vast majority of those 'Southerners', their own true countrymen government, who un-believingly could not have cared less. Oh! What jellyfishes must live down South who had no affinity with scorching hot days, 365 days of the year.

True Desperanians told the Pricklebush people that they were apostles of all matters local. Fringe mob, the edge people, said they did not believe that. The Pricklebush schoolchildren continued their studies, and one day, came running back from town. These children stood full of themselves in front of the old people and proclaimed loudly, that the folk of Uptown could be masters of their own dreams. Yes, like stonemasons, who in a night could relay every single stone in an invisible boundary surrounding the town into a wall so solid it had the appearance of a wall surrounding an important medieval palace. *But where were stones to be found in the claypans?* In these times it was assumed that any outsider to these dreams would never see the stones of Desperance, if he carried a different understanding of worldly matters originating from ancient times elsewhere. The outsider to these dreams saw only open spaces and flat lands.

The Pricklebush mob saw huge, powerful, ancestral creation spirits occupying the land and sea moving through the town, even inside other folk's houses, right across any piece of the country. Nothing but no good was coming out of puerile dreams of stone walls, big locked gates, barred windows, barbed wire rolled around the top to lock out the menace of the black demon. Pricklebush decided the Uptown boundary must be a gammon one. Then the folk Uptown showed their boundaries which they said had been created at the beginning of their time. The town boundary they showed the Pricklebush mob was there and there, on paper. To prove what they were saying, they said it was invisibly defined on the surface of the earth by old surveying methods, methods long in the grave with the original surveyors, when the original pioneers came along and developed the town.

When the name Masterton, the new name given by an infamous State government to change the name from Desperance, appeared on all the modern maps, along with contrary degrees of latitudes and longitudes to the old methods, the locals of Uptown said by their actions – a two fingers V shaped in the air – *Go and get stuffed*. The town kept all of their nicely painted Desperance town signs up and waged an intense battle with the disinterested proletarians of the Main Roads Department whenever they arrived in town with an arsenal of sign-making equipment, along with government trademark 'silver bullet' mobile living quarters to spend a few days erecting more Masterton signs.

The enraged residents would band together in full force for the town. They took on the appearance of red-faced ogres who threw buckets of verbal abuse and other things, while those government workers who were full of nonchalance, sat around and did nothing until it was time to go away again. The workers just went on humming through gritted teeth, *Keep remembering, pay day on Friday*. Desperanians ripped down any new Masterton signs the workers managed to erect and in the process of acting out purposeful community pride, they hammered into the ground many more signs along the side of the road into town just to make sure no one would mistake Desperance for the name of some past his use-by-date Southern politician who wanted to plant his ego in the minds of the future generations. Pricklebush complied, by saying they too vomited at the thought of Masterton, to please Uptown.

With all the official road maps to Masterton regarded locally as some place different, strangers only had a snowflake's chance in hell of ever finding their way around these parts. *Nah! Nah! You got the wrong map, buddy*, lost souls were told as they limped up to the single petrol station selling Shell only. Uptown never liked to talk much to strangers. The impasse between the town and the government led to a high road mortality rate in the red never-never land.

You is in hell, Pricklebush could have told them travellers, but name the traveller or the one single tourist who ever goes to the Pricklebush for a piece of advice. And as far as the local hierarchy of Uptown were concerned, but never posted anyone down South a letter about it, their town remained Desperance, named after the founder, Captain Matthew Desperance Flinders. Needless to say, no one in Uptown accepted the fact that Flinders was a prize fool to go about saying he discovered a deep water port that turned into a dustbowl when the river changed course, and a century would pass before the giant serpent ancestral spirit made that track again.

Uptown people said all people were born without lands and came to the new world of Desperance carrying no baggage. When you think of all this philosophy, it was easy to see how momentum was building up amongst the wet throng on the beach watching Elias Smith, a vision splendid, walking in from the sea. Their teardrops joined the showers of rain which had started to run down their faces. People became full-hearted, loving the memories of their personal histories, even if it was an aberration from a history only as old as the cemetery down the road.

But alas for Elias, it was not an even-tempered day to be taken on the wings of angels, even if he had been saved from drowning amidst the lure of a sea churning and rolling with storm-shredded seaweed and meadow grass. He could have stayed many fathoms down on the basement of the ocean floor amongst the remains of ancient shipwrecks, lost forever to the tranquil music of thousands of bits and pieces of chipped and broken china – sugar bears, yellow chickens, spotted dogs, and pink babies of lost cargo, hanging and clanging against each other, all over the reef ledges in an other-worldly abyss.

But poor Elias was temporarily blind. His eyes stung from the night of lashings by the sea, and were made worse, as he walked through the waters into straight winds blowing out to sea from the south, dense with the choking smoke from bushfires clogging the atmosphere. One can only dream if things could have been different. If he wished for good luck, he might have taken a closer look at those gobsmacked people huddled in the misty drizzle, standing there doing nothing to lift a finger to help him. He might have been better off not feeling so good about himself. Wiser, if he had felt less like a miracle escaping the fate of becoming an ornament of bones, dressed in algae, for little fish to swim about in.

If God had shown grace, Elias would have seen all the Pricklebush mob hiding about in the long grass, and like one of those big hammerhead sharks out there in the water, cruising up and down by the beach, instantly recognised the fear in the eyes of the mob of people huddled on the beach. A hammerhead shark would have seen the real way those people looked at strangers. Elias by crikey, being half drowned, was no excuse. You should have seen it written up there in thin air above those people's heads, that if towns like this were granted three wishes a day, they would sharpen up whatever God blessed them with like knives for brains, and as quick as you could say, *Bob's your uncle,* stab one another in the back, including Uncle Bob if he was around.

A wiser man would have dived straight back into those grey milky waters and swum off with the receding tide, straight back over the twenty-five kilometres of mudflats he had come from, and be gone and done with it. He should have thought about that like the edge people, who know off by heart how deluded will-o'-the-wisps from nowhere reigned in a glorious separateness from all other humankind. Elias should have said, *Hey! It's just a tiny, whimsical seclusion of xenophobia, just like all the other isolated apostrophes along the claypan horizon.*

Since no one in the entire local history had ever seen anyone actually walk into town from the sea, and the miracle was appreciated by everyone gathering to watch, the old people worried about Uptown's ability to cope with their uncertainty about new things coming into their lives. It was normal for their approach to fluctuate between confused joy and confused woe and on this day it was no different. He could have been what? An angel carrying the message of the one they called the Almighty? A ghost, spirit, demon or sea monster? Or a man? The closer Elias came, the more the little cloud of people moved backwards to higher ground. Even the edge mob, standing way off in their Eastside and Westside camps in groups of their own with their black heads high above the long grass, could hear those Uptown folk describing to each other the vision splendid as a marvellously hideous *other kind*.

As morning wore on, the old people witnessed the cloud of Uptown, now unconsciously grouped in the shape of Australia, speaking more wholeheartedly about the apparition in ghostly terms. Yes, it was true that they were saying what they thought, even acknowledging the ghostly phenomenon in realistic terms. Their children, covered in play mud, looked as though they were part of some kind of ritual. Their ears, tuned like radar, burst wide open when grown-ups said they were witnessing the emergence of an aquatic aura, a God-sent water angel.

Without shame, married too, emm! emm! Shocking messages scurried along the long grass tracks about what those besotted women were saying, watching his thighs. Oh! Oh! Look at that! What a sight those golden thighs made, wading through kilometres of shallow weedy waters, leaving a little feathery trail behind his knees. Heavens only knew what thoughts were luxuriating in depraved minds about the faraway look in his ironic Slavic eyes. The old people had to duck down, look away in shame; they just looked quickly through the long grass at those women with sneaky eyes. They gave long, slow whistles to one another through the grass, as they watched the mirage of hot air building overhead, spelling nothing but trouble, rising through the cloud like it was spurting out of the mega-sized chimney stack of a mine with a very large processing plant. *Tell everyone their men are blind*, the old people hand-signalled each other above the grass. If black could blush, if only. But the steam-making women standing on the beach, downright proper, respectable Uptown women, could not escape the spell the mariner had cast on them, simply from looking at his bare thighs walking through water.

Oh! Of course it pained the hearts of the old people who had to witness those sad women quietly remembering hot nights of childhood imaginings, when parents once read them European folktales, where gentle horses went clipperty-clopping through the stories of mist and fading images of other lands and lullabies. Where appeared from fog, the lone male skater, gliding effortlessly over a white ice-covered lake with edges surrounded by sodden reeds, and moaning elm trees drooping heavy with spirits wrapped in cloaks of snow.

All of this happened on the water's edge, after Captain Nicoli Finn – someone else from Uptown who also claimed to have originally appeared in Desperance from out of nowhere – had said he had discovered the person walking in from the sea. Finn was an old man, a local feature on the foreshore landscape, whom Uptown commonly referred to, not by his actual name, but as a thing: *The crazy whatever!* On the day of the discovery that changed everything in Finn's life, he was engaged in his usual surveillance of the coast-line that was now temporarily relocated right next to the town because of the king tides.

Finn was all rigged out in his crazy clothes. A *get-up* of full, winter serge, the olive-coloured uniform of the Australian army he slept and worked in, which was commonly regarded as a public health problem. Perched crookedly on his long, oily, greying hair was his sergeant's cap. He could have been called, *Look at him*, which was what perspiring people habitually whispered in dismay behind his fly-attracting back. But when they were smart they avoided looking at Mr Finn, especially on days that were scorchers, so as not to break out in a terrible prickly heat rash themselves.

Since Finn remained oblivious to most things, he never noticed how the long spells of humidity in the air made his unkempt, dank-smelling uniform a home for hundreds of nestling moths visiting Desperance after the rains. The invading insects left numerous holes behind when they moved on to chew up more of what he wore, before spreading their larvae like couch-grass pollen wherever he walked around town. Until one day, Uptown made it their business to formally thank Finn for the permanent plague of moths besieging the town.

Finn's career of undercover work, which he claimed he did as an enlisted soldier for the Australian army, was uneventful until the day Elias rose out of the waters. Every day he followed a set routine. When he proceeded on 'operation', he would set off very early in the morning on his 'secret' orders to the water's edge, whatever its current distance was from town. He was commonly seen as a blob moving in the early morning fog-filled atmosphere covering the land that stretched right out into the sea to hide the horizon between earth and sky. Head down, with a stern expression of concentration stretched across his lips, he marched on up the beach in search of signs to report to army intelligence. He was fastidiously particular about filling the requirement of his cover, by pretending to be a madman in army uniform, but for all and all, he was the inventor of confusion about his actual line of work, and it was hard to know if he was a habitual liar, or really did work for the army. He created a foil by collecting all of the empty bottles lying about the water's edge. These he would neatly and painstakingly stack until they produced giant-sized walls of amber glass at the back of the Fisherman's Hotel. Anyone could go and watch him sitting at the plastic table on a chair in front of the walls of bottles. This was where he ate the counter dinners the hotel gave him for free.

Before the day Elias came and things changed, Finn's cover was so strong that he could elicit spiteful scorn as easy as you could click your fingers, wherever he walked in town. The women hated him: *Don't look, pretend you're not looking, but there goes that old madman wasting his life again – just like a general fool.* Uptown matrons, who once looked like kewpie dolls, now voluptuously overfed to sustain their elephantine memories, whispered out loudly behind his back just to spite him from across the street. You could feel their jealousies moving up and down the streets of Desperance, leaving you breathless for days.

Silly old Finn never gave two frigs – he kept on walking, no, he did not walk, he shuffled in a zigzag fashion from one side of the footpath to the next on Main Street, bent with whatever hawks he had shot while hunting alone on the beach slung over his shoulders. Shooting hawks was a useless preoccupation and Finn spent a lot of time hunting the skies for them. The sun-frocked matrons in their sun-bleached dresses shuffled by, blood draining from faces like dried pears at the mere thought of having to cross right next to him on the footpath, and as they did, snubbing him with jaws atrembling and eyes glaring ahead.

But Finn's life changed for the better as he stood in his mud-caked army boots on the beach that early morning when the mist was just starting to lift, and the air was still full of red haze. It was at that precise moment of the red morning, when he would commence firing, wasting army bullets on a group of hawks circling above the sea, as he always did, that he had first noticed the miracle. The birds too must take credit for their part in Finn's miracle. Finn was affected with the dero shakes, wobbling one way or another to steady his position, as the hawks, looking down at him, casually flew out of range. It was a game the birds played with the army captain, flying in and out of range, up and down, occasionally one fell foul – a fluke hit – but for years they knew he could not aim straight enough to save himself. It was while he was jerking himself around in a haywire frenzy to keep up with the birds, screaming at them to keep still, switching the rifle's sights from straight up to the sky to dead level with the horizon, that he made the discovery.

For a long time he watched the man walking across the mudflats through the muddy waters choked with reeds at high tide. Finn knew the lie of the land, and he watched Elias making detours past the decades of half-submerged car bodies – Holdens, Fords and semi-trailers laden with mud, homes of crabs and gluttonous man-eating sea fauna. Finn wondered why the man seemed unaware that it was the season of the box jellyfish with their long, stinging tentacles invisibly spread across the surface of the water. The man walking through the calm looked almost spiritual to Finn who stood transfixed to the spot, like he too was made out of clay.

Poor Finn. Crocodiles, sharks, gropers, stingrays, box jellyfish, stonefish, hundreds and hundreds of the invaders of childhood dreams swam around his mind. He heard his head pulsating with voices reminiscing over every single tragedy in Uptown fishing or beach picnic history. Voices saying they could remember it all, as though it only happened yesterday. Living next to the sea was like having tragedy for a neighbour. He watched, half expecting the waters to swirl at any second into a bloody vortex of the man being devoured by a giant sea carnivore. Until just as suddenly, as if out of the blue, *Finn tell yourself*, a distant military voice boomed from his memory, *fright was not right, or expected of the one and only Australian Army defence force personnel for miles around*. At that, Finn climbed onto the top of one of the dumped, empty diesel drums left lying around, for a better view through the sights in his rifle, in case he had to shoot.

He swore on oath afterwards that he had even heard music rising out of the waters from a pedal organ playing to him as clear as day. It was God's music, he had said, and softly started to hum the bits he could remember. Everyone recognised the piece as Handel's *Messiah*, exactly as Beatrice Smith played it on her pedal organ in the solitude of her house, whenever she was overtaken by spiritual light-heartedness.

The Captain could not contain himself any further and decided he would have to share the news with the whole town. Forgetting his limp, he ran straight through the mud up to the middle of town, arriving exhausted and out of breath, but still able to muster the herculean strength required to yank the rope of the town's new bell into full ear-piercing peal, without permission. The large bell had, within months of its arrival, become rusted from the thick salt-moistened air, where it hung from its steeple on the neat, front lawn of the new Council Chambers.

The first response came from Libby Valance, the big, plump town clerk who really should have been the one to ring the bell in case of emergency. Unless, of course, on those days he felt down with the weight of middle age and heavy humidity, he wanted someone else to do it.

'What are you doing with my bell, Finn?' Libby Valance hollered as he came, striding in slow motion across the lawns, to stop Finn yanking the rope.

Finn stopped and stared, then ran off back towards the sea, unable to speak, gesturing with his arms for Libby Valance to follow.

In no time at all, with the children yelling out about Santa Claus coming to town, everyone in town was heading down through the yellow grass towards the beach. The children who had been drilled since they were just toddlers in nappies to the heavy ding-donging bell, charged out of their homes, knocking each other out of the way, and ran, yelling out, 'What is it? What is it?'

The kids stood close to the edge of the waters to watch the strange man walking across the kilometres of shallow mudflats before they joined the deeper waters of the ocean behind him. 'He's got mud-curls,' they yelled, and the women who had been transfixed by the sight of his bare thighs replied in muffled voices, 'That is because he is a miracle.' It was the first time anyone in town had seen anyone with dreadlocks.

The more practical-minded amidst the crowd announced they

were going to find a boat to rescue the man. Regardless of all else, they said, 'Obviously he will need rescuing.' They went off, the young men itching to partake in something like a sea rescue, the older men trudging through the mud, half knowing already it was going to be a futile attempt to find a boat in working order.

The trouble was that nobody went out fishing during the monsoonal season. All except Norm Phantom, the only real nautical man of these waters, and he was already out somewhere fishing the estuaries. It was the Wet and the town's boats were sitting up idle on blocks having repairs done. Every motor had been taken apart, and left lying about on old newspapers in one hundred greasy pieces inside the fishing sheds around town.

At the waterfront, prayers were remembered and the crowd, some kneeling, said them out loud – Our Fathers, Hail Marys, Glory Bes, Acts of Contrition. By the time the man arrived safe on dry land, the talk on the beach had gathered to the height of wonderment. It was amazing. They agreed that nobody had ever seen anything like this before. For once something good had happened. Anybody's wishes could come true. What a day. The town stood well back in a circle staring at the man lying face up on the sand and ordered: *Give him room. Give him room.* You could tell from the look in their glassy eyes that they had placed the richness of prophecy squarely on this man's shoulders. It was only logical, on the face of things, something good had happened, but underneath the mask of appreciation, there was also a pot of apprehension bubbling away in their brains.

Time passed. 'For God's sake you got to tell us who are you?' Libby Valance, beckoning and pleading on behalf of the town, tried to persuade the unmoving man to speak. The man did not speak. He asked in every way he knew to entice a reaction. Suddenly, several others piped up, since they could not help themselves, and answered Libby Valance's question. They said he was a saviour.

The town clerk spun around and looked at them in disbelief. Libby prided himself in being educated. Blood drained from his abnormally red face. His wife, Maria-Sofia glared at him so hard, he bit his tongue and said nothing.

Libby Valance did not give up. He kept trying to work through the lunacy talking in the background, squatting with his portly stomach slumped on his knees, balancing himself awkwardly next to the man lying face up on the foreshore. He tried to be a comfort. A long time passed. The sun shone directly above the beach and Libby thought he was being singled out. How could the sun just shine on him? He was determined to keep his interrogation up until the matter was finalised. The wet man could not answer, but continued breathing heavily and seemed in a state of total confusion.

Yes, who are you? irritated Uptown mimicked, losing patience. They wanted to go home. The whole situation of the perfect man lying before them, exposed on the beach, presided over by hovering, plump Libby Valance in sweating black, was just too perplexing a matter for anyone's mind to chew over. They told Libby to get on with it because they wanted a good answer there and then.

Since Libby was useless, all eyes began casting around, looking for someone else to speak to the stranger when a voice said, 'Get the bloody law and order man.' All eyes fell onto Constable E'Strange, same name, Truthful: someone whom they had previously written off as more than useless. The Constable stood back, observing everything and everybody in his own tranquil way, loving the fact he was living in Desperance, and being totally ignorant of his reputation. Tut-tut! Poor bugger, a black hand signalled from the long grass: *Come quick and have a look at this*. The kids ran their index fingers in a circle around their ears.

Radar! Radar! All disgrace for poor Truthful. A policeman without a good pair of local ears? Perhaps it was best to be incapable of picking up all the whispering tongues hissing behind your back. More than a few years ago, the Constable had arrived in Desperance but the truth be known, nobody had use for a policeman anymore, so E'Strange had became very comfortable sitting down there at the police station doing nothing thank you very much. In his abundant spare time, the mild-natured law enforcer had created around the grey besser brick building beautiful rose gardens that Uptown women now liked to walk in and admire. He spent hours honing up his hoon town bribery skills with withered plant cuttings, to crash the treasured plant collections of all those slack-cheeked Uptown matrons. They had even strolled down to the police station in broad daylight to help him transform the barred cells into a hothouse for *Ficus elastica* and *Monstera*. The plants grew into jungle proportions of twisted vines. It had not occurred to Truthful that if the need arose one day, there was hardly any room left in the building for locking someone up.

Even now, Truthful did not recognise the vibes of the town against him. He just saw himself as part of the crowd. He had forgotten he once had a passion for crime. 'Oh! Leave him,' some woman said in a dry, acid voice, typical of the North. The word around town was not nice. Whisperings in the ear claimed he had been left to his own devices too long. It was plain to everyone that Truthful was not really interested in Elias lying face up on the beach, a complete stranger who had not said, nor satisfied anyone, if he were friend or foe to the town.

Truthful kept checking his broken gold Rolex watch, guessing the time. He longed to go back to his office, where he spent his working hours undertaking a personal rehabilitation course with a tax-deductable, mail-order counselling service which promised a one hundred per cent success rate at the end of thirty-six months at very little cost to his pay packet. At times, whenever he appeared out of nowhere, down among the edge mob in the prickly bush, trying to make friends, he would purge his conscience to the old

71

people. 'I am trying to make a new man of myself,' he explained. He talked about spiritual journeys, including self-hypnosis, exorcism, self-analysis. *I'll kill the bastard if he tries any of that shit on me*, echoed the old people after he left. Above all, the Pricklebush people were scared about what would happen to them after being apprehended by Truthful. But listen! This man built for dealing with trouble said he had moved a long way from being a thug copper from The Valley in Brisbane. He said people from the prickly bush should think of him as a friend, like a true, rural gentleman cop. He said he was even thinking of changing his surname to Smith like everybody else in Uptown.

The situation in Desperance might appear bad on the surface but the law did not fall into tatters just because a Southern Queensland Valley cop could not fill the shoes of the old sergeant when Jay Smith passed away. A good man Jay, who had spent sixty-one years one month dedicated to the police service without missing a single day's work until, after having apologised, he dropped dead. What a resignation. Everyone talked about it. Now, the numerous dynasties of Smith families kept lips zipped about the town's sins. The town had ways and means to deal with pub brawls, rape, robbery, assaults, family violence and fraud among themselves. So, up until now, with it being obvious to everyone that Libby was doing such a balls-up of a job, Truthful was free to stand about, looking on with the rest of the crowd gathered around the man on the beach.

You could see how oblivious he was when the glaring started and the whispering began. A plethora of worries! A deluge of ill fate! There was no joy to be had in not having a proper policeman, and the algae man was still lying on the beach, and all of that hot sun was making people think weak thoughts and voices were raised. Well! Now everyone up the beach from the Pricklebush in the long grass could hear the consternation of Uptown and how they could go on.

What if the man is dangerous, contagious, riddled with all kinds of incurable diseases, a violent maverick, or a murderer or a foreigner trying to gain illegal entry?

What if he is a maniac and a menace?

What if he is a spy collecting data on our confidential capacities to defend ourselves?

What if he is an alien?

Uptown was running on hot air because everywhere else on earth was sweet: *they were changing guards at Buckingham Palace* but nobody in the world cared what happened to Desperance. Nobody could laugh at these things because aliens were a serious consideration and the town had stories about these aliens that could send a cold shiver down your spine. There were real people who could tell you the stories of how they had been taken away for weeks on metallic-disc spacecraft with red lights flashing across the sky, and who knows, they said when they came back, if aliens were invading the whole countryside. There was so much space in the Gulf, no one would ever know. Those stolen people who acted very sane when they spoke about their adventures, acted like a rabid dog the next.

It was hard to get your mind together when anything could land on the flat lands of the claypan country, and why not? The world was turning upside down, everything was coming apart when you expect to see red days, boatloads of illegal people, sea angels, unhappy spirits of dead people, stinking dead whales, even truckloads of contaminated fish, turning up on the foreshore of Desperance. Now, a man had walked in from the sea.

The man on the beach took on the appearance of the surreal. The sun had dried the mud on his skin until it curled into creamy milk-chocolate-coloured flakes. The layers of seaweed and algae flapped with the slightest breeze. Little sea mites crawled through the litter and into the blisters, fêting on his raw skin. The big-eared children listening to the adults talking about aliens were shooed off right back to the school ground. *Fetch the water bag*, they were told. *Which water bag?* the kids screamed back, stalling, trying to be clever. *The bloody water bag hanging on the school verandah.* They were told to bring it back immediately with threatening gestures, *And bring sandwiches for the man, too.*

Get it yourself, the little bullies answered back at their parents, who seemed to have forgotten it was a school holiday. They were reluctant to go in case they missed out on anything. They were ordered off again very smartly with *Git*, by fathers known to wallop a good punch. Off they went, racing each other back to town, collected food and water, and were back within minutes.

The semi-conscious man's skin oozed with blisters and putrid flaking skin. The circle widened because he really stank. His lips were swollen and chafed. His eyes were squinting from his long exposure in the sea and from all of the smoke coming off the fires. Finn, who had been pushed to the back, even by the children, because he was the town's idiot, felt angry about how he had been ignored. He decided he was not going to act like a mangy dog at the back. Why should he? He was the one who guarded the coast-line, why should he be struggling to get a look-in? The Pricklebush mob, watching Finn, was coming alive for him, hmmm! hmmm-ing, *We want the army*, they jived, elbowing each other and grinning. Everyone wanted to call out his name – *Finn! Finn!* Call out to get the man in the uniform up front there – but they didn't. People got to know their place.

Finn looked around at the noisy crowd. He was the only one among them who knew how to deal with the unexpected – refugees, boat people, any foreigners seeking illegal entry, how to apply mouth-to-mouth resuscitation to injured aliens. He was the only one who had a certificate of first-aid training for injuries received from being in a secret army camp. He pushed his way to the front, snatching the waterbag from a child. *Yes, yes*, Pricklebush cheered in their hearts for Finn. He sat down on the ground and held the half-filled bag to the man's lips, that were cut like strands of cotton, and very slowly, tipped drops onto his tongue. After he considered that the man had drunk enough, he took small bits of mashed-up egg from a sandwich, which he placed in the man's mouth. Everyone watched and waited, looking at their broken watches. From the corner of his eye, Finn saw Libby Valance pull Truthful aside to gee him up on how to interrogate his potential prisoner.

Truthful moved in excitedly, after all he was the cop, but reluctant anyhow, because he was thinking about how he was going to have to move all of the plants from the crowded jail. He stood with his shadow over the man's face, and started to ask random questions, like, 'What ship did you jump, Mister?'

'What ship did you jump!' Shocked, Finn repeated very slowly and loudly the question back into Truthful's face. He muttered on and on about jumping ships, about the pointless need for that kind of realism, about silly people needing to clutch the same old straws in moments of spiritual elevation given by the Lord himself. He couldn't stand another moment of Truthful trying to muscle in, and he shouted at him, 'Stand out of the way, civilian.' The crowd approved, stood well back, and let Finn take charge.

Finn gently asked the man again who he was, waited, then almost jumped out of his skin when the man smiled back and in a low voice said, he did not know who he was. He pointed weakly in the direction of the bushfires in the south, and towards the rain clouds far out at sea to the north that everyone was hoping would eventually bring in the rains to douse the fires. 'I!' was the only word he struggled to say into Finn's ear now bent close to the man's head. Those who heard, looked at each other. He got lured into a lost romance in the fish markets of Asia they whispered, *You could tell by his accent.* Finn smiled, 'Of course,' he kept saying for there was a communication, a very large outpouring of thoughts, flashing like torchlight into each other's mind, a kind of osmosis that Finn understood perfectly. He suddenly remembered Saint Elias from the forgotten distant land of his own early childhood and exclaimed his annunciation out loud, 'His name is Elias Smith.'

Oh! Light of day! It was alright to be the anointed one, the guardian, perhaps even the guardian angel of this melancholy coastal town of Desperance. Elias Smith had gotten up from the beach and survived. No matter it being a hot town with a freezer full of stored facts, local facts cherished as truths and permanently slung over all those stooped local backs of fishy-smelling people eating fried fish on Friday night in humidity-flooded homes of talking memories. Of misfortunes at sea in a storm, relived through the suffering of the surviving fishermen who moaned through rainy days that never stopped, while the landlubbers, dismayed over the cattle lost in flood or the following year's drought, compared rain gauges like sad trophies, which was the only distraction to helplessly watching buildings destroyed by salt erosion and wind, if not, then termites, damp rot, or plagues of rats, grasshoppers or locusts. Sister! Brother! It was just calamity after calamity for Uptown. What else could a person expect before the reprieve of a lonely grave? And the manna from heaven? Schools of prawns and barramundi never where they should be. Why not then an answer to decades of prayers and religious devotion for things to be better? All for one and one for all for God's creation in a place where the Lord's hand was always at work in ways that often defied the comprehension of the local people. Why not then – a gift from God?

Yes, it was like God had given Elias to the town. And it was true because they said: *We prayed long and hard to the Lord for help.*

And prayers were answered.

God gave us Elias.

Over the years Elias came to live in Desperance, he would tell many stories about himself that rang true with the strong local beliefs of Uptown explaining how such a person who had been given gifts of prophetic dimensions ought to behave. 'How else?' he asked, after trying to intellectualise his own legend of being dispatched like a letter out of heaven into a storm and surviving all the atrocities of hell. But at the end of his high-faluting pontificating, Elias Smith was just like a normal man who found it impossibly hard to believe something special should have happened to him.

'No! No! Go away.' Sometimes he would sulk because homage piled on homage was like cream cake. A person can only take so much. Elias vented his spleen in secret places, screaming for mercy, for normality; he thought he was going mad. Correct the Pricklebush for saying they actually saw Elias Smith standing about on the claypan in the dead of night screaming his lungs out. Correct the old people coming back from a leisurely moonlight stroll for mentioning they saw Elias out there again, gazing at the mid-winter stars. *He was a very strange white man*, they agreed. They built an identity for the one he lost. All told, they said he was a man of ancient ways who was planning his escape route from Desperance. He told the Pricklebush elders he most definitely was not.

What were you doing out here looking like a madman then? they asked him. He told them he was adding new stars to his collection of novas and auroras. They also sat with him to count stars. Everything was hush-hush in the Pricklebush. No one ever told Uptown a single thing of what Elias was doing out on the claypan. You learn a good lesson when you get told, *Oh! Yeah! And pigs have wings, huh?* Invisible things in nature made no sense to Uptown because of their savoir faire in being Australians. Once, a long time ago when they first heard Pricklebush talk like this they kept them out of town for a long, long time. *Can't come in here if you want to talk mumbo jumbo like mad people*, Uptown said. The old people they had tactlessly taken to calling simple-minded retaliated with a hundred months worth of evil curses and sorcery. In the end, black and white were both crawling on the ground in reconciliation. Both saying that they were plain jack of each other. So, the old people said, *We have to keep it a secret*.

This was the reason no one said anything about Elias's nocturnal flights of fancy. About seeing him lifting up his bony arms, outstretched palms level with the horizon, standing in one spot, swaying from side to side, trying to imitate the flight of a bird or fins of a fish. Whispers circulated only in the Pricklebush about how he looked like a crucifix ticking in the moonlight. And he would shrug sometimes, if anyone questioned him, as if he too found it difficult to believe in his own story.

It was always a difficult time when Elias lost faith in himself. He was melancholy about being unable to recall memories about himself, for instance, his childhood – what of it, where had it been? He became despondent knowing he was not the same as normal people. It worried the Uptown folk sick right to the pit of their stomachs on the occasions of high humidity which marked his anniversary of coming to Desperance. This was when Elias would go around spreading his arms like wings of doubt, saying he didn't exist, or even saying things like, 'Why me?' In town, it was considered strangely funny for a man to be questioning his status as a celestial being. *You either are or you are not, and you are*, they told him.

In doubting himself, he also created doubts about the town's *specialness* in being unlike any other place in the whole nation. A town unlike all the capital cities, or all the towns with radio and television broadcasters, where all the so-called lucky people had a stranglehold on the nation's better-class goods and services. 'Nowhere on earth had Desperance's specialness in having acquired an angel,' Libby Valance reminded the town at the beginning of every speech he made. 'There's no place that gets more privileged than that.' He sang the praises of 'This Town'.

The esteemed Finn, now highly regarded around town, had gained a reputation for his sharp sense of predicting and gauging levels of humidity in the summertime. He became expert in knowing Elias's degrees of fretfulness. When Finn sniffed a change in the atmosphere, he would head straight up to the Council and have a small talk with Libby Valance in his office. Soon afterwards, Libby would have eagerly-beavering people rallying about his clean, cream-painted office to carry out his instructions. In town, aromas of cooking pans would filter out of every kitchen so that everyone felt hungry all day long from the wafting aromas of stews, fried fish, roast beef or corned beef and puddings all cooking at once. The normally downcast Uptown, threw off the heaviness of humidity for light-hearted excitement by throwing themselves into round-the-clock talks, meals and singsongs with saronged hula women – dragging out old favourites like 'Tie Me Kangaroo Down Sport', inventing solve-the-mystery games like if you took four men at sea and only three came back what happened to the one left behind, and joyfully reciting old prayers and inventing new ones in a shed that served as a chapel.

Some other people had a different reaction and gambled by the light of kerosene lanterns on the spare allotment covered in buffel grass at the back of the pub, betting the reasons why Elias was thinking the wrong way. Talk, talk and more talk, this was when the traitorous Eastside mob came into dominance. They made Westside sick looking at the way they encroached onto the spare allotment, blending in their non-stop talk with old Joseph Midnight in front leading the way. *Welcome! Welcome!* Uptown invited those crawlers in. Dogs, pussycats, a million flies, all jumped to the spare allotment for talk. Just slowly, surely, the crisis over

Elias Smith passed. A little something someone said, a dull, little gem picked up by somebody else who mulled it over at home until they could see the light of day, and a solution was found to add to the endless scroll of truth about Elias.

The telling of Elias's story as white-haired man, or night-time angel, or crustacean-covered aqua spirit just grew old until one day all anyone remembered was that he had appeared one time, out of the pale blue yonder, and built his own place by himself just like they all had to, and there was nothing unusual about that. Local stories were more reliable than what anyone had ever heard from the big shots on the radio. These were the Southern politicians who talked about themselves and what they were doing but had nothing to do with the little people of Desperance. Uptown said nothing good about these people.

Although Elias never remembered his origins, he was able to acquire other people's memory. They gave him their imagination. Through adopting their childhood memories as his own, he was able to close the gap on the past he could not remember. The faintest recollection he had left of an original memory was that he thought he had been thrown on the night sea from a bolt of lightning. He was able to describe in vivid images how he had entered the atmosphere at sound-breaking speed and because his memory could not keep up, it was left behind. He told his story so persuasively he was able to convince people of just about anything. Nothing was said to the contrary, like his having a screw loose, perhaps. He told the people who gathered around his hut just to hear him speak that when they heard thunder warring out at sea they ought to take care.

Since one angel was unable to care for all of the sinners of the town, he said, 'What you are really hearing is God arguing with the Devil about bringing down other angels on earth to fight the wicked people.' People believed he made storms come in from the sea to Desperance. The way the dark cloudy skies loomed low in storm above the flat claypan country could make you believe Elias was telling the truth. He had become almost as crazy as Finn.

'Look out!' Elias would cry, running out onto the rain-drenched streets in an electrical storm. The old Pricklebush people looked at him out there in the pouring rain and said he had been bitten by a flea. He frightened Uptown by yelling out with his booming celestial voice, pointing his long holy stick towards the heavy clouds, and saying, 'More angels are coming.' It was true how those dark clouds stretching across the long, flat horizon, resting low above the town, seemed as though the heavens were about to break open. Anything could happen around Desperance.

Alright! We will get out there and draw the covers, and the council workers drove out in the Council's trucks to each corner of the town in the rain and they cast an eye, and threw the invisible net invented by Lonely. Lonely was a misnomer. Lonely was not lonely at all. He was just another Uptown outcast said to have *jumped the back fence*, which, in the language of Uptown, meant marriage by a white man to an Aboriginal woman. Together, Lonely and his wife, Glenny, had twelve kids who all lived together in a noisy little corrugated-iron hut in the Pricklebush, all yelling and screaming at each other, laughing and crying, surviving the good times and the bad, as you do. Anyone had to be plain stupid to call his life lonely just because he did not have a white life. Their circumstances were pure dire straits, you better believe it, and poor old Lonely fished all day long in the estuaries to feed them all.

This man's real name was A.D. Smith, who came from some-where and died with every single one of his family crowded around his bed. His grave no longer existed because the year he died a cyclonic flood washed out the cemetery. The yellow waters were like whirlpools tearing through the mud, searching for the bodies of all the old fishing men and their wives, and when the arms of the earth gave up clinging to their wooden boxes, the coffins shot up, poof, to the surface and were carried off to sea. Sometimes, the coffins of Desperance can still be seen floating around in the circular currents of the Gulf. Nobody ever had the nerve to haul them in, even if it was their dead Aunty or Uncle. You could just wave to them. There was nothing else you could do. If you touch the home of dead people it would bring bad luck for fishing. But what if you knock on wood? Doesn't that cause good luck?

There was nothing to be done about the holey cemetery except to put a grader over it and build a new cemetery right over the top. The disastrous burial ground of Uptown made people react like dog-bitten sailors, demanding that a family had the right to bury their freshly dead at sea, even though the Council's by-laws had put a stop to sea burials. So much consternation caused by the heartache of fish versus pollution versus dead people: Who was right or wrong? What were basic human rights, family rights, town rights when the dying called up the Town Council, begging to be allowed to be buried at sea? Nobody knew the answers to any of these insoluble forays of life and death. Nobody could agree about changing the law because the bottom line was: What if it meant more bad luck? Really! At the back of people's minds what it really boiled down to, was who wanted to end up being dragged by their dead corpse of a neck by some old rotting-guts reptile living in a submerged Holden station wagon, somewhere out there in the shallow waters of the bay?

In a vivid dream before he died, A.D. Smith had envisaged a defence system in the form of a giant net made of prayers and god-fearing devotion – a protective shield, saving the town from a cyclone. The legacy of this dream was glorified every November, at the onset of the Wet, at night, when some of the Council men could be seen congregating in secret. You knew the net was being drawn, because you could see the mysterious flashing of torchlight in the long grass. In the Pricklebush, everyone stopped to listen when the bush creatures became silent. Crickets and frogs were the guardians of the night for generations of Pricklebush folk. The old people said, *Don't worry*. They explained the men were checking their magic nails in the fence posts in case anyone was stealing them. In early March, after the Wet, the Council men were instructed to drive out again and draw the net back – *Make the town nice*. So, they went out to retrieve the net and let the fresh air flow in after the rain.

Yes! Sweetening the nostrils. Beautiful mango blossom scent filled the air wafting down the broad streets into the widely spaced-out houses and passing through the many spare allotments in between. And inside sat the lonely spinster women crocheting and knitting blankets or repairing holes in the net made by seagulls. They laboured with good works through their winter nights, gingerly picking out, here and there, trapped morsels of other preoccupied so-and-sos' lives who were otherwise tied up with woeful marriages in clammy doonas, until the net was renewed, back to its original condition, and the Dry had passed.

One day it was decided that Elias should guard the town. For no good rhyme or reason, Elias had the big job handed to him on a plate. Why Desperance was mad about surveillance was not un-exceptional, because everyone in the nation was crazy about peace of mind. Sallyanne Smith, the town's scribe, had been running back and forth to the Shire Council office reminding the Councillors that the town had always had a guard, so they decided Elias should do it.

Not long after that, old Joseph Midnight tried to have an affair with Miss Sallyanne on the sly. He said it was in retaliation for making Elias guard. Even his wife teasingly asked him, 'What? You want to become the guard or something?' He said if anyone was smart like him they would be doing the same thing. He said he was going to steal her brains even though everyone told him to stop wasting his time. To steal the story on Uptown, he should have snuck down the white lady's prickled and bindi-eyed backyard, then with a rock broken into her padlocked shed and stolen the 'Book of Books'. Joseph Midnight would be a very useful man to know if he had her books in his possession, the complete collection of the Smith family's sagas, in volumes wasting away in dozens of dusty cardboard boxes in her rusty old shed.

In those yellowing pages chewed by defecating vermin lay thousands of blue-inked words describing countless years of hot-collared Shire Council meetings debating imagined threats of invasion. The countless whorled words described numerous inci-dents of spyglasses snooping along the unguarded coastline of crocodile-infested, mangrove mudflats lacing the northern frontier. 'Of course everyone on earth longed for such a landscape,' she wrote. Hordes of Asians swooping down across the Pacific ocean were screaming, *We want it! We want it!* And where was the national military? In other countries. Southern states. Pretty good job vermin couldn't shit on what the Pricklebush had locked up inside their heads.

Every day, a job being a job, at precisely four-hourly intervals, Elias would drop whatever he was doing to walk the buffel grass, spinifex, prickly bush circumference of town. His best fishing mate Norm Phantom now went to sea without him. It was no use taking him out on a boat fishing anymore, because right on the hour, with-out the aid of a watch, he would start off to his job on the edge of town, even if he had to tread water to get there.

'Where hid reality?' Elias asked in the Pricklebush, yet who could say what existed in one ordinary coastal town plonked at the top of the nation? Who knows what wars Elias thought he was looking for? What war, which war, in whose mind? Somebody could have said, *Elias, there is no war*. War was somewhere else, something to do with the USA or those foreign countries in Europe, the Middle East or Asia. Yes, all of those kind of things were just passing by, far, far away from the things people would talk about in Desperance.

Years later, some very unfortunate things happened while Elias was on patrol searching for clues about what he should be guarding against. There were several mysterious fire incidents in town – grassfires, burning of the Queen's picture, backyards set alight. Then Sallyanne Smith's Book of Books exploded into a bonfire when the roof lifted off her shed. On the very same night, another explosion. The Shire Council office became a gaping view onto the pale blue yonder. And with a simple dong, the toll bell fell off the burning inferno, flat to the ground. Who would have thought anyone would burn the history of Uptown? So much, thank you very much, you could say about the net of security. Arson became a new word for Desperance to deal with.

By late that night Elias Smith's fate was all but sealed by every adult from Uptown who had crowded into the stale-beer-smelling Barramundi Bar of the Fisherman's Hotel. Even though it was the middle of the week, people had to come to terms with new meanings in life. No one was spared. Every flashy Uptown person regretfully slipped into their plastic raincoats and, trumping and slurping with thonged feet through the deep mud to the only pub on the main street, silenced countless million frogs croaking in the ecosystem. There was nowhere else to go, no prospering community centre in spite of sitting on a Solomon's treasure – the so-called mineral rich provenance winding underground across the Gulf country.

Men came marching into the pub in their work clothes smelling of perspiration built on old odours dried slowly over several humid days. There was mud all over the floor of the pub for Lloydie the barman to clean up later. Anyone would have died for a whiff of fresh air and every couple of minutes the townswomen, who seldom frequented the pub, sprayed themselves with lavender-scented water. Many who had been directly affected by the arsonist(s) said they should speak first. They said they were accusing Elias, it was their basic human right, since their lives had been ruined and they expressed their agreed wish: *Let us take him outside and shoot the bastard*. Voices reverberated from wall to wall, talking about: *shooting, getting rifles, killing being too good for the bastard(s)*. Everyone competed to be heard. Nobody would have thought there could be so many ideas of how Elias had gone around causing so much damage to the town. There was such a frenzy inside, someone from the edge mob, peeping through the window, eager to get a look, ended up running away whispering to himself, *Oh! Spirits*, when he saw all the shadows of Elias's accusers, laughing around the ceiling.

Outside the pub, all the children played in the muddy waters spread about like great shallow lakes. It did not matter to them that it was night-time and they were out in the storm. They were using bedtime for running up and down the street in the rain, kicking water onto each other in all the deeper puddles made by car tyres in the muddy clay under the floodlights along the main street. Their wet bodies glistened in drenched, clinging clothes. Only the seagulls hovering in the rain around the streetlights kept an eye on them. The parents were far too preoccupied to notice that night had fallen, or even that there was a storm brewing outside, but who would have noticed? Desperance storms were like second nature to these people. Inside – their hearts and minds were inside.

Lively local youths, with girlfriends in tight clothes who were standing around hanging onto their jittery emotions, watched while pool balls rocketed all over the ripped green-clothed pool table in the weekly competition. In another corner a group of older, pot-bellied men wolf-whistled moderately at each other's scores, as they took turns to fling three darts for a bullseye in the comp.

Meanwhile, at the other end of the bar, people from the Pricklebush sitting in the snake pit were stretching to look through a small opening into the Barramundi Bar, watching Elias defend himself. Whispering back to the others gathered behind them: *Poor thing! Poor thing!*

Wild white-haired Elias was standing in front of everyone else, alone, looking proud-faced, everyone talking over him. He never had a chance. What argument did he have against a stick-up of prominent residents? He had been speaking all day at one place or another and his voice was dry. No one offered him a drink. Hmm! Hmm! *Shameful! Yesterday's people who could not do enough.* Smug faces surrounded Elias as they pushed up closer, their voices becoming louder, and he strained to be heard above the racket as he answered the repetitious accusations.

But listen! Listen? Quiet, quiet, at the back. Listen. You are not going to believe this but good old Elias was telling them straight. Alright! Go for it man. No one believed it. The whole pub became silent when he told them what a total, unsurpassed act of ignorance in the memory of human kind it had been for a town to have singled out one person on which to hang its destiny. Don't say? Never heard him talk like that before. And he told them that the town must surely be registered up there somewhere in God's book of records as being the most ridiculous place on earth. Well! That went down like a lead balloon. Desperance had standards. What a nerve, Elias.

Of course everyone got into the rush to say something after that. *You accusen me then, Elias?* Everyone started screaming and shouting, taking his criticisms personally, and all pointing a travesty-of-justice finger at Elias. *Jesus, didn't he know they were the mainstream, and if anyone thought different, they must be the one with the problem?* But the act of a community closing in on itself was not an isolated act particular to Desperance alone. Go anywhere, and it was the same, same, same.

If only the town could see the power of words at work, if it could have, just for one instance, imagined what it was like to throw words around nilly-pilly, like string to create a confusion, a pile of twists and turns, all jumbled up in a bowl like spaghetti. This was what the strings of accusations did to Elias Smith who was thrown out like dishwater by all those good Smith families of Desperance. Could he have had the time on his hands to have caused all of the town's recent misfortunes?

Could Elias be blamed for Y. Pedigree's dog being driven over yesterday while it was running aimlessly on the main road in broad daylight, and through no fault of anyone's, except it being a pure bred inbred born without a brain? *You know who we are talking about.* Or, could Elias take the blame for I. Damage's husband whispering about warped sexual encounters to a dis-interested brothel girl long distance from the corner public pay-phone on a hot summer's night, and I. Damage not knowing how to speak about infidelity? Or, for A. Clone's family, *You know who we are talking about*, with nothing on the table to chuck out anyhow because the social security cheque didn't last when every last cent of it was gambled away on pension day? Or last night's public on-again, off-again love affair of the conservative U. Torrent fuel attendant with the equally conservative B. Easy? *Soo! You know who we are talking about?* Of course you do but who speaks against the prevailing view of Elias?

Mrs C. Caucus, the local diva from down at the It's Flaming Hot Fish fish and chip shop, saved others from speaking reams by saying with a wink of an eye and a 'Ho! Ho!' through her side lip, 'You know who?' She might well have been slapping the newspaper-wrapped bundle of fried local produce on the counter in front of you. Then adding for good measure, 'Darling, you'd need to blame a much higher authority making them decisions, than him (Elias), my lovie – if you know what I mean, if I can point to the ups and above for a hint.'

But who? Who was claiming responsibility for burning the Shire Council office's records of floods and fires unprecedented in one hundred years of impeccable recorded history of natural and other calamities in the local vicinity? A valuable record, now a flake of ash. Or, Sallyanne Smith's Book of Books? An arsonist! A water diviner! No one rang up, left a message, or came forth to claim the responsibility. No one. And Elias Smith could be all of these things. Perhaps, in the fullness of time the world would agree with Desperance. Their verdict that night was that the rest of the world should have Elias Smith. He was asked to leave town by the morning.

Surely, then, on this day of all days, it was another God-given miracle that Elias Smith could wake up with a precious mind so free of worry, it weighed less than a chookie fowl's feather.

Light feathers did fall outside of Elias Smith's place, as he awoke to a beautiful dawn filled with trilling calls from flocks of sandpipers lifting off the mudflats to fly in swirls around and around his tin hut.

'These little brown speckled birds are the *Limicola falcinellus*,' the new schoolteacher remarked at the beginning of his first class for the morning. He explained that the birds 'were catching an unusual collision of winds heading from north and south.' He wrote it down in the class journal. This act of writing down was significant since the loss of the town's records in the fires. It would be the first statement for the new history of the town that would not be based on suspended reality. But the occasion was lost in the classroom of mostly missing students. Those few children present leaned their heads on their elbows and would soon be drifting away in their own dream world. Poor kids! Assailed with threats to get off to school. So little sleep last night. Birds were so common to these parts that no one took any notice of them except Danny Real, the young schoolteacher with bubbling enthusiasm for the local nature, who had only been in Desperance since the beginning of the year, and it was still the Wet season.

Everything was new for young lean Danny from Brisbane with wire hair, who was early to bed and early to rise. He had heard some of the gossip in the classroom about Elias, but he did not go in for what he had judged was a circus. He was an educated man and a kangaroo court being held down at the pub confirmed his belief that country people were just hicks and cretins. What would he know? Danny was an outsider. The teacher chatted on about how the birds had glided on unusual breezes, blowing out to sea, south to north, flying on a silver lining. He was just relaying what he had seen as the only other resident to be awake so early in the morning, when he went searching the grasses for nests. He was new so he could not have noticed that there were other thoughts floating in the vicinity, far above the local grasses of the flat plains.

Could every cloud have a silver lining? Thus it does, it does, Elias had mused to himself as he listened to the words in the quiet of the morning, spoken somewhere as daybreak spread over the flat lands, now with the season turning from the Wet, a metre above sea level. For some time he stood and looked around the treeless view in all directions. Often, during his long residency in Desperance, he wondered whether others in the town woke up in the morning thinking exactly the same thoughts as the day before. Not that he really expected other people to have the same thoughts as him, although such notions would now seem an agreeable proposition, but just say, to wake up thinking the same things as you did the day before and before that, was what interested Elias. He wondered if the world could be as though someone had struck a button twice to give the town's residents their instructions for the day. First, telling him who he was in this flat world in which he had been living and secondly, that the day was good.

A short memory was sometimes better than a long one or having no memory at all and this was what Elias Smith thought on the day he left Desperance for good.

Chapter 4
Number One house

Looking straight out of the window, way across numerous heaps of storm-given driftwood stacked for firewood, over the pungent-smelling salty flats towards the water's edge, Norm Phantom watched his friend Elias Smith. The first thing Norm thought about Elias dressed in his long dark olive trench coat as he headed out to sea, was how he looked even more other-worldly, like a fugitive from another time, as though he fished in an icy sea, instead of the tropics.

There he was: Elias, pulling behind him a bit of green tin, an excuse to float on water named *Choice. Who sails in a boat called* Choice? Norm Phantom watched and mumbled this question solemnly to himself, just as he had done every time he saw Elias towing his boat. Sometimes, he looked on the scene of reckless endeavour in total puzzlement, but mostly, in resigned endearment for his friend, he had regarded it as the finest sign of peace in paradise. Who was he, Norm Phantom, to say what another man should do? What business was it of his how each man designs to be at sea?

Now, for the first time, Norm thought the old grey-green boat resembled a sea coffin, not the piece of tin Elias liked to float around in at sea. He listened to the sea murmuring to Elias, *slaap, slaap.* Even flocks of white cockatoos flying in a cloud along the beach like an angel with flapping wings, raucously cried for him. The noise chased away schools of sardines, while Elias's abandoned butcher bird sitting outside Norm's window sang for its feed of fish. The bird's tune rang out across the grey woodpiles like a flute.

Norm knew before Elias could begin his journey, he would slowly lug the boat over a kilometre of muddy shallows towards the inky sea. Out there, the sea joined heavy rain clouds spreading to the basin of the Gulf from a weak trough sitting over Cape York. In front of Elias the *yidimil* star of the morning hung low in the sky above the dark sea, looking down at the town. Norm looked at the star in the way men looked at a woman who causes trouble in their families. He spat. The stories Norm knew about the morning star would make your hair stand on end like a porcupine. He and Elias had spent hours at sea discussing the skies. 'She is Venus,' Elias said, smiling at his knowledge of stars which the sea had restored to his memory, while telling Norm excitedly, 'who is also the beautiful Aphrodite born of the sea.' Out at sea, she pulled heartbroken sailors and fishing men to her beauty where they were lost forever. 'She is a harlot then,' Norm laughed. Elias responded with silence.

Back then, in the good times, neither man spoke to the other again of stars or fish, neither the next day or any day following while they were at sea. Their fishing became a silent business of intense matter-of-fact concentration so spooky, it even scared the fish away. The very spirits that plagued the Gulf seas would not have known these two men were in the vicinity. The small tin boat had become a tanker, and when they returned from the sea, both men parted company in silence.

'And yours?' Norm simply asked one night of Elias's heart, continuing the conversation a year later when they met at sea while fishing at the same black-blue cod hole. Both were alone, the fish not biting, and all that was left was the sphere of honesty, which felt as close as all of the stars of our galaxy passing above in the Milky Way. 'And yours?' he remembered Elias had replied absentmindedly, concentrating on the line, 'And yours?'

'Elias always believed in his own stories,' Norm said through his eyes, while his jaws tightened with a sense of resignation, while he continued to look out the window at the dragonflies – blue, red, green – flying around Elias's boat. Norm knew Elias. Knew when Elias would have seen the star which had stolen his heart, hanging in the sky waiting, and full of confidence, prepared to follow her signal. Norm remained at the window, resigned to watch, understanding the wishes of his friend's heart, yet believing in the complete opposite to Elias – *She only comes for death.*

In this country, where legends and ghosts live side by side in the very air, inside the Pricklebush home no man, love-forlorn or not, sets to sea while the morning star shines above their fishing boats waiting for them. Have you considered he might already be dead? Norm was surprised at the thought. No, he could not be sure as he watched Elias. Imagine if he was actually watching Elias's spirit. Norm was able to look out his window in the morning and see in the mist, the spirit of dead men pulling their own coffins. Men whom people had heard saying goodbye to themselves as soon as the curlew called. Norm dispelled such morbid thoughts, though he remained fatalistic in his realisation that once his friend followed the star, she would pull him away forever. And that was the truth.

'I suppose I should go down there and bid him farewell,' Norm mumbled, firmly telling himself it was the decent thing to do – for a friend. Eh! That was right: regardless of whether that someone was pretending to be dead or was really dead. But he could not move. The muscles in his legs tightened like his jaws, as though he was pulling the boat himself, yet, he knew he could not go. The town, driven by its own paralysis, determined the fathom of where its law dropped – and Uptown was watching hard from their houses too, to make sure nothing was interfering with their law.

What was a good law or bad law, huh? Nobody, particularly

Pricklebush, could just go out there, and say things to Elias, such as – *Don't go!* The Pricklebush knew how rights were miniscule. How could anybody, even somebody like Norm Phantom, interfere with the boundaries of someone's fate? You want to be called a troublemaker, Norm? Everyone was pleased enough to accept his or her own fate from the natural flowing dominating law of white governance. Who was thinking himself too good to say, say among the black community, whether an individual was going to receive a box full of life's jewels or an empty box? Norm found he was telling Elias all of these things from the window, yet they were pulling the boat across the slimy mud, side by side, as they had done for ages. Then a funny thought occurred to him. 'You know, I am doing all of the talking as usual.' He looked across at Elias, perspiration running down his golden face as he looked back at his boat, and Norm realised there would be no conversation between them again and was weighed down by the heaviness of his heart, while knowing what he had always known, that Elias belonged to another world.

Gulf people have something to say about fish: their Norm Phantom was the big man of the sea. Regardless of the isolation of country people, because talk reaches out and grabs people's attention everywhere, all nature of people strolled into the Fisherman's Hotel just to clap their eyes on the sea man of Carpentaria. In sea men's circles, yarns of Norm Phantom of Desperance were imagined far more than the truth. This was the only man they knew who lived in the world of marine splendour, riding the troughs on God Almighty seas, surviving cyclones one after another, following a fish to where other fishing men had perished just for the sake of it, and once in a while, returning to port to check on the family, before leaving the very next dawn. What a man! An asset to the town, an asset to his race, mind you.

Yet a pure person can burn with pain. Oh! Goodness God, helplessness was a terrible thing at times. Norm stayed transfixed by the window, he was like glue, he hardly believed it possible that he was losing the only other person in the Gulf waters of Carpentaria whose sea skills matched his own. But Norm stayed inside anyway, watching Elias go.

Then, something strange snapped in Norm Phantom's mean heart. It might have been the combination of the butcher bird's song, the dragonflies, the significance of a crisis having dawned on him, or seeing the nesting swallows that shat everywhere fly out of his roof – because what he decided to do instead of going out and stopping Elias, was a much more over-the-top gesture for his loss. For people who never wanted to see the sight of Elias again, who wanted to wipe his memory from here, there and everywhere, he would be a consistent reminder of their law – the good and the bad. A forgetting people would be hit in the face with Elias. They would wish life to be normal again, and wish without luck to celebrate the stories worth remembering, but it would never be the same, because when they thought of Norm Phantom and the sea, they would think of Elias. So! *Norm Phantom does not fish anymore*. What kind of story would that be? In this way, Norm decided to destroy his legend. He felt pleased: this was sacrifice. This was the retribution the town deserved. By crossing the margin, fudging acceptability, he knew he would end all sense of hope his life gave to others. Erasure! A total unconditional response for someone who had no heart to call Elias to come back.

Yet, why not call Elias? Norm had plenty of voice for calling out to the whole world when he wanted to. He possessed such an enormous voice, the pitch of it could reverberate up and down the spinal cord, damage the central nervous system, and afterwards, vibrate straight up the road to the town and hit the bell so hard, it would start ringing its ear-piercing peal. This was how Norm Phantom reached whoever was in earshot when he wanted something like, 'Could you pass the butter, please?' Who, what, jumped up straight and listened and replied in shock: 'What? Who? What? Is he calling me?' Norm Phantom could have used those lungs of his to call Elias back. He could have roared at the whole town. But, 'Oh! no, can't do that,' he would have said, even to Elias as he walked away. 'One day you might listen now! You know the limits. You can't go upsetting the white people.' Protocol! Elias. Such an important piece of information, Elias, for harmonious living.

Many, many times Norm stretched this deep voice down to the elusive shoreline from the very same window, yelling at any one of his seven kids to get back to the house – 'What kind of idiot are you? Get in here! Can't you see a storm's coming?' Always the world responded. The sea lady bowed submissively, momentarily, she let him say his piece over the roar of her song. If his children did not listen quick enough, she suddenly drew up the wind, over-taking them in complete surprise as she threw her waves higher in chastisement, slapping his children in stinging blows across their arms and legs, enclosing her arms around their brown bodies and forcing them to ride in the rips before throwing them face first, back on the dry sand. 'What are you fucking well doing?' You should have heard Norm roar at the sea and the kids when that happened.

Never mind! Why speak up for Norm Phantom? The big, hard-nosed Westside man of house number one had closed the book himself. What did it matter to him? He had not contributed to the decision made by the 'good people' of Uptown. Westside always said, *We are just plain, simple, Aboriginal people, never been born white, and proud of the fact*. Norm always said, *We were not like the local mafia*, which made Elias laugh. He could not become involved, jump any invisible wall of separation, break it down with an axe, just because he, Norm Phantom, should say so.

Everything was changing. The town was a different place to the way it was when Elias had first plopped like a giant cowry shell on the beach.

Desperance had become a boom town with a more sophisticated outlook now, because it belonged totally to the big mine. When the mine came along with all of its big equipment, big ideas, big dollars from the bank – Well! Why not? Every bit of Uptown humanity went for it – lock, stock and barrel. The mine bought off the lot of them, including those dogs over Eastside. They would be getting their just deserts, Westside told those traitors who ran down to the mine crawling on their stomachs for a job. They were all doing deals.

Norm remembered he had told Elias that there was no point getting involved. But Elias let himself be bought off for a few lousy dollars. Just to guard the town from what? What next? Norm had asked him. Norm told him many times what would happen once someone owned you. But Elias, poor, no-memory Elias had forgotten about the fish in the sea. He thought he was on top of the world. No time for fishing, he told Norm, then watched the back of his friend set to sea after Norm had told him it had come as a shock to hear Elias had agreed to take on the job of guarding the town. Nobody could have tried more to warn him of the consequences. Norm said he knew things he could not say because of what the mine had done to his family. Remember who your friends are Elias, Norm had told him enough about being the guard, although he was mindful that when a man spoke in Desperance, who knew where his words ended up and how they might come flying back to hit him one day.

The old people in the Pricklebush growled more now about how their words were being stolen by the bad people – *Spies from the mine going around in the bush*, horrible devils that the gigantic yellow mining equipment scraped out of the big open-cut holes. Everyone talked about seeing the spy agents scratching about in the bush. Eyewitnesses saw strange men near the river. They were seen everywhere, all wearing thin wires on their heads, driving around the dirt tracks, looking at nothing. People said they wanted to know what those strangers were up to in their bush. You want to know? They were picking up the sounds of who knows what, explained the old people.

The children did some research in the storybooks for the old people about white men who wore wire on their heads. This was the start of the old people becoming *scientify*, talking technical talk. *Your words*, the old people had explained, *were important now*. Your words could end up being a thousand miles up in the sky riding on a satellite disc, zapping across the world on invisible beams. *Don't even worry thinking about what beams are*, they said in their stories. *Beams are things you could never even dream of*. It was some kind of gadget that can take away all your myall words, transcribe what you say in better language so people can understand what you are talking about. And then the beam flies on orbiting through space, straight to the boardrooms of rich multinational mining people in Holland, Germany, the USA, even 'Mother' England, or who knows where, to listen to you, before you have even had a chance to end your sentence. *So, watch what you are saying. That's why*, they said, *a man had to stay quiet like a mouse while he snuck around getting his cheese in the big people's house*. Uptown, hmm, hmm! This was what they called belonging to the mining company who owned speed, and orbit too.

The sound of the sea lapping tranquilly along the shoreline carried Norm's thoughts out to join Elias, wading further out to sea. Norm felt the familiar pressure of pulling each step out of a metre of sucking mud. The water left trails behind him stretching over the surface like silver ribbons. 'Keep it going,' Norm willed Elias, 'keep it going, old mate.' Soon, both men could feel the other's presence pulling together on the wet rope, hauling *Choice* through thigh-deep water, breathing in the strong fishy smell. Seagulls hovered over the boat just as they always did when the red-eyed birds followed men to sea.

Elias stopped, eased himself into the boat and took the oars. Norm waited, but Elias never looked back. He just rowed as if the gap between their thoughts was unbridgeable. And suddenly they had parted company forever.

And when Norm had finished watching Elias become a dot that faded out of his life, he sighed, for that was that then. Except a fitting silence did not prevail, for it was no longer quiet in town. The makeshift, resurrected bell on the Council lawns started to toll loud and long, anyone would have thought it was Sunday. Car horns honked and beeped from all over town and Council vehicles headed to each corner to draw the net while the mad woman's organ filled every ear with Handel's *Messiah*. The blasted noise lasted for a total of ten minutes. This was how Desperance celebrated the last sight of Elias.

'Jesus let me tell you,' Norm shouted, 'what no end of spite on your earth can do!'

With Elias gone, Norm thought he ought to try talking to the Council again to find out when they were going to stretch the net over his place. Westside mob in the Pricklebush said that they thought there was no reason why the safety net should be stopping short of their homes. Just because of the gap of wasteland, half a mile, called the distance of tolerance, that surrounded the town and where black people were allowed to live on the other side – all Pricklebush people were complaining that they had rights too for the same municipal goods and services as anyone else. 'Go and be a troublemaker,' the old people called out to Norm from his front gate, and said if he had any sense at all like his father had, he should go Uptown and tell them that.

Norm came out through the gate to speak to the old people. He told them that burning hair was what trouble smelt like because when his father was a small boy with weather-bleached hair, gone tinder dry all through winter, it went up in flames like burning spinifex when lightning struck the rivergum he had been sheltering beneath. Again, Norm repeated the story of his father, exactly how his father told it, copying his old voice, which seemed to comfort the old people, and members of his family: they stood around the front yard and listened.

'The tree, you hear me, exploded on impact into a long streak of fire that sent hundreds of arms out in every direction, several raced towards him, in a vortex, grabbing his hair and setting it alight. Luckily, he was saved by the force of the lightning charge that threw him clear onto the soft sandy riverbed. Unluckily, it did not rain, and life resumed. Running with the smell of singed hair into the desert country, hiding in rocky hills and living without water. Running away from the men on horses, nostrils burning, sniffing the air, horses snorting, dogs racing with their noses set to the ground, the human scent of fear trapped in the scent of power.

'In the evening twilight came powerful, strong men, heavy with rawhide coverings. He watched through a pin-sized peephole between the boulders, moving pictures of leather-skinned men dressed in leggings and jackets, moving in and out of frame as their horses danced through a heat mirage towards the foothills, searching. He caught glimpses of how they sat relaxed on leather saddles, wore leather leggings, leather boots, leather holsters for guns and leather whips. Stopping to dismount, horses sniffing the air, stopping – starting again – *in stretto*, men rolling tobacco, part of one figure quietly smoking, checking the cartridges, spinning the barrel, nodding directions, taking a drink from the waterbag hanging on the horse's neck, cracking the whip, never stopped cracking the whip as they moved on up the hill.

'Paralysed with fear, dry-mouthed, his body remained stock still with his eye squashed against the rock. A pinhole view of the world collapsing in a kaleidoscope, of his parents, patches of bare body moving into view, blood spraying, men's trouser legs dripping with blood, sunlight flashing off knife blades, death screaming in his mother's voice, noise like thunder – bang, bang, bang, cracking sounds as the tongue of the whip flicked by. His body was a lather of sweat and he felt shocked by the feeling of coolness in the mild breeze pouring over his skin that set off the smell of his hair. Like a lizard he slid with the gravel into the dirt and rolled into a tight ball that rolled sideways like nothing alive on earth through a small opening under a rock ledge. He rolls on until he becomes lodged against the rock face at the back of a dingo's lair. His mind fights his trembling body until he becomes still like rock, and dirt, and ancient times, and darkness, until his breathing stops and he is invisible.

'That,' said Norm, coming near to the end of his passionate deliberation, his ode to his parents' memory, 'was what trouble smelt like. And being lucky,' he whispered to his audience, 'was when nobody else could smell your trouble.' Norm had a hypnotic voice, his eyes cast spells, he distilled memory like the flooding river emptying into the sea. He made people wish they were there when it really happened. He made them feel that it was better to have been alive in the times of the real people, his ancestors. What Norm could do with stories he had practised down to a fine art and glued it to surviving relics, like the still-to-be-found fire-gutted ghost gum willed by providence to the families' memories of Westside, where the local pastoralist whipped Aboriginal men and women, the boulders with a peephole view where cartridges were as many as stones on the ground from the massacre of the local tribespeople.

Those stories of trouble never lacked lustre in Number One house. Norm often told his sad stories to his listener, an abnormally huge, white cockatoo bird, named Pirate, over their breakfast cup of tea. Just chopping wood for practice, he called it, declaring it was his natural-born right to pluck history at random from any era of the time immemorial of the black man's existence on his own land. 'Too true,' rattled the bird, an enchanter inciting more to be said. The creature was unbelievable to watch. The more animated Norm's storytelling became, with hands and arms akimbo, face, eyeballs glaring under his smooth face and straight greying black hair, the dirty sump-oil-and-meat-fat-feathered bird either sat solemn like an owl in thought, its black eyes fixed on every movement of his lips, or jumped up and down crying out like a woman, 'Stop it! Stop it Norm!' with people running to see who was getting murdered.

The disgusting animal usually perched on the back of a chair facing the table back to front, making it easier for him to eat what he wanted from the table. Nobody in the Westside camps was game enough to say a word against the greasy-feathered bird, which had become holy after it went with the pilgrimage to Alice Springs in the 1980s to be blessed by the Pope. To the Phantom family, the bird was more than holy. Westside claimed Pirate was extraordinary. Why? The bundle of feathers had appeared in everyone's dreams one night and insisted it had psychic powers – so the old people declared the bird to be a prophet.

The whole of Westside came to Pirate to have their fortunes told. They held their empty cups close to the bird's head to make it easy for him to inspect the spectacular designs made by the dregs of tea stuck together at the bottom. Sometimes, if the bird felt inclined, he might answer, *yes*, *no*, or *perhaps*, or anything else from his huge vocabulary which included questions such as – *Am I going to die?* Or, *Does anybody love me?* Without judging his merits, they considered him to be a truthful bird, even when the truth hurt. But the proof of the bird's talents came from a large flock of resident cockatoos, thousands of them, flying over the town, screaming in a spectacular, uncoordinated chanting, *What are you doing youse bastards?* It was thought to be a miracle of the English language, that simple birds had learnt to talk English too, just like everyone else. When the birds flew around town, magic sparkled in the air, and people raced outside, looked up and waited for the birds to ask them the question. Then everyone replied, *Nothing! We are doing nothing*. It made people think that they never knew from one minute to the next what was going to happen.

'Tut! Tut!' the insufferable bird screamed repeatedly at the sleeping white dog Dallas, who unlike the Jimmy Dale Gilmore country and western song he was named after, had never been to Dallas on a DC9 at night. The dog was such a big fan of country and western music, it had no time to listen to Norm's stories, as it lay with its back on the dirt floor, piebald belly belly-up, showing its fleas. The bird demanded the same story to be told again and again whenever Norm stopped talking; its hunger for the family's history impressed Norm more than his own family's. Openly, he praised Pirate, boasting he placed more faith on the twenty-five-year-old bird retaining the family's memories than any one of his six children, who, he said frequently, had done nothing but let him down. There were really seven children in the family but Norm chose not to recognise his third and once favourite son Will. He was disappointed they had gone off and married the wrong people, and all were gone and had left him alone, except the three girls who had brought their broken marriages and a string of kids home, and the youngest, Kevin, who was sixteen.

Kevin could have been the brains of the family, everyone kept making it their business of coming around and saying to Norm after the accident in the mine.

'What kind of consolation is that for a brainy boy, being rendered a mental retard?' Norm knew how to end a conversation about Kevin quick smart.

Well! I was only trying to help so don't get stroppy with me. And one by one, anyone who thought they could offer sympathy left, and stayed away.

None smarter than your Kevin, the white people used to say all the time about Kevin. Before, schoolteachers just about wore the road away, tramping down to the Phantom's place every other day just to make sure Kevin was alright. *Mr Phantom. You must keep on encouraging Kevin with his schoolwork now won't you?* they would tell Norm, and he said he was starting to wonder what schoolteaching was all about. 'Well! What will you be doing if I have to teach him?' Norm asked. He said the family already knew how smart Kevin was. That was the reason why he was going to school. *He has to amount to something*, the teachers wailed, biting their tongues, trying to make the family understand that Aboriginal people needed to succeed, and to succeed they needed to be educated.

Norm Phantom reiterated how proud he already was of Kevin but nobody needed to make a trophy of the boy either. 'You do your job and I will do mine.' By agreeing, he wanted those teachers to make sure they did their job to help, since nobody wanted more than Norm Phantom for Kevin to be able to get the hell out of Desperance, and away from the family too, for that matter. 'Kevin thinks he is way too smart to be tied down to school,' Norm explained, wondering why the teachers had failed to capture his imagination by just telling him straight that, like them, he could have a good life with lots of money.

'I don't even feel like I belong here anymore,' Kevin complained about why he had to sit around uselessly trying to do essays about books talking about *them* white peoples lives. He would look out the window from the kitchen table strewn with pencils, paper and books, and see his best friends enjoying the good life, standing around in the sun, preparing to go fishing down on the foreshore, talking to the teachers going fishing as well. Later, he would look up again from a pile of Tim Winton novels, to lock on a last glimpse of their boats crossing the seascape horizon, or would be just out of hearing range of their laughingly spent hours, tinkering over improvised outboard motors. He became the silent non-participant, listening to epic tales of sea journeys he kept missing out on. He was the warrior most unlikely. *Only in your dreams Kevin.* They told him of expeditions, where renowned sharks were preyed upon in nocturnal hunts. Finally, Kevin was left only to hear stories. His essay on Tim Winton scored A plus, but you tell me, who on earth cared?

Then, school days were finished for Kevin. When he left with his friends, they hung around town for months looking for something to do. At home, Kevin grew into the role of being the unchallenged brains trust of the family. He and Norm sat around for hours discussing television news, the political state of the nation, the way the country stuffed up the wool industry, who was who in the wars in countries nobody else in the family knew existed or were interested in, because they left the television for something in the fridge whenever the news came on.

But that was alright. Nobody, in any case, including Norm, expected Kevin would actually get a job. 'No, look at Kevin,' the brothers teased, and Norm let his eyes slip over his thin son. He was all skin and bone. 'Aren't he the most unco kid you ever come across?' Norm refused to have Kevin on his boat even if he begged to be taken because he was too clumsy. All the family knew that if there was something to drop, Kevin was going to drop it.

Gradually, all of his school mates were recruited into the road gangs working on the yellow roads. Up the track for weeks at a time mending chopped-up roads after the Wet, Brahman-cross cattle for company, they drove graders and trucks for the Town Council. They joined the crew sitting on their heavy machinery on the side of the road, waving at passing traffic, waiting for the foreman to arrive. There was plenty of work. Too much work. A perpetual round of work, repairing flood-damaged roads hacked to pieces by road transports carrying heavy machinery and grinding their way up to the mine, then loaded, returning to the coast, hauling the country away to pour into ships destined for overseas refineries.

'Kevin? You got to be joking!' The works supervisor was a straight-up-and-down kind of man who grew up with Kevin's older brothers and uncles. 'The Council has no call for Kevin.' Everyone in the town and down to the Pricklebush knew that Kevin, the fidget, would be useless on a job on the road. Over on Westside, Kevin's hands had already destroyed thousands of dollars worth of torches, electric appliances, motors. He must have had a little devil inside his head telling him to take other people's precious things apart. Even though the whole world could accept the fact that a table must have four legs, if you left Kevin alone, it would be on its side with three. *Kevin! Kevin! Why did you do that?* Unguarded machinery, instruments strung, screwed or balanced, or anything that operated on fuel, electricity or battery, was no place for Kevin. It would kill Kevin. Kevin would injure himself. But Kevin went down the mine for the money and the bosses took him on because how would they know? They did not even pretend to know who fronted up for work from Pricklebush.

Inso and Donny were the two oldest Phantom brothers. Everybody in town said these boys did nothing for anybody except for money. They worked in the mine from day one. They were both hulkily built men who liked a boxing match and dreamt of becoming professional. Once the pub tried to raise money to send them to the State championships. In a ring, drawn in sand on the saltpan, Inso and Donny trained local kids to stay six rounds. They fought anything from Eastside that walked in sight of them for stealing their land. 'I saw you.' 'No you didn't you weren't even there.' 'Yes I was and I heard you.'

White boys, singled out for making racist remarks years before, were flogged. Boxing matches were a menace to everyone. Gangs of youths formed from Eastside and Westside and Uptown with an arsenal of weapons. On their way home from the pub, you could hear them laughing as they roared by in their four-wheel drives, up through the muddy road, stopping only to attack anyone standing in their way, or out of their way, or whenever they smelt trouble. Well! Enough was enough. The town did not need any of their money. The elders struck when Norm was out at sea. *Get out and don't come back.* They took to those drunken boys with iron bars, sticks and weapons, causing a bit of a mess in Norm's place.

But still, the family had Kevin, the beautiful last child who had inherited all the brains, who Norm believed would never survive the world in which he was born. 'Why did God give us this child for?' Norm would despair as he watched Kevin grow. 'He could have been smarter, if he had had better teachers who knew how to teach someone like Kevin,' Norm accused the school when the accident happened.

What was he going down the mine for? Inso and Donny came home to accuse Norm, and whenever they came home and saw Kevin, they said openly they could not comprehend how anyone could let him go to work in a mine of all places. But asking questions around Norm did not help. Questions about Kevin caused arguments. 'What you want to come here picking fights for?' Norm challenged Inso and Donny. 'We are not picking fights.' 'You are always picking fights.' 'If anybody's picking a fight it's you.' What a story! Inso and Donny banged their way out the door of the Number One house, got into their cars, and shot straight back up the road to the Fisherman's Hotel. My! My! It was astonishing how cold beer rolled down their necks. Hot heads cooled. They checked their gold wristwatches to decide if this particular visit home had lasted – what? five minutes or less.

So nobody came to terms with what happened to Kevin, and they just kept on saying how brainy he used to be. Who, anyone might well ask themselves, would have given a skinny lad with not one single physical attribute to show for himself, a job in an underground mine? It only took one day. He went down the mine on the day he got the job and came out burnt and broken like barbecued spare ribs. He heard the ancestor's voice when an explosion with fiery rocks went flying at him – left, right and centre. The boy they dragged out of the crush had been rendered an idiot and it was plain as day no prayers would undo the damage.

Even after the last scab healed nothing could put out the fire in his brains. Call it God's will, or call it facing the ancestor in the face, or call it someone like Kevin knowing darn well that what was in that hole would come looking for him, but he went in anyway. Call it coming face to face with yourself and asking – who are you? Call it trouble too. Uptown people said it was a tragic accident that should never have happened. Norm Phantom took his son home and blamed the Shire Council because they had refused to extend the net to cover his place.

Thinking about trouble always made Norm think of Kevin, and thinking of Kevin made him think of fear, and then he would think of his grandfather's stories to the bird. Kevin was one you would not bother yourself telling the family's history to anymore. More! More! And the bird, true to his word, as if he could read Norm Phantom's mind, had heard more trouble on the way. Now, Norm could hear Kevin coming along the twisting corridor, not only disturbed in the mind, but drunk too, and it was only seven o'clock in the morning.

Norm heard him first, dragging something along the corrugated tin walls of the twisted corridor heading towards the kitchen, then finally, saw Kevin running at him, flashing his knife through the air and screaming like a wounded animal. On this occasion Kevin was wearing a torn T-shirt covered with fat swastikas painted in blood. The T-shirt was the first thing to hit Norm in the eye and the sight of it shocked him more than anything else, even the departure of Elias whom he had just finished watching.

'Get that thing off,' Norm barked, 'before I rip it off of you.' Norm thought he could get used to anything new in the strange world of Kevin, but this was too much, because if Norm said he hated anything, he hated what the Nazis did to the Jewish people. He had always said it, and Kevin should have known better. Kevin stopped in his tracks with the knife still pointed towards his father's face, but he looked as though he had received a mortal wound. 'Why? You ever saw what happened in Germany or Europe? How would you know?'

'Jesus! You take the bloody cake,' said Norm, 'Get that thing off – I am warning you.'

Norm roared out to his household in his booming voice. You could hear him down the road, even Uptown heard him, calling out the names of his daughters, 'Hey! Girlie, all of you girls. Come out here!'

Norm started to move from the table where he had been sitting with his bird. He wanted the whole house to see Kevin, see what was happening in this day and age, right there in his own home.

'Come and have a look at your brother. Have you seen anyone dressed like that before, like a bloody Nazi?'

'You! You!' Kevin's spit spluttered everywhere as he looked Norm straight back in the eye, trying to block him with his emaciated body from going back into the house to find his sisters.

'You're fucking nothing to me.' Kevin felt hatred for pity, for pity was what pity gets. He felt betrayed by the family whose honour only he had had the guts to defend. It had been one hell of a night fighting the 'enemies'. An incident that had begun out on the claypans with a spilt drink, a piece of broken glass picked up and thrust through someone's hand; a fight that had extended through the bush with spotlights, and the pursuers hunting for the chase, and him escaping like an animal. It had ended outside of the family's house in the wee hours of three o'clock in the morning.

Why was it that the reputation of homes in Desperance were built on other people's judgements? Norm asked his family to answer this question. Any passerby could say this or that house was nice because of the way it looked, from out on the road, and be plain wrong about what happens on the inside. Or, they could say the house next door was full of trouble, or that house across the street was full of no-hopers, and no wonder just look at the place. But Norm knew a house made its own life, regardless of the family who chose to live within its walls. Why was it? Ever since the day his house grew to be an eyesore on the landscape, the place felt as though it was always ready for a fight.

Even that night when the white town was trying to intellect-ualise the behaviour of the local demons and blamed it all on Elias, wondering if he was a harmless bream, or a town-eating piranha, the outsiders in the Pricklebush were making do with their lot in life and attending to family vendettas. And you know what? Their houses never slept. It was not long before the Phantom house pricked up it ears and let out an enormous – 'What's that?' Waking households of mothers and kids on Westside who were sleeping on top of each other, fell back onto their sleeping heaps, when they heard who it was. Only the Phantom household's ears stayed pricked to listen to the sound of Kevin screaming, running and falling up the road from his pursuers. The men doing the chasing were the self-acclaimed tough guys gang, from the other side of town. Now, they were on Westside territory, hanging out of their mud-encased Toyota Hilux, and staying teasingly on the heels of their victim.

'Left! Left!'

'Now Right! Riiiight! Hold that fucking thing still, you moron.' The yellow beam from the kangaroo spotter jerked all over the countryside, picking up images of Kevin staccato, then in slow motion.

'What are we going to do with him boys?' Over and over again they repeated the question.

They almost ran him over but somehow, the part of his brain which deals with flight functioned sufficiently enough to steer him out of the way.

Then, suddenly, someone shouted – 'Feed him to Abilene.'

This loaded thought caused momentary silence.

'Yeah! Let's feed his bony little arse to Abiiiilene.'

As soon as they reached hearing distance of Norm Phantom's house, they started wolf-whistling and shouting to each other, 'Noooorm. Say sweet dreams to Kevin and Abiiilene. Oink! Oink!' They laughed at the silliness of each other's jokes.

Panic set in – Kevin dreaded the name Abilene. They knew, he knew, that everybody in Number One house knew about Abilene. Abilene was more than a nightmare. She haunted the eroded river-bank eating herring, where the river runs out to the sea. A true, live wild pig whose grossly overgrown, black hairy body and a head filled with brown, rotting teeth, roamed with her legend across the whole length and breadth of the Gulf of Carpentaria.

Abilene was a merciless killer, hunting down local men fishing on the riverbank. The story was told to little boys by their grannies to make them be good, how the animal lived forever, and was everywhere, grunting, stalking and hunting down the local men on a pitch-black night.

The story continued to be told. Even if it was hearsay. It also had a reality, since living people had actually seen her, amidst the stark, naked proof of flattened grass where carcasses of cattle were found, or half submerged in the running water. Nearby, fencing was destroyed and witnessed: *Ever seen the wire stacked up neat on the side of the road like that before?*

There was talk that Norm Phantom was the only person alive who had really seen her, although he never said so. But why would he? Rumours spread from Eastside accused Norm of having trained the pig to kill people. Joseph Midnight said Norm Phantom used the pig to attack people he disliked. Like! Norm never liked Uncle, who owned that Hilux those young men were now driving after Kevin. When he was killed, the Toyota was found in the bush with the car radio playing country and western music for the mess and what have you of poor Uncle's remains spread all over the place. Made you sick to see it. Joseph started these rumours even though he and Norm were equally related to Uncle. 'Nobody can prove it, but one day, Norm Phantom, people are going to see you for what you are. You are the devil incarnate. A very bad man. You just wait and see.' This was Uncle's Aunty. When she became a widow, she went bustling down to Westside, throwing her weight around in traumatic grief. She told Norm Phantom off – to his face.

The Toyota sat in Joseph Midnight's backyard for months, even after it was smoked. Nobody wanted to touch it again. For a long time, nobody would even look at the vehicle. Now the boys drove it around. Vendetta, vendetta, such a strange word for the Gulf.

The fracas coming off a combination of the jumbled voices of wild men pitching for trouble, making pig noises, and the Toyota's distinctive revving, was reverberating from corrugated-iron clad wall to wall in Norm's house, down through the long curving corridor which resembled the shape of a cochlea inside an ear.

Inside this ear the sound grew louder as it travelled, jumping the puddles of water seeping under the tin, just as Norm said it would, in the unfolding years of the house he had designed to have its own built-in alarm system. He mentioned to his wife no less than a thousand reasons justifying his security device. She called the unwieldy construction a trap for fleas, crawling around in the hair of rats, whose eggs had fallen with the dust from the ceiling. At various points along the partly roofed corridor, rooms had been erected as the need arose in the family and trashed when called for as well.

When the sounds of their brother's terror raced through the corridor with increasing amplification like the pain of an ear infection, the Phantom sisters appeared out of total darkness, from various exit points, like witches spouting steam. They walked out to the front yard together with six or eight dogs running in all directions and barking their heads off, including Norm's old white one called Dallas. It was showdown time. Other families gathered up their flocks, and listened while they hid in their houses.

'Have the first shot.'

'No you. You first bitch!'

'No, I give it to you first. Go ahead. Have the first shot. Then I'll kill you.' That was Girlie, youngest of the three Phantom sisters, just three years older than Kevin, skinny as a bacon rasher, with bright yellow dyed hair in rollers and dressed in a cotton nightie, always minding how she looked, just like her Mother. Girlie was standing in the middle of the road in the middle of the night, aiming her rifle. She was blocking the Toyota, the jeaned and Bob Marley T-shirted, gammon Rasta men from the prickly bush ghettos of Eastside, their own cousins mind you, all armed with iron rods and one or two rifles aimed straight back at her.

The other two sisters, more heavily built, always pregnant Janice, and always flogged Patsy, stood behind Girlie. Everyone said these two girls were deadset – just like Inso and Donny.

Standing behind Girlie, in Nike shorts and Ed Simpson T-shirts, each held their iron bar gripped between both hands.

'Come on dog, or second thought: worse than a dog. You hear what I am saying? You are worse than a fucking mangy crap dog following around sluts on heat all night long with your diseased pricks dragging through your legs on the fucking dirt. Shoot first. Go on drunken men who fuck dead women. Have the first shot because then I want to kill you dead, so I can watch the crows eat your useless body in the morning.'

The man Girlie challenged to the duel was her own womanising ex, her own cousin Noelie whom she was currently saying she was off with for good this time, in their off-again, on-again relationship. Goodness knows how they had managed to spawn four reasonable-mannered children over a decade to date. The Toyota, resurrected from Uncle's demise, was so loaded down with the weight of Aunty's rumours, the axles almost touched the ground.

Noelie, a tall young man with a big ego and minimal good looks lost prematurely to liquor, glared at Girlie with her rifle aimed at his temple. 'Who you kidding Girlie,' he yelled back up the road, still not able to work out if his Girlie wanted him back dead or alive. But what did it matter: Girlie was not the only fish biting in the sea. 'Why don't you come over and see your bloody kids sometimes you useless moll,' he quipped. He bit his lip about her obsession with mickey mouse courses which had taken her mind off of his interests. All she talked about was TAFE this and TAFE that. And how she was getting herself a proper education that the useless primary school had not given her.

Girlie did not respond. She had handed over his children when he had demanded it but she was not prepared to give up her opportunities. Her ticket out of this dump of a town. Norm agreed, telling her to be done with the gene pool from what he called that scum from over there. 'You made mistakes, more than most people Girlie, now put it behind you.'

'Stop wasting your time and get your black ass over to my Dad's place and do something with your kids for a change.'

Noelie had forgotten Kevin, who had run stumbling into the yard and then disappeared into the darkness. But, after a few moments, he decided Girlie didn't look like she was in the mood for a *quick one*, which was what she was worth now he had the Hilux. He knew she wasn't worth taking on along with her two sumo-wrestler looking sisters, not when he and his mates were cold plain sober. He liked the look of Girlie though, and thought it wouldn't take much to get into her pants. But it could wait for another night. He would come alone, carrying a carton of grog to impress her with. 'You win doll,' he said and backed off, waving the others back, until they had all tumbled into the vehicle.

The Toyota threw a wheelie and a spray of mud hit the women. 'Fuck you,' Girlie screamed. She took aim and fired the rifle. The bullets sprayed off the sides of the vehicle. Janice and Patsy did a Chubby Checker twist then, noticing their dirtied clothes, they decided to go on the warpath. They screamed like wild women, and were soon chasing the vehicle as it swerved up the road in the slippery mud with dogs barking at the wheels. The big women slammed their iron bars on the side of the heavenly blue-painted vehicle, until it gained on them, and headed off back up the road towards town.

'Why you sitting around, man? Why don't you go and fight? Stick up for the family, man,' Kevin was at the back of the house goading Norm who wanted no part of it. A man was old now. He had been sitting in the darkness enjoying the night. The cloud cover had broken and a bright new moon shone down with so much light he could see his own hand.

It had been the perfect opportunity to read the future across the entire sky. He knew if he could sit for the rest of the night, examining the constellations of stars travelling across the sky road on their journey to the spirit world which wandering souls must reach by dawn, he would be able to read and decipher the messages. But he could not concentrate. Not because of the noise around the front. It was something different that forced him to stop what he was doing. He could not bear to hear the distinctive motor of the Toyota crying of other people's sorrows, screaming at him to come around, and have a look. He sat there, stony faced, not hearing a thing.

When Girlie heard her brother screaming loudly around the back of the house, pestering her father, her blood still pumping with the adrenalin rush from the fight on the road with Noelie, she switched. She wanted to kill Kevin now. As far as she was concerned, a strike at Noelie could just as well have been a blow at Kevin. She stomped around the back of the house, saying she wished the accident had finished him off. 'You are nothing but a pest to the family Kevin.' She started jabbing Kevin in his skinny back, 'Fight me if you want to fight, you useless bastard.'

A crazy look of madness made his face twitch uncontrollably. He was not far from a convulsing fit where he would totally lose himself in a world that had overwhelmed his brain. When he reached this point in his madness, it disabled whatever skerrick of common sense he might have had even to save himself. She knew she only had to jab him hard once, to send him off into this state of paralysis. She threw herself onto his stick body, while Janice and Patsy grabbed his arms. Each of them took turns hurling him through the house until they reached his room and forced him onto his bed. Whenever he tried to get up he was knocked back onto it again. Finally, he collapsed into unconsciousness.

'Well! He's either asleep or dead,' Patsy remarked, and the three nodded agreement, feeling relieved that they had restored some order to their lives. 'Lucky we are here,' Girlie said, and Janice grunted as she was apt to do, rather than getting involved in longwinded talking. Tiredness returned, and each went back to their separate parts of the compound to tend to the children who luckily had slept through all of the noise. The night turned quiet again except for the frogs croaking on top of a mud pile every fifty centimetres, for hundreds of kilometres, around the Gulf of Carpentaria.

Chapter 5
Mozzie Fishman

From out of the dust storm the Fishman drove home.

A long line of battered old cars heavily coated in the red-earth dust of the dry country crawled wearily behind him, leaving in their wake a haze of petrol fumes and dust. The red ochre spectacle belonged to Big Mozzie Fishman's never-ending travelling cavalcade of religious zealots, which once again was heading home, bringing a major Law ceremony over the State border.

Bearers of the feared secret Law ceremony, these one hundred men were holy pilgrims of the Aboriginal world. Their convoy continued an ancient religious crusade along the spiritual travelling road of the great ancestor, whose journey continues to span the entire continent and is older than time itself. They come and go, surrounded in a red cloud of mystery, travelling along roads where the only sound is the ghostly intermittent chime of a single distant bell, ringing out of the ground, echoing throughout the bushland.

The long dusty convoy, passing through the pristine environment of the northern interior, seemed to have risen out of the earth. There it goes. A simple other-worldly in appearance crusade, that looked as though it belonged to some enchanted agelessness touched by a holy hand.

In the thirty-car procession, moving, eating, sleeping, living in second-hand Falcon sedans and Holden station wagons of 1980s vintage, travelled men of every adult age were covered with days and months of dust. They breathed so close to the earth, the night might have mistaken them for the spirits of the dead. On the spiritual road, which was indeed hard and bumpy, the life of these vehicles had been refashioned many times over. In an astonishing modern-day miracle of recycling by those spiritual men of Fishman's convoy who had artisan hands and the minds of genius, using tools and parts found only in nature, all of these vehicles survived over thousands of kilometres of the country's hardest rock and gravel.

Aboriginal folk living along the back roads spoke in whispers about how they had encountered the half spirits – *Men, bedraggled*. They hid from the dirt-encrusted cars with the Australian flag flying from radio aerials all along the convoy. It would be difficult to dispute that the journey undertaken by the Fishman's convoy was as pure as the water birds of the Wet season's Gulf country lagoons flying overhead, travelling through sky routes of ageless eons to their eternal, ancient homes. It was this sound they heard one day, coming their way, and bush folks called it the breath of the earth.

The clear day into which Mozzie Fishman's convoy travelled was so different to yesterday on the southern edge of the Gulf of Carpentaria when a dust storm suddenly appeared in the plains country. It rolled down from the skies, darkening the land, howling like dead people in the night, and swallowed up the weight in the heavy minds of these spiritual travellers while they slept with backs against the wind, so they could be released from the bond of months, even years, on the road, dedicated to religious duty. This was the story for the journey passing through this part of the country. No one in the convoy had been surprised; the dust storm was expected to appear before they reached home.

The convoy crested spinifex-covered hills, dipped into red rock valleys, curved round the narrow bends, and created a long snake of red dust in its wake. Ahead, the road, a wound cut in the country, was as clear as a day could be for Big Mozzie, who was so happy country and western melodies sprang into his mind from a buried heyday, jumping from his soul out to the world through his steel-grey beard. Listen! He was singing his favourite songs in a full voice, loud and infectious, on the north wind travelling back down the convoy, everyone laughing. The landscape passed by in a yellow-green and red blur of enchanted spirits listening to the riotous choir of *yippee yi-ays* heading for Desperance, home of the country and western big man, fitted like a stuffed black glove in the bucket seat beside the driver of the leading car.

Not everyone on earth knew how the religious leader acquired a name like Mozzie. Some small thing that happened sixty years ago when he was born into this world can become the hardest thing to remember. His childhood was of times when big secrets grew in families. Nor did everyone know that once upon a time, his name might have been Paul, or something Old Testament like Joshua, for it was never said. It was best to remain prudent and not invite common talk about a cultural man like Mozzie. The Pricklebushers never asked how people acquired names. Instead, they preferred the jargon of deference, talking in sentences, like, *Nobody remembers any old jingalo trivia about names anymore around here.*

Gasbagging talk was what other people did behind your back, whispering if they liked – for it was a free country. This is why the world never fails to astonish, no matter where people live, for there will always be some who sink so deep into the valley of dishonourable pursuits, and chatter amongst themselves about the humble beginnings of the religious and holy, like Mozzie Fishman. One poor old limpy woman and one ageing crippled-up leg of a man, who by chance of miracle, lived into modern times. So what if they had conceived a son at their age? This was what people do, they were in love; there could have been worse freaks of nature.

Ten thousand fish still swam in the bay and as many birds still flew in the skies.

If it was not enough for gossip to fall like the blow of a heavy piece of lead, straight on the heads of this one poor, elderly couple, but they soon had more bad humbug to bother them. They were ruthlessly urged to move their sparse household, a dozen times a day. People were complaining endlessly about the old couple with the troublesome son who was causing half the mischief and running about, they claimed, wherever he pleased. Justice was nothing. They appealed, but seeing there was no use in talking, they would end up talking less and less, and in the end, what happened? Well! They were squatting like a pair of dogs sheltering under one prickle bush to the next, in little *yaji* nests, and going about bewildered, cowering from one nothing place to another. 'Shameful and a thousand curses too,' the old couple complained to the big *walakuku* humpy people. This was only muttered behind their backs, but the embittered community heard and cursed back. *Go away you people!* They called out to Mozzie and his elderly parents. *Go! You are too much more spreading diseases, if you please.*

Those were the days of people rushing around mad with too many modern ideas which did not belong in their heads. Strange things were said by the *maranguji* doctors about the boy's blood being full of boiled lollies. Some people, women in particular, who were blood relatives to the *maranguji* men and women, spoke of collision theories which they had formulated over a quarter of a century of card game talk. These women spoke of what happened to people if you had seven decades of accumulated sugar racing around in your body – like what had happened to the old couple. You could feel the irritability in the air by the way they flapped the cards, feeling the old couple must still be around somewhere, still there some place, and would have to go. Their impatience was the normal way people of the modern world of the white man went about their business, the general attitude to your fellow mankind's acts of intolerance. Afterwards, complaining of the others who had participated in that marathon gambling and talkback event, they whinged, *Their mumbling and grumbling made you sick*. It was no wonder why the spirit of the country was raw with unkindness.

The harmless parents of Mozzie Fishman moved obligingly, repeatedly, only mentioning from time to time, 'It was no good being so persistently nomadic in modern times for you cannot keep up with people, always jumping about the place.' No truer word was spoken because jumpiness creates a tidal wave of problems. You have no place to call home: nowhere to send the mail. Nomadism was no longer the answer.

Wherever the old couple's boy was seen to be in those miserable days of unkindness, the spies in the Pricklebush swore that they had seen black clouds of mosquitos swarming in his wake. Wherever the boy walked, the Pricklebush resonated with the irritating sounds made by these unusual swarms as they moved around in the air. The boy had to walk somewhere. So, everyone got the chance to see the phenomenon.

Mozzie Fishman grew out of his childhood affliction, and not a single mosquito followed him around anymore. He proudly claimed that he was conditioned by his parents to be ready to move for the benefit of other people.

Such tales were alluvium, pay dirt to the Roy Orbison sunglass-wearers who often travelled by nightfall like so many bats, with the windows of their cars wound up, so the devil-devil spirits of mosquitos could not get in and inject them with the dreaded encephalitis disease. *Aborigine* people were different now, they knew the scientify as well, like the sophisticated naming of what mosquitos carried around in their little bodies. And if mosquitos were bad, the devotees of Mozzie's convoy would get the Mortein

Plus out, like the television advertisement, and hit them hard between the eyes.

The spiritual Dreaming track of the ceremony in which they were all involved, moved along the most isolated back roads, across the landscape, through almost every desert in the continent. The convoy, which had grown with cars of all colours and descriptions, kept a wide berth from the gawking eyes of white people's towns, Fishman called them, 'those who just wouldn't know even if you gave them something on a stick.'

The men in this moving mirage of battered vehicles felt they had well and truly followed the Dreaming. Travel had become *same, same* and mandatory, as the convoy moved in reptile silence over the tracks of the travelling mighty ancestor whom they worshipped through singing the story that had continued for years. The crossing of the continent to bring the ceremony north-east to the Gulf, to finish it up, was a rigorous Law, laid down piece by piece in a book of another kind covering thousands of kilometres.

'Start em up again!' The Fishman's voice would ring out each morning. The men would rise from the face of the world where they slept like lizards, dreaming the essence of a spiritual renewal rotating around the earth, perhaps in clouds of stars like the Milky Way, or fog hugging the ground as it moved across every watercourse in the continent before sunrise. The convoy journeys were a slower orbit of petrol-driven vehicles travelling those thousands of kilometres each year. The pilgrims drove the roads knowing they had one aim in life. They were totally responsible for keeping the one Law strong by performing this one ceremony from thousands of creation stories for the guardians of Gondwanaland.

The feared ceremony crossed the lost dusty roads of ancient times, running across one another like vermicelli, passing through many empty communities. People in these isolated communities had simply gathered up all their sounds and left silence in their wake. The high degree of secrecy and sacredness surrounding the convoy extended in an invisible radius beaming hundreds of miles in every direction. Only an idiot would ask about it. Only a stupid person would stand in the way of the approaching convoy. Unless, they wanted to end up being drawn into the whole realm of this sacred business, for once absorbed by the snake lizard moving along the roads following the path of the great ancestor, you were hit with a ton of responsibilities that common people could not even dream about. Whole communities of hundreds of people living anywhere ahead of the convoy ran straight for the bush when they heard via the two-way radio, the morse code warning that the convoy was getting closer. *Must be nobody going to live here anymore*.

People quickly came down from the skies where they were walking the tightrope of existence and armed themselves with rifles for protection against the zealot mob. Women and kids who were not allowed to see anything of the convoy on the road headed straight to the sand hills or ran into dense mulga scrub – covering up all tracks behind them. This was where everyone sat quiet as a marsupial mouse not doing a single anything, just whispering, that's all, until word came at last that it was safe to return home. Not all men or all older boys wanted to be dragged away into a religious pilgrimage that would heave them far from their home-lands for endless months, maybe even years.

As time went by, hundreds of sick people would have waited on the hot, parched road for the Fishman to come and take them away. They were the ones who said they had thought they were going through life for what it was and then, all of a sudden, some other terrible thing happened, and their life would never be the same again. Fishman would pick them up and they would go on pilgrimage to the ancestral resting places, until the end came. Fishman treated sick people with reverence. They had his respect and he buried those who died properly, in a sacred resting place. Why? Fishman explained he helped his people because there was no good whitefella government governing for *blackpella* people anywhere. And the sick pleaded to go with him.

When Fishman came across the sick people waiting beside the red dust blowing dead spinifex balls up the road, he would stand for a long time on the outskirts, just looking at their ailing communities as though he was expecting the people hiding in the bush to come back. The pilgrims would stand around their cars watching the wind blowing past the empty houses – studying the lives of ordinary people. The young men tapped their car roofs to the tune of *I got you babe*, all eager to move on, as soon as the petrol supplies were replenished. It was on these occasions, so close to the empty communities of fellow countrymen, that the Fishman felt a much stranger, frightening sensation of what was left of his own humanity. These times when he stared into space were the times when he talked to himself.

Mozzie saw visions when he drifted off with the hot temperatures or the silence and began speaking to himself. The men would over-hear him saying things like 'The skies have become a sea of hands.' 'There are too many, everything moving too fast and thick like a nest of worms twisting, hands turning, convulsing hands, attacking the place like missiles.' Nobody claimed they ever saw what the Fishman was watching, while looking where he looked, following his eyes glinting in the sun. Some old wise men moved closer behind the Fishman in case, they said, 'We might capture his line of vision.' They were determined people the old wise men. There was also a lot of nervousness in the convoy. But the more inquisitive wanted to know what he saw. So, Fishman explained. He said it was hard to keep up with all the hands sliding everywhere, created by a special luminance caught in the fractures of light. He described how he saw hands touching everything in the community. 'Hands too many,' he whispered, coughing, 'running like mice all over every dwelling, trying to reshape, push, mould, trying to make things different. White hands.'

Must be how they would like it, hey? What do you think? Mozzie always had someone available to give a little back-up commentary.

The old wise men were astounded by the vision of white hands. Perhaps it was presumptuous for them to assume they ought to be black hands of black people when most other people believe the colour of spirits is white.

Fishman would be taken over by these visions, and would speak out very loudly, as though they were all witnessing the monumental event, like they had all been thrust into the front line of a war zone where the attack he was witnessing was deafening, and he would be shouting out the bits and pieces of information: 'See this, see that.' It was as though he could not hear himself speak. And Fishman? He cringed, lowering himself, and stepping back, arms wide, as if he were trying to keep everyone safe and out of the line of attack. He never liked what he saw in the visions because it was too frightening, he said. Sometimes he saw thousands of these hands at work. He could see them killing Aboriginal people. He believed the hands belonged to all kinds of white people, some dead, some still alive, and he knew because he was able to recognise hands, that some of those hands belonged to people who were still living and still sitting themselves on top of traditional Law.

'You know what?' Fishman asked, as he did, before explaining what he saw.

'No!'

'Their unconscious thoughts have been arrested in a limbo of unresolved issues which must be preventing their entire spirits from entering the afterworld. Their hands and thoughts have been left behind. They are locked up in their own injustice.'

These were the kinds of visions which made the Fishman decide on new rules. His number one rule was that the convoy was never to enter a community together. He of course never went into a community while on the road. Only a few were allowed to go into a community if the purpose served the convoy.

Frequently after his visions, Mozzie would complain of chest pains that only affected him in these empty human places. His followers would begin moving him back to his car, sighing to each other in relief as the other vehicles returned from the community, and the senior men ordered the convoy to move on. Then, turning to whatever ailing people were waiting on the roadside, Fishman would say, 'Come with me and be released from the cages of poverty.'

On the road, Fishman picked up anybody, even if there was no room left in any of the vehicles. 'Get out and walk,' he emptied cars of young men. 'Make do,' he ordered others. 'Catch us up.' Fishman's visions did not die with the distance placed between him and his men. In the following days on the road the pilgrims drove while listening to the crying of the frightened voices of the sick people, pleading not to be taken to a whitefella hospital where they would be treated rough, like they were strangers: 'We are not taking you there, we are not going to.' It was hard to build trust.

More times than not, the convoy would stay clear of communities they passed on the roads, because visiting was too stressful, particularly on the old people who would dream about what they had seen for days afterwards, about how they saw a whole industry of invisible hands at work on those places. By staying away from them, they felt they had won a battle because this was what Mozzie told them. His voice winning down the roads – winning he claimed, over the cold and heartless ambitions of politicians and bureaucrats who came flying in from faraway cities and capitals to destroy the lives of Aboriginal people.

They say, people in the right circles – academic people, who use their brains to talk about such things as cult movements – that there are not many religious zealots as big as the Fishman in the *Aborigine* people's world of today. It might be true. He might be too big, or it might be equally true to say that his reputation was more dazzling and more amazing than the actual man.

Norm Phantom, a close friend of Mozzie Fishman, who was himself a big man of the contemporary times, said quite plainly he never wanted to have any part of his friend's convoys. He said Mozzie got on his nerves. Everyone knew in the Pricklebush camps that Norm Phantom was a follower of spirits out in the sea. The Fishman, on the other hand, was a failure as a water man. Two minutes on a boat and he would be hanging over the side. But Norm could not deny Fishman his unbeaten title of water divining. The men travelling with the Fishman saw this miracle every day. He would get out of his car, sniff, and, without fail, detect in the dry air the moist smell of water coming out of wet ground and plants a hundred kilometres away, or of a hidden soakage in the flat spinifex plains. 'He never used a forked stick either,' the Fishman's followers bragged in the Pricklebush contest of whose extra-ordinary gifts were bigger and greater, but it could have been that he simply knew the country that's all, like the back of his hand.

'Fishman is the most uncommonly uncommon person walking alive today.'

'So he only used his nose then?'

'Yes.'

'Big nose like Pinocchio?'

'No, not like Pinocchio.'

'Well! How does he do it?'

'He just sniff the air like an animal.'

Everyone had a story to tell of the Fishman this and that. But it was not all glamour on the religious road. He extracted a big price for his pilgrimages into the redneck country of small towns and vast cattlemen acreages where he and his whole shebang were considered an affront to white decency. Pure white nanny-goats running down the dry riverbeds and phone callers echoing to each other: *Can you see what I see?* Dead keen to excite each other up, those isolated white folk, any stranger to the entire continent would have thought Mozzie's convoy carried a huge deadly chimera of a virus from the third world. Oh! Joyless one day life turned out to be in the openness of the cattleman's kingdom, when a blot of strange-looking blacks appeared like an eyesore on the horizon. Who knew why there were *boongs* squatting down on the riverbank? the maddened men announced as they did what they normally did: defended their boggle-eyed kin with rifle fire. This was why Mozzie Fishman knew he could not stay with the white people teaching them about reconciliation, and moved the convoy on. He never saw himself as a target and would never get used to the idea of being used as target practice either.

All the little country towns, dotted here and there on the back roads, hated the sight of Fishman's convoy in the main street: dirty people and whatnot. The words about dirty people and whatnot, which travelled like wildfire, spread down the bush telegraph: *Of seeing them hordes of blacks on the road again.* The story did not go away like in the newspapers where yesterday's story was old news. *The what was likely to happen,* a question of huge proportions and consequences, grew up into big talk, which must be big talk when town people were talking about killing the black hordes.

So, there was no bringing out a Red Roses box of Australian chocolates to share around but instead, there were gawking people wherever there were shabby cars full of black men filing into a town. *All we want to do,* the residents chimed to each other behind locked doors in a mighty big hurry, *is to guard the decency of clean-living people.* They had a respectable place and there were

Aboriginals travelling foot to mouth. Worse than even...? What? A bandwagon full of politicians. *Why don't you go out and blow up the roads when you see people like that coming here?* Those tiny town shires spoke hard logic when sunshine was threatened.

No, Mozzie's life on the road was not easy and back home at Desperance, he was expected to return.

As soon as a fair breeze blew in from the south, going straight through the Pricklebush and out over the coast to converge with the seasonal change of the Wet, there would be someone with an acute sense of smelling no one else had, who might say they could smell trouble coming up the road. *How could that be?* There was no reason. It might turn out to be true or it might be some people were born liars. *Trust nobody* was the motto.

Pricklebush waited instead for the red wall. This happened when the breeze picked up and turned into a wall of red dust spanning from left to right across the southern horizon, visible up to twenty miles away from Desperance. Then they really knew Fishman was coming home. The red wind ran through their homes and the specks of dust gathered from Mozzie's convoy hit people right in the eyes.

Days like this stayed around like a rot, and every day the wind would start up again, as soon as the clock said eleven. The wind blew and blew until six p.m. and people with sandy blight in their eyes jumped with relief, as soon as the wind stopped. But still, no one would admit Mozzie was on his way, until one day, a red-ring-eyed person, some pea-brain person, for every creed and race has got them – an Eastside person – would start to make trouble. You ask yourself, *What's that noise?* And it would sound like a stick being dragged along the ground. And it was a stick. The stupid person was dragging a stick around the ground, making little noughts and crosses, in a full lull of boredom on a sunny afternoon, perhaps, Sunday! When, without thinking about it, this person who you had been watching and just turned your back on what they were doing for a second, had gone and written the name Mozzie Fishman in the dirt and walked away, leaving the name in the ground behind them.

It was too late to run over and rub away what was done. *What's that?* Some old person who could read English came along and stopped, shocked. He stared down at the ground mind you, and could not believe his eyes. Mozzie Fishman's name written in the dirt. Soon the old person would be screaming – *Come out the stupid person who wrote that man's name in the ground, who got to have a sound slap over the head*, and then he would scrub the name out with his feet before walking on. But it was far, far too late by then. The deed was done.

Ever since Mozzie set off down the south road on his first convoy, there had been many times when the Pricklebush people thought they had said their final farewell. *We hopes he never comes back*, the poor old skinny people said wholeheartedly as they waved goodbye. They were jack of him causing trouble with Uptown. He was like a dumped cat, always coming back, always claiming the people who had thrown him away.

They said they only had themselves to blame for causing their own bad luck. Awful days passed waiting for the conjurer to evoke himself into Desperance. The build-up in people's minds was as though some spell had been cast over their brains. Up and down the Pricklebush people went, chucking around their suspicions about each other and casting aspersions around hilly-pilly with their hostile staring about what other people might be thinking, and cutting up the air into thin little ribbons. Silly people tried to excuse themselves by saying, *Oh! Jesus Christ I never meant to be bad*. But it was too late, *You idiot*. The change was on the way and one day, materialising out of thin air, Mozzie Fishman would be amongst them again.

'You forget your troubles easily,' Norm Phantom was forever trying to defuse the obsession created by Mozzie's visits. He often went fishing, sat in a becalmed sea, just to get away from the talk about whether Mozzie was doing this or was doing that. Calmer people often tried to persuade Mozzie to act normally when he was in Desperance – to stop his outlandish behaviour.

'You want to stop running around town like a white man,' Norm told Mozzie.

'But brother, it seems to me you accuse any black man in town of being a coconut. I seduce Uptown. I get them to eat out of my hands.'

Mozzie was a wizard or some kind of magic man with a cauldron of tricks brewing inside his body. Many, many Pricklebush people went up to Uptown and cautioned him, *Be quiet about white people*. He paid you no attention. *You don't go and tell white people anything. Not the police especially*. But no, he went right ahead walking around town saying he was like nuclei. Did anyone knows what was nuclei? No. People in the Pricklebush talked about killing Mozzie.

'Well!' He explained in wild talk, his cigarette bobbing up and down in the corner of his mouth, saying how, 'Everyone had to go through me. Everyone had to because they were like negatives on a roll of film and nobody could see their picture.' He said when he joined the negatives up with the great spirits they would turn positive, instantly like a polaroid photo. The people of Uptown were convinced something was happening when they listened to Mozzie's speeches, because they said they felt the heat of fire burning the side of their faces.

Mozzie claimed he had the power to cause an enormous nuclear fusion which nobody on this earth had ever seen before, and goodness knows what will happen next. Whenever he spoke, using his grandiose words, he would lead people into agreeing how he could have been a great President or a Prime Minister in another life – if he had not been born in the Pricklebush. The policeman just stood there listening to Mozzie talk while his baby-blue eyes almost popped out of his head. Even with full uniform on and a cap on his head it was a waste of money paid for the power of authority. Nobody was in charge. When the policeman came down to the Pricklebush to see what Big Mozzie was up to, Mozzie told him the story about nuclei. He had the nerve to call out that story to the police, while knowing full well the law was being aided and abetted by all the governments in the whole country – state government, local government, government calling themselves Aboriginal Affairs, or whatever else coming from Canberra, because who knows by what Act of Law the white man calls himself in his many disguises. All the friends of the law were standing well behind Truthful while he was being set upon by Mozzie. They were hissing this and that advice, while being forced to breathe in Big Mozzie's words like they were poisonous fumes of loose radicals: carbon dioxide, carbon monoxide, carbon tetrachloride.

All those poor Uptown people who did not know any better were really frightened of Mozzie. *We know all about fallout, Mozzie Fishman*, someone shouted at him, even though people in the Pricklebush who were watching knew the speaker did not know what he was talking about. They never knew where Mozzie Fishman had been, disappearing and reappearing into their lives. They thought he must have been living in a nuclear dump if he said he was *nuclei*. But apart from what was happening in Mozzie's life, everybody knew one thing, people had a good right to be frightened about breathing nuclear air and Mozzie should not have brought his radioactive body into the Pricklebush.

It was things like this which were the last straw. Uptown people started running around telling tales, until the whole town was jumping around about Mozzie Fishman making bombs. Soon enough, everyone had an expectation rattling in their minds. With a major explosion in sight, old people had their eyes trained on Uptown with spyglasses from the Pricklebush. *Look who was who ordering the law and order around.* Reading lip talk, they said to interested spectators what people were saying Uptown. They said, *Get him out of here, get him out, he's a bloody troublemaker.* Nobody could believe their ears, and said they did not think it was that bad, listening to the telephone wire twang in panic for hours between Desperance, and down South. The children, who were used to dangling themselves along the wire, said it was the line that was hot, that even the mad crows flew off in fright with smoking feet dangling below in midair. No one knew what the earth was being talked about that stopped the night owl from trying to go hoot! de! hoot! at two or three o'clock in the morning. It was such an uppity town sometimes.

People united like never before to confront the Fishman with their shiny rifles aiming right at his fat belly button, which looked like a good target, but he told them to forget it. He stared at them with hard eyes. The look he had on his face had not been seen in the Pricklebush for many generations. He said if anyone got two foot in his way, he would explode like the bloated carcass of a bullock someone had run over, and when that happened he would be more or less obliged to spill his guts right into their faces.

All he had to do was sneeze he said. 'Yes, just sneeze.' Such audacity. And the crowd, standing too long on Uptown's hot bitumen road, hallucinated how they would all die one terrible death of suffocation in the rotten stench of Fishman's exploded guts. Only the men on the convoy knew the harmless sound of his cough. A sound, similar to the faulty carburettors of their vehicles, came from deep inside his throat all day long. 'Look out for unseasonable dust storms,' he warned as the riflemen began retreating, heading instead to the rifle range out of town, 'It will make everyone sneeze.' Before they could move very far, he gave one sharp clap, and their twitchy fingers closed on triggers, with a volley of shots reverberating overhead.

When everything calmed down, and he had their full attention again, Fishman said the sound he had just made was the sound of instantaneous death. 'That was all they would hear,' he explained with an honest-felt melancholy in his voice which made their eyes twitch faster. Perhaps Uptown already knew that the sound of death sounded like a sharp clap of the hand. 'You will die one day,' the policeman warned, wagging his finger at Mozzie. 'You will know,' Mozzie repeated, with a mocking sputter of spit, a little choking, and then silence. Only his cigarette continued to glow and burn on his Clint Eastwood face, whenever he inhaled its fumes into his lungs.

The trouble was Mozzie Fishman was from a different dimension to other people who had to get on with their lives. Fishman should have known too: nobody should lose respect for people who had to get along with others for the peacefulness of the situation. But, that was too good for Mozzie, he decided he would stay in, or return to his own particular time warp, unable to get it out of his system. The art of compromise was too good for him – to get on with life. No, he lived solid to the past, to relive it all when he came home like a curse. Neither would it take him long to drive everyone else back into the past with him – two minutes of plethora to reorient Pricklebush lives into the past was the record so far. Two minutes back, and off he would go, harping on the piece of bitumen in Uptown about the time when the mining venture was first established twenty years ago on his grand-daddy's traditional land. This was not the big, multinational mining company which came recently, but an old prospector he was talking about, digging gravel with a shovel.

The very next thing which would happen, he would come marching around, like in one of them old street marches – a demonstration, and people who were just out shopping for the day, would look and say, *What is this?* Nobody knew what was happening, or what caused it, since he was acting like twenty years ago was only yesterday when there had been so much water under the bridge for everyone else. Kids grown up. Grandchildren on the lap. Mozzie was oblivious to all that. He continued marching along, left – right, left – right, stirring up the possum's nest, bringing all those painful memories pouring back, if anyone could remember so far back in time.

The old skinny Westside mob who went out with their spy-glasses, peeping through the thorny bush hideouts and in unison tut-tutting, said: *Boy! We wish he would just piss off.* Insidious nightmare. Et cetera.

Well! Nobody thought it was a joking matter because his talking caused talk everywhere, big talk, all over the country. Oh! Imagine how people felt when they turned on the radio and the television even, and there he was, speaking: talking on the radio about the mine. Even the television had his big face on it. Well! Big talk caused no sense but trouble which came along in full force. All the police flew into Desperance on an aeroplane for the day to pick up Mozzie Fishman, manhandled him forcefully to the edge of town, and chucked him out like he was nothing.

If he was not enough nuisance there was more bad talk like nobody had ever witnessed, coming out of the fat lips of the Queen of Sheba herself. She, Angel Day, had eyes all over the place, even though she was still married to Norm Phantom then. A lot of people said they saw the wickedness of the devil's face when she smiled although none had the courage to tell her to her face. Old Mona Lisa would have looked like a sour lemon beside Angel Day on the rare days she put a smile on her dial, laughing with her friends when some new man was in town. The old women yelled out to those hussies, *Haven't you got a kitchen to attend to instead of*

sitting around ponging like backstreet alley cats? Dressed all hoity-toity.
Angel and her friends laughingly yelled back, *Well! Old women you
would know about what goes on in the backstreets.* The old women knew
what was being said as they waltzed around each other's homes in
the Pricklebush, whispering among themselves and listening to
their rot.

'He was like an opal,' Angel purred through red-lipstick lips
about Mozzie Fishman to her other moonstruck friends.

'No! He's not. He is like a really bright sapphire shining
through the night.'

'How come he be like a sapphire when the biggest diamond in
the entire world was what he was like?'

'He like topaz too because his very skin look like warm, delicious,
golden trickle of topaz.'

'Sister, that's not at all what he's like. He was for sure all of the
precious stones, opal, sapphire, diamond, topaz, all rolled into
one.'

Perhaps it was the time of year when Mozzie returned to
Desperance, which coincided with heavy doses of pheromones
in the air with the Wet. They held open their hands to show a
small innocuous looking insect. It was, they said, the secretions
of this insect which caused younger women to become downright obsequious, although the unctuous charms of Mozzie
Fishman were known across the continent, and perhaps he had an
unhallowed relationship with all the insects of the earth. To
those who could speak of moments in life shared intimately with
another, if briefly (who could ask for more?), he shone. It was word
of mouth which created this jewel of the imagination with its
refracting beams of light so intoxicating for the female eye, swelling
with unrequited emotional longing for the experience of the
celebrated shared moment, more or less. Mozzie believed he tried
no harder than other men to have women love him, but for some

extraordinary reason, he was unable to deny that he was a beacon of light in the fog of men, flickering brighter than any other sojourner to Desperance, loitering in the Pricklebush of religious and political fanatics, evangelists, bigots, shamans, philistines, and passing-by self-appointed gurus.

Angel's philandering did not stop the petulant Norm Phantom and Big Mozzie from being the best of friends. All the confused mummies told their children that both Uncles were the brightest shining stars flown in from the night sky for the people of earth. Stories, stories, the truth became so blurred, except the owl with big eyes saw everything in the night: all sorts of people were visiting each other, whenever they got half the chance. But who was anybody to butt in and dispute anything a big woman wanted to tell her children? The world would be a very sad place, little children would be lost, if they could not believe in the fantasy of a mother's story.

Whereas Big Mozzie with the Clint Eastwood face was nothing but a bag of bones standing tall in an ancient pair of dusty R.M. Williams boots, Norm Phantom was physically and intellectually the bigger man. Their friendship grew out of Big Mozzie's drive over those other competing religious freaks who turned up regularly to the Phantom household with their fugitive attempts to exorcise the demon, or the snake spirit, whatever it was, living beneath Angel's house.

The Phantom house took regular forays into other-worldly matters. There had been moments of magic, precise times of exorcism, countless days of solemn prayers and undying reverence. A Catholic priest, Father Danny, drove into the Gulf one year and in the back of his car he had one thousand little crucifixes which were erected all through the house, and around it outside, and he left them there for a month. The biggest discovery the priest made was that the Phantom family were the clumsiest people alive. They knocked the crosses over whenever they moved, and the priest observed that not one member of the family was able to walk in a straight line. 'Tell him to get this stuff out of here,' Norm told Angel who had insisted on these matters. She told the priest to take the obstacle course away, and blamed Norm when the exorcism never worked.

Then she got a guru man to start hanging around. It was a mystery in the Pricklebush how she managed to find these people who kept turning up at her door. Everyone watched as the blond-haired guru seemed to slide around like an angel in white gowns over at the Phantoms' place. He left out a piece of bread for the devil every day for months, bashing a drum and chanting, some-times up to eighteen hours a day. Norm's family did not like that either. The kids ate the bread before the spirit had a chance to get to it. At night, under the guru's instructions, Angel made all her children go outside and beat the ground with sticks, without fail, whatever. Nothing worked. The only result was that the lurking spirit bestowed generously on all of the religious visitors a strange will to hang about, wearing out their welcome, until Norm had them evicted. All of the fanciful and fanatical became driven with obsessions like those that kept driving Mozzie Fishman, kept him dreaming of coming home to Desperance alive, to be shackled to her skirts, and to plead to be freed.

This was until one day, even with his strong connection to the spirit world under Norm's house, his neediness for acceptance by Norm, his passionate heart for Norm's Angel who caused only calamity for devoted men, when who would have thought Mozzie's heart would be broken – Well it was! Whoosh! out the door. So much came unstuck from a heart torn to shreds. She said her piece to Norm like a whirly wind whistling across the flat, everything flying in sight, smack! smack! then she was gone. A middle-aged woman, run off with a...

Mozzie told Norm he could barely conjure up the vision, it was so disgusting, how a woman so magnificent in every way, who spun gold from the rubbish dump, could have stooped so low. To take up *honky-tonking* probably in the *animal bar*, who knows where, run off, with a thing, worse than any useless thing he could think of, not even a white man, but a fake. Not just one of those New-Age self-styled guru people who came looking to exorcise her demon. It was sorrowful. The so-called winner, a common black man, a coconut, even had the audacity to call himself, Uncle Tom. *So additionally*, he said of those times, what he had in common with Norm Phantom was shared devastation, although it was truer to say, Norm Phantom never lost a moment of his time to her memory. When she left he told the kids she had run away with a money spider.

'What for?'

'To chase the spider.'

'Did you run after her?'

'Sure, I did.'

'Where did she go?'

'A house full of spiders.'

There were lies in the Pricklebush and life was a mess when two of the biggest men around had been jilted for a gladbag full of whatever had drifted into everyone's lives from the global winds of the world's religions – Apache, Hindu, Buddhist, Jew, doesn't matter what else. Five minutes worth of each, the wise men said. The old women wept for the man with no shame, running for grog, the white man's piss they fed by the bucketful to poison the Pricklebush folk. They said nothing about Angel. It was the modern man's dream of the Mona Lisa clawing at his heart which caused Big Mozzie to cry like a baby over many hundred kilometres of road.

The novices plucked like desert flowers to be taken aboard the motorcade community initially found the name to be highly deceptive. They had difficulty with the idea that nothing in Big Mozzie Fishman's world was how it appeared. Big Mozzie growled at the newcomers and told them he was not connected with anything to do with fish – 'No, siree.' Lesson number one. Any debutees in his following who took it for granted that their spiritual leader would bring forth fish for the hungry wherever fish could not be found, discovered pretty quickly that was simply dead wrong, and being wrong would not do at all in Big Mozzie's eyes. A thing done wrong was the right key to wind up the boss.

'Biblical stories lived in somebody else's desert,' he would start up and talk on in a monologue with his long grey beard bobbing up and down, mesmerising every one in sight, as he talked throughout the day, if the mood for talking up big took a hold of him. Big Mozzie was at pains to make it clear that eons of indoctrination heaped onto the hapless by bible-bashers were the scourge of the blackfella's earth. He said he believed Christian beliefs had indoctrinated Aboriginal communities like grog and it was true to say it was even the cause of grog. So, grog and other people's religions would never do, never on the big Dreaming track. 'Never, never will do,' he explained. 'Biblical stories about baskets of fishes and loaves of bread belonged to the Jewish people or some other people,' he said, with the often-seen pleased look on his face of hardly believing his intuitiveness for hunting out the true nature of things. Time and again things happened on the road, he explained, saying that debutees must make a clean slate in their mixed-up little minds, on their hands and knees and using their own face for a rag. Big Mozzie Fishman said not to ask him about fish because he couldn't give a dead dog's eye about fishing, in fact, he hated fish, preferring to eat freshly hunted bush meat which the debutees had to produce for him on a daily basis, until it was proven beyond doubt that they had become true devotees.

This morning, everyone was talking about going fishing. 'Why do they do it?' Fishman asked with loathing and muttered a string of undecipherables into his beard. By the time the glorious sunrise grew into a hot day, he was still pouring out a venomous lecture to the people travelling in the number one vehicle of how he hated people taking it for granted that he would catch fish for them.

He spent the entire day conducting a monologue of his thoughts, speaking how he would be hard-pushed to remember the last time he had ever eaten a bit of turtle meat. 'Stop the bloody car,' he ordered a dozen times at least throughout the day, bringing the entire convoy to a standstill again, so he could walk down to another car and give the occupants a mouthful of his mind. 'I should kick the whole flaming lot of you out of the convoy and just go by myself in future.'

The day was a heatwave, and the zealots, covered in sweaty dust from head to foot, were all jammed up against each other like tins of oily sardines. The dust flew through the car windows and stayed trapped inside the vehicles, swirling around in little whirly winds of country dreams. Well! Breathing dust all day clogs up the lungs, and all the vehicles were full of men with heaving coughs, or sweating skins, shaken up and down from travelling every inch of corrugation of outback roads.

Each vehicle managed to motor on, while dirty oil spluttered over overheated engines, and exhaust pipes laid about in the dirt several thousand kilometres behind. The motors were pieces of modern art held together with rusty wire and leather belts or whatever it took to keep the cars on the road. The drivers were cherished by the convoy for their expert motor mechanic skills learnt on the road. None had never shopped at the service station for the Hi Tech Carburettor, or the Fast and Efficient Brake Service, or spent time playing around with the state of the art equipment at Correct It Clutch Repairs. Nor had they ever seen the full range of spare parts and accessories for the cars they were driving, or knew what the Beaurepaires salesman sold for a living. But out on a lonely dusty road of the never never, Mozzie's bush mechanics would have picked up enough man-made rubbish to fancy-dress a car, or do a complete engine rebuild, gearbox overhaul, the upholstery and welding done to suit.

In the middle of the day, the vehicles were travelling along a narrow, hilly road, twisting like a goat track out of Mozzie's fishing nightmares. This stretch of road always caused Big Mozzie to break into nervous singing with a great deal of soul to the spirits. 'Goodbye Joe, me got to go, me oh! myo! me got to go for the codfish ladies down the Bayou.' Seriously, he told Will Phantom, a young man in his mid-twenties, who was travelling in the same car right next to Big Mozzie as his driver, he was a living expert on every Hank Williams song known to mankind. Older convoy members pretended this was true. It saved the peace. However, they knew, he knew, he never remembered the lyrics of any song, and simply invented new words to suit himself. But why not! 'The son of a gun, hey, Will?' And he broke into a jitterbug, singing on about some place as if he knew where it was: 'A buzzin, having fun down the Bayou.'

Mozzie was so comfortable sitting there, wishing and shaking about with his Roy Orbison glasses on, humming on, saying his monosaccharose was playing up again, not acting his age, juggling his extra glass eye with the blue iris. The only blue eye in the convoy. Will watched the glass eye rolling through the air, landing from one hand into the other. It was a mesmerising act. The driver became so drawn into the eye, he could not keep his own eyes on the road. Mozzie usually kept the eye in the pocket of his trousers and liked to juggle with it on winding roads. It was for this reason nobody liked to drive for him and if they complained, Mozzie had one response: 'Get out, if you don't like it, go on, get some other so-and-so up here. He can drive the bloody car from now on.' The rolling blue eye stared into the back seat as it bounced back and forth. Four pairs of frightened eyes in the back seat moved in time, going left, right, staring at the false eye flipping to and fro, looking back at them, catching a glimpse of what they were thinking about: ready to jump out of that number one car, moving or not, with some so-and-so driving like he can't wait to get to hell.

Unfortunately for them, there was one thing stopping anyone jumping from the reckless speeding convoy. It was the giddy sight down the gullies below the twisting road which had been formed and re-formed from years of washaways, and now hung like fish gills, out over edges of the limestone substrata. Who wouldn't become recomposed, after looking down to the graveyards full of rusting car bodies littered on the bottom in a hundred degrees of heat? Before they had commenced the climb, Mozzie stopped the convoy like he had done on previous occasions and told his men assembled around him how to stay healthy by following a piece of his advice.

'If the spirit has its eye on someone's car on this road, if your car starts rolling backwards down the road, and no matter what, this car of yours is unable to make it up the hill, then there is only one course of action. Let the ancestor have the car and be done with it. Let him drive it around if he likes, after all it's his country. You don't need the car. Be happy, because one day when you go to whatever heaven claims you, you will need a car to run about in, and your old car might be good enough to be waiting there for you. So don't be a greedy person. Let it go. Always remember there isn't going to be a guardian angel on this rubbish heap of a road to push your car up the winding hills. Instead of poisoning yourself and anyone else with your greed and selfishness, it is better for you to chuck the useless car and let it slide to the floor of the valley below.'

Feeling satisfied, Mozzie finished the speech-making taken from his epistle without end, sighed deeply, and jumped out of the heat back into his car, after ordering the convoy on its way again. 'One time, the spirit, he wasn't so greedy. He only used to go for fancy wagons and animals,' he told Will, who kept his eyes on the road. He had heard a million and one stories so far on this trip with the Fishman. Fishman continued: 'Bones, pure white of dead horses, cattle and mules, plucked clean. You would see all of them down there being consumed by the spirit, but now he only eats cars.'

The convoy finally reached the turn-off for the last night camp before home. This stop was always a lagoon at the end of a non-descript, rocky track into the thick undergrowth of spearwood trees and turpentine scrub. Suddenly, as the country opened, and the cars crawled down onto flatter ground with a view of the water, nobody could believe their eyes. They peered through the paper-bark foliage at the water's edge onto the mirror image lagoon. Fishman put his eye back into his pocket. Those driving in the front cars wondered how could it be that someone else knew about their secret fishing hole.

As each car came over the rise and crawled down from the hill, and their occupants peered out of the dust-caked windscreens down into the lagoon, they all saw the fisherman. Right down in the middle of the lagoon, a white man was sitting out there in his boat. He was sitting as casual as can be, just like he had paid good money for the place. 'Now, what are we going to do?' Shallow and brackish, they all realised the lagoon was drying up until the Wet arrived. They also saw the significance of the white man being there first, and knew they would soon pull out, although still exhausted, and tired from their long travel over the dry country to get to the water, hungry for fish. Will Phantom did not speak, but he thought they outnumbered the white man, one hundred to one. Mozzie, reading his thoughts, quipped, 'You know Will, it would be one hell of a world where the truth of reality weighed nothing.' After a few minutes of quiet talk amongst themselves in the spearwood forest, someone who had taken a sidelong glance down through the paperbarks out over the lagoon's edge, loudly whispered, 'You know something? I think he's dead.'

It was a pretty big thing to say about a complete stranger. A funny sort of joke to cause a commotion. The men jostled for a better view while their whispering grew to a crescendo, muttering to each other and trying not to notice the fisherman, while sneaking glances.

'He's not. He's fishing.'

'No! Have a flippen better look.'

'He is dead.'

'Told you...'

Everyone started to have a good look, staring out there, waiting for movement from the fisherman, but he stayed stationary, like a painting of a still life. For a split second, nobody knew whether to laugh or cry, it was a relief, they were by themselves after all, and there was no white man, just a dead one. But, even if it was true, their minds snapped to another truth: the convoy would have to move on.

Nobody would be hanging around for long, not if there was a dead white man sitting out there. It looked bad. It would be bad for them if someone came and started to put two and two together, making connections, constructing scenarios not worth thinking of; imagining the consequences. It looked as though his boat had become set in mud where it had moored itself, when the floodwaters had drained into the ocean, after the last wet. Now he was separated from the sea by stretches of land and dry creeks. A halo of salt lay encrusted in white crystalline moulds around the sides of the boat. It was a freaky sight, the man just sitting there, tanned skinned clinging to a skeleton. It was the most terrible thing in the world in those moments of wondering what to do. Nobody thought it was a good idea to touch the body, or to be seen bringing it into town, so they said to Fishman, just leave him sitting there.

'Someone else will find his body eventually.'

'He's dead anyway.'

'Let the water take him out, poor thing anyhow.'

Fishman nodded briefly and said, 'Alright then. Let's go.'

'We are out of here.' The word spread.

Soon, perhaps that very night, with the smell of rain in the air, and the dark clouds in the north, it would start raining, and within hours the first flush of the rivers in flood would rush out to the sea. The bush echoed with the movement of men returning to their cars, and within fifteen minutes, when Will Phantom surveyed the area, he thought nobody would have ever known there had been over a dozen cars around him.

On the road again, someone said he thought the man in the boat looked a bit like old Elias. He said he recognised the way he was just sitting there was how he remembered seeing Elias out at sea when he was a boy. Fishman said, maybe it was, how would anyone know, they only got a distant view? It could have been. The idea that it was poor old Elias travelled like some strange osmosis down the vehicles as though the convoy might have been an animal with its own brain, agreeing: *Yeah! I think it was his boat too, now I think about it.* It was strange indeed, they were all talking about it being Elias out there in the boat, all through the late afternoon and evening, until they crawled into the prickle bushes of Desperance about midnight.

'Yes, it was strange,' Fishman yawned, reserving the last words he had to say for the day for himself. He was caving in to the deep tiredness that overcomes a person returning home after a long absence. The sea air opened his dust-fevered nostrils to the fetor of rotting fish that lived permanently in the air of Desperance. It overpowered the sweet smell of fish being cooked in dozens of homes on a Friday night which too was still lingering in the air.

Mozzie lay down to sleep beside the car on the blanket he had thrown on the ground. He heard the night owl somewhere in the trees close by, and in the distance, the guitars strumming in the drinking camps over on Joseph Midnight's Eastside. The music of *Heartbeat why do you miss* on a car radio, voices and laughter. Oh! For sure, some people have a whale of a time womanising, drinking, having mates. Further off still, he heard the sea woman heaving her breasts onto the beach. The familiar sounds of his past were falling from a magician's wand, waving around specks of memory in a trail of glitter, until the specks became millions of flooding, crashing helter-skelter visions in the stars, flooding through his mind. All those deeply buried emotions relating to home had resurfaced, rising out of a cauldron in clouds of steam, to strain against each other. For a long time, Mozzie lay on the ground waiting to drift away into sleep, thinking he would go mad if his mind did not stop running until, finally, escape came when he slipped into dreams that plucked their way through Desperance and back to the events of the day.

He knew now, recapturing the sight of Elias sedately sitting in the boat as a dead man would, that this was a message given to him from the spirit world. While he stood on the brink of his dream, watching Elias in the lagoon, Mozzie felt the spirits saying that he was alright. Nobody ever knew for sure what had become of Elias after that fateful morning, when he turned his back on Desperance, and was last seen dragging his boat back to sea. Now, they knew, Mozzie thought – *Elias was fine, he had gone to the spirit world in the sky across the sea, safe from the wickedness given unfairly to him at Desperance.*

In his sleep, Mozzie dreamt of the moments after the convoy headed back on the gravelly road, he was sitting in the passenger seat, just staring at the empty road ahead, and thinking about Elias, and checking in his mind, taking a mental tally, walking through the rows of groaning cars, and realising what he had originally thought, that Will Phantom had left them at the lagoon and was no longer travelling in any of the other cars. His mind slipped quietly back down the spearwood-lined track, and he stood behind a cluster of trees, surveying the landscape, until he found Will sitting alone by the lagoon looking at Elias. Mozzie crept over, his feet on padded leaves, until at last, he was able to look so closely into Will's undetecting face, it was a wonder that Will could not feel the intrusion of someone searching into his eyes, trying to dig out his soul. Mozzie, withdrew, *just be satisfied*, he told himself. A deal was a deal, Mozzie Fishman – *You had delivered Will, as you promised, safe and sound back inside of his country*. The sound of the owl brought Mozzie back to the night, and he lay half awake, thinking of Will Phantom, who had many responsibilities for one so young.

Hours of fitful sleep passed by as Mozzie Fishman retraced the journey to and fro from the lagoon, where he again hid behind the spearwood trees with the spirits of Will's ancestors, watching over the corpse of Elias. It occurred to Mozzie that the silent spirit men were listening to the sound of Will Phantom's country, to the dull, monotonous clanging made by heavy machinery churning and gouging into the land. These thoughts annoyed Mozzie into wakefulness, to sigh resignedly, and again, to roll over on his other side, muttering in his half-sleep to question the night: *Was there any good carting around your malaise? Spreading it around the camp? Inflicting others? Where had it led to?* Mozzie knew he had tried, more than some people, more than Will Phantom's own father whom he had told two years ago: 'I am taking Will on the pilgrimage – convince him of our ways of renewing the strength of the country.' Norm had not batted an eyelid and continued gutting fish. 'Nothing's changed, Norm, you win,' Mozzie acquiesced, seeing Norm Phantom in the dead of night, gutting a wriggling fish. Will had carried a mountain with him across the desert and in the end, everyone in the convoy carried a replica of Will Phantom's mountain.

In some ways, Mozzie recalled feeling lighter when they left Will at the lagoon, and the convoy, even though it must have motored up the steep gravelly road again like a clumsy, panting animal, had at the time felt like a breeze, floating with the dust and untangling itself from depression. How surprising had been the feeling of relief of not having Will for company anymore, although he had cherished the young man like his own son.

'Ah! a man does not need to sleep, ain't worth the trouble,' Mozzie said to himself, sick of his troubled night. He sat on his bedding and dragged dead grass and sticks into the fire with the cherished long stick he used for bashing snakes over the head. He set the billy to boil. In a few hours time it would be sunrise at home for his men.

He gazed casually through the darkness, scrutinising Norm Phantom's place, contemplating the stubborn old coot. When he saw a light on, flickering dimly through the Pricklebush, Mozzie Fishman flashed the Clint Eastwood smile. *You stupid old coot, call yourself tough, couldn't help yourself, could you?* The light intrigued Mozzie because he realised Norm had stayed up all night too, in spite of himself. Mozzie twisted his grey beard, elated about catching someone out, even in the utmost privacy of their inner-most emotions. He knew Norm would not acknowledge that he was waiting for Will.

Will was never expecting any big homecoming from his father. No one imagined Norm Phantom rushing out, carrying the fatted calf on his shoulders as soon as he got the news that his son was coming home. There was no use for some angelic child rushing to tell the patriarch, *See the prodigal son was coming, walking if you please, through the spinifex, over the rise.* 'Yep! Time will tell,' Mozzie sarcastically quipped. 'And pigs have wings.' Will would reach Desperance in his own good time, so let the light burn in a house where a fully-grown man only had time to recognise six of his seven children. The house with a slogan: *A man gets sick of running for his kids – I run for none of the buggers now.* 'It's like that is it?' Mozzie mouthed the words, remembering asking Norm when he had heard news of the rift between father and son. *What did he say back?*

He just glared for a moment, then he kept on scaling the big fish he had in his hand. Was he mad? He was mad alright. Scales were flying everywhere. What did you say then? *You were a stupid man when you were young, and now, you have turned into a stupid old man*, Big Mozzie remembered cursing Norm Phantom. Cursed him easily for rejecting a son like Will. Was he not made with the same blood and bone that made a good man? Indifferent, Norm spat in exactly the same way he would at a less than perfect fish on the end of a line, a puffer fish: *Chuck it to the dogs*. What was the difference between the patriarch and the zealot who grew out of the same Pricklebush thicket? Time would tell.

Listen to this. The talk was all over town. He did not? He did. Will Phantom of all persons mind you had absconded, flown the coup, walked. Walked where? Walked to Eastside. What did Norm say, his son and all? He swung the axe. He was hot with fever for a week. He kept swinging the axe around. All doors were slammed shut over on Eastside. A thousand nails bashed into the coffin which parents make for themselves when they throw their children away. This incident between Norm Phantom and his son gave birth to intractability on a grand scale. Oh! Well! War was war. When you have been at war for four centuries a son cannot overrule the father even in modern times. Old Cyclone, the mastermind of the old war in present east and west hostilities, long dead as a doornail, did not change matters. 'Enemy never die,' Norm quipped in his first and final words on the matter when he watched Joseph Midnight's relatives carrying Cyclone's coffin to the cemetery. Dead and good riddance, the mob on Westside remembering the good times and the bad went *Hip! Hip! Hooray! Kudala!* when Cyclone died, but what a man!

Memory, honoured in death, incorporated blood ties. This was what Norm meant when he referred to the enemy amongst them. Then, downcast whispers spread, unbelievable whispers full of truth and what have you, stultified the air in the Pricklebush over on Westside: *Will! Oh! Dear Lord, not Will, his father's image in every way, walking off with his own mind, apparently gone to live even, in old Cyclone's house.* The lad was stolen to the other side of town from under the father's nose by the grand-daughter of a bad man: *One for you and one for me.* The nuisance haunted the living from the grave.

Cyclone was old and clever, *binjuna Malbu kuluwulugu.* He believed in magic and became the first person in contemporary times to turn imagination into reality. Instead of being a rain man, or weather man, like he ought to have been, he brought lies to life. One of his extraordinary stories about the 'once upon a time' was a fictional pig story that became a real life nightmare.

In one of his elaborate once-upon-a-time inventions there lived an illusory porker of exceptional longevity with unwholesome attitudes to Pricklebush people roaming the riverbanks. Cyclone, messing with magic in his fingers, crawled into the guts of his twentieth-century story and brought it to life. He called his creation Abilene but she came to life and left mess after mess in real nightmares. This was what happened to the Uncle from Eastside who was the original owner of the blue Toyota. Westside pricklebush people said it was a fluke of nature that Abilene only attacked members of Cyclone's family. Cyclone had run to the police, the law, the white people when Uncle was killed. He stood around the police station in his old baggy pyjamas complaining, 'What about all the deaths relating to only our kin?' The new policeman pondered what he heard. 'How come only our family is coming to this grief?' he asked. The policeman became impatient and jumpy to use his gun. He made inquiries, made it quick smart. He called homicide up and they came up to Desperance and said: 'It was time for some action, man!' This was what happened when the favourite Uncle over Eastside was killed and Cyclone was running down to the police station every five minutes, and his family joined in the running after the police, until they were there all the time, jumping up and down, slapping the walls, complaining louder and louder, making threats, throwing their fish guts around and pointing their finger down Westside, over to Norm Phantom's place.

When Norm Phantom was arrested as a murder suspect he said he had nothing to say. Proudly he walked off with the police. It would have been good if the whole world could have seen the way he just walked as though he never had any fear inside of his body. The old people reminded everyone on Westside for months afterwards what a good day it was to see someone walk like that. When the day came for him to sit in court he sat there like a rock. He said nothing to anybody. Westside folk swelled with admiration. The rallying families of the two Pricklebush factions sat on either side of the temporary courtroom set up in the lime-green Council building meeting room. Both sides were eyeballing each other. Then the whispering started. Then the all-out abuse could be heard up the street. 'Good Lord! Thank you it wasn't the Sabbath, because the good Lord needn't have been in town,' the district judge roared for silence when he made his appearance after nobody had noticed the usher had announced his entrance. He found out very fast how your ears could turn red after hearing what one of those families could say about you.

The witnesses on Norm Phantom's side of the family said they saw no fluke there, no coincidence that the other side got the chop all of the time whilst their side didn't. The oldest witness from Westside got up and explained that the pig was territorial and, 'It was just going about its natural self, like Adam and Eve, pardon for using white man diction, that was why it got to hunt everything it believed belonged to itself within the precinct of its boundaries.' The judge told the old man his story was plausible and he would consider it.

The other oldest man on Eastside, Joseph Midnight, in fact, Cyclone's son said: 'It was understandable why Norm Phantom was the prime suspect in matters of crime relating to Abilene.' The judge asked him to continue his evidence even though everyone knew it was only grog talking. 'Who knows even how close he was to the big set of gristly trotters, since, wasn't it known how Norm Phantom could talk just plain too nicely about all matters fauna and flora in these parts?' But the judge explained something important to old Midnight: 'You cannot rightly accuse a man for all of them deaths just on hearsay, without hard evidence, just because he talks to the trees.'

Norm's blood relatives testified as sober people with bent heads. They never frightened the judge or any of the Australian law because they spoke their English calmly, which they knew would not frighten white folk, who never liked black aggressors. They turned out to be reliable witnesses. Drunken people did not make good witnesses slipping around across the nice shiny, linoleum floor, running around in court with delirium tremens, not remembering who was dead or alive, disappearing for hours at a time down the pub for more heart-starter when they should have been sitting like solid citizens in the court room.

The atmosphere of the courthouse changed dramatically with a shift in emphasis on the case when Cyclone's kinsmen came to the court full drunk, and engaged in slinging accusations at each other. The Eastside witnesses claimed Norm Phantom drove them out of their homes to live on the east side of town. They should have blamed Angel Day for that. She split the families. Then, something totally unexpected happened to the case.

The judge became impatient and sick and tired of tapping his fingers up and down on the judge's bench as he studied it for days, figuring out the age of the pine knots and circles, in order to avoid looking at the motionless mudflats through the window, or the hawks and crows soaring in the hot thermals over towards the rubbish dump and wondering why he had not become an ornithologist instead of a judge presiding over a murder trial, while waiting for the prosecution witnesses to arrive. Suddenly, out of the blue, he snapped to the assembled law men, 'Case Dismissed.'

Too good, cheered the Westside gallery, as the judge jumped up from his swivelling chair like he had ants in his pants, slammed his papers and judgely possessions in his Queensland port and walked out of the courtroom. Outside, the judge demanded the car keys for the Paddy Van waiting outside to pick up the drunks loitering the footpath from the court to the snake pit. The vehicle headed out of town via the footpath. Neither the judge nor the Paddy Van were ever seen again. The old people sitting in the grass with the binoculars knew what the crazy old white man went through. No secret could be kept from their prying eyes. *Oh! Yeah, we know where the warri, warri ngabaya went to*, they claimed. In very serious tones, reserved for a senior Law person, they explained how he had gone off to Surfers Paradise. Oh! poor, *damu ngabaya*. He had reinvented himself down there amongst the surfers, going around incognito in a refurbished surfie van, like a vagabond. They say you would not recognise him now, living in abandoned warehouses with the city pigeons crapping in his hair. Nobody from the Pricklebush ever told the policeman the story, otherwise, *damu, damu ngabaya* would be facing pretty serious charges back in Desperance.

Sweet reminiscences. Dawn crawled over the eastern horizon and Big Mozzie reckoned to himself, that his second name should have been Reminisce. It felt grand to be back with the memories of the ludicrous trial, junk foods, unhealthy intrigues and other musings about what souls do in their search for truth. The truth about the pig story. What truth could be found in watching a man concentrating on scraping fish skin with his skinning knife? What price silence?

'They got their just deserts the pack of mongrels,' Norm told Mozzie on the day before Mozzie took the convoy on the road again. Norm had whistled, skinning another fish, and with a twist in his face as he concentrated on the job, said, 'Couldn't wait for more of the bastards to go down either.' As he listened to the dull sound of the knife scraping, Big Mozzie could not help noticing the blue guts and fish flesh spilt all over a newspaper article about killer bush pigs. Mozzie caught Norm looking at him reading the soiled newspaper. Pulling and tugging at the fish, Norm broke the silence. 'Walking about in country, country that don't belong to them anyway, they should be in the Territory somewhere else, am I speaking a true word or not, and that's what happens when you do the wrong thing.'

Mozzie, not wanting to buy into the old arguments about who belongs where, said he would not know where those people should be or if there was any killing pig. Norm dropped his fish, and it went bang as it fell into a green bucket, and wiping his hands with a dirty towel, said he had more fish to catch. As he was preparing to leave, he told Mozzie he only believed what other ordinary people believed: 'If they say there is a pig, I say the same thing. If they say he was a killer and he would kill again, I say the same thing. I am no better man than other people.' It was no wonder you created suspicion, Mozzie thought, watching Norm Phantom walking off down the track in the tussock grasses towards his boat, 'You bring on trouble.'

Chapter 6
Knowing fish

Will Phantom thought about many things while sitting on the side of the lagoon. It was a moment of regaining his own sense of self after living for so long in Mozzie's shadow. The sound of the groaning mine reminded him there would be a lot of things to be done now he was back home. The dark shadows surrounding his father sung into his mind. He hoped things might be better between them, but if not – who cared? Business first, he thought, looking over at poor old Elias. A deep furrow formed between his eyebrows, just like the father's, as he frowned at the little boat sitting in the middle of the lagoon.

There was no telling where you will find fish...

This story, Joseph Midnight said, must be told, because there were all kinds of particular people – government people, important people, money people, nuisance bugger people, anyone who can take your thoughts away on pieces of paper, just like that, and put it, wherever they like, inside white man's technology in *whatchayougoinama* call it? Computers. Yes, that's the one the old blackfella man had been *tinking* about, racking his brains for it: 'It come to my head for a look around.' Yeah! Alright. 'They lock em up all the information inside for them own eyes only.' That's how he was talking now because he loved the young rebel Will Phantom who had disappeared from the Gulf after being accused by the

State government, and the Federal government too, of sabotaging the development of the mining industry. A media frenzy generated by city based government, searched high and low for Will in the Gulf of Carpentaria. Well! Sweet sugary governments in the cities were not going to spend vast sums of money in a place like Desperance to find an Aboriginal. You listen to an old man's story if you want to know how.

Every day, never miss, the white city people started to metamorphose themselves up there in Desperance, and they were asking too many questions, millions maybe, of the white neighbours. Will Phantom was that popular. A big troublemaker but nobody had a photo of him. *Got nothing to give*, for the white people – too insular. What they got to know? Got nothing. You could see they were city people who were too plain scared to go about, and come down there in the Pricklebush and ask the *Aborigine* people sitting at home in their rightful place. They looked, Oh! this side, or that side of town. *No, not going*, they must have said about the Pricklebush. Waiting and waiting instead. Those reporter types hung around town not knowing what to do, then they all looked outside of the fish and chip shop, and guess who? One old blackfella man, Joseph Midnight now, white hair jumping out everywhere from *he* head, he was sitting there. Him by himself: Uptown.

He looked over his shoulder at those city newspaper people and saw they'd even got a Southern blackfella with them. A real smart one, educated, acting as a guide. He got on a tie, clean white shirt and a nice suit. He goes up to old man and called him, 'Uncle,' and he says: 'What kind of person you reckon, older man, you say Will Phantom?' Old Midnight he looked back for awhile, and he says: 'Who's this?' He was thinking now for must be two minutes before he was squinty eyes, still saying nothing, and then he speaks back, 'Well! You, you, say, I never, and I never believe it. You say I am your Uncle, then listen to this one, boy.

'No, this or that is ever going to happen when Will Phantom was around. No way! Ever seen a brolga dancing in a mirage? Our Will, he moves lightly through the bush to the beat of the muddied and cracked dancing feet of a million ancestors.

'Will Phantom was not full of bad luck, always whingeing and saying, *Expect the worst*, like other sort of people. Nump! Hmm! Like the ones who in ignorance can retrospectively call up the evil spirits, turn on the switch for melodramatics, make tranquillity run amok, then cut loose all those motley-skinned bush pigs with the spiky hair – to come out to play. You hear them tearing at your brains to get through to your nightmares – you hear them saying, *Give me a three. Click, slow click, quick click, with their little trotters – up high, down low, too slow*. Then woof! Out of the night dust, they manifest themselves into wild killer boars you never believe who come out of your head in their one, two, threes, and more than likely counting non-malevolent sheep to sleep, crazed, on their little black piggy-wiggly tracks for miles around, to make your hair stand on end when you walk around in the bush here with those kind of people who bring you bad luck. Those kind of people never made you feel safe at all. Never.

'Or, just say what could happen in the broad daylight, worse than a circus, if you were walking down the street of a loony town – Soosh! Here, but don't tell anybody I said that – walking with someone like that. If you were just plain dumb to go walking with those kind of people, you even minding your own black person's business – Well! Can't be done! You still had to keep a good eye out for the nearest tree or maybe, even a jolly fence to run to and then, you got to fly up the top.

'There are some people in existence, just one or two, who make dogs want to froth at the mouth. Then what happens to poor old you, who just happens to be out walking with them sort of people and you didn't know?

'Well! You gotta know all the time, just in case those pack of another people's biting dogs – real bad buggers, are going to jump out of nowhere and ambush you. And some diseased dog isn't going to waste his limited time on earth being discriminate about you because you come from the city, because it's going to bite you good and proper anyhow.

'Then, what say? You could even be out fishing, sitting with your lonesome, singing a lonely song, except that nuisance flotilla of man of wars as far as the eye could see, kept following you around all day waiting for you to make one slip so they can leave your carcass floating and bloating in the sea. But Will Phantom was a different kettle of fish. Oh! Yes! He would come along whistling some happy old song he composed about the sea, and those jelly-welly creatures just turned around and happily be on their way. Not interested in making trouble. They left his fishing waters for good. And then, what happens next? Will Phantom left you, gone, shot through, never stick around one minute. Left you sitting out there in the middle of the ocean. Must be all your bad luck come running back just like clicking your fingers, just to show you, you got no luck at all and it would be – what next? Woom! Boom! You never heard so much noise.

'You know what? More bad luck. Your boat's *catched* on fire. There is probably going to be an explosion. And you are that jolly well scared you are going to die in the ocean, you just about run across water to get home.

'See! Well none of that. That never happened to Norm Phantom and he passed all of that on to Will. So! Will has a good way with nature, all of the natural things, except he is not too good with human nature. That boy was in one hell of rush to throw fuel on man-made adversaries. If it had anything to do with mankind, he had the knack to rub it hard, right up the wrong way. His father was like that too. And if you thought the falling out with his father was not a good thing – you are wrong about that. It was a blessing compared to what he had gone around accomplishing in his life to date. Oh! Poor me – What a history. This lad was writing memory with a firestick that made lightning look dull.

'So, if you want to know what Will Phantom looked like – He looked like that.'

When Will Phantom had caught his first glimpse of the fisherman on the lagoon from Mozzie's vehicle sliding down the gravel track through the spearwood trees, he knew it was Elias even though the emaciated shell barely resembled the man he once knew who had helped tame his childhood spirit. He knew it, as true as only water people with a natural cunning have of recognising another fisherman by sight, from a huge distance away, even across heavy seas, from the particular way he sat, stooped over a line.

He felt a tinge of guilt about not telling Mozzie at the time, but for some strange reason he knew he had to stay quiet about poor old Elias while the convoy was at the lagoon. He felt he had to respect Elias's death and privacy. It would have been how Elias would have wanted it. He remembered a private man who shunned opportunities for the company of other people. He saw Elias, a tall, shaggy white-haired man in his fish-smelling hut stacked inside and out with fishing gear, and watched his hard-skinned fingers longing for salt water, skilfully fixing lines, fashioning a spearwood rod, mending nets, his whole existence one of a fishingman's life. Elias, with shy downcast eyes away from the sea, said he never had time for socialising and mixing with strangers.

All of these childhood memories flooded through Will Phantom's mind, and he accepted the gift of Elias's spirit, who had been waiting to pass these memories of his life onto him. The stranger to others, who had taken him fishing, growing him up in the sea. The last thing Elias would have wanted would be to have strangers pawing over his remains, staring at him close up, trying to read his soul with who knows what kind of thoughts they were likely to be carrying around in their heads. But as it turned out he realised he need not have worried himself about Elias's wish for privacy in death. Although Elias might have been a dead man for weeks or months, he still had enough life in him to protect his personal privacy. The discovery of a body had set off pandemonium amongst the convoy, and within minutes, everyone had bundled themselves back into their jalopies, and were rip-roaring up the track in a stampede to get back on the main road.

A gentle northerly breeze had started to blow through the spearwood after the last of the convoy was heard – zem, zem, crackling up the track. The breeze had come down from the sea, passing inconspicuously over the noisy motor cars on the Gulf road, touching Will in a gentle caress, as though the ocean seemed pleased to know its son had returned.

Time was a fleeting whisper for Will sitting on the edge of the lagoon that had been carved by an eternity of rushing floodwaters inside the remains of a forest that lived a million years ago, and had, after a moment of shock when drowned by high seas, petrified into rock. Time accumulates thought or vice versa and Will Phantom, in no hurry to return home after years, since he had been travelling on sacred journeys, took his time deciding what he ought to do about pulling the boat in, until he felt a cold shiver of fear running down his back. Swiftly he glanced around, and in the silence nothing moved, except where a thudding of ancestral footsteps was pounding loudly in his head, and his fear shifted, across to Elias in the lagoon.

He began to think how strange it was for Elias to be sitting out there, peculiar how someone who had never left the sea's edge could be so far inland from the coast. His best memory of Elias was the coastal man forever staring at the seas lost from his memory. Now Will, who had spent too long following the illusions of the Dreamtime, was thrown back into the real world, where men became clowns and clowns men, which was another string of illusions altogether. How could he have come so far, particularly if he had to carry his boat over long stretches of dry land? How far would he have reached before the sheer exhaustion of the effort of carrying the boat overland had overtaken him? Surely, he would have needed at least one or two other men to help him upriver?

Will began to chart the river course from the sea that might have been how Elias had brought his boat inland. Will knew this river backward, like the palm of his hand. The river and Will Phantom had many secrets to share. So, Will mapped the journey and stalled at the many gaps in the river where Elias would have stalled too, to catch his breath and to contemplate the boat which would not have made it through the narrow causeways, prevented by the jagged, petrified remains of the ancient trees, perhaps once fig trees, that had become rock. There were places where the water was just a trickle, where only a green ant, on a floating piece of weed, would have been able to forge its way ahead. Elias would have been forced to carry the boat, not heavy, but a real burden over a long distance as he negotiated each step with the riverbank, climbing up on the side of the creeks, up along the wallaby tracks. Frequently, he would have been forced to stop, where he would have hesitated, and hoped he had taken the best of the long, slender tracks running beside the creeks.

Elias, manoeuvring the boat barefoot, would have wound his way through an obstacle course of dense prickle scrub, burrs, spinifex spikes, stomping bloodied feet through the long spear grass as he felt for the potholes, and twisting over and under a devil's playground of hanging branches. It would be no good thinking about being somewhere else. Think if in one loose moment, and Will Phantom's own heart slipped a beat for Elias, following the unknown river course, slipping down steep banks, where strangers could break their neck.

In the minds of local people there had always been an infallible certainty without evidence or proof of Elias's knowledge which was said to have come from travelling the many seas of the world. It was just so, for the spirits who had stolen his memory had left him the sea. This was what happens with the magic moments – a skilful coil of a rope, a special knotted hook on the fishing line, slyly observed shrouded mysteries given a story by people who had yet to reap bounties from travelling distant seas. Yet, instinctively Will knew Elias was no river man, and in fact, could not remember one occasion of Elias ever going to the fresh waters to fish. On the other hand, Will knew this area well. He, having grown from a child with yellow spinifex hair, had walked through all these tracks, *a billygoat's kid*, the Uncles proclaimed, and his father, the big man Norm Phantom, had joined in with the laughter, complaining with pride in his voice, *the goat's got no school-work on his mind – ever*. In the happy days, following his father's shadow all around this country, he already knew a little tin boat could not go through the steep-sided gorges on a wallaby track.

If anyone had the mind to be taking time thinking about some-body else's life until his heart was content, or cannot leave a thing alone, someone like Will Phantom, then they would have to think what else Elias would have had to do to be sitting dead for a very long time, waiting for fish, with his line out in a stagnant pond laced with salt? The only straightforward answer to Will Phantom's mind, was that after having been forced by the path of the creek to lug the boat up ridges of stone and petrified forests, on banks of flaking earth, Elias travelled across the high plains. Elias, single-handedly, would have carried the boat cross-country through the spinifex until the watercourse had widened and he would have taken the boat back down to the creek again. He would have had to repeat the exercise at least a dozen times in following the river from its mangrove-lined mouth to where he had ended his journey in the lagoon. And who was there to help Elias to go fishing miles inland, when everyone for miles around knew all the fish had gone to the sea?

Will considered the circumstances of the day Elias left Desperance forever. He remembered what the old people said about the terrible night of Uptown: *accusing Elias of burning up the Queen's picture*. They often told the story of how offended Uptown had been about the Queen's picture burning, and coming down quick smart asking the Pricklebush people, *What kind of low-down dog, a complete useless loafer, would burn the Queen's picture?* The old people thought they were expected to say they done it, own up to it, but instead they responded to Uptown: *Unfortunately, you can't exterminate a Queen by burning her picture*. That was the kind of treachery Elias was accused of when they said he had chucked four-gallon tins of kerosene all over the brand-new Shire Council offices and burnt them flat to the ground. Nobody touched the Queen. Uptown found Elias guilty of sedition and treachery to the throne because he was a new Australian whom the whole town had seen walking out of the sea, and when he went home to the sea again, no one had even bothered to go out to say goodbye. Nobody would have helped Elias to go inland. They had screamed like a landlord at him to leave their continent forever and never come back.

Will stood up. If anyone had seen him standing there, they would have believed it was Norm, fishing this lagoon years ago, at the onset of the Wet season as a million fish teemed up the river, when he was twenty-four. Will with bare chest, no shirt to his name, covered with weeks of accumulated desert dust, his jeans, no longer blue, were ingrained with dirt from months of travelling through the dry country. One muddy lagoon was not going to do a hell of a lot more damage, so Will Phantom walked knee-deep through the mud, breaking the crust of salt crystals which sparkled where hit by sunlight, as enchanting as snow.

Will knew that Elias could not have undertaken such a trip to the lagoon by himself. He listened to thunder in the storms brewing in the North, but the skies were clear, and the afternoon sun shone like silver on the mud, glittering salt and water. As he walked out, Will was disturbed by juxtaposing images, flashing across his mind. In one image, he saw white men, perhaps from the town, he did not know, making a mockery of Elias's death. But there were only a handful of people outside of Mozzie's convoy who knew about the existence of this sacred lagoon. *Uncles!* He needed to think of the Uncles but they failed to appear through Uptown! The suffocating net! He put the thought aside, knowing he would have to think about who knew how to find the lagoon – titles, names, faceless people jumped momentarily, a split second only to show themselves, to announce they existed.

He saw the occasional strike of lightning from the storms in the North, the day would soon become darker, everything would be covered in darkness, within thirty minutes, when the storm had set in. He moved through the muddy water which at its deepest level came up to his waist, and did not take long to reach the boat. He said a quiet hello to Elias, *What are you doing here?* He began to investigate the human remains smelling of the ocean's salty brine. Interference, the slightest touch can open a Pandora's box, and Will leaning on the side of the boat, found the aroma of the sea was as distant as the sea, compared to the overpowering stench of decomposing fish which emanated in a heat of steam from two sugar bags, lying on the floor of the boat.

Will recognised the bags the instant he saw them. He remembered how he had often stood back as a child, out of the way, wishing to become Elias, cramming things into any old sugar or flour bag – tackle, food, his belongings, rowing away to sea whenever he chose, coming back, jiggling a bag of fish in front of his nose. Will expected maybe Elias had bagged one or two old barramundi. The ancient ones that lurked in hidden places of diminished lagoons waiting for the Wet to arrive. Elias, a skilful fisherman, would have pried them out of their underwater cocoons. He believed only the old hunter Uncles could achieve such a haul. Any other hunter of the barramundi fish would need to be some champion fisherman to have found a fish left in this mud, let alone catch it. The other fish Will expected could be hooked, perhaps, a few reasonable-sized freshwater sooty grunter, rifle fish or bream, if the boat was in the main water arteries coming up to the coast from the spring-fed river systems. Not the useless little tributary jutting off into a mud hole at the end of the Dry.

He got rid of the flies that had picked up the whiff of rotting fish in the air. They were swarming in from every corner of the bush it appeared, for miles around. Hundreds of flies covered his body. The larger march flies, which also flew around the boat drunk with the stench, began to attack every part of his body exposed above the water. It was then, in those fleeting moments, as he caught sight of the rotting slime-covered remains of fish spilling out of the putrid bags, a cold shiver ran down his back, and he spun around, his brown eyes surveying the banks and into the bush, right around the lagoon. He looked at what was coming out of the bags. One fish fell after the other, still with their flesh intact, and it was easy to discern that they could not have been caught more than ten days ago. Sea fish! These were fish no man had ever seen this far inland. Will turned to the spearwood as though expecting the spirits to answer, tell him what surely they knew.

Sea water was lapping its last little flip! slip! for sea creatures living where Will Phantom now stood 500 million years ago, when the sea levels had been as high as the surrounding hills, when time and life on the deep-sea plain of the Pacific Ocean was not even advanced enough to beget a fish. Yet now, on this uncelebrated occasion, Elias had apparently fished saltwater fish from the mud hole. Elias's beautiful coral trout, pink ten days before, its putrid remains clearly recognisable falling from the bag.

Will could remember the deep trench in the ocean where Elias fished, with a line baited and dropped 200 metres deep. In the other bag, emptied perfunctorily, its contents a revelation of other sea fish, strangers to these parts of the country, were hardly given a second glance. Queenfish, snapper, red emperor, mangrove jack, bream, all reef fish, and one giant trevally, a tidal fish – so what? Will retrieved the line and pulled it in, discovering what he had expected, Elias rigged up for deep-sea trolling.

The white-breasted sea eagle's flight was almost noiseless as it dropped out of the sky, falling down, descending down, so quick, until it flew, whistling in behind Will to scoop the stinking trevally up from the mud. Watching it perch on a dead log on the north side of the lagoon, it surprised Will that while he had noticed it hovering in the sky, he had not taken any interest in it. The large bird was yet another unfamiliar sight, almost ghostly looking as it sat motionless, claw on the fish, staring at Will, the boat and Elias's body. The sea eagle was also an unusually long distance from the sea. Will believed it must have followed Elias.

The Phantom family knew the sea eagle well enough, although they never gave it a name. Will remembered being out in a high sea on a grey day, in a stormy sea with his father and Elias, years before, when he was ten years old, and saw the sea eagle when it was a fledgling then, injured by another sea eagle perhaps. They all saw it drop out of the sky and Elias plucked it out of the sea. For perhaps a year it hopped around on Elias's boat, never leaving it. A greedy, demanding bird squealing non-stop to be fed, whenever he saw a person move. Then, when they had all just about given up believing it would ever learn to feed itself, Elias took it back to sea. He was gone forever it seemed to Will's young mind so he went around telling everyone that Elias was dead. One day Elias came back and told Will the eagle was in the sky, but it stayed at sea, and lived on the perpetually passing traffic of transport barges, ships and fishing boats.

The eagle always came back to Elias when he was out at sea, sitting on his bent back while he fished, wanting to be fed, and getting a bellyfull of good fish, until Elias headed back to land. Now, evidently, it had come to a muddy lagoon, fishing with Elias for reef fish, hovering hungry for days, waiting for one of the bags to be opened and fish offered to him as though he was incapable of fishing for himself and had to be fed, as though he had again been injured.

It had grown hungrier and more disoriented, waiting for Elias to feed it. Yes, yes, Will whispered to Elias, it would be put right soon when the eagle picked up the sound of thunder rolling inland from the sea. Will watched the eagle watching him for a few moments. He hoped that now he had his fish he would be smart enough to fly back to the sea once he heard the thunder clap and roll. The bird dropped the fish and sat looking forlorn on the log. Will turned his attention back to Elias. With a deep breath, he confronted Elias's empty eye sockets staring straight into his face. Elias's presence felt so real, if it had not been for the missing eyes, Will would have sworn he was still alive and was playing a joke on him by pretending to be dead.

The clouds were approaching, wind started blowing through the trees and the unnatural darkness which came with storms was settling in. Alone, with Elias, he did not want to look at the dead man's face which might tell him things of the other world he did not want to know. This was when Will saw dried blood stains all over the front of Elias's cream cotton shirt.

The same stains covered the floor of the boat. Elias had lost a lot of blood when he died. Again, Will saw the image of white men flash by the other side of the boat. They looked as though they were laughing at Elias's body, as though it was a joke. He placed his arm around Elias's body and picked up the human shell, weighing nothing. Words, which even surprised Will Phantom, raced out of his mouth, 'I am going to avenge whatever it was that happened to you, Elias. I am really sorry, old man.' Easy now to make such a commitment for the first time in his life to somebody else, and mouth the words with conviction.

He knew the old Uncles always said there were bad omens surrounding the lagoon in that heavy foreboding of the land before the Wet. They pointed to where the spirits had lain in the atmosphere, before moving freely in and out of the lagoon, while they turned normality into a nightmare.

The clouds ran overhead, and in the distance, he heard wild winds tearing through the woodlands. He moved frantically, automatically doing what had to be done, to get the boat out of the lagoon. Blue plastic rope had been used to tie Elias down to his seat and more rope had been used to secure the boat. The rope was looped tightly around the boat twice, looped over the front and back. Working to untie other men's work dissolved any idea he had which suggested Elias had carried his boat cross-country as just a foray into fantasy.

The cloud front had reached the lagoon and a dust storm was only minutes away, so Will took a grip of the pile of loose rope left lying on the floor of the boat and started to lug it towards the edge of the lagoon. The wind blew red dust in ahead of the rain with the pungent smell of wet gidgee warning Will to get out of the lagoon. It was time to find some shelter. He knew if the rainstorm set in, there would likely be a flash flood through the area, and he would have little to no chance in the morning of finding the boat again.

If he had not been so preoccupied with his thoughts about the mystery of the fish and why the boat was in this particular lagoon, he might have recognised there were sinister undertones to this unusual situation which had been designed to look so ordinary. He did not hear the droning engine of a machine in the distance until it was almost above him.

The sea eagle's blood sprayed over the lagoon like early rain when the bird took off in fright and hit the rotor blades of the helicopter descending at high speed over the spearwood. Will dived under the mud as the helicopter bubble, coated with blood, roared down towards him as the pilot tried to regain control and ascend the other side of the lagoon. Then, it returned at full speed and began to circle slowly above Elias's boat. The whorling blades stirred the mud into a turbulence that boiled into the air. Will went under again and when he resurfaced with mud falling out of his eyes, he saw the bloody machine moving off over the spearwood, just far away enough to position itself to return. Will waved frantically, hoping they would see him, then as the machine drew closer on its return, Will caught a glimpse of the pilot and another man through the blood and muddied bubble. He watched while the man in the passenger seat positioned himself to lean over the side of the helicopter with a rifle to his eye, aiming the weapon directly towards him. In disbelief, he did not react, or try to figure out how to save himself. There was so much happening in those moments as the helicopter swooped nearer and the flying water whipped his face, that he was not able to determine the identity of his pursuers. Assuming they were white men, simply because they were in a helicopter, he could not comprehend why they looked so dark. Precious moments of saving his own life were slipping away, when it suddenly dawned on Will Phantom, who was unprepared for a trap by the company, that they were mining men, dressed in navy uniform, expecting his return. Idiot! Of course they looked dark.

He re-entered the sightless world under the mud, knowing that somehow, if he could avoid being shot at, he would have to get out of the water. The machine hovered close above him. His mind running, calculating distances, his own down in the mud and theirs above, and breathless, knowing he must have taken them by surprise, if it was him they were after. If he could get out he would have to run, but where to, he was not sure. All he had to gamble on was the helicopter not having enough space to land, convincing himself that this was so, otherwise why did it not come down?

Not sure if the man was firing his rifle into the water, Will moved away from Elias's boat, hoping it would be difficult for them to see him. He crawled along the mud floor, camouflaged by the turbulence in the choppy waters covering the surface. Which way? The image of the log where the bird had sat sprung into his mind. He was almost breathless as he made his way towards it, hoping, convincing himself that it was the only cover, his only chance, to escape. He moved, quickly estimating he had correctly pinpointed the log from under the water, hoping that they thought he would stay near the boat.

He calculated right, the right length of time he could stay submerged, long enough to bump into the end of the log. He resurfaced behind it. Safe for the moment, he looked back towards Elias, only to see the boat sinking lopsidedly in the turbulence. They had fired at the boat thinking Will would stay under it. Now, the helicopter was taking up position again directly above him, then it flung itself back across the far side of the lagoon.

He knew it was time to get out of the water – if they had not already seen him, they soon would. He ran hard towards the spear-wood with the deafening noise of the machine closing in behind him. He could not hear the rifle being fired. Random shots into the gravel ricocheted beside him, from left to right. Shots hit the ground in front of where he ran, behind, and right to left again. Will thought he was being pursued by a psychopath with high-powered sights, or else someone was trying to scare him off. He ran as a wild zigzagging animal in full alert to danger, knowing it was being hunted down, became like rubber, flexible, bouncing, too hard to catch. The helicopter, accelerating to get up ahead of him, turned for the gunman to get a crack at him, face on. It was too late. He was running with a power he did not realise existed in himself, and he was approaching the cover of rocks in the gullies. But what neither party realised was, they had run out of time. The storm hit. Wind and rain fell in horizontal sheets across the valley, and the helicopter made a hasty retreat to the west, in the direction of the mine.

Will knew that he now had the night before they could try again, but if the rain kept up, it would not take long for the roads to become impassable for days. He sat on the rocks and became just another dark shadow in the premature darkness of the rain, except when every minute or so lightning struck, and he was able clearly to see the surrounding landscape, and he and the lagoon in white light. In his mind he began surveying the open space that separated him from the town. Where would he find the best cover if the mine sent out more helicopters to find him? Perhaps it was just a coincidence? He decided to be on the safe side he would assume the company had a memory as big as his of their battles fought over mining in the Gulf. He would have to stay out of sight of search parties as much as possible, if the helicopter was likely to return in the morning, and then he thought about how careful he would need to be in Desperance, after this.

The rain fell in torrents and he knew even before he caught his breath, he would have to go back down to the lagoon for Elias's body before the psychopaths from the mine had another chance to tamper with his body. Mozzie had told him about the poison festering in the souls of the men who disturbed the earth. 'The spirits went Blah! They just spat on the ground like a piece of rotten meat. They were listening to the truth, and they knew, and they looked to you, Will. You keep doing what you got to do.' Will felt Mozzie Fishman's presence, standing behind him, grinning and pointing between flashes of lightning to where the spirits flew around in the wet skies, speaking quietly about the mining men, saying how he believed their work was just beginning by using Elias as their vessel. Will could never escape the words he heard in his heartbeat. But, if the rain kept up, the creeks would flood through the lagoon in the night, and who knew where the body would end up, if he did not take it out now?

He went back into the lagoon, anxious to save Elias before the water rose, and his own spirit shadow, one old ancestor, limped along to keep up with him. When he finally touched the boat in the dark, he found it was not entirely submerged and he was able to straighten it enough for towing out of the water. In the hours that followed getting Elias out of the lagoon, Will took the tin boat and hid it behind a spearwood thicket leaning against a rise, about a kilometre away in higher country above the flood levels. Carefully he concealed the vessel with spinifex and dead branches, until he was satisfied that he had created a hide as though nature's hand had constructed it. Then he went back for Elias to take him up further into the high country. He was not difficult to carry. 'We will get you somewhere safe, up in the hills,' Will kept on talking, speaking to and replying for Elias as though he were alive. 'How could you be dead Elias?' 'Well! I can't tell you because…because…because I don't know what happened to me.' It was comforting to hear the sound of his own voice, to feel he carried a real man, not to think of the dried-out remains of the person who had helped to condition his life. He felt each step of wet, loose rock with his bare feet, as they climbed the rugged terrain as swiftly and with the sensitivity of mountain goats in total darkness, higher on the hill.

Satisfied he had them both secure in the hills, and sheltering from the rain under a rocky ledge he had located by sniffing where the kangaroos sheltered, he looked down in the distance and saw headlights below. He observed the lights of two cars coming in a hurry through the rain in the direction of the lagoon. He could see how the car lights weaved about in the darkness, that the drivers were finding it difficult to keep the cars on the road at the speed they were travelling.

'Elias, I don't know what is going on here but someone seems to be in a big hurry coming along that road,' Will spoke propped up against the rock wall, sitting beside him. 'Yes, if they are not careful they will be dead too,' Elias replied. The vehicles continued to swerve back and forth across the road.

Will slipped back down the hill, without ruffling a stone, to get a closer view of what was going on. The two vehicles stopped at the turn-off, and he listened to the voices discussing whether to take the vehicles down the steep dirt track, which was slippery now from the rain.

Headlights and searchlights on top of the vehicles beamed down the track through the rain. Water raced down the road like a river and Will watched the navy uniforms of six men, including his two older brothers – Donny and Inso, who worked for the mine. It was a wonder they did not hear his thoughts. Perhaps his thoughts were blocked, concealed behind the rocks on the other side of the main road. He watched the big dark frames of Donny and Inso, sliding down the watery road to the lagoon in the black wet, with their torches jumping ahead of them. Two others followed them.

'What we supposed to be looking for anyway?' one brother

spoke. All four were talking, and someone said he'd been told there was a body down there.

'We have to look out for a little tinnie boat.'

'What's that smell anyway?' Donny asked Inso, who said he did not know. 'It smells like an animal, probably kangaroo fur.'

'Fish! You idiot, it smells like fish.'

'What fish? Animal fur when it's wet.'

Will followed, moving through the spearwood on the side of the road. In previous times he would have sprung out in front of them to pick a fight, their fighting marathons, fought until one remained standing. Donny and Inso kept talking to the other two men about the rotting fish smell.

'Can't you smell it?'

'Yeaaa, I suppose so.'

Will heard his thoughts leaping out of his mind so loudly, he believed they were hanging around in the heavy humid air, like illuminated balloons. Donny and Inso, or the other two men, jumpy with the torch, often swung the light around to shine straight through the spearwood trees, as if they were trying to locate where the stench of old fish was coming from. 'There can't be any fish here.' It was too dry for fish, they said, laughing at the repetitive topic of their conversation, and the absurdity of the lingering smell, until finally, because they were in good spirits, they agreed that the overpowering stench was the work of indigestion – *food poisoning*. A fish percolating in their own intestines.

Will moved in closer, moving next to them through the spearwood. Silently his feet joined the paws of the wallaby and kangaroo, feeling the ground in the darkness, belonging as if to nothing of life. So, close, he listened to their heartbeat, so nearby, almost standing as his brothers' shadow. He penetrated their laboured breathing inside their lungs, and could see when they waved the torches across the flooding lagoon. Yellow beams cutting across the bucketing rain, sheeting across the rippling water with the wind. He saw the shock on their faces when they could not see the boat. Oh! Glory be. He could almost hear his brothers pray. They argued with the other two workmates, about whether it had sunk and whether one of them should go out into the lagoon and check. Just to make sure.

Curiosity killed the cat. Will knew Donny and Inso's motto in life. Not one of the four men volunteered. No one wanted to go into the muddy water that was already rising with the rainwater racing down the steep surroundings of the lagoon, running black liquid over their boots. They heard all the dead things thundering down the hills from miles around with the leaves, sliding snakes, awakened crocodiles, rushing into the lagoon. It seemed as though all the wind and rain on earth was funnelling inwards with the spearwood trees bent, pointing straight down to this little lagoon. Will knew that even Donny and Inso saw the spearwood trees become the spirits blowing spears which whistled past them into the water.

The technical bosses, talking back up on the main road, were minding the vehicles. 'Who was to know,' the four men agreed, 'that we did not go in, looking for the tinnie they up there are after?' Will was relieved that the other two men followed Donny and Inso, and his brothers were true to form: the story of their life, always willing to shirk duty. No one was arguing; there was total agreement. The four headed back up the road.

While they walked up the hill through the running water and rain, occasionally they would shine their torches through the bush, perfunctorily, perhaps thinking of having heard a sound of an animal. Many times the beams cut straight across Will, but he was a mud man not seen by others. They tell the others, the two supervisors, waiting with the vehicle, that the lagoon is starting to flood and the boat must have sunk. Their voices, practised, have a genuine ring of truth. 'That will do anyhow,' the technical men say dismissively, with authority.

The technicians continued speaking, discussing the possibilities of losing the evidence in the floodwaters. In voices that speak quietly and without emotion, they discuss the forecast, the rainfall patterns, the jet stream, flood rates, all with a blank look on their wet faces, dismissing the 'local knowledge' given by the other four, whenever they spoke. The technicians talked about concrete evidence – not the dead body nor the one they had earlier tried to shoot. The conversation becomes too detailed and monotonous for the likes of Inso and Donny. The mine in their mind meant good food, as much as the money, and they did not want to miss out on dinner, not for one day, not for anyone's business. While the technicians stand in the rain, Inso and Donny and the two others sit in their vehicles, brand-new four-wheel drive troop carriers, navy blue under the mud, talking of stews and casseroles, excellent fish curry. Good food cooked properly by chefs, not just chucked around in a frypan in a pile of fat until it burned, and nobody to fight you for it. They smile and wait – nobody ever had it this good.

They wanted to say if given half a chance about what was right – *In the nocturnal world you leave the dead alone*. It was not dead people who feed you. Inso and Donny lounge back in the company's vehicle. They are comfortable, just like they are in their own cars. They are thinking big, because they can, earning good money down in the mine. They make veiled threats of leaving the mine for good, waiting for nothing, keeping an eye on the time, watching the technicians point up the road in the headlights, and thinking sourly – *they can stick their flippen jobs*.

The four working men tap the car dash, the gear knob, the steering wheel, waiting, thinking about what the kitchen staff will leave in the oven, thinking about manoeuvring the vehicles back over the sodden roads. They light up and wait in a cigarette smoke haze, listening to the commentary on powerful car radios, mostly they say nothing to each other, except to comment in expletives about the uselessness of the local football commentary on the local radio station. Listening to their favourite team making the same mistakes over and over, when, *even a girl would know better*. That useless referee again, *Didn't anyone know people listen to the cunt of a radio and even depended on the friggen thing once in a while to get the proper information?*

The technical men in navy raincoats and yellow helmets still spend time hovering over the front of their vehicle. They seem to relish rain dripping down their nose, spilling off their faces and hands. Will, standing behind their vehicle, hears of their lengthy experiences in the tropics as seasoned troopers of many Wet seasons, recalling all they remembered about floods in those parts.

The smell of rotting fish hung glued to the air, as though it had came from the rain and dirt mixing together, but they did not notice. 'What about this lagoon?' They speak about the speed of flowing waters in the height of the floods, travelling floodwaters, racing at the speed of 200 kilometres an hour, and pausing at the fantastic knowledge of this idea, they come to the realisation that if there was a remote possibility of recovery of the body along the river in the Dry season, it would simply be noted as a flood victim. Another poor soul lost to the river. *What else?* If by some sheer fluke, his body washed away to sea and was discovered, it would be like he never left the sea in the first place. There was nothing to connect him to the mine or the lagoon except, except what? They said it was a dumb, stupid idea to put the body there in the first place. 'We had to flush him out somehow from amongst those religious freaks.' But Will Phantom had got away. It was an accident – the storm came. 'Well! A right cock-up. But we'll get the bugger; it won't take long.'

There was a further shorthand version spoken over the

two-way radio: 'The target was off course.' Their voices sound confident: 'Of course the target will be recovered.' Whatever they do they are always confident. Why? They always have a strategy to keep the bad ball rolling. The technical men get back into their vehicles, then, as Will watches, the vehicles swing around on the main road, again the headlights pass over him standing in the bush, but he remains invisible. Will Phantom is mud.

At home on the sea, at home on the land…

So sang the windy night through the slender, bow-bent spear-wood forest below where Will Phantom slept in the surrounding foothills away from the road. The ghost-white under-leaf of the wax-green foliage of the stick trees became a procession of spirits moving across the soft earth of darkness, protecting the country of the water people.

'I will keep you out of the rain,' he had promised the poor deceased Elias, carrying the body so light it hardly weighed a feather, hanging over his strong slender shoulder. Will had climbed higher into the hills, until eventually, he came to a large rock cave. Inside, the walls were covered by ancestral paintings telling stories of human history, made and remade by ochre paints, as the fore-fathers whispered the charter of their land. Will acknowledged their presence, touched the walls in places to embrace the timelessness of his own being. He felt humbled, honoured to be in the home of birds, animals and clans people of time passed. He had eaten the meat from a small wallaby he had caught off guard earlier and cooked; it had been a glint of silver eyes shining in the darkness, startled in its solitary cave, then its life was snatched with bare hands. All night he kept the old man warm, and when occasionally he stirred from sleep he stoked up the small fire made with dry twigs and leaf litter accumulated on the floor of the cave.

The rain stopped early in the morning, but far off to the north across the coastline, the dark clouds were building up again at sea. The hours would pass and Will knew it would be raining again before long. He felt cleansed by the refreshing air steaming off the damp earth as it lifted in pencil-thin columns of mist from the sodden bush. The atmosphere relieved him of his longing to return home after his lengthy, dry journey through a string of deserts with the Fishman. Now, in the context of having to look after Elias, he had time to adjust to the vicinity of home. He thought he needed to spend a few more days in the bush adapting himself to being alive again, to breathe in moisture from the frequent showers of the storms. The discovery of Elias was a clear reminder of the reality of what it meant, at least to himself, to be back in the Gulf country.

He sat outside the cave, killing time, wondering about the prospect of Elias killing time for eternity, while enjoying once again the sight of his country's blue, green and red paintbox landscape, surveying the road from the northern tip, down to the southern horizon. He was surprised to see a vehicle, still a dot some distance away. It was the last thing he expected to see coming along the road which had overnight metamorphised itself into a long glistening snake river of muddy water.

He watched the dot grow larger as it ploughed through the red water, listened to the roaring engine, and even though it had been years since he had heard the particular sound of an eight-cylinder funnelling water, he knew the mud-covered vehicle belonged to the travelling priest. He turned to Elias and told him, 'Some decent person around here is going to write to the Pope about him one day.'

The bohemian priest, whose mind was that of a sixties hippie, was driving his car like a bat out of hell up the flooded road. Every year he repeated the last minute journey with one challenge in mind – to beat his luck in the Wet just to confirm that God was on his side. In return, the black Valiant's souped-up engine roared profanities throughout the pristine neighbourhood. Will pictured the big hippie priest, a red-skinned gargoyle with flowing white hair, settled comfortably back into his red vinyl bucket seat, basking in his Father's glory, listening to the Philadelphia Tabernacle Choir singing in full throttle on the cassette player, occasionally taking in glimpses of the surrounding countryside, but taking no notice of the loose exhaust pipe rattling along in the mud. A gambler by nature, it was not just the Wet the priest loved to beat. 'The priest must have heard the rumours, Elias.' Will paused in his thoughts for a word to Elias, who was resting up against the wall of the cave. 'What do you say Elias, do we or do we not know Father Danny?' Will knew the priest was on his way to visit Norm, to compete with all of his godliness to win the old man's devotion against the zealot Mozzie Fishman and his devotees.

As he watched the car edging closer, shimmering through the sacredness of the flowing water snake, gathering storm clouds, the divine nature of red earth, what came was a holy car from the pale blue yonder, as though sent from heaven to commence the journey of taking Elias home. Will thought how fate, although bewildering, was the nexus to hope. 'You know Elias I could easily drive back later on from town to get you.' Will was surprised by the hollowness of his words, spoken without thought while knowing, staring down at the road, it would be cut off by the rains for weeks.

There could be no question of leaving Elias behind, even though it would be easier to come back later on to fetch his body in a borrowed car, driving stealthily on some still night when men unknown to anyone in the world went about their business undetected. So easy Will could almost feel himself reach out and claim such a night for himself.

He watched the priest's car ploughing along the glistening road across the claypans. Red-coloured water sprayed out from the sides of the car. It was now or never, Will thought, knowing he had to decide what was the best thing to do, deciding to leave Elias in safe care before he continued on with his life, and because he could not help himself, slipping in begrudgingly, 'I don't want to say it but I have got plans Elias, I have been away for two years you know, I have been putting my plans on hold for too long now, I think I am going to run out of time.' Yet lingering still with the caution of a jack rabbit, he sniffed the air, resisting the temptation to start heading towards the road, to be ready to flag Father Danny down as soon as he was close enough.

Somehow on that day, instinct kept Will up in the hills, inching him back inside the cave as though gravity was working against him, and all the while watching Father Danny twist his way around the gullies, as the car climbed the road through the hills. It was just as well because Will heard the familiar droning coming from the distance in the east. It seemed that someone else had their eye on the red serpentine road as well, because, the drone grew increasingly louder, and very soon, the helicopter from the mine landed on the road just below the cave where Will waited for the car to arrive at the turn-off to the lagoon.

'Where are you headed?' the men in uniform asked solemnly.

The imposing bulk of Father Danny remained glued to his bucket seat, a feature which was deceptive to people who had not looked up to speak to his extraordinary six ten frame. He hardly moved an inch as he poked his head out of the car window, while in the true tenor's voice of the Irish dales, and possessing an air of authority that did not go amiss when amplifying the voice he was renowned for boasting about, he announced cheerfully over the blasting Tabernacle Choir, 'The Lord's destination is Desperance, my good man.'

The two men respond in mock cheer, eyeing each other cautiously, by telling him he ought to go back to the mine with them because of the flooding along the road. *Abandon the car –*

Father Danny envisages a stratosphere of riffraff and pillagers already spoliating cars galore in his mind's fancy. Father Danny deliberately notes his face in the rear-vision mirror outside the car window, just to make sure that he does not look like somebody stupid or something, who leaves his car on a road out in the sticks for nothing. He was an old hand on people who spoke in veiled threats. He could count them all on his fingers and toes, and stayed put in his car, while eyeballing the two lean security men through his bushy eyebrows – *con men*. This was no sitting duck to be ordered around, so the mine men talk generally about the worsening weather. A mere trifling matter. The blasting music, not reduced one notch, continues to flow beautifully into the static of the surrounding saltbush, conveying the aura of the religiously spiritual in all worlds.

The priest smiled nicely, mentioning he understood their concern, and speaking in a firm voice, leaving no doubt about the authority of the Church, so he thought, said, continue he would. Sermon-like, he said the truth of the situation was, that he had raced through saltpan floods a thousand times in his life, and always arrived at his destination, purely and simply because he was blessed. Blessed be, to have driven through the path in the waters God's holiness created for his servant. Could he, he asked, tell them the story from the Bible of the parting of the waters? This was the time when God drove the mighty sea back by a strong easterly wind, to let Moses lead the Israelites to safety from the Egyptians. Thousands of Egyptians were drowned when they had tried to follow Moses, did you know that? So let us begin to pray.

The priest begins, but the men interrupt him, first with apologies for being unbelievers of any – all religions in fact. They still insist he goes with them, because he cannot go forward or back – *The road's blocked*. Father Danny's speech continues, he has after all perfected the same routine thousands of times in the past for the unbelievers of the story of the Israelites' dash through the parting waters. Next, in a sudden change of tempo, it was no longer a cordial conversation of well-wishers accompanied by sermon. Then came the vexatious shouting of who was going to make him leave his car sitting on the side of the road in the middle of nowhere for all the useless, thieving scoundrels of the world to plunder. 'Not me, not for no one at no time – get it?' Sprays of spit for the helicopter to be removed from up the road.

'You got no right to park that piece of rubbish in the middle of the road like that,' the Irish voice, a far cry from its salicaceous lands, rose up the sides of the rocky hills coated in yellow blossoming spinifex in a clear booming tone, while down below, Father Danny was continuing to stir the morning heat with a folksy barrage of wharfside pub abuse imported from the Motherland's sagas of wars and rebellion, now applied to a lead ore mine in the modern day – like they think they owned the place!

'Father, Father,' in between the shouting came the responsive soothing, water-off-a-duck's-back tone of a uniformed man. He tried to be reasonable, his hands levelling the invisible weight of things in front of him in a gesture for calm. When the priest paused, he continued, 'You don't know how quickly these roads become impassable and once that happens, it is going to be months before anyone can get through. Father, we are sorry but we have been instructed by the police, so we can't let you get stranded in an isolated area with the roads flooding.'

'Don't tell me what is or isn't impassable, I have been travelling like a bloody donkey up and down these roads for years, so get that contraption out of the way,' the holy voice rose. 'Or I'll be getting out of my car and be moving the contraption, holus-bolus darn it, off the bloody road, with my bare hands, myself, if I have too.'

The men steadfastly refused to take the helicopter up without him on board and the priest's voice echoed through the hills for the Holy Ghost to deliver his church, be it but a humble motor car, to safety. Then Father Danny revved the vehicle until the engine was full throttle and roaring. Will, smiling down on the impasse, wished Donny and Inso were there to see their old coach having a go, in broad daylight, instead of sneaking around the bush at night. The helicopter pilot who had been standing across the road having a smoke, froze, his blood-drained face registering total disbelief, then turned, ran and jumped into the helicopter. One of the other men wrestled with the priest for the key to the car which he was trying in vain to pull out of the ignition. The other mine man, brandishing a knife he had taken out of the sheath attached to his belt, circled the front of the Valiant in a primordial crouching position, and slashed all of the tyres. Air rushed out of the wheels within moments, leaving the car sitting on the wheel rims. The two men tried wrestling with the pugilistic priest, now red-faced with anger, who had by God's will, so he announced, been given permission to fight like an ordinary man.

The priest spoke in a grave voice to the two men circling him, one with the knife, saying he had no intention of leaving his car or ever to fly in a helicopter. 'The only flying I was prepared for, before you desecrated the holy tyres of the Lord's cathedral here, was rally car driving, and the final day when hopefully, I might lift off on the lightness of stored virtue if it pleases the Lord to fly to the kingdom of heaven.'

A little bit of local knowledge always went a long way, and it was considered as being respectful in these parts not to pick a fight with the priest. Father Danny was a prize of the Gulf. Locals knew his background as an ex-heavyweight fighter when he was young in his former diocese down South, in the big smoke's poor streets in a formidable place like Sydney. If that was not enough for reverence, they also knew the kind of Irishman he was, because he had told them he had been bred on brine fish, and the sea winds, and a good fight on the Irish docks. He had in former times been an advertisement of triumph for the common masses, a poster of promise hanging on the bedroom walls of the country's youth, the nation's hope for Olympic gold. But the good Lord called him up right on the eve of the big fight and said to him, 'Hey! Danny, I will be needing a strong man like you elsewhere.'

Well! Father Danny just dropped Ireland like a hot potato, and he cried out behind him, as he walked off, 'Flame fame!' In haste to be gone, he barely left enough time to say goodbye to his Mother, let alone farewell to the Motherland, before he jumped with the excited energy of youth onto the next ship sailing halfway around the globe. He travelled for six hundred days through numerous lands, soils and weather, impatiently asking the Lord if this or that was it, until he found the place of his calling. So it was, the late sunlight shining on the wide tussock saltpans in the bush diocese of the Gulf of Carpentaria was for the Irish pilgrim. If you watched Father Danny over thirty-odd years of teaching Christianity through the art of boxing, song and abuse, you saw for yourself that holy sacrifice could be given and received with joy, through the many good fighting Catholics Father Danny had created in the makeshift boxing rings from lines drawn on the beaches of the Gulf, through salt down in the salty claypans, or on the red soil with the spinifex shovelled away.

'You better be off you boys before I get me temper up,' the priest snapped, and started to whistle the hymn playing on the cassette, while edging the men towards the helicopter. With the dockland instinct of perceiving every Joe Blow on the street as being out to fight you still pumping in his blood, the priest hoisted the two men into the helicopter then slammed the door of the capsule shut behind them. The helicopter blades went spinning for take-off, filling the air with sucked up bits of dry grass, turpentine scrub, plastic bags and dust, that covered Father Danny standing next to the door laughing, until it nosily lifted itself up from the ground and with an immediate swirl, all that was left was the sound of heavenly voices in a Te Deum of three massed choirs accompanying the plastic bubble darting across the sky. The priest, triumphant trumpets accompanying, rubbed his hands with the pleasantness of having just completed mass, although the words he uttered through a mouthful of dirt were Irish jewels best left lying on the little known roads of the outback.

Overhead, the heavy clouds moving their empire south began raining steadily while Will eased his way down the side of the wet hill sure-foot on slippery rock, carrying Elias over his shoulder. Father Danny, wet to the gills, was repairing his four punctured tyres as fast as his heavy weight allowed. From the side of his eye, he caught sight of movement through the rain but the strangeness of the form did not interest him as he laboured over the tyres. He kept working, lost in thought, counting the minutes of the heavier rain moving up ahead, miles away over the coast, to hit places in the claypans where he envisaged the rising waters would spill over the yellow river road and turn the whole plains country into an inland sea. Who would get through then?

'Should have known I'd be paying for something connected with you,' the wet, and now muddy priest mumbled nonchalantly at Will, from under the chassis, where he was lying, as he continued denouncing the car for being a useless bucket of tin. Will could hear more than he could see of the struggle under the car to keep the jack from sliding and the car from falling on top of him.

'And if you got a problem, don't bother me with it, or bother me with any of your futile excuses about why this happened or that happened. I've had a bucketful of lies already today. Look! Stay there will you? I'm not talking to you! I am talking to this bloody car here before the bloody jack slips. So what's your problem this time? God! This used to be a safe place before you lot started arguing and mucking around with that bloody mine. And another thing, since you are here now, you want to tell me why you got a dead man hanging over your shoulder? Are you going to tell the police about it? No, don't bother, I don't want to know, young troublemakers! I bet you can't even be bothered in your thick skull about going to the police. Well, I won't be burying him if that's what you want unless you go through the proper channels, so don't come pestering me to do it.'

Father Danny hurled himself out from under the car with the grace and noise of a wounded elephant. Will said nothing. He never spoke much to the priest anyway, never saw eye to eye with his religion. Instead, he took the liberty of easing Elias's body and his sacks across the back seat of the car. The priest took no notice, preferring to concentrate on removing the tyre from the wheel rim at the rear end of the car. He told Will to get a move on and help him with fixing the tyres if he wanted a lift, so they could get the hell's name on the road or they would both be swimming to Desperance.

'Double blast for that helicopter, hey, son?' the priest said mockingly, in a better mood, when twenty minutes later, he threw the tools back in the boot of the car. The car was ready to go.

The car flew up the road drawn like a straight pencil line through the flood plains. The priest kept his foot flat down on the accelerator. His dexterity and control over the steering wheel belonged to an inhuman kind of power, Will observed, but it did not matter, if he succeeded in keeping the car on the road while slipping and sliding from one side of it to the other. Meanwhile, they both saw that the floodwaters, spreading across the flood plains, would soon obliterate the road.

'Perhaps,' the priest hissed as he lunged over beside Will's ear, in order to be heard over the engine and rain, 'perhaps, it's going to take the combined force of you and me, camaraderie, my friend, an esprit de corps between two men, to get us through. What do you think, Master Will Phantom? You reckon we can trust in God to get you home?' Will chose silence. Let the holy man talk his legs off. The land was full of spirits which might help the heavenly power of the Irish to tilt flat land and push the Valiant home. He thought of the dead man spread across the rear seat of the black car, stared ahead at rain splashing the yellow waters, feeling the cool air moving across the flood, and that was enough satisfaction, to be on the road home.

Father Danny said he felt good. Will thought the mud-caked priest was pumped, spurred by the success of getting the car back on the road, a triumph in dire conditions. The monologue rolled on and on, as Father Danny spoke with enthusiasm about the craftsmanship of the humble Valiant and the ingenuity of the lone traveller on bush roads. Will searched for the watery road across *kunbulki* – flat country. He felt the silence. The priest did not see silence by acquiescing to silence. For him, the land opened his crammed mind. 'Out here a man can get a chance to let some of the good ideas escape into the wilderness,' he claimed. He proceeded with a stunning commentary about the potential of bush mechanics, their ability to get through any crisis, and what he would have done if he had been travelling without this tool or that.

'The question is, would a man cope? Would, for instance, an ordinary man, not an astronaut, someone scientifically trained, but a practical-minded ordinary man from the bush, if he became stranded on the moon, have the potential to make his way back to earth?' It was because the potential of bush people was underrated that this kind of research was not being done.

Will, at this point, became mildly interested in the talk, linking what Father Danny was talking about with the old people's stories of Uptown. Periodically, Uptown folk claimed they had been taken away by UFOs and had, somehow, either been placed back in their homes, or scanned their way back through the galaxies, simply by applying the cut and thrust of practical bush skills. Will said nothing and let the talking Valiant swim its way through the floods. Always sceptical of Father Danny's theories, he would not allow himself to become a captive audience, like his parents, and all the others who listened and watched, waiting for the legs to fall off a chair.

The sound of a human voice, even if it was his own, seemed to help Father Danny's concentration on the road. 'Watch out *jurrbu, jurrbu* – hole in ground here.' The priest spun the car, righted the outcome, and the oratory continued into a lecture about road bandits – heavy vehicles loaded with mine machinery headed for the mine, using the road, who thought they had the right to take over a man's right of way. 'There were laws that protected the public user of public roads,' he said while the car slid and Will looked at Father Danny, who did not seem to notice. 'It's what happens when men lose sight, lose their vision, of democracy. Power, that's what destroys democracy, education used to destroy the rights of other people. It's gone too far this time Will, too far, this mine, using technology to control people. Very unwise. They cannot crush people just because they have the power to crush the landscape to smithereens.'

So many good words were wasted that day as Will Phantom stared past *kunbulki* and into the past itself.

It was still raining and even though still afternoon, appeared to be almost night-time when Father Danny dropped Will off with Elias's body at the bridge on the edge of town. He roared off into the lights. The first place he was going, he told Will before they parted, was straight to the police station to tell Constable E'Strange he had a fat lot of complaints to lodge about mine staff attacking him on the road. Will thanked the priest, then set off into the darkness, camouflaged in his mud-stained clothing by the dense olive-green undergrowth of prickle bushes.

He skirted along Eastside, then passed Uptown, past others camping on Westside, staying out of sight, carrying Elias, until he reached Norm's place, where he moved unnoticed through the shadows of prickle trees at the back of the house. The house was quiet, and Will, knowing his father was able to identify a person approaching the house from the distance of a kilometre from the sound of their movement, was pleased there had been no one around in the late afternoon. He made his way to the old man's fish workshop which was separated from the house, although it was an extension to the fortress itself. Both buildings were joined together by the long crooked corridor constructed of corrugated iron which appeared always to be half finished by not having a roof. He laid Elias's body and the sacks down on the dirt floor of the workshop. 'I will have to leave you here with the old man,' Will whispered to Elias. He knew his Father would want to look after Elias himself. It was the reason for bringing him home.

In the golden half-light Will gazed around this familiar, favourite room. Soon, without realising what it was that was happening to him, the faint odours of chemicals that had hung in the workshop forever, robbed him of the years of absence and troubles. Like autumn leaves, bad days fell away as though the genius of the room could not retain them. Will became tantalised by the seamless possibility of rushing widdershins back into boy-hood habits, seeking the latest piece of magic his father was working on. It was here in the amber womb that each member of the family had come to lose themselves in their father's world of fantasised hidden treasure, as they watched Norm intricately creating fish jewels of silver, gold and iridescent red, greens and blues.

'We used to spend a lot of good times here, didn't we old man?'

Will talked on, whispering to Elias while gazing around at the walls covered with fish. Norm Phantom had been given the great skill of robbing the natural function of decay, by the act of preserving all species of local fish, and the walls of the room were covered with mounted barramundi, coral trout, bream and salmon. Will studied the crowded rafters which were decorated with hundreds of butcher's hooks, and from each hook hung preserved fish in gleaming silver attached to a strand of fishing line, three or four to a hook. The dangling fish in the workshop always appeared more alive than dead. Hours had been spent by the family watching Norm patiently scraping out the guts of fish, boning the flesh like they imagined a surgeon would have done, and they went Oh! and Ah! when eventually Norm held up the bare fish skin for inspection. There were secrets inside Norm Phantom's head about the plants pickling in bottles lining the shelves. The liquids he brewed came from the plants he collected in night journeys in the grassland bush. He used the juices sparingly to tan the thin skin of the fish specimens given to him by all kinds of people – redneck fisherman, rich businessmen, politicians, scientists. *What do you reckon mate?* All kinds of people turned up at Norm's rusty gate to drop off some fishy thing wrapped in newspaper.

Norm unwrapped the fish at the gate, quietly studied it, and after several minutes, he would say so if he felt he could do something with it. Even the guardian angels hovering in the skies above were in awe of Norm's decision to return life to dead and rotting fish. Norm waited for the response as though it did not matter to him while the stranger's money antennae shot up, eyebrows twitching with excitement, to haggle what was fair: 'Ten dollars ought to cover it.' World-class professionalism, Leonardo Da Vinci for a bargain. *How will we know you will finish the job?* Norm might have done the job for nothing. His mind was light-ages away, mingling with the axis of symmetry in the spirit of the dead fish. Only craftsmanship could resurrect what lay stinking in his hands. The kids, running with the men to their cars, overheard the fishermen feeling hard done by, slamming the car door behind them, grumbling as they observed the Phantom kids. *Well! You don't want to be ripped off by them either.*

Will ran his hand haphazardly through the open bag of horsehair used for stuffing his father's fish. He loved the texture of the hair, and for a split second, an old habit wiped away the years of their disagreement, and the time returned when horsehair would be washed clean and dried by him until it shone for his father's liking. He stood examining, inside an enamel basin, the skin of a barramundi soaking in the tanning mix. He moved by, passing his hand over bottles of preservatives, sealers and lacquers. He remembered how Norm would give him the task of patiently stitching the skin together around a mould of the horsehair. His small fingers had become so adept to using a needle and thread, he was able to make the stiches so small and tight, the seam was invisible to the naked eye. Will studied his hands now, fully grown, and wondered with light mirth, how his father's huge hands achieved the task of an elf. Afterwards, Norm spent many hours and several days to paint the fish with painstakingly steady movements with a small paint brush.

This was the time when there was total silence in the workshop. Norm painted, and the children watched over his shoulder, at the miracle he performed restoring the original colours with paints he made from ochre and plants. These, he said, were mixed using the secret measurements of life, and pearl shell crushed into a fine powder. All his painted fish possessed a translucent gleam of under-the-sea iridescence made from the movements of sun rays running through the wind currents. God creates God's friends. The angels helped him, the children were told. Perhaps, Will thought, viewing a glistening coral trout's ocean-blue dots, slowly spinning at the end of a thread, children were mischievous elves, while men with big hands were angels.

From time to time Will still thought about the childhood beliefs he had of his father. Sometimes while sleeping, he felt that his father went to live under the sea in his sleep, in a world of colours that normal people would never know existed. This image he sustained, of Norm living under the sea in his dreams, was the only explanation he had of why his Father was able to paint fish so delicately and true, as though it were his second nature.

In the accumulation over time of hundreds of bottles, none labelled, lining the shelves, the startled-faced children watched Norm reach for whatever he wanted, without checking first if he had the right one. Somehow he could remember what he had stored down to the last bottle. It was like magic, and children talk. Phenomena like this was what interested the thoughts of the people of Eastside, the *jarrbikala*-policeman and the Uptown *kadajala*.

The family had lost count of the times that Norm had replaced the bottles, and restored the collection to its exact position, after the workshop was searched and his collections of poisons temporarily confiscated by the *jarrbikala*. When the policeman came, the Phantom kids cringed like the dogs, with their backs flat against the walls, trying to attain a powerless invisibility. Immobilised by fear of being seen, they listened to their thumping hearts race when they watched their father being taken away. Each time he saw his father leave the house with a policeman, Will thought it would be the last time he would ever see him. On these occasions he implanted the image of his father's face in his mind, in case it was forever. He would always have the stoical expression on the face of his father leaving to remember, and being too frightened to think of the terrible consequences if this would be the last time they would ever see him again.

Will fingered the wooden workbench, running his fingers along where Norm had instilled in him as they worked the fish together to never have one thought, one vision. 'One idea could get you into so much trouble, boy, you might never know if you are dead or alive for instance. Sideways, you always want to be looking out when someone serves you up a drink – might be a cup of tea or a glass of water. Never let them. They could be serving you up the worst kind of poison.'

His father had found a dead countryman once. He said he found him at the tip, when he smelt a human being rotting where he poked a stick around in the muck. 'My country what are you doing here?' Norm asked, angling for the man's spirit to come forth and purge the wrong done, and when he got no answer, Norm had walked around in the putrid mud searching for clues, while a million flies, buzzing to and fro in one big black mass, never stopped following him. He was convinced, he claimed, that the flies tried to push him away. Perhaps they were hiding something. He kept waving the black demons away with his free arm and a stick from a bamboo thicket bulldozed from the artesian bore up the road, and dumped at the tip. Although the vile stench tried to pull him down into the palace of death, he continued blindly forward, choking back his vomit, until he stumbled upon a pile of dirty housewife's kitchen rags and pieces of cardboard marked Cocoa butter, which he flicked away, and there he told police, he un-covered the corpse. The body was actually stirring about, and Norm, both repulsed at the sight and thinking it was the devil in personification, rising up to get him because he never went to church on Sundays, said, it was in those vital moments until he came to his senses that he believed the cadaver was floating off in midair. Then he realised it was riddled with maggots. 'Get the police, run quick,' Norm said he snapped at his children, who he claimed were with him at the time.

Well! Aren't no business of ours, that was what the police said. They said, through Truthful, it was not reasonable to expect them to muck around with anybody's body in such an awful state of decomposition. *Other siders' business*, that was what the muffled voices said behind the industrial masks, as the whole stinking lot, treated like any kind of animal carcass, was quickly and unceremoniously shovelled into a body bag, zipped inside of another and another, and air-mailed off that fast to a city hospital. 'The police,' Norm said with a spit reserved for whenever he referred to the police, 'had spent that much time pursuing him just for finding the body, there could not be enough hours in a day for *squestion* this and *squestion* that. Well! They could have been out doing what the decent taxpayer paid them to do, catching the real criminals,' instead of making him look like the guilty one. But some people said, it was no good what Norm Phantom could have done. So, throw enough mud – some sticks.

It was any wonder everyone started thinking Norm was a murdering criminal type, with the police just about wanting to marry up with him, by the way they were hanging around his property. Even his wife Angel Day started to get jealous of all of the attention Norm was getting. She threw things at the police when they came. She demanded to know what was really going on. 'Your Mother is a very suspicious human being,' Norm casually mentioned to Will at the workbench after the police had come cruising up and down, passing their place at all hours, staring in, searching the premises and then driving away in their police cars with bits and pieces of his hobby. *Whatever for, well, who knows?* Over the next few days everyone started putting two and two together and ended up with light bulbs flashing! *Forget evidence, forget police investigation, forget fact. Here we have forensic scientists in every household who had no need to surrender themselves to fact.* The Phantom household tried in vain to keep calm too.

Than the chemical analysis revealed the man had been killed straight out. Analysis came back, not quick smart from the hospital, but saying anyhow, *This man was killed with the worst poison, 1040.* 1040? 1040! Everyone knew about 1040. Word got around about 1040, saying it was being made locally – Aboriginal-style. Will remembered the endless string of people coming to their house, standing around in the yard with Norm, speaking in whispers with the palms of their hands capped to the side of their mouth, as if it would block the kids from hearing what they had to say, that someone with this 1040 was well and truly up to no good. At the time, people would arrive one after the other and he could still feel their presence radiating fear around the yard, and saying whatever they had to say to Norm.

The yard was the place where all theories about the mysteries in life were tested that, later in life, Will would reconstruct as he struggled to remember the stories of the old people on the road with the Fishman. *That 1040 someone*, it was whispered, *might have run away now to somewhere else because he knows he is in trouble with the law, but, it could be he is still around, trying to make people weak with poison. I saw him in my dream and he was the death angel who looked like swarming bats packed together, taking the shape of a giant bat shadow flying across a starry sky in the middle of the night, crooked and zigzagging, like lightning, then he shook himself out flat to make himself appear in front of you like a human being with sly, downcast eyes.*

Even if the 1040 killer stopped doing it for a while, you cannot be too careful – He might say he is finished fighting with you, but you never know, he be friends with you for awhile – Oh! good way, but not really. When you are not using good eyes for looking, not thinking about anything, he will put something in your drink to make you get weaker and weaker, then you die. Always watch this. Then people stopped coming over to the Phantom place.

These were the reasons why Norm Phantom had always told

his children never to let anyone get them a drink even if it was only water, because it could be the 1040 killer giving it to them. Norm believed there was only one fundamental principle for longevity and this was never to depend on others. This he would suddenly announce to his children out of the blue – 'Because, who could you trust, eh? No one really.' As children, Will recalled the deep impression his father had on each of them, as someone of such total adroitness they were convinced he could fathom anything he chose from the depths of life. His children should have been in the forefront of survivors in this wicked world with a father like Norm Phantom to guide them. His persona, his aura, lived constantly in their line of vision, constantly diverting, even hanging around in their sleep, always ready to catch the bad dreams.

Dream and reality blurred, of children standing on the foreshore watching their father fade over the sea horizon only suddenly to turn back, coming never close enough, to hand signal an almost illegible message. Other times, they were distracted, when suddenly he would appear behind the backs of people he did not like, using hand-signal language at a rapid speed to say whatever derogatory stories he wanted about them, to the utmost embarrassment of his children. *Never trust this bat-eyed dog. Tell this smelly piss trousers to get going. HE IS AS USELESS AS A BROKEN-BACK SNAKE. Tell him to piss off.* The banter of hand language subsided only when he got them to do what he wanted.

Their place was guarded by black angels. Will remembered being told that by the old people who said when it was a good clear day, they saw plenty of these angels going about the place clutching their javelin weapons, looking for the snake that stuck to the place like glue. Will said they were hawks. Blessed or cursed, or whatever Norm Phantom believed, his face was unnatural, almost as black grey as the head of a fish he once caught. The old people called it worry for the snake. Will did not believe the snake lay in the ground under their house. The snake he once saw was the living atmosphere. Its body stretched from horizon to horizon, covering each point of a compass, and encasing them all. His father looked in all the wrong places, for the air flowing in and out of his nostrils was the snake. Will dismissed the vision, but he could call it up, if he wanted to.

Will sometimes saw the dead people who sought out his father in the workshop. They were local people mostly, coming over as soon as they found themselves becoming dead persons, frightened, not knowing what was going to happen to them. They could show up, in person, or else send someone else instead to grieve for them. Norm had as little time for the deceased as he had for the living, telling one and all: 'What you want to come here whingeing for? Am I God? I am not God, so go to your church, you idiot.' It could have been that Norm talked too much to himself without realising it. This was what he said he believed. He claimed he never knew the difference. He did not know whether those people turning up in his life, popping around his place to have a good old cry, or telling tales, were either dead or alive.

So, once, he chased all the illusions, apparitions, spectres, persons of the otherside, off his prickly bush patch, and back up the churned-up, mud-dry road and through the main street of town as though it too were an illusion, a town that never existed. Who knows what anyone thought about seeing him chase nothing, telling it to go to hell. Did he stop, come to a halt, like an exclamation mark, when everyone of good nature shouted at him to stop as much as the spinster aunts, agitating like tarted-up Pekinese dogs because he was frightening the children? No, he just kept on running like middle-aged men do, with his green stick, until he was two steps short of entering the other side of town. Once, Will recalled, following his ghosts, Norm did momentarily stop to ask, 'Did you hear that pin drop?' It was no wonder the whole town thought Norm Phantom was mad. Forever calling him to explain himself: 'Don't you go snobbing me Norm Phantom,' one of the aunts shrilled, her voice cracking the air like a whip.

The only good thing was that the Uptowners did not know what to do about certifying black people, and claimed they had learned to live with 'harmless' insanity. It was part of the North. Although their town was very old, the Uptowners never knew what demons were being chased. Nobody living in the middle of a war zone knew it existed. Even in a war of extreme intensity which had been conducted with such a high level of intelligence it had lasted at least four hundred years. But that was Uptown.

Will lingered, looking over to where Elias sat, thinking about the town, about being back home. He was beginning to feel as though he had never left being Norm Phantom's son, who had gone against the conventions of the family and their war. He broke the rules. It was the first time in history, or so it seemed to all and sundry in the Westside Pricklebush. Could it be that he was different? It did concern him to have flaunted responsibility without conviction. Why did he not cart the ancestral, hard-faced warrior demons around on his back as easily as others in his family were prepared to do for land? They were good people, and the old people were bent over, so stooped with carrying their load of this responsibility. He had asked himself, and again now in the workshop with Elias: 'It was good enough for them, why isn't it good enough for me?'

Will sighed deeply, gave the bench a final light tap before leaving the workshop. He knew he had already failed the obstacle course, had slid down this track many times before, wasting time on a futile examination of his conscience, knowing there was no answer. It was just no use trying to feel remorse for letting others carry their war, his war, an inheritance that belonged to him, as much as he belonged to it. He could only give a clinical glance at the proudly worn combatant scars of his relatives when they boasted of the battles in the middle of Desperance. Will carried no scars, only the dark brown birthmark straight down his left leg. The old people recorded the reappearance of familiar old family scars in the newborn, so that four hundred years worth of events could be remembered in stories of ground battles, sea battles, and not forgetting the air battles either, they claimed. *Don't ask how*, the old people said, just because it was widely recognised that the white man invented aeroplanes and the black person was believed not to have had aeroplanes. *And a good job too, because you never know if they are going to land at any right place, except probably, into a big mining hole in the ground; you go into it and that will be that. Don't trust engines. Trust your intuition and of course you will see Aboriginal people flying themselves around and no reported crashes yet.*

They said Will's scar came from such a battle that took place in the skies with sea eagle spirits over the Gulf sea, long before he was born.

Away from the house, Will felt great throbs of sadness vibrating through the rain from Norm's grief when he discovered Elias. The rain fell over the saltpans and over the sea for hours that night, then Norm heard the oars swashing through the shallows, as Will rowed out to sea.

Chapter 7
Something about the Phantom family

Last Wishes…

The fishroom never kept the silence of the dead. For years Norm Phantom knew this. Peculiar things happened in his workroom where he competed with the spirits of who knows what, to make fish from the sea come back to life, to look immortal. To hang in schools by the dozen, suspended in oceans of air, stranded, attached, much like himself, unable to swim off into distant horizons. Mortality did not belong in this room.

Occasionally, he lamented that one day he would die, and saluted his premature epitaph, *Who would look after all of this then?* Oh! Sad. His was the lot of an isolated man. The twin in his isolation: quiet, unassuming, humble pie. Was it any wonder such a man would make other peculiar claims too? After hours of laboured work, when finally holding in his hands the masterpiece, he claimed it was not he who had created it. Why would he make up such a story the old people said: Listen! Who did he think he was kidding? He was kidding himself. Everyone knew the hours of toil Norm Phantom put into creating his fish. Desperance being what it was, a modest place, humble people believed in real facts. Only real facts created perfection. So it was. People were not fools.

When nobody believed the story spread by Norm Phantom about not being the maker of his work, he kept his beliefs to himself. These were the fascinating secrets of the fishroom.

Secretly, Norm remained convinced that others helped in such exquisite creations, something much more powerful than himself. A supernatural master artist who created miracles, a dalliance of God consuming the room as an experimental studio, a type of exposé for life in the decaying world, where the air smelt like a beach.

In this bewildering scenario, Norm acknowledged himself only as being the original creator of the workroom. This was true. It was through a glimmer of thoughts like that, that Norm realised what had really happened to the room he had built with his bare hands. In a fascinating growth, when the preciousness of the new fades with no one noticing, the room had changed, evolving into something else. Inexplicably, without messing about, in came and dwelt a powerful spirit with grander goals, a perfectionist who spat dead lizards of scorn at human beliefs of what was perfect, who loved to play 'touch up' with a humble man's work. So, Norm Phantom, with such gorgeous ideas flooding his mind, was able to skirt around the true origins of his genius – the twin unfetching forces of envy and competitiveness, matters that often sustained him in dealing with his family. Plain old truth was undeniably becoming the diminishing factor in his work with the fish.

The seeds of thought can be very enterprising. Once, when very weary in the middle of the night, and while still stooped in his intricate restoration of each colour-drained minute scale of a king trevally back into silver, one at a time, so as to have the job completed by the morning, for a common 'madman' who did not deserve to have caught such a magnificent fish, Norm had been disturbed by the light flickering, pulsing like a heartbeat.

Steeped with ideas so enormous they could be tracked as chaotic enterprises, matrices of chaos, and suspecting the reason why the light was pulsing, he began to understand that the room was like a pickpocket, robbing people of their memories. Norm accused the room of becoming a hoarder of other people's secrets of the heart. What he saw for the first time that night was as real as anything he had ever seen in his life; it opened his eyes, and from then on, he was able to see other things in the room. As the room matured, Norm saw it was bending inwards, steeped with the weight of holding one miraculous discovery after another. It occurred to him that all truths were being accumulated. Poor truth sucked straight out of the minds of all the unrighteous people who came to admire his handiwork. Sometimes, the room appeared to be absorbed by quietness, as though it was reading its secrets. He continued his work, and paused, when he heard the rustling of a page turning inside the walls.

Over time, Norm preferred not to take his eyes off his work until it was completed. He merely blinked when he heard the room working, and carried on, rather than have to endure the time lost from a distraction which served no purpose. He especially did not want to see what other people thought stacked up around the room like bundles of newspapers. Finally, with the last dab of paint drying on his trevally, Spanish mackerel, long-whiskered catfish, codfish, whatever, with the same single-mindedness, Norm Phantom renegotiated his way out of the workroom through the crowded space.

Norm suspected that nobody else could possibly be aware of where the unexpected heaviness had come from, the heavy breathing people said they felt in the room, which they said was swimming against their skin. Norm kept the room's mad secret from other people. For those who had experienced its weight, the fishroom was the one pitiful place in the whole of Desperance where most other people, except family members, were eager to leave, unknowingly with less. All manner of people, usually oddball fishing men of all walks of life, from all places of the globe, made similar excuses to let Norm get on with his work –

Think I caught old so-and-so's flu again. He had heard people say it a thousand times. They said they preferred not to interfere with the great artist at work. The old people never went inside. They said they did not like to go inside strange houses.

Norm saw unsuspecting people, uncomfortably but impulsively, give up their tight-lipped family secrets which had been passed down through the ages. What poor people! Especially those that did not even know they had been carrying the secret knowledge of generations passed. Well! They spilt the beans to the fishroom. One time, Norm told the old people he had a dream about the room. He told them that every house had a spirit, and in his house, the spirit's brain lived in the fishroom. The few who heard Norm talk about his theory said it was too far-fetched, but Norm argued that once the spirit consumed the original room, it became the likeness of the room itself. In fact, it was a complete replica of the original room. His story was too strange even for the old people, who in return, accused him of making up stories to frighten them away. Norm kept thinking his own thoughts anyway. He said nobody could stop him.

It was during this time of realisation, a haunting that the old people wanted nothing to do with, that Norm had become distracted from the calling of his art. He felt he had lost something. He felt he had lost his touch. He spent more time listening to the hawks harking above the roof. He said he was too distracted to conspire against death with his fish. He lost faith. He was wasting time casting his eye around the room and seeing the walls watching him with a sustained look of amusement. The fish from the sea just remained plain dead. Work was never finished. Decay and rot began to take over. The room taunted him and everywhere he saw death, robbed by the years, now laughing in his face. Great schools of fish conjured from the sea were sent scattering in every direction through the cyclonic air. Norm fled the room, running through enormous weights of water to drown his conscience in the hub and tub of a psychotic Pacific ocean collapsing through eons of compressed time.

A truce was made however, and whatever Norm did to re-create life in the fish he preserved, it was amazing. His fish looked like priceless jewelled ornaments. Each piece was better than the last. He became a master known throughout the land. This was the reason why people came from all directions of the world to Desperance to have their fish preserved. Yet, no matter how masterful he was, he knew the ever-watchful other-worldly spirit had more work to do. It remade the fish more beautiful to the eye, casting a replica of colour through the empty nail holes in the roof, shining where the dazzling rays of sunlight, hitting onto the scales of fish, left them forever glistening silvery gold on colours of green, grey, blue and pink.

Years passed with the winter winds blowing south-easterly in weekly rhythms after midnight. Like nobody else, Norm loved the grand old composer, the rapturous melodies which swam along the tin walls of the corridor from the house to the fishroom. The music arrived in the middle of the night and tapered off after midday. The breath of music at this time of year made the old people camping on the cold ground outside move their blankets as far away as they could from the house. They said the house was haunted. They did not like the old star in the night working close by to where they were camping because it was flaunting the after-life. Norm sang *Gloria*, alongside the old composer conducting his mass choir of crickets that sang *Glory! Glory!* in time with the rattling walls. The crickets, part of the fishroom's metamorphosis, lived in the dark, musky, fish-smelly environment. Packs of these creatures had moved into the room in magic droves, having come out from under a maze of stubby grass and leaf litter in the bush, to live in the nooks and crannies of dark places inside the walls, behind jam jars full of chemicals, or under benches groaning with the weight of plastic baths full of fish-skin tanning fluid. Dozens of the gleaming fish hanging off the rafters sang eerie songs in shrilled, mezzosoprano voices that floated out of their mouths from the crickets' hidden nests, from deep inside the fishes' horsehair bellies.

'Bloody this and blast that about the ozone layer,' Mrs Angel Day lamented in her heyday as Queen Bee of the household, after yelling across the rooms of the house for the confounded radio to be turned down. Norm Phantom refused to listen to people complaining. In his quest to find answers to his theories, he was addicted to news on his radio. Constantly twiddling the volume knob, any news item about the hole in the ozone layer would be blasted to a crescendo through the house. For he had a puzzle: 'Was the chorus in the fish-room a new strain of crickets caused by the hole in the ozone layer?' He told his wife such a thing had never happened before. He asked the question: 'Could mere crickets, normally a curse to mankind, have developed the ability to chirp through the noise barrier?' A thousand times he had asked her: 'What do you think?' For Mrs Angel Day, the sound the crickets made was like listening to plates smashing. 'What do you think?' Such goings on in one ear and out the other, drone, drone, meant nothing to her. She said she did not give two hoots, but the sound was driving her mad, and he could stuff any stupid *scientify* ideas he got from city people talk up his butt. 'They wouldn't know about here would they? If they did we wouldn't be living here like this, would we?' Norm excused his wife for not acquiring a modern sense of refinement, such as a fine ear for the kind of music he liked listening to. She said the crickets were mutants addicted to inhaling those chemical fumes he used for tanning, 'Gone mad, like yourself!' Explaining further to prove her point, she proclaimed, 'They don't live anywhere else in the house, do they?' This was the truth.

Norm kept his old ventriloquist cockatoo away from the workroom, in case it learned to chirp like the crickets. The bird was regarded as a genius for its unusually quick knack for picking up sounds. 'Mark my words, you keep that bird of yours away from there otherwise I'll guarantee you this one thing Norm Phantom, his little pile of bones will be licked clean by every baldy old camp dog in Desperance to kingdom come.' Mrs Angel Day, as the old people referred to her in those days, had threatened many things on numerous occasions, more than her other veiled threats about leaving Norm which she finally did, although not on account of the crickets. She always started off or ended her threats with an added conjecture – 'Mark my words,' and you better believe it, sooner or later, she did whatever she threatened.

In the early days when Mrs Angel Day ruled the roost in the Phantom household, reigning supreme out in the front yard, she often sat in a pram kept from her last born which she had converted into her chair. This was the spot from where she complained to the old people about the loud chirping noises of the crickets. She said it would drive her to divorce one day. The old people said the noise must be too great for her nervous constitution. If she ever saw her husband pass by, an occurrence which was not frequent, she complained to him, saying it was always left to her to save the marriage: 'If you had any sense you'd shut up your noise.' Veiled threat! Veiled threat! Norm always felt she was insinuating that he was personally responsible for summoning up all the devils that came into her life. 'Inadvertently you might be,' she claimed, and the old people looked away. 'You will ruin our marriage by your ignorant inadvertent.' 'You're hearing things,' he told her. In truth, she did blame Norm for all of their bad luck, often stringing out piece by piece all the things that had gone wrong, starting from day one, New Year's Day a long time ago, when they first met. 'What New Year's Day was that?'

Norm Phantom did not remember any New Year's anniversary. Every time she mentioned it, it was like a slap in the face, but he never told her that she was wrong about the date. He let it be a reminder to himself of her infidelities. Instead, he accused her of having a disease she had picked up: 'Must be from one of those other men you were with before me.' He furthered his claim by announcing to the old people sitting around pretending not to notice what they were arguing about, that she had passed the disease onto her children when they were born. 'What disease?' she retorted, although not denying her experiences before Norm. He told her it was a disease which makes people too sensitive to sound, where they turn into maniacs, they become *like police*. He said he would not have been surprised if his children wanted to become *jarrbikalas*.

Norm Phantom went around telling the whole world that his family had some rare disease which made them overly sensitive to noise, although he claimed they were 'stone deaf when a man wanted some simple thing done to help him around the place.' At the time Norm was spreading false facts about his family's hearing disabilities his good friend Elias was one of the few who disagreed with him. Elias claimed it was not logical that the entire family had hearing problems. He told Norm he did not know what he was talking about, because anyone who was half deaf in one ear and stone deaf in the other, was going to hear less than a person with normal hearing.

Norm was annoyed by Elias's insult and retaliated, saying if a man could not remember who he was, then surely he was not in the position to make sound judgements on any other matter. Norm was so fully convinced of his own superior hearing in spite of his inability to hear most normal sounds, he decided on the spot to write out another attachment to his many scribbled last wills and testaments he kept in a locked toolbox. In front of Elias, he plonked on the kitchen table an inch-high pile of 'last wishes' to be performed after his death. He wrote with a heavy hand, another document with a biro running out of ink, in broken traces of red writing that tore through the ruled page. 'Upon his death,' Norm declared, 'his eardrums be gouged out by the police, butcher or any nurse, anyone (up to performing the request), except the one connected with the underneath date (namely Elias Smith),' then he instructed – 'Put em into a sticky-taped clean plastic bag.' Instructions followed for the package to be covered with clean ice in a six-pack esky (which should be big enough), and stored in a cool room at the hotel or the butcher shop, until the arrival of the mail plane. 'Then send the lot to science,' he finally scrawled at the bottom of the page.

It was Angel Day whose wishes came true. After a devil of a windstorm made the final decision, blowing south-south-west by eighty degrees, the fishroom was rebuilt away from the house, at the end of the twisting snake of a long and rusty corrugated-iron corridor that remained featureless, and provided no windows.

Another requiem was being chanted when Norm discovered the body of Elias in the fishroom. In fact, it was the intensity and loudness of the sounds made by the crickets that had brought Norm running through the house, down the long corridor, with a million wild thoughts running through his mind. Scenes of death surrounded him. The music was so strange. The sound tumbled through his heart, mingling pulsing blood with the music for the dead.

Norm froze the order of his reality. He struggled to maintain the surreal fresco of fishermen coming to collect their trophies. It was a day when he had to get the tanning fish skins ready to mount. He had a lot of work to do. With the requiem sounding like engines drumming, he felt his hands shaking as he fumbled to open the door. The sound did not stop as it normally would have when he entered the room. A cold shiver ran up his back, around his head, flashes of nightmarish times spent in hazardous seas jumped in front of his face. In the midst of the wreckage of all these storms, now racing through his mind, he looked around the room, suspecting his family, expecting to see a little pile of white feathers, the cockatoo dead. The mere thought abhorred him, and then he was surprised to see creeping into his mind the banned son, the one whom he never thought about anymore. He stood uselessly, searching, knowing it was pointless to push the unwanted away. The treachery felt in the room was profound, but the obstinate father let him remain.

He needed to check the skins, and as he tried to walk over to the tanning baths, only his eyes responded, darting warily to left and right in time with the flickering phosphorescent light overhead, while his mind became more disoriented with the noise whirling him into a vortex of blue-black clouds, spinning with his memories.

His legs felt disconnected from the rest of him as though they were walking ahead of the rest of his body. With his long arms, he reached for the bench to stop himself from falling heavily on the ground, only to feel his hands land on something soft. Under them he saw the crumpled bags he could not remember seeing before, not lately, or ever. His eyes caught sight of a putrid coral trout and in disgust, he immediately pulled his hand away. As he looked at the rotten fish in the bags in a stunned silence, he immediately thought someone was playing another trick on him. Similar things had happened before. Stupid sorts of people would turn up with old fish with an expectation that he could work miracles. He would look his admirers in the eye and say that there was no one on earth who could make their wishes come true. Had they ever come across such a person? Someone better them himself? A person who went about converting rotting decayed bodies into jewels? He threw their fish in the stinking bin at his front gate.

Dreams come and go, or come to a halt, as had the crickets, as though a certain shocking vibration had simultaneously struck their antennae. The alarming silence was almost as deafening as the piercing high-pitched orchestra had been. Norm looked around him, convinced something terrible had happened, and knew in that instant, that there was someone in the room looking at him. This was when he saw Elias, recognising him straightaway, profoundly ghostly, enveloping them both in death, then disconnecting, as his heart cried out loudly with the pain of being torn apart. His friend sat slumped against the wall. Norm cried from the pit of his stomach, like a lost creature of the earth, until the end of all things roared from his mouth.

The tragedy did not end there. It had only just begun in the Phantom family that day when Elias had come home. 'Look! A felony! Look! It's a bloody felony that has been committed against Elias,' Norm screamed repeatedly at the three sisters, his daughters, who had come running, jostling each other like getaway thieves through the corridor, and thinking their father had had a heart attack. The youngest brother, Kevin, was still strapped to his bed, thinking his father was being killed by the 'othersiders'. He hollered incoherently and jerked the straps around like a madman to free himself. His mouth became full of froth and he cursed his sisters in a stream of spit, but was ignored. Easily exhausted, Kevin ended up moaning long, breathless guttural sounds, as though they would break his captivity. No one came to untie him.

Janice, Patsy and Girlie stood there in the fishroom, staring in absolute puzzlement at their father's outrageous behaviour. They were speechless – *He wasn't having a heart attack*. Then they saw he was pointing to a man sitting on the floor against the wall. In the wildness of the moment, seeing a dead man with skin tanned to the colour of old parchment, long muddied, hair tangled with twigs and grass, none of them recognised it was Elias. Girlie said it looked like one of those mummified Egyptians you see unwrapped in a foreign museum for a television documentary. None saw it as male or female. They looked blankly at each other, ignored Norm who was still screaming about felonies, then saw the decaying fish. Together they thought aloud, 'Evidence.' Then Girlie said, 'P-O-L-I-C-E in capital letters. The police will be coming here.'

Knowing that the whole town already suspected their father of being a murderer, they talked rapidly about how to get rid of the fish, how to get rid of the body, how to rid the workroom of all traces of evidence. None of the daughters went near the father, who was now leaning in a slump over the workbench. All three were apprehensive about what they thought in the presence of their father.

They stood well back. With a long piece of wood, a disused oar, Norm swung around wildly in the room sending the tanning fluid splashing through the air. The crickets were silent. The sisters were relieved. Patsy said, 'Let him do it if he wants to. If he wrecks anything, at least it will be his own things, not ours.'

Then the sisters worked fast, even Janice who was complaining she did not want to miss Oprah Winfrey. They ran back and forth across the room, avoiding Norm, who, even though exhausted, occasionally swung the oar at them. Then they raced up the corridor, through the house, past Kevin who was told to shut up, and out the front door. Minutes later Norm was distracted by the suffocating smell of burning rubber.

When he looked out of the window to locate the source of the smoke, his heart felt as though it had jumped into his mouth. He saw the blaze of fire and billowing black smoke pouring off the molten blue bucket dancing on top of Kevin's collection of play tyres which were being twisted around like a hurdy-gurdy in the intensity of the heat. He ran out of the room, cursing the stupidity of the incredibly long twisted corridor, then through the house, ignoring Kevin, who intensified his feeling of being a cursed man who had been dealt another blow of stupidity by his family: they were destroying the evidence.

'It's the bloody evidence. What do you think you are doing with that?' he yelled. 'You idiots.' The girls ignored him. The fumes of burning plastic and rubber were continuously refuelled as they threw more and more metho onto the flames. He lunged vainly, trying to grab the metho bottles, as each daughter side-stepped out of range.

'Put it out, put it out,' he roared at them, but, it was as though he was not there. 'What a bunch of no brain idiots,' he could not believe it. He banged his fists together. Girlie looked, but took no notice. She had just seen the monkey beating his fists without his tambourine. He shouted, furiously stressing each syllable, saying he could not believe the mongrel breeds he had brought into the world. They took no notice and kept looking up the road in case anyone was coming. *Where were the fishermen – why hadn't they come?* He looked up at the black smoke to see which way the wind was heading, if it was heading towards town, and sure enough, it was just as he expected. The black smoke was being picked up by the south-easterly breeze, which was sending it like a giant black worm, straight into Desperance.

God's truth! How unlucky can a man be? Norm knew the whole town would be standing out on the street, looking up the road towards his place. Everyone would be wondering – What the heck was happening! Why was Norm Phantom burning tyres? Why was he burning them in a big bonfire in the middle of the day? They would be surmising to each other about what he was trying to get rid of. In a small town like Desperance, people knew about burning incriminating evidence. Anybody with any sense burnt tyres at night-time like the mining company.

The black smoke stretched out, spreading across the rooftops, and the soot fell onto the white-painted walls of the houses of Uptown. Phones rang, ringing, matching thrilling voices, exclaiming to each other their indignities against Norm Phantom for doing this to them. It was thrills for everyone. Norm Phantom knew there was a certain drill that operated against him amongst the houseproud, double-chinned maidens. The busybody matriarchs were quick smart, already jamming the telephone line, calling up the nice Constable about those Aboriginal people in the humpies over on the west side of town. They were at it again – burning rubber. 'Could you be a dear and go down there and see what you can do about it, Love?'

Janice, Patsy and Girlie worked on in a haze of fumes, possessed by the mesmerising height of the flames; still ignoring Norm, they stoked the fire to even greater heights. Suddenly Norm noticed the big daisy chain dress was missing; Big Patsy was nowhere in sight. His heart slipped a beat, then another. He yelled at Girlie and Janice to find her. He thought she had been engulfed by the fire. His chest tightened, he felt he was going to have a heart attack. But Patsy returned. Now he could see her struggling towards the fire with the body of Elias. Norm tried to stop her by pulling her back from the fire, and almost collided with Janice. With a panicky voice, she told him to get away from the body.

'We have to get the police,' Norm shouted, pulling at each of their clothing, trying to haul them back from the flames.

'No, get away from us,' Janice said, shaking herself out of his grip.

'The police will be involved, you can't stop it. They know.'

They edged closer towards the hideous bonfire. Norm was unable to hold back the two big women working with all of their weight against him. They would burn all of the evidence, Patsy said, and that would be the end of it. He could almost taste their anticipation that all would be well again.

'Burn the evidence? You can't burn the evidence. What are you, an idiot? You can't burn Elias like that,' Norm tried to tell her, in disbelief that they were calling Elias the evidence, a man who was like an Uncle to them. 'Who do you think you are talking about?'

'Get out of the way, Dad. Just you keep out of the way,' Patsy kept saying, trying to push past her father, while he held her in a headlock.

Girlie ran back into the house after she heard Kevin making an almighty racket on the corrugated-iron wall next to his bed. When she went rushing into his room, she saw him shaking his head violently from side to side, hitting the tin wall each time with a horrible loud thud. His baffling eyes were staring into space. She knew he could not see her when he became lost in this other nightmarish realm. Nobody knew Kevin's world anymore. She felt sorry for her brother. She saw white froth and vomit all over his face, falling back into his mouth and nostrils. Kevin was drowning in the stench. Seeing his face had turned purple, she knew they had to untie him very quickly and get him into an upright position. It was not the first time the family had almost killed Kevin by tying him to his bed. Each time only sheer good luck had saved him when someone got there in the nick of time. Soon enough, they were all trying to save Kevin, while Elias's body was left on the ground, out in the yard.

'I told you you shouldn't go around tying up your brother. I told you I never liked it,' Norm reprimanded Patsy, as she struggled to undo the straps that were tightly buckled across his chest, stomach, thighs and ankles. Kevin wanted to speak to them but his mind felt ancient, as though it needed to come back across the mountains of a million years, to learn many languages, to be understood. He wanted to tell them he had seen Will, who had also crossed the mountains and come back to them. Will had come to visit him from the graveyard of a thousand sailors in the sea. Kevin had grown up believing that Will was dead because no one would mention his name in the house. He imagined himself searching an armada of war ships becalmed on a flat sea, searching the faces of those long-forgotten sailors, trying to find Will.

Conversation remained elusive for Kevin. He could not choose to tell them, because it might have been a dream, or they might think he was seeing things, because he did see ghosts, and the snake spirit, and other spirits of the ancestors, and spirits of the dead people who said his father had killed them. They all came to tell him the future but nobody believed him. Will had come back home and said, 'Hello bro, why have they got you strapped up for?' And something happened that never happened before. His bro touched him on the head with his hand and it had felt real.

He wanted to tell Patsy that, while her head was bent so low and almost touching his, but it would be better to choose Girlie because she listened to whatever he had to say, understood his lingo, even while both of them knew that he was talking stupid again. But his head kept throwing itself from side to side and he could not stop it. The more he tried to control himself, the more upset he grew, and his stomach tightened with the vomit which kept coming up the back of his throat, and he was struggling to stop himself from choking again. Even in the midst of all of this, Kevin was determined, because Will said he should hold on, because he was going to come back and get him. That life was going to be really alright, Kevin thought, slipping past the faces staring down at him. He wanted to be with Will; he always wanted to be with Will.

'Can't you see what you stupid people have done. I don't want any of you girls around here anymore, you hear that? Bring nothing but trouble. For heaven's sake, can't you useless idiots see he's going to die like that, he is going to die,' Norm was crying loudly, almost in Patsy's ear, but she took no notice.

'Patsy stop it,' Girlie demanded. She was frightened and nauseated by the smell. She thought she would fall on top of Kevin if she could not get out of the room.

'You are useless, useless, you are all useless,' Norm cried, tears running down his cheeks, as he unbuckled the straps and grabbed Kevin, pushing him up into a sitting position and holding him tightly to stop the convulsions, until the choking sounds subsided.

'You know, this must be the worst day of my life, seeing my poor friend like that, poor bugger, Elias,' Norm said to his daughters when Kevin had calmed down and fallen asleep. Girlie made a pot of tea and they sat around the kitchen listening to Norm talk despairingly about the day being worse than anything he had been through in his entire life – cyclones, his wife walking out on him, the lot.

'A storm at sea was better than this. Trapped for days with a broken leg in a swamp full of crocodiles. Malaria too, and don't tell me you can't get malaria in this country. Your Mother never believed anything except her own self. Even when she left – it was a celebration of good fortune. I said good luck to her. I felt like I won the lottery. I felt plain bloody rich compared to this.'

The girls ignored him. They were thinking up ways of talking to him about the body. They had to get rid of the body because it would eventually end up being tied to the family. It was still out in the yard.

Absentmindedly, Girlie tapped the teaspoon – *rat-a-tat tat*, over and over on the table. Norm told her to stop it; it was making him feel mad. She kept tapping. Finally, Norm grabbed the spoon from her and said he had made the decision for the family. 'We got to tell the police.'

'You can't tell the police,' Girlie snapped. It was not the end of the day, nor the final decision. It was just the start for Norm Phantom's daughters in dealing with their father.

'What are we going to tell the police, "Someone put him in there"?' Janice said. '"Who do you suppose put him there?" They'll say you did. That's what they are going to say.'

'We got to tell them we don't know because that's the truth, the start and the finish of it,' Norm replied.

Girlie was pouring more tea into her cup but did not notice that it was splashing over the table. As far as she was concerned, although she never said so to her father's face, he brought them shame. He got accused of being a murderer or being mixed up in one after another of the strange deaths in Desperance, or whenever anyone died. She already suspected him of having something to do with Elias's death. She kept asking herself how well she knew her father. How many times was she and the rest of the family, not counting the big brothers because they were big champions around Desperance, who loved a fight, but the rest of them, weren't they the object of ridicule in the town because of him?

What happened when she and Janice and Patsy were abused by the other idiotic families from over the other side of town? Well! In a nutshell, no one intervened, not even the policeman who liked to watch women fight from a distance, when the big ugly cows struck, ganging up on them in broad daylight, in the middle of the main street with pieces of broken bottles and whatever else their slack-arse hands could grab to use to fight the Phantom sisters. What did the bystander do? Well! He just watched. It was a circus, that's right, a circus for white people, hanging around like dogs to watch black women fighting. She had lost count of the number of times she had been chased out of town, like a dog, by those mongrel cows with their beer cans and bottles they hurled at her back for target practice. Then, after a few days, with a smile on their nasty faces, they said hello, as if it all never happened. That was what black sluts do as far as she was concerned and she had the scars to prove it.

'It's not up to you Girlie,' Norm snapped at her as though he had been reading her mind and it annoyed him that she lacked the nerve to tell him.

'Police don't care about our truth,' Patsy spoke. She had vivid memories of putting together her Mother's house again, and again, and again, after the police had rampaged through it to their heart's content, with or without a search warrant. It did not matter because if the police had not done a thorough job, the white men from town came afterwards and wrecked the place. When that happened, they were flat out putting themselves back together, let alone the darn house their Mother had loved and forsaken all else for.

'Police don't care about our truth,' Norm repeated in a sarcastic tone. He said they had to make them believe their story of what happened, because if they said nothing it would all fall back on them one day. 'Just you wait and see.'

'Anyone home?' a male voice from outside disturbed the discussion in the kitchen.

'Anyone at home? Anyone at home? There's nobody at home,' Pirate, the grease-coated cockatoo who had been carried to the desert to be blessed by a pope, called back from his perch in the cedar tree. The mean-spirited bird was plucking cedar berries and throwing them down onto the mess it had created on the ground, where the Constable stood, staring at the smouldering fire.

'Well! What did I tell you? I knew this would happen,' Norm said, almost whispering, in a tone of satisfied resignation.

'You tell them nothing Dad, or you will get us all into trouble. Do you know who brought Elias here? Do you know? It must have been Will, that's who,' Girlie explained.

Norm looked straight into her face, 'You've seen that bastard haven't you and you didn't bother telling me? If it was that bastard, too right I'll be telling our friend out there, you just watch me.'

'No you won't Dad, I'm telling you Dad,' Girlie stood her ground, 'I don't care what you think about my brother, your son, what you do to him is going to affect all of us.'

'When was that bastard here?' Norm demanded, glaring into Girlie's face to force her to answer. It was this stubborn one who stuck up the most for her no good brother.

Girlie shrugged her shoulders, and he looked around at the others with blank faces, and saw that they were looking at Girlie for an answer as well. Before he could say another word, the Constable welcomed himself into the kitchen. He had become a fat man in his years at Desperance and was still looking for a woman suitable enough to become the wife of a country policeman. Yet his heart-strings tugged for Girlie.

'Make yourself at home,' Norm said, his eyes glaring at what his language called the *waydbala jarrbikala*, whom he had never welcomed into his home.

'Sorry, old man, but I did call out,' Truthful replied, giving Girlie a sweet smile.

Girlie did not even look up, while her sisters went out of their way to make him welcome. There was a rush around the kitchen as the two bigger women hurried to make a fresh pot of tea, to heat the food, to clean the table, wash up, make a proper place for the Constable to sit down. Sometimes, Girlie thought, they would do anything so as not to talk to outside people. Norm and Girlie remained in their chairs, unresponsive to Truthful's pleasant chatter. Neither had a thing to say, leaving Patsy and Janice replying – 'Hah! Hah!' or 'Nope.' After a couple of minutes the room fell into silence.

'Quite a bonfire you got there outside,' Truthful finally said.

'If you say so,' Norm replied.

'Had a couple of phone calls, people complaining about the smoke, that kind of thing. So I thought I'd better come by and check it out.'

'We lit the fire to burn rubbish, so what if the wind started blowing the wrong way, that is what the wind was doing around here for thousands of years before Desperance ever existed.'

'Well! Love, I was just doing what I have to do, you know what some of those people are like,' Truthful never liked getting off on the wrong foot with Girlie.

'Then you go back and tell them what I told you as soon as you finish that cup of tea, okay?'

Janice went and stood at the kitchen door with her back to everything. She lit the first of many cigarettes she would smoke for the day. She watched the smoke still heading towards town but she sensed the change was coming anyway.

'You can take your time honey,' Patsy cooed at Truthful's hurt face. She thought Girlie should consider her lucky stars, the cow that she was. She gave Girlie a mean look every time she stood behind his back, bending her body in so that her breasts touched his shoulders, while she topped up his teacup. Girlie looked back in mock exasperation. She felt like wiggling her own tits at Patsy but decided against the idea, as it might give the pig something to get excited about. She had always thought those two fools were meant for each other, if only they could see it.

'Gee, Patsy looks after you,' she said with a tightness in her voice to Truthful who was watching her every move, while she was just short of stopping herself saying, or haven't you noticed, you overweight lump of shit.

Truthful responded with a smile which reminded Girlie of a crease in a turnip. He knew better than to get into a debate about anything with Girlie in front of the family. She was at it again, trying to palm him off with Patsy as if he was hard up for a woman. He knew ways of making Girlie scream for being mean to him. Well! She knew what she was asking for, he thought, if it was pain she wanted.

Norm stared at Truthful, while the room bristled with long unresolved tensions about dead bodies, finding someone to blame, how to classify the terms of victimisation, trashed homes and ram-shackle bodies recovering from sexual abusers who wallowed with joy, like they were opening presents on Christmas day. Each of the daughters recognised the body language. Norm was sitting at the table, rigid, like one of his stuffed mullets. They raised eyebrows at each other – he was brewing again. Truthful was chewing gum.

Girlie looked at the clock on the wall and knew it was just a matter of minutes before the explosion would hit the room. They had seen it all before. First, he would slam his fist on the table, offer to give Truthful a full fist in the eye, abuse all of them, especially Girlie, whom he called the fornicator with no shame who slept around with a cop, and what have you. She would instantly react with a raucous laugh, and say: 'Can't you say slut because that's what you mean isn't it? And that's what the whole world calls a slut around here.' She had already anticipated what he would do next – let the cat out of the bag about Elias, whose body was still in the yard. Norm would follow up by offering to challenge Truthful out the back. What suitable means of blackmail would it be this time? Acceptance into the family by endorsing the big ugly prick who was fucking his daughter? It never worked. Girlie knew the cop's job and Truthful was the full box and dice. He would do his job, questioning and questioning until Norm became that rotten mad he would drag Will into the firing line, or all of them even.

Janice was still standing at the doorway staring at the smouldering fire, looking at Elias's body through the black smoke, and anticipating how the whole town would once again become involved in the private lives of the family, when the anticipated smell of rain hit her in the face. She looked to where the rain was coming from, and saw a windstorm approaching from the south behind a wall of red dust.

'Rain's coming,' she said, throwing the cigarette butt out in the yard. Turning back to the kitchen, her gaze met Girlie, and she said with her flat, matter-of-fact voice, 'We better shut up.'

Janice had given the signal for Girlie who looked down at Truthful, looked directly into his snake eyes, while reaching over to tap the table with her hand directly in front of him, the only indication she wanted to give him to follow her to her room. Since he had managed to worm his way into the house, she knew he would hang around until he got what he had come for. Everyone in that kitchen knew he intended to stay the day, or night, or until he had got Girlie into her room. In the many months Truthful had been coming over to the Phantom household, if Girlie tried to ignore him, he just hung around the place for hours waiting until she gave in to the pressure he placed on all of them. It would have been a different matter if the boys were around town. Their presence would have made him leave them all alone.

But with Inso and Donny working down at the mine, Truthful felt free to come around whenever he wanted, as though it was his job to look after the family. Girlie sneered at Janice and Patsy as Truthful flirted with them about how he had become their man about the house. Swaying between his lust and his ability to keep on his toes, even revelling with pride in having a close relationship with such a capable man, he never forgot Norm was his prime murder suspect, and it was his job as a professional policeman to snoop around the locale. Oh! Yes!

A man like Truthful thought it might be kosher to have his fun, but he knew his job. He would solve the unresolved crimes in Desperance even if he had to die doing it. The waiting game offered the extra bonus for Truthful's happy calculations. The handcuffs in his pocket pressing into his groin roused the sensation of good times ahead. He could almost smell the lucky break in Girlie's perfume, the smells of her body mingling with his, knew luck was just around the corner. All he had to do was fuck the sister, sweet talk the others, become a top fisherman. If ever the scoundrel of the town, Will Phantom, became homesick, and came running home to daddy like the spineless cur he was, all the better.

Girlie looked over at Janice. 'Don't worry about shutting up the windows,' Janice said, 'Me and Patsy will do it.'

Chapter 8
Norm's responsibility

Secrets...

Thousands of dry balls of lemon-coloured spinifex, uprooted by the storm, rolled into town and were swept out to sea. From the termite mounds dotting the old country the dust storm gathered up untold swarms of flying ants dizzy with the smell of rain and sent them flying with the wind. Dead birds flew past. Animals racing in frightened droves were left behind in full flight, impaled on barbed-wire spikes along the boundary fences. In the sheddings of the earth's waste, plastic shopping bags from the rubbish dump rose up like ghosts into the troposphere of red skies to be taken for a ride, far away. Way out above the ocean, the pollution of dust and wind-ripped pieces of plastic gathered, then dropped with the salty humidity and sank in the waters far below, to become the unsightly decoration of a groper's highway deep in the sea.

Wild weather was happening all around Norm Phantom, as he rowed through the darkness, pushing with all his strength over the breakers of the tidal surge, taking his clever thoughts with him. His mind had a certain kind of craziness of not caring what happened to him. People said that, but people were wrong, because Norm Phantom was one of the most calculating men on earth, second to none when it came to self-preservation, who normally set out to sea under the cover of a storm.

Those big pretenders sitting in their long grass camps were not in the slightest bit astonished when he told them that those who searched for his secret fishing places had failed. *Lucky! Lucky thing! Too Lucky!* They knew the names of the old white people in Desperance who had sat around miserably for many wasted years, trying to translate the secret conversations Norm had with the heavenly spirits at night. *They will never know.* Those white folk believed that if they could learn how to translate the voices of the stars, their sons would be safe at sea too. They would become invincible, like Norm. Their boats would never return empty, bringing back fish from one end of the street to the other as in the heyday. A little bit of luck was what was needed for the town to rejoice in fish once more. The old people respected Desperance custodians because they felt sorry for them. The graveyard in the sea was full of their sons.

Everybody knows that there are big groper in the Gulf of Carpentaria, but those that joined Norm Phantom on his journeys were the ones nobody else had ever seen. Norm told the old people how he could camouflage himself as a big fish, fooling the local pirates of Desperance when he disappeared over the waves. The old people said he must have sprayed the robbers with Mortein fly spray, to divert them off of his tracks. *It was a very tricky thing to do*, they claimed.

When Truthful went with Girlie Norm had remained seated at the kitchen table brooding about the possibilities of life – if only he had his way. He mumbled something about how it felt as though a foul air had departed. 'What did you say?' He ordered his mute tongue to speak. He willed the words jammed in his throat to come out of his mouth, roll around the kitchen, roll down into Girlie's bedroom. He waited for the words to break through, the words saying he wanted to kill Truthful, to put his body parts into a bag and run off as quick as he could to feed him to the sharks, and that was the truth of the matter. He waited while watching his daughters run around the yard picking up what should not be blown away, closing windows and doors, preparing for the dust storm to hit. He could kill the cop, but the words stopped him from doing it.

Patsy and Janice looked once or twice in the kitchen as they ran around the house. Both knew that if they were not living at home, their father would just sit there, while the wind blew its merry way through the house, taking the lot. He let the house go when they were not around to clean it. He let his daughters sleep with a cop. He let so many things happen. Norm thought they could think whatever they wanted, for it would be a sweet day if all of them got out of his house. The truth was, when Truthful had left the kitchen with Girlie, Norm was incapable of moving. He was immobilised in the glue of his own blood, pinning him like a dead weight to his chair where he wrestled with murder, while the law of the Ten Commandments held his body captive.

Truthful had left the room mumbling something about *reality*. He knew the father played his part, second by second, with enormous intrigue and secrecy. He had watched Norm sit at the kitchen table, uninvolved, detached, immorally complicit, thinking he knew about cat-and-mouse games to outsmart a cop.

Norm's thoughts on the other hand had been running in a different direction, sifting through the pores of the many different storehouses in his mind. First was the obvious truth of resignation. He would let the white man get what he wanted; wasn't it always the way with Truthful, growing fat with his own greed, getting whatever he could to gorge himself with? Then, two, he sought someone to tell him it was alright to kill a white man. Where was the Fishman? He knew Mozzie was in town but he still had not come over to see him. He had been half waiting for Mozzie since he heard his cars driving around town. Even now, he was half expecting him to turn up. Mozzie knew how to get to the heart of the matter. He would tell him if he was right about what he felt he should do, play it straight, or play around the back. Well! Why doesn't he come; he should know something's up, Norm reasoned, tapping his cup, since he had not gone in search of Mozzie when he hit town like he normally would. Mozzie should realise something was wrong. It seemed that a man could be lying in bed half-dead, waiting for someone to turn up. He had forgotten that Mozzie never came to his place anymore.

Norm thought Elias's body was most likely Will's doing, since the girls would have been correct about that. Norm knew it was not his imagination why the cop, watching like a hawk, was in the house. He recaptured a past scene in the kitchen, seeing Will's fury exploding, kicking his way out of the house, reversing at breakneck speed back down the road he had just arrived from, and screeching to a halt in a ball of dust, to yell, 'Watch the cop, man!' Then, with not a moment to lose, foot dead on the gas – that was Will, and the last time he was ever seen around the traps.

Will drove off, leaving the family staring at his dust trail. And somehow, maybe it was because there had been no chance to finish the argument, no resolution, no reconciliation, Norm wanted to help the cop to hunt his son down. Norm knew himself to be a naive man, and too intoxicated with his passion for the sea to abandon it at Will's request. He believed the world would look after itself, infatuatedly, against the odds, because it always did and because the white world cared little about people like Norm Phantom. Norm still pictured him packing and firing his words like bullets, 'You are wrong, man. You want to take a reality check on the situation, man.' Norm remembered those words, very insulting, new words around these parts. He frequently had a chance to think about what Will said, so much so he often used his son's handful of words on others, to be impressive in an argument. This was what memories are made of. Things like Will's blue ute, left on the outskirts of town heading south. The abandoned car was still there like an ornament on the roadside. A piece of memorabilia, dedicated to the history of the Phantom family, which the father refused to tow home.

The Fishman was in town but where was he? Words were like water sweeping by, taking the memories of Will away. Well! Will was never a proper son. Norm sneered at the oncoming storm; if Girlie did not kill the cop soon, then he might just about do it himself. He pictured the two of them, he and Truthful, out at sea. 'Would you want to go fishing tonight son?' It could easily happen – an accident. He had taken Truthful out enough, though not far, never too far, because he judged a man's seaworthiness, what he was worth out there. The trips inside the shallow water line, not journeys, were far enough to get him off his back about fishing, time enough to give Girlie a chance. He could have taken Truthful twelve hours out to sea to find the body of Elias, and just as they both looked down in the water and saw the body lying on top of a shallow undersea ridge, it would be then that Truthful would stand up in the rocking boat to get a closer look, saying, 'Where? Where? Keep it steady,' and these would be his last words before he fell, after he had leant too far over the side, just as Norm leant across to pull him back, the boat unbalanced on Truthful's side, just as they were floating on top of the groper's den. Unfortunately, things happened too fast, the cop was drowning at sea, dropping quickly into the depths with the heavy force of his overweight body, fully clothed in uniform, his mouth open in the absolute shock at seeing passing pictures of himself drowning. Truthful would think someone else was holding a slide show of his death, *click, clap*, and Norm saw himself, many hours later, stricken with regret, apologising to Girlie. Norm had finally relented to the kind sea, and he was unable to reach down far enough into the water to bring Truthful back.

He opened the kitchen door again to let in the fresh air of the dust storm, so he could look at the wind flying past. He was waiting for that tall, skinny man with the untidy rat-coloured hair to come along. Gordie had inherited the tin combat hat that had once belonged to the madman Nicoli Finn, before he was found belly up and picked at by every fish in the bay, way out in the low tide. The ladies of Desperance said Nicoli died fighting like a soldier. The few witnesses attending the annual picnic day had watched Finn in his final encounter, but said afterwards, even though they had talked about what they could do, and had even decided to take a closer look, they decided to keep walking along the beach kicking the seashells out of the way so as to appear as though they were not watching his birds. At the wake they said: *He was pretty particular about his birds you know*. The witnesses said Finn was fighting the hawks which kept diving at him, diving out of an ordinary blue sky, just like missiles. Someone remembered remarking at the time while Finn was doing his work: *This is what the war must have looked like*. The old maidens attending the picnic could only imagine what took place in a war, just as they wondered to which unfortunate battle in what corner of the globe their knitted socks and blankets for the national war effort had been dispatched long ago.

Officially, he was doing his own business, and the maidens said they were not to get involved in someone else's affairs, even if they should have, for it would have been improper to interfere in a man's work, and they had grown fearful that if they had interfered, they could have done nothing to prevent the attack, and what if the hawks started attacking them? Saving Finn was a job for the police, they remarked without offence. What was being asked of them was a job a decent wife would do if Finn had been sensible enough to acquire one. Well! He was dead now and useless to anyone.

After Finn died and Elias left, poor Gordie inherited the

mantle of neighbourhood watch. Gordie was magnificent. You could watch him, always with a compass swinging around his neck, and a hammer in his hand, in case he had to tack down the net. If he did not have these things, then you would have to think something was wrong, something was out of order. Gordie forgot nothing. He was good at his job. The best. When he became the official watchman for the town he taught himself to walk fast, first by running, then gradually slowing the running until he got it down to a trot, and from a trot, to a fast walk. Had to. He had to circumnavigate the town every three hours come rain, storm or nothing. And be better than Finn, who had a background in surveillance.

With the storm under way and Truthful ensconced out of sight in a tryst with Girlie, Norm waited for the moment Gordie would appear, striding his way across the horizon. He had seen him pass earlier in the night. The cloud cover was heavy, hiding the light of the moon, but the white dog had groaned in its sleep when it heard the passerby crackle the stubble grass underfoot. More intently, Norm watched again at midnight when the clouds had lifted and the moonlight shone like a torch. He watched for Gordie's eyes on the prowl.

Once he saw Gordie was heading back towards town again, marching on a track through the salty marshes near the beach, Norm listened for the startled sea birds squawking as he approached their nests. He quickly gathered his sea gear together. Matching the extraordinary quietness of the night bird in the blackness outside hopping past the house, he moved past the bedrooms of his sleeping family. Truthful snored peacefully. Norm paused outside Girlie's room before continuing to the fishroom. He returned, carrying his fishing tackle, then paused once more to see Kevin, still sleeping.

Outside the house he picked up Elias, and along with his gear and fishing tackle, swung the body over his shoulder. He moved off towards where his little aluminium boat was moored in the shallows, where the murmuring sea with its incoming tide kissed the shoreline. An owl was speaking to the night. These were the only sounds. With the thought of going on a long ocean trip after being on land so long, Norm felt light-headed, but he packed the boat and was ready to leave within minutes. 'We'll go together, just like old times,' Norm told Elias, as he pushed the boat further out on the water. Repeatedly he told himself it was the right thing to do. He was not too old. He could still do the journey.

He had taken Elias to the gropers' place in the middle of the sea before, and had been surprised that Elias already knew of it. The gropers started to rise in the water all around the boat, mingling closer and closer than they had ever done in all of the years Norm had gone on this pilgrimage. Norm had been sure that there was communication between the fish and Elias. Then, he saw the gentlest expression on Elias's face as he looked up from the water. It was a child's face, smiling at the look of Norm's concern. Elias turned back and slapped his hands under the water.

Hundreds of the big gropers surged towards the boat, until in the moment when they looked like colliding, the fish had pulled away, creating a foaming sea in their wake as they sank back into the depths of the ocean. Norm had often thought about what happened that day. It was the memory which had come flooding back to him as he sat at the kitchen table, ready to destroy the world around him. The memory fought off the devils until Norm saw what Elias had wanted. Elias had come back to tell Norm to take him home.

Norm knew if he mapped the route well, he would reach this spirit world, where the congregations of the great gropers journeying from the sky to the sea were gathered. The gropers would wait for Norm before they moved on, far away under the sea, before returning to the sea of stars, at the season's end. He was still feeling annoyed about the girls burning the fish. The coral trout belonged to Elias's spirit and rightfully, they should accompany the dead man on this journey into the spirit world. Having to take Elias away without his belongings did not prepare him well for this other world. He knew it was the wrong thing, if Elias went without his fish. He cursed. The wind that had been ready waiting for him died and there was an incredible stillness. It had to be a sign, as though the wind had refused to take them, Norm thought. So there he was, standing out there in the water in the middle of the night, sweat running down his face, all that work for nothing.

Norm trudged barefoot back up the beach, back towards the house to collect the old fish. He felt like a fanatic, a madman, searching for a precision that did not exist in his terrible obsession with fish. He realised he was out of time halfway up to the house, but he kept going, dodging around the back of several piles of driftwood, almost crawling along on his belly so that Gordie would not detect his movements. He expected Gordie would turn up at any second, he could picture the long, lanky streak running almost, coming in to check.

As he retraced his steps inside the house, he knew he now had only minutes to leave in order to follow the course he had charted for himself. He knew if he set sail any later, the seas would be giving the wrong signals, the tides would be wrong, he would not be able to recalibrate, and after that, whatever he did would bring him further askew.

The white dog, happy he had returned, was following excitedly behind him. He thought he had disturbed Kevin, but the lad was just talking in his sleep, talking to Will. Norm knew it would not be long before Kevin was up and about. Truthful was still in a deep sleep – it would be so easy to smother him. He reached up and pulled down about six of the silver fish and four coral trout that were hanging from the ceiling, and put them into the bags that had come with Elias.

Norm threw the bag of fish into the boat and pulled the boat out to deeper waters, just as he had watched Elias do on the day he had set off, leaving Desperance for good. The coolness of the water was refreshing on his skin after working in the humidity of the hot night. He set course by the star of the fishermen that was setting low in the northern horizon. Then he climbed on board and started rowing away as the cloud cover again returned blackness to the remaining night.

A steady rain fell while Norm rowed into the tide racing over the seagrass meadows of the flat sea. Once again, his thoughts turned to the Fishman not coming to see him. In the darkness, he felt Elias's presence, sitting at the end of the boat, looking at him, as he usually did on their way out fishing in the good old days. Before the kids grew up, before the madam of the house caused her trouble, and the Fishman came and went as he pleased.

'You remember that, Elias?' he said, speaking softly, as though the dead man had been listening to his thoughts. This had never happened before in the ups and downs of the in-between years. 'Fishman always came around, didn't he Elias?' There was no answer, and Norm rowed, hissing his story in the rain, 'Despite the sheer irresponsibility of it all, she drove off with him.' He remembered both of them, Mozzie and Angel, huddled like a couple of teenagers, in the huge expanse of the back seat of the main man's flash car, driven by the membership.

'It ended for me on the day she ran off with the Fishman, Elias,' Norm said on the forward lift of the oars. '28 January, 1988,' swinging the oars back. 'You know why I remember it?' Swoosh. 'It was precisely four p.m.' Swish. This was the time of day when he most vividly felt a loss of heart. 'It was a hot, hot day to remember.' The hot wind had been blowing it was true. He had circled the date in green on the calendar, and fourteen years later, the same calendar with the Snowy Mountains stream picture remained on the wall as a reminder to the family.

'No, you are wrong,' Elias's deadpan voice came back through the night, the way he usually spoke to Norm while they were fishing, back to back to each other, waiting for a bite. Elias had never budged from his belief that it was a different day. The 27th day in January 1988. It was ten a.m. A hot bugger of a day. Angel was walking, her shift made of some fine material, he did not know what, clinging against the front of her body as she walked in the hot air. The wind was that hot it made your blood boil. Piles of rubbish at the tip had combusted into roaring fires. People were fainting in their houses in the middle of the morning. Oxygen was draining from the atmosphere.

Everyone was perishing for rain. There were people who were too breathless to speak, but Angel had spoken to him. She said in her dismissive, flat voice, in her usual manner of speaking to the likes of Elias, men who did not stir her feelings in the right way, that Norm was already down looking at the boats. Elias had argued that he too, would always remember that day because he had marked it on his own calendar. It had a picture of two galahs sitting on a perch, screeching at each other. He had kept the picture because it reminded him of the occasion. Norm remembered seeing her thin frame of a body in that dress, walking in the mist along the track through the wastelands, heading towards the rubbish dump. He refused to believe Elias. He argued vehemently that in January of that year, high tide was at precisely four p.m. in the afternoon, the same as the day Angel left, so this was why Elias had to be mistaken. The argument lasted for days on the sea. This was fishing with Elias. He rowed on.

Devoid of blue, a strangely coloured creature was man, the intruder, who ventured at his own risk into these faraway, watery domains of the ocean...

It was a long journey Norm Phantom had set upon into a world that by day belonged to the luminescence of the ocean and above, to the open skies, and by night, to the spirits who had always haunted this world. They say this faraway place belonged to the untamed spirits of fishes, women and sea creatures. This was the realm of mischievous winds and other kinds of haughty souls from above. Who goes there? the quiet wind asked. The following wind answered. It said there came a man of pain and another, who looked disinterestedly at the world as though it did not exist.

The sea wind following Norm along in his little boat was a spirit of intemperate disposition, who woefully blew little gusty breezes for days and passed through the night playing nocturnes that droned over the waves, or else, left, running away from the toiling seafarer in its wantonness, searching for a wild idea on the other side of the world. On those days of hot calm, the air was heavy with a humid clamminess that drove Norm half crazy. Everything on the boat felt damp. As he rowed on, looking back at Elias all day long, he started to detect a grey mould growing over the dead man's face. With no escape from the sight of Elias's face, he watched for the spread of new patches of mould advancing over his friend's body.

At night he slept, half curled up in the cramped space in the middle of the boat in a puddle of stagnant water. Although his body felt sluggish in the heavy air, his mind was as attuned as a wary night bird passing his boat. Even the slightest movement of water breaking with a fish surfacing would awaken him in fright. 'What's that! What's that!' he called out, half asleep, ready to abandon ship. And from the other end of the boat in the darkness, Elias said calmly, 'Relax, go back to sleep, it's nothing.' Unfortunately, once robbed of his sleep, he could not sleep. Instead, driven with annoyance, grumbling that it was alright for Elias to be calm – he did not have to come back alive – Norm would start rowing again in the middle of the night, navigating by his memorised map, following the star of the fish.

He would row into daylight, his mind absorbed with directing his monotonous labour, until a startled cry from a seagull winging close to his head, ricocheting off every surface of the sea plain, echoed like madness through his mind.

Elias's version of the argument, which altered and swayed in many different directions over the years, was based on seeing Angel Day walking to the rubbish dump in the summertime. Elias said he was not blind, he knew what he saw. All the Pricklebush people living on the edge of town were sloshing around like wild pigs in ankle-deep mud to get anywhere all along the roads in town, after the heavy Wet season rain.

The world was no longer under the spell of the monochrome grey-coloured Dry season. The land was covered with flood plains alive with frogs calling to each other in waves of sound running across the atmosphere, closing to absolute silence near to the magical footsteps of Elias, before resuming the pitch of the highest decibels behind him again.

Next, Elias used the brighter paints on his palette to portray the scenario, describing how he had watched her moving in the mist and long grass like an angel, a spirit no less, along the path, skipping to avoid the puddles. Elias was not taunting Norm. He spoke frankly without any realisation that the truth of the lost wife was painful for his friend. The way Elias spoke about Angel astonished him because his wife had never been angelic.

The way Elias spoke of what he saw was no secret, not something he had seen alone, because everyone in the Pricklebush felt haunted whenever she approached them, like a hummingbird, in the bush, along lonely paths on the outskirts of the town. She was the one who made people scratch their heads and say, 'What kind of woman was that?' To many others, she was a memorable, marvellous sort of woman who printed herself on your mind with red lipstick, while you watched. Elias said she was too good for sure. He had stood by the side of the track like a stupid man, he said.

'Hello Elias, Norm is already down at the boats,' she purred catlike at Elias gawking at her again, then rolled those luxuriant brown eyes, and just like the queen she was, she floated off.

Norm paused at the call of a seagull. His mind floated back to the thoughts that had preoccupied him in those days. All of the many preparations he was engrossed with, even for such a small sea craft. The inconsequential trappings to ensure survival. Elias never worried come rain or storm, while Norm was forever moving about with his all-weather jacket over his head for shade, checking equipment from one end of the boat to the other, fanaticising over hairline cracks becoming gaping holes overnight. 'You never used to be like that, fret, fret. I reckon you live in the ruins of married life.' Those were Elias's true words about his good friend Norm. Norm threw Elias's words back now as an accusation, 'How come you were saying things like that about me?' Elias looked him back squarely in the eyes and kept on staring, until Norm answered for him, 'Why didn't you ask me that when I was alive?' Norm mumbled he would have, but he did not want to cause an argument, so, 'It did not matter.' Unable to continue this argument with itself, his mind slipped back to the days of golden yellow, and boats of capillary red, when a man walked home when he felt tired.

Norm moved awkwardly, his legs severely cramped from the long journey, and checked the four fishing lines hanging over the side of the boat. He changed the bait with pieces of flesh from a small shark he had been saving from his catch from the previous night. 'See!' He showed the lines to Elias before throwing them over the sides again. Looking into the spot where the lines were sinking into the blue-green depths, he saw his companion following, the manta ray with its greying form moving through the depths of ocean below. Norm became intoxicated by watching the prolonged movement of the suspended ray. The creature moved so tantalisingly slowly by suspending itself in the drift of tidal movement. He no longer cared to stay above. His vision slipped into and out of the waters, breaking the surface so many times, he became lost in time.

The grey sea creature willowing below carried his subliminal mind on its back, absorbing those captured thoughts of Angel Day walking out of a submerged track in the sea towards him. She walked out of the water not far from the boat in a dazzling ray of sunlight, and she walked away, back on the track that led to the rubbish dump. Norm gripped the vision, staring straight through reality to watch her for the first time that long-ago day when Elias had seen her. Looking so closely into her face, he was astounded at its clarity. He was shocked to see a secret intimacy residing within her. He had never before seen this face from her childhood transcending through the travesties of their life together. He thought he had never seen her before. She walked with a tranquillity and a beauty that was her normal face, but which she had carefully folded up and stored away, saved only now for stolen occasions of when she was completely alone. He felt ashamed to be hiding behind the long grass, peering out with the grasshoppers, slipping along behind her, following on the path of what happened on that very last day he and Elias had cast the peaceful spells of being just simple men working on their boats.

It had been a very ordinary day of whiling away the time when suddenly the blue nylon line ran straight across the water, and

Norm Phantom was propelled out of his daydreams. He was being challenged by a fish of great strength that held the end of the line taut after it plunged into the depths, as though it had turned itself into a rock. The strange object in the distant sea line that he had been watching still edged its way through the water, slowly bobbing like a balloon, moving against the slight breeze blowing across the sea from the mainland. Norm scanned the surface, vigilant, yet far too preoccupied now with the sun hanging low in the sky, as he struggled with his first catch in what had become a long day.

The war raged on for what seemed like hours between the old man weakened in his travels, and the fish, the long, narrow, silver body of a giant Spanish mackerel, spinning through the water with one of Norm Phantom's lines hooked into its mouth. The fish sprang out of the water, twisted in the air to eye Norm with the hateful vengeance caught fish have of men, and ran the line flat chat – twang, twang, back and forth, from one side to another, cutting through the thousands of little bait fish that regularly swam in the shade underneath the boat, and like a great trickster, twisting the half-dozen spare lines into a single knot.

Afterwards, success was not great. The perverse deep-rooted sea man's euphoria did not etch deep in his bones. Instead, he felt humiliation wash over his skin, exposing him as a marauder of the sea, a stranger in a strange place. He felt vulnerable in his little boat. Self consciously, he used his knife in a butchering act to gut the fish, then he noticed the strange shape of a giant stingray, as big as the boat itself, flying across the sea like a passenger of the wind.

The sun sitting low on the horizon threw its bright rays across the water which simulated liquid gold. The tantalising phenomenon moving towards Norm reflected a blinding light, as its ploy to distract his scrutiny, while it scrutinised him with predatory eyes. Several times Norm was forced to avert his own eyes to the safety of the sun-glistening waters, or more guardedly, to the shining silver of fish blood swimming around his feet. Yet, drawn back time and again, he would lift his eyes above the shield of his tiny world on the vastness of water to capture another glimpse of the giant creature's hypnotic power. Drowning in his distractions, Norm suddenly looked across at Elias as if remembering he was not alone after all, and saw the dead man smiling at him. 'If you are in charge of our little journey Elias, you better start telling me what we are going to do now,' Norm said, relinquishing control, no longer sure if he ever had control. He ate some of the raw fish flesh, staring around like an animal, waiting for another animal to eventuate, to steal his food. He heard fingers clicking. He looked around and there was nothing. But it was enough. He found what he had mislaid. He saw the route of their journey laid out in his mind, from woe to finish line, and knew he was again on track.

'Right! Right! Right! So if this is the case...' Norm spoke softly this time to Elias, without ending his speech, as if Elias was also studying the same map he was looking at. He must never question his vulnerability to the elements of the weather again. He looked across the sea, this time he could see wind and storms held in the arms of the saltwater spirits, which had always been there, all through this journey to the graveyard of the men of the sea.

He now understood the travelling phenomenon he had watched was the sorrowful woman, a cursed spirit of death who had come to find them. 'Can you hear her Elias?' That night, he was convinced he could hear her cries in the wind whistling across the waters, that her cries were curses in a language that was foreign to him. He knew what the old people said about her. In the long grass they would hear her wails coming in from the sea, or even from land along the beach, if they listened closely at night. The old people said if you could hear her way out at sea, she was warning those who heard her to stay away. No fisherman would ever actually see her because she would make herself *moonba* to them, yet Norm knew what he was looking for. He had an image of a white flowing hair witch, whose very skin he knew was like slime, and off her body trailed seaweed for clothes.

Men such as Norm Phantom kept a library chock-a-block full of stories of the old country stored in their heads. Their lives were lived out by trading stories for other stories. They called it *decorum* – the good information, intelligence, etiquette of the what to do, how to behave for knowing how to live like a proper human being, alongside spirits for neighbours in dreams. In the local stories handed down through the generations, the sea woman was a death angel. She appeared from nowhere in her endless search to take men back to her dark, empty world in the deep waters at the bottom of the ocean. Norm knew what this world looked like because he saw it in his dreams.

On the floor of all oceans was a world overgrown with a forest of living black coral. It was a place that harboured a final darkness, where light never penetrated, and where men who were captured through some form of bewitchment, lived for the rest of eternity, pulled and tugged, while suspended in the streams of water running back and forth across the globe. The old people always spoke of this limbo world, where fish never seen by man were really spirit women who lived and swam through holes in the captured man's ribcage, and perpetually fiddled with his brain to make him forever yearn to be rescued.

Another little wind blew an old green rubbish bag into the boat. Norm guessed it must have flown hundreds of kilometres, whirling its way across the water from Desperance's dump. Believing it to be a second omen, a curse from someone in Desperance, someone from the Pricklebush mob on the other side, he kicked the tattered plastic overboard in the darkness, as though it was something alive, a Goddess woman who came flying low across the sea. When it blew straight back into his face, he read the change as a sign telling him that there were wild winds beginning to pour back into the Gulf from the north-east, bringing more storms.

Norm carefully watched the green form spiralling around the boat, once, twice, each time as if it wanted to land and attach itself to him. With his arms flailing aimlessly at the plastic thing in the night, he told her straight: 'Don't you come here.' Oh! Yes! What a thing. He was convinced this was a sorceress of a wife. A witch who had borne his children and then behold, in front of his very eyes, walked off, wilfully wrecking their marriage. He heard her rustling as she hovered between them, whispering secrets to Elias – 'Norm's lost at sea.' Then the wind turned, and she flew back with it towards the coast. With her departure, Norm felt a heavy shadow passing over him. It was the change coming, and he told Elias in a low, steady voice to get ready. 'Make out nothing's happening. Brace yourself man.' The sea remained as flat as a tack but Norm waited. The wind did not turn into a storm and the boat sat in the flat, humid sea with Norm, sticky and hot, returning to the last dying days of his marriage.

So far, the journey had taken Norm more than two weeks of rowing all day long, living on raw fish, and drinking rain water he collected on a sheet of plastic made into a hollow dam. He stored the water he captured in soft-drink bottles. Then, knowing the place where the gropers lived was drawing closer, he stopped worrying up the storms as he journeyed through the humidity and flat seas, realising that all these obsessions of what was not right, were metaphors for his failed marriage.

One clear morning, Norm knew he had reached his destination, when he caught a glimpse of a groper swimming with his huge back fin clear of the water, no further than twenty metres away. He waited, watching while it swam over to the side of the boat.

Once, Elias had told him that the groper was the descendant of the giant dinosaur. Norm did not know whether it was true or not. He had other stories. Their whole area was covered with megafauna once upon a time, Elias said. This he explained was millions of years ago, before it stopped raining, and the claypans were covered with rainforest. Elias explained that when you went around parts of the country thinking you were walking on rock, it was really fossilised tree stumps from those times. The rainforest trees were massive, he said. It was hard to imagine. Norm saw both these worlds wherever he looked at one.

Elias said it was not hard to imagine at all, for he had seen such trees somewhere, but he could not remember the places he had travelled. Norm knew there were fossilised bones of the ancestors of gropers and other animals being found by the palaeontologists and flown by helicopter out of the country by the bag load. These old bones which had lain with the ancestors for millions of years, were being stuck together again with araldite and wire, and covered with fur so all Australians could visit them in museums to see what these creatures used to look like.

The Fishman was full bottle about the palaeontologists, so he came along too, saying to Norm it was only natural for Elias to say those things, for the groper was a creature that used to have legs for walking on land, but it returned to the water to live sometime millions of years ago after a drought. 'We are having the same drought right now,' he said, sniffing the air for temperature. Norm and the Fishman had once watched a groper die. Fishman patted the dry skin of the creature, and called it the giant Queensland groper, *Promicrops lanceolatus*. Norm was amused with the Fishman's knowledge of science. Fishman smiled, and said maybe it weighed nearly a ton, and joked, 'All that scientify stuff is easy. You could learn it in a day.' Norm knew the Fishman picked up everything he knew, foreign languages, cooking, taste in music, just from listening to the broadband radio. He declared, 'The radio has been my education.'

The creature had lain on the beach motionless. Norm looked at the tyre marks of a Toyota four-wheel drive vehicle. It had winched the animal out of the water and up onto the beach. They had sat down on the beach beside the animal. Perhaps they were waiting for it to die by keeping it company.

Well! he just goes on looking at you. He just goes on breathing and breathing through his lungs, pumping steadily, waiting. Its body had dark mottlings of brown and grey, which slowly, over time, dried out. The animal took on the appearance of being coated with thick armour, with its hard little eyes on either side of its broad head, still staring. 'I can feel him staring right through me,' Fishman said at the time. The white fishermen from the mine were hacking the flesh off the body of the groper with an axe. 'He takes a long time to die.' Meanwhile, they heard the animal grunt with the torture of each blow until its heart, buried deep inside its massive fleshy body, caved in to its long, agonising death. Norm knew other stories about the groper coming from the Dreamtime and continuing its story along the tracks in the sea which he had followed for Elias. And other kinds of stories about bad luck.

The old people would say never go to sea with a fisherman who had killed a groper. Everybody will tell you that. Better to let the groper live, or his ghost will live in the dreams of the fishermen who killed him, and when they go to sea, he will know what is in their heads, but he knows more about the sea than any fisherman, so he will be able to steal their luck away. This was the only way the spirit of such a colossal fish would ever go back to the sea.

The groper hole was in an abyss, an ancient reef crater of a sea palace, a circular fish city full of underground caves where the huge fish liked to live. A place where they could have returned to from the land in ancient times like the palaeontologists say, or skies if they flew like the elders say in the Law of the Dreamtime. Millions of years ago, what was it like? Remember! Were skies blue then?

Once before, Elias had brought Norm to the ocean's *pavonazzo* which shone from the depths to the surface with the colours of a peacock's tail. It was where the gropers had lived for centuries and even though they swam together, lived solitary lives in their own separate caves.

The groper caressing the side of the boat was instantly recognised by Norm as one of his friends who swam right up to his beach in the night, calling him to go fishing with them. 'Well! I'll be darned,' Norm said, awestruck perhaps, that he would actually reach his destination. He began whistling *Auld Lang Syne* of all things to the creature who had once been his groper's friend. Elias had become misguided like a fool into the politics of Uptown. He was far too busy to go fishing, too busy for the sea. He abandoned the lot, everything he knew, just for Uptown. Then it was just Norm, instead of Elias, who set off following the gropers along their sea tracks until they were out on the reefs. There, they would leave him behind while they herded up the reef fish, holding them in a tight circle around his boat, allowing Norm to spear as many as he wanted before releasing their hold.

There were other times on strong moonlit nights, when the giant fish swimming in packs would lead Norm up the river estuaries of yellow waters with the tide, to show him something special, places anyone would want to see, where the prawns were running in their millions. Ahead, the gropers swam in a semi-circle formation, trapping the prawns in snags of dead trees piled up by floods near the riverbank. These big fish living in schools of several dozens, contentedly stayed around Norm, then, without any visible sign, they would leave for the sea. Norm watched them swimming off quickly, knowing it was time for them to follow sea tracks which did not belong to him.

Relieved that he had not set out on an aimless journey, Norm followed the giant fish guiding him, steering him along a corridor above a steep underwater canyon. During this last phase of the journey, he had rowed most of the night, knowing he was nearly on top of the abyss where the fish lived, and the place from where they left to go on their spiritual journeys into the skies. Now he knew this was real again.

He noticed a different breaking pattern in the current line and when he touched the water, felt its temperature had risen. He thought he saw glimpses of the giant spirits as they clung, swimming closely to the sides of the underwater chasm. He imagined them looking up to the spirits of dead people twinkling as stars in the night ocean of the skies. While looking straight past Elias, he saw where the green-coloured water of the sea was beginning to swell as though there was something huge moving under the surface, forcing the water to surge up over the under-water reefs. Then, still many hundreds of metres away, he saw the sun spreading and hovering over the swell, the flashing, lit wings of all of the sea birds. Orienting his eye through the glare, he saw the birds diving into giant schools of sardine fish and returning to the sky.

More gropers appeared, following the side of the boat; their fins cut through the water and in their wake, they left small trails of swirling water. Many of the sea birds, after noticing a place to rest from their hovering in the hot breeze, flew in to land on any available surface on the boat. They assembled in large numbers, squabbling over space, forcing Norm to brush them off as fast as they would land. Norm was overjoyed. He swept the birds away with his hands, while still trying to row to keep up with the gropers, happily telling Elias he had found the right place.

'So, here we are old friend. Here we are and we actually made it. I brought you home.'

Norm gradually stopped rowing, contented to look on, while the sea swelled into life with the assembling gropers ploughing together through the water, vying for space next to the boat. He thought how remarkable the big fish were as they swam to join in with other groups, until many hundreds were clustering. Strangely, it reminded him of the Pricklebush families gathering at funerals. Even though the day was growing hotter and stiller with humidity, it did not lessen Norm's exuberance. He felt joy flooding from his heart. He swooshed away the white seagulls hovering between him and Elias and cried out, so far from land, 'This is paradise.' The birds lifted themselves up from the water and floated through the hot thermals like angels high up in the skies where the night meets the Milky Way. What say, he thought, considering he too could possibly fly. If he went back to Desperance or not, it did not matter, for in this place, he felt alive again. He had brought Elias's spirit to his final resting place while discovering man could do almost anything if it was meant to be. Even knowing he was an old man in reality, he could go to sea again and again, if he could still read the signs.

The fish completely surrounded the little tin boat, and it was any wonder to Norm that they did not bump into it. Initially, citing Acts of Contrition, and other prayers for the Stations of the Cross, Norm anticipated hell instead of heaven, after the moment where the weight of the milling fish would collide into and capsize the boat. The fish nudged the back of the boat through the water while Norm sat and watched, looking sadly at Elias, in the knowledge they would soon be parted forever. Finally, the fish moved away, creating a circle of clear water around the boat. Norm waited for several minutes, not sure of what to do next or what would happen. The fish did not move, and even while delaying the inevitable, he knew that he had to let Elias go.

'So, it's time old mate,' Norm said, as he balanced himself in front of Elias to untie the ropes holding him in place. During his journey, Norm had become quite nimble as he moved around the small vessel, as though he had always possessed a corklike buoyancy with the movement of water. 'It's time for you to go home.' He remembered the coral trout and undid the lid of one of several plastic containers kept behind the ends of their seats for storage. The fish in their bags were emptied from the container and Norm placed them in Elias's folded arms. Then he lifted his friend, knowing he had to let him go, but not wanting to either, because once he did, he knew he would be alone. Betrayed by feelings of loneliness, and a sadness which was only half reserved for Elias, he sat holding the body. He could feel Elias's spirit resisting his hold. Very carefully and reluctantly, Norm lifted Elias over the side of the boat and placed him into the strangely calm emerald green waters. Elias sank deeper and deeper, gently through the giant arms of water waiting at every depth to receive him, until finally, Norm could see him no more. Then he knelt down in the water on the floor of his little boat, and prayed for Elias, and was thankful he had brought his spirit safely to his final resting place.

In time, when he looked up again, he found himself alone. All the gropers had departed and the day was almost gone.

An unusually early darkness fell over the ocean on the day of Norm's burying Elias at sea...

How quickly the day had passed, and how incredible it seemed that burying Elias could have taken all day. Norm Phantom lay on the bottom of his boat reflecting on all that had happened. He longed for sleep. It occurred to him that perhaps the day had not passed quickly, and the eery half-light was actually his own eyes failing to see clearly, after weeks of water-reflected glare.

'Have you thought you might be going blind?' he asked himself, warning himself while staring upwards at the clouds, but too tired to care. He thought of the stingray's efforts to send him blind for invading its territory. It had made him its prey. Deliberately it had lingered within his vision throughout the day. Yes, deliberately making him stare into the glare, while it waited for the sun to fall low enough in the sky in an attempt to blind him by its reflection. Ho! Man overboard. Who? Where? You, you idiot who's yelling out mad. Poor Elias had called. Don't fall prey to the stingray. He knew he would have to be more careful if the stingray came again, or else no one would call *Man overboard*. No one would hear, not even himself. He would fall overboard, trying to chase after its smile.

They say the devils sitting around at sea could swim through a fishing man's mind like a virus, waiting for the perfect opportunity, in which very carefully, a devil switches your thoughts for his. Thinking about the sea could turn a man mad, although there were other things too that could change the look of the world, an old man's eyesight was not that reliable. He would be flat out seeing a dollar on the ground, Norm thought of himself crossly, for being old, looking at his white beard which ran through his fingers. Perhaps he would not make the journey back to Desperance this time. Exhaustion crept over him, entered his blood, and he could feel its flow pulsing through his body like lead. He settled down for a long sleep. He was overcome by the emotion of the final farewell to his one trusted friend. He told himself he would rig up and set sail tomorrow.

He was wrong. He should have set course home immediately and rowed away. Millions of small fish were journeying south underneath his boat. Near and far, the waters rippled with moonlit silver as they passed by. Norm did not notice this, nor their crowded bodies nudging his boat, as if signalling him to leave. He took no notice of the watery spirits in the distance to the north-west throwing themselves up from the sea as they warred with the warlords of the skies. He should have left straightaway while he thought of sleeping.

If he viewed the threatening skies or felt the fleeing fish, he refused to acknowledge the warnings. His whole being flowed away, rolling in the slight south-east swells which were both familiar and lulling, while he slept. Through his exhausted mind rolled an incoherent jumble of pictures, of guiding stars, sea currents flowing from all points of the compass, crossing the route of the sun. He grabbed from the forest of stars, selecting gliding currents from bundles of spears, and sun rays stacked for choosing as he began plotting, jigsawing bit by bit to form an imaginary nautical map for the journey back to Desperance. It was all he had to do, all it was going to take, and in the morning, or later on in the night, after sleep, he would be on his way.

He slept fitfully, forced to a state of wakeful consciousness sifting and sorting time, place and current. Sleep finally evaded him because his mind was alive, it was electrifying inside his head, where the sea kept dividing itself into greater and smaller horizontal and vertical columns, forming tributaries as thick as the matted hair of the universe, from where all manner of ocean currents were flowing, full to the brim with floodwaters. As he walked in this place, searching for an escape route, streams of water were running in every direction as though it was the history of his knowledge crisscrossing itself until it formed a watery spider-web, a polygon structure tangled with all of the local currents he ever knew in his mind, all tracks leading home.

Sleep finally arrived through a state of restlessness reminiscent of the meandering of an ant moving endlessly and abruptly, this way and that, through its world in the dirt. With each sharp clap of thunder he was drawn from dreams where he half expected to see Elias springing up from the depths below, as he imagined him trying to force his way through the water's surface until it tore apart. Norm could feel his heart racing as he watched the desperate face of Elias continuing his struggle to come back to life, while he in turn gasped for air on Elias's behalf, and battled to keep his own head above the surface. Then, drawn to the sight of Elias's hands gripping the side of the boat while trying to haul himself dead and all over the side, Norm woke himself up, just to escape his nightmare.

Peering into the moonlight he saw it had been nothing except large fish, a queenfish, a jewfish, a snapper, flying through the water and hitting it again side on with a thud. It was nothing compared to the sound the ghostly squawking seagulls made, and when he opened his eyes more fully, there they were, dozens gathered on every available space in his boat again, white wings lifting off with his slightest movement; and, white wings landing again, all of them, sitting there like angels staring at him.

Norm felt pains gathering in his chest, pushing his body in on itself. *Glory be to the Father* – he thought he was going to die, or else what? Already dead in the escort of angels? A beautiful prayer he liked, reaching the end – *As it was in the beginning, is now and forever shall be*, he called out in his sleep, only to be awakened again minutes later and again. The birds were ferocious and helped themselves, fighting like unscrupulous beggars at the full larder, gobbling down all the dried strips of fish from the Spanish mackerel hanging over the sides of the boat.

After a time he fell asleep again. He dreamt he watched the stars fall deeper through the water, where their light lit up the watery world of the gropers' palaces. He looked down into the depths, through the effects of water moving to and fro with the waves, until he saw the abyss that descended down the many levels of a Mesozoic bluff. The deep hole could have been the result of a Dreamtime volcano, or a meteorite the size of a mountain, or a city that had sunk deep down into the earth.

Every layer of this world was covered in sea gardens of coral, coloured all shades of red and pink, and glistening green sea vegetables, amidst olive seagrass fields waving in folds in the currents. A fish lives far better off than a dry old blackfella from Desperance, Norm Phantom considered, looking at this spectacle. He saw himself walking through these quivering gardens, searching for Elias, but all he found were bluey-green lobsters and crayfish mooching. They froze like little statues as soon as they saw him approaching, walking how a fisherman walks – guarding his every step, and singing out – *Elias! Elias!* Well! It was none of their business. They were only crustaceans darting under cover in his wake, exchanging fright for flight, escaping quickly, slipping back down into their burrows.

Awoken by the scuttering and scurrying of small creatures escaping with his dreams, he looked over the water and saw the big tank fish – gropers swimming together in congregations of fifty or more like dark clouds arriving from the distance. As each group moved upwards, they surfaced loudly in volumes of water, raising their bodies high out of the sea, which were splashing down like waterfalls behind them. The creatures did not stop when they reached the highest level they could before falling back into the sea. Norm wiped their salty spray from his face, as he studied them swimming through the ocean of air, to ascend into the sky world of the Milky Way. They became specks in the sky until they were so far away in the distance, they became a cloudy blur in the celestial heavens of stars and spirits.

Afterwards, the only disturbance they left behind were little eddies in the water that made the boat roll more frequently. Norm, drifting in and out of sleep, caught a glimpse of the fish become stars shooting back in the skies, and finally, the night caravan moving further and further away on its journey. He knew at once Elias was up there with them. Gone thank goodness in another form than the old hunched-back dead man who would have gone off to heaven carrying the basket cases of Desperance along with him. Elias was taking the journey back to his own country, or the place he wanted to call home. Norm was ecstatic with his generous vision of Elias. He knew for the rest of his life he could stop looking out for him. He would no longer resemble a man. He would be like a star. A man like a star. Fish stars. Numerous reminiscences slipped by in Norm's search for the sign which would distinguish Elias and make him clearly visible for all times. Nothing happened. The book had been closed on their friendship. So, by jingo this was it. Nothing left, except the wretched shell left behind in sun and sea-salt worn-thin cotton clothes who wondered if he were a man.

In the early morning, Norm woke to the startled cries of the seagulls. He pulled his jacket over his head to keep the light away from his face and lay there inert, deciding whether he felt exhausted from dreams, or from too little sleep. Above the harsh awakening, the vivid memory of the Groper exodus stayed clear in his mind, until the deafening racket of squawking birds resounded in his ears, echoing as though the sound was being slapped back from distant hills.

Peering out from under the jacket, he was shocked to see an even bigger assembly of birds had gathered on the water and in the skies since yesterday. As far as his eye could see, more and more birds filled the skies. The surrounding sea had turned almost stark white with the huge flocks that had assembled on the waters, lolling to the slight rise and fall of the flowing waves. As he stood up and clapped his hands the birds flew off his boat, but instantly came back. Then he understood and said, '*Kangolgi.*'

It was the time when the migratory birds were coming back to the coastline of the Gulf, some travelling on to other parts of the country. Above the travelling birds he now saw the long morning glory cloud of the Wet season looming over his boat. Any local knew instantly what the long tubular cloud was. Stretching from the western to the eastern horizon so low in the sky, Norm thought it might touch him as it descended to the horizon of the sea. Now it occurred to him that the birds were travelling along a special route made from the evaporation left by the heat in the cooling atmosphere by the trail made by the big fish on their journeys into the sky world of summer. The cloud band would soon evaporate, but would return again and again in the morning, until the air became saturated with the humidity of the gatherings of enormous storm clouds. Then when the heavy rains finally stopped and the waters became calmer the following year, the big fish would return, as was the natural cycle of things.

A world without end, *Amen...*

Whispering prayers, Norm Phantom awoke at dawn on his second morning at the gropers' place to a seascape locked inside a heavy mist. The birds had lifted high into the skies and were nowhere in sight when he set his lines for fishing. The day was good, fine weather, and Norm had decided he would fish first, replenish what the birds had eaten, before he left on the long journey home. Phew! Behold! Valuable time failed to blemish a stubborn man who decided he needed fish from one part of the ocean and no other. His mind was made up, and once the task of fishing was under way, lines dropped, there was really no stopping him. The journey back would just have to sit around and wait it out with the fishing, where time stood still. Norm Phantom's time was a spectacular clock which rang the alarm once he caught enough: exactly ten lines bearing a large snapper each, more than enough to last a few days, after throwing a few back into the ocean, after hours of boring *andante* breeze, then it would be time to go.

It was a funny day because the mist, godamn it, did not lift, nor did the fish bite. Norm sat patiently in his boat rolling with the waves all day long and waited for a line to move. The oars idled, he lost track of time, the captain did not row away.

On the third day there was still no sign of fish and scarce movement in the hunched figure of Norm, dispassionately waiting over his baited lines while looking off into the misty distance of hidden wilderness. The sea now a divine limbo under a membrane of whiteness, undecided how to create a new day. Norm felt sure of the movement of ocean swells underneath the boat, still rocking very steady in his map of the rhythms of the south-east winds passing from the other side of the globe, while he kept a pinpoint image of his exact location. Otherwise in the stillness and quiet, he looked like he had died; no fish tugged on the dead lines. No surface waves rose for the absence of localised winds. He saw nothing through the murky grey waters aswelling.

Obsessed with a single mission, he hissed through closed lips, 'Give me the bloody schools of sardines.' He remained adamant fish would come sooner or later; they had to for this was an ideal spot. He kept watching for the large predator fish herding the bait fish. In a location such as this, they become locked in a terminal corral, but where in the sea could they be?

Not one fish of any size, large or small, appeared above the surface under his hawk-eyed surveillance. There was a detectable sea swell changing in the deep water currents many fathoms below, but Norm, the sea king of fishing in the Gulf, did not notice anything happening at all. He was deciding, if not how morose he felt, whether he was experiencing the loneliest and longest day of his life.

He cut his hair, hacking chunks off close to his skull, with the sharpened edge of his fish gutting knife. Staring down into the water, not noticing the fast moving current, he watched the long strands of his hair, then his whiskers, fall into the water, and the indeterminable pattern of their floating away. The sea, occupying his thoughts, reminded him of how life is always haunted by death. How off-guard had Norm Phantom been when the dark shadow of the sea lady engulfed him – nobody would ever know.

The mist lifted rapidly, as though the grand curtain had been swiped apart by a magician who in his unexpected performance, banished the broken pieces of small ethereal clouds off into the sea. With the horror and shock of her unexpected arrival, Norm flinched at the wind driving him in his shoulder blades with the inhuman heaviness of two very strong hands. First, she pushed and kneaded, willing him to *stand up*, shaking the boat. Her invisible touch she replaced with a bolt of static electricity which dipped his every movement into her stinging body. A crackling feminine wail ran around him, embracing him, coaxing compliance to her desires. There was no denying it, the voice of the wind was relaying her needs, and could easily have been deciphered, even by the silly old fool Nicoli Finn, if he had been alive to hear it. Norm did stand, still as a statue, and looked into the sea as she beckoned for him to leap. *The fine sea birds have made an opening just for you*, she hissed. *Leap.* Each time she repeated the word, it rang like the echo chamber of an enthusiastic audience at a spectacular performance of the wizard magician, cheering on the faint-hearted volunteer to his act, *Leap! Leap! Leap!*

'But Elias has gone,' Norm kept repeating to the sea lady, as though it was his duty to correct her. He stood in the rocking boat, steadying himself while he argued with her, half captured just by acknowledging her existence, while from the sensible part of his mind slipped an ever fainter desire to go home. After so long alone talking to himself, he enjoyed the sound of a womanly voice. He of course longed to go with her to look for Elias, already knowing if he found Elias he would leave her, jilt her, leave her flat. He even saw how comfortable he would look, reliving his story, how he escaped the sea lady, back at home together with Elias. But he still denied himself abandonment to her body. His wily stubbornness to fight against lust was exhausting. *Stop making excuses*, listening to her hiss on uncontrollably. *See those warriors coming! Look right and left! This is their fighting ground! Go now! Save yourself! Jump!* She made the sea heave.

Heavens only know how he managed to keep standing in the rolling boat, but his body, wavering with the rolls like a spring, somehow maintained balance, while every last bit of his bodily strength planted his feet to the bottom of the boat. She shoved him roughly in the back again, before containing him in her embrace when he looked like falling, then changed tactics by whispering in his ear about the old wars of the families. She was high speed, like an adding machine rattling off the local history of centuries in minutes, exact time, precise location, whose boundary it really was, the reason why others thought it was theirs, then explaining again and again, by going back over time in endless forays, the mistakes of each battle.

She knew too much. Naming the people involved, the pain and suffering inflicted, who fell, what misunderstandings lingered on and grew again like cancer, she was a running account of battles which had gone on for centuries. Minutes later she called him *War Lord*, and started naming his battles, showing him a celebration of his life in pain, while intertwining the speed of her dictation by whispering the way out, an escape from the same family wars continuing on and on and on. *Go on now, come out of the way of the unhappy dead, be with me.*

Her tidings were bereft of glory. Could she have lied? Norm tried to understand the barrage of her verbosity by choosing at random, names to slot into rows in the crossword puzzle of forgotten history. As the puzzle grew larger, forming new offshoots, she would jump in front, too smart like, trying to squeeze in her own words, but Norm knew the game better and would keep crossing her out with the right word. He understood perfectly that the winds were coming from two directions now – south-east and north-west, colliding in squalls, after the mists had long ago been blown apart. She continued trying to distract him by calling out the names of all the dead people he had ever known. She described the battles they were now waging with each other in the afterlife. He succumbed. Her knowledge was greater than his own. She had condemned him as a person of ignorance. She had crippled his mind. Defeated, he saw a new truth in himself. He was just an old sailor of such lackadaisical efficiency, he could no longer see the seasoned helmsman. In truth, he was dependant on a captain to navigate the way home, and in great peril of losing his life.

More was the pity, the old fishing men at Desperance would say, to find a fisherman at sea acting like a gambler losing the game, after he became too greedy for fish. Sad loss for a sort of person who had lost track of the end of the day. You hear of the ones addicted to fishing who could not leave the fishing hole, not knowing when enough was enough. These fish gamblers never knew when to stop. Well! It was the truth of the matter.

The story goes that those doomed men became lost in a sea boiling with dense schools of large fish – like salmon on the run, balling the bait schools. So, they followed the dark patches like clouds in the water. It was the worst kind of fever, following fish night and day for days, pulling fish in, throwing them on the pile, stacking up more and more. By the time their overloaded boats sank, even the birds had become fat. They sank with their boats, craving with their whole heart and soul the odour of rotting fish gut. There have been some fish gambling survivors. You got to pity them, the ones you see hanging around Desperance with that funny, faraway look on their faces – like a stuffed mullet. They skulk around looking like flea-bitten dogs, running from corner to corner, hiding behind fences and in other people's yards, escaping from no one because they think someone is trying to stop them heading back to sea. It was hardly surprising to see their crying and gnashing families rushing up and down the Shire Council's roads, swinging around their long sticks, trying to chase their crazed relative away from the boats. Do not feel pity when you see a family flogging the fish gambler half unconscious. Don't waste your breath calling the government who own all the essential services like social welfare in cities down South. No one can shake the magnetic forces put in a fisherman's skull by the sea woman.

Caught in the sphere of the sea lady, Norm saw, over in the distance, ghostly dark waves moving like haunted spirits. In the air he heard a melancholy swishing monologue humming and drumming the advance of the front moving helter-skelter towards him, while up in the skies, its spiral disappeared into the heavens. Norm, centre stage, prepared himself, for he was a brave man, and he was warrior-like, in readiness to face her army of mourning ladies.

He remembered the old people watching these clouds from the long grass along the shores of Desperance and turning away, they always asked the same old question, *Say! Do you know who they are boy?* Yes! Norm knew the widows. They belonged to a life-long premonition – one which linked his destiny and theirs: the eternity of the disappointed dead travelling in the seasonal storms of the summer monsoon. Watching these clouds in their haphazard race around the skies, he saw their glorious watery costumes of mourning colours lined with silver sprays that looked like torn lace, decorated with little unstitched pearls.

Each widow rose to wail in majestic heights, showering him

with teary froth, as they tore forward with the faster north-west winds. The haunted spectres loomed higher and higher into the skies until they could no longer hold their dignified pose, and collapsed down on themselves with a spectacular and extravagant chain of lightning and thunder above his head. Norm applauded. Bravo! he called appreciatively to each dramatic gesture. Salty tears poured from his windswept eyes. Each flawless performance made space on the celestial stage for a throng of others, each as large and foreboding as the other and with as much power to whip up even more exciting winds.

By executing the dwindling south-easterlies, these new winds produced in Norm a lightness, a spring in his step, he would have run if he was not in the middle of the ocean. For half a year, particularly in their peak, the south-eastern winds had roared through the cracks of houses after midnight, looking to snaffle humanity from sleeping people's hearts. Now this dying force, outnumbered and outflanked, could only fight back with the weapons of those Desperance homes: so many disappointed dreams and the doomed tenor's song of unrequited love. Oh my! Norm reminded himself he had better stay alert while sizing up the strength of the storm, unless he wanted to be remembered as a theorist who drowned in his own daydreams. This was how the opposing trade winds interlocked in war, blew the top off the lid, and out would fly the navigator's mental map of the groper's travel line.

The storm intensified. The currents resulting from the two opposing trades colliding with each other lifted the surface waters to look like an enormous wart jutting out from the sea. Norm locked his arms around the steel seat of his boat while it rolled and tumbled into the lull. He prayed as his body smashed down on the bottom of the boat and swore, before tumultuous lashings of sea water tumbled over him. He had moments to spare when the boat rose rapidly out of the water, and only enough time to gasp a mouthful of air which he fully expected would be his last, when the boat tilted to ride out the next wall of water, before falling again into the watery dungeon below.

He could have been an ant on a leaf for all that it mattered. Hours went by and his body felt as though it had been broken into a hundred pieces, his flesh pulped into a bloody mash. He screamed for Elias, 'Come and get me brother, I don't want to die alone,' but could not hear the sound of his voice. Reverberating back in his ears, was the thunderous crushing of waves exploding one after the other. Over and over he was thrown up or thrown down, but his arms stayed locked to the boat. He thought perhaps he was already dead but through his spirit, in some bizarre twist of fate, was destined to remain conscious of everything that was happening to him.

Through hoarse lips swollen with bruises, he tried to whisper, forcing words to form in a throat that felt dry as a desert stone from taking in too much sea water. The effort stuck like a ball that was lodged painfully in the back of his throat. 'Take me,' he whispered when the words finally came, willing Elias to come, and believing he would just slip away. What faith he had, listening hard, convinced he had heard Elias tapping under the floor of the boat. Yes! Yes! Elias had come back but could not do anything to help him, Norm knew, Elias was there, trying to come aboard to help him.

Finally, the legions of warring spectres ceased fire, the waves dropped, the storm subsided, and in the skies, the viper's box sprang open. The victorious north-west winds, still crazed into conquering the seasonal change, blew the heavy rain in horizontal lashings that blistered through the sea. Norm lay broken and semi-conscious in the salty waters on the floor of the boat. His body throbbed, his skin was raw to the flesh, and his ears remained deafened by the sound of the world into which he had intruded. He shifted himself with relief out of the stinging sea water, as he felt movement underneath his little boat driving him away with great speed.

Lying there, too injured to move, unable to lift his face into the screeching rain, Norm only saw patchy clouds resting low on the water, whenever the rain eased. Occasionally, he saw large flocks of sea birds travelling in the same direction. Even in the storm, he knew the birds would not lose their orientation. They would re-route and head for land, and sometimes when he looked closer, he could see that the birds were actually sailing with the wind, barely working their wings, as though they were being blown along.

Many hours had past since the storm had started and every time Norm closed his eyes, over and over, wanting to sleep, he struggled to stay awake. Remembering to pray, he started reciting the Act of Contrition, 'Oh! My God We are sorry. Forgive us our trespasses,' and then he stopped. Church had been a long time ago. Pausing momentarily, he tried again to recite the prayer, before stopping to linger once again on the perplexing word *trespass*. Trespass had been a big word in his life. It protected black men's Law and it protected white men. It breathed life for fighters; it sequestered people. The word was weightless, but had caused enough jealousies, fights, injuries, killings, the cost could never be weighed. It maintained untold wars over untold centuries – *trespass*. Trespassing was the word which best described his present situation, and it occurred to him that he was wrong to have taken this journey with Elias in the first place. He should have just let the girls dispose of the body. Yet he called, 'Push the boat Elias and don't worry about me.'

But he could not stay awake, and the last thing he saw spinning through a labyrinth of maritime tunnels was himself. He knew at once that he was entering a spiritual country forbidden to all men and their wives and their children's children. In his dream he saw himself, as if looking from above, in the aquatic seafaring vessel called *Trespass*. As he watched the boat, he saw himself gliding along with the wind-driven current in a straight line. He passed place upon place where people once lived in the sea. All were devastated but each destination in turn propelled him into another, while pushing him further away into stranger places that had once existed. Each of these sacred places was wretched of hope, yet somehow capable of snatching the faith he himself had difficulty in holding, until he felt so depleted he knew neither where he was, or how to retrace the route he had been taken through to navigate his way home.

If he hoped to find his way back, he knew his hopeless task was to visualise and commit to memory the multitude of landmarks. An unfamiliar voice pointed out that these were the wrecked artefacts of an ancient past fossilised in parts of the sea where the likes of people living, who ought to leave well enough alone, should never have ventured. What he saw he knew should never have been seen again, but all the while, he was unable to turn his head and look away. He heard the names of places in a harsh language which was both strange and uninviting. Passing through the tunnels of the watery labyrinth, he noticed the sides were lined with a flowing substance not unlike slime, but when he looked closer, he saw these were ancient webs. The longest broken threads of these webs joined others in an entangled mass. They reached out like tentacles attempting to ensnare the boat as it passed through their half-woven sacs. He envisioned himself entombed in their secret places of antiquity. Forever, until one day his spirit began crystallising into a towering wave where the trade winds meet locked in battle. In this future of eternity, he lived on as a fighter of wars that were never resolved in life by becoming a death spirit, a thing so strange, it was perpetually salvaging little pieces of humanity by preying on lone seamen such as he once was himself.

Norm awoke suddenly, startled by a breathless sensation of drowning in his dreams. The rain had eased, and the little aluminium boat continued to move at a rapid speed, as though being pushed by the invisible hands of the sea on and on in its flow with the currents. Norm knew he was moving in a north-easterly direction, and there was nothing he could do. All he could feel was that Desperance was now a long way south-west from the direction of the flow. Sometime in the night, the wind dropped suddenly, and the world seemed a better place. For a further two days the boat drifted with the movement of the north-east flowing currents. Whenever Norm had the strength to try the oars, he would attempt to row, but found he could not against the will of the sea. Each time, his oars would lie flat on the surface, and would be swiftly wiped back to the side of the boat. Norm knew it was hopeless for him to change course for Desperance.

Throughout the day, he trawled for fish, and was able to catch enough trevally to start eating regular meals again. When the sun was overhead, he sat with his jacket over his head for shade, even though the heavy clouds stayed close to the waters. Sometimes he quietly sang country and western songs as though borrowing well-used treasures from his house. While he was lost in the music he visualised each of his children growing alongside a particular piece. Otherwise for the life of him he could not remember what any of his children looked like. Always he took careful notice of the movement of birds reappearing over the sea, observing their direction, where they were heading, where they had come from. Then, on the third day, he was awakened by a sound he had long forgotten. In the first dull light of morning spreading across the waters, there were several green snakes streaking across the skies. As the formations moved closer, he was relieved to see many birds flying towards him. 'Land! Yes! Land! Where are my oars?' He knew at once that these were only common old seagulls, but they were like the angels of the sea. He was glad to see them, now he knew land was not far away. Quickly he began to row. At last, across the rise of the dented prow, as the boat rode the first breaker over the bar, he was able to see a spectacular cloud of mist sitting on top of the ocean. The surrounding waters were encased in the silver rays of sunlight. Soon, he was over the next, then others, until the boat slid through the shallow waters up onto the beach.

Standing tall, resembling an exclamation mark on the putrid-smelling beach, Norm Phantom had no idea where he was, except that he was as inconsequential as the millions of dead fish strewn with other decaying marine life at his feet. No more, no less, and as futile and forgotten, but he could not accept that this was how it was; he was screaming, with all the ravenous sea birds gathered in their tens of thousands in a white flurrying cloud up and down the misty beach, 'I am not one and the same as...' Dead fish. Dead fish. The two words were locked in his throat.

The stillness of the wet bush behind him reached out like an open mouth over the edge of the sand. The sense of foreboding that he interpreted as his doomed fate made his blood run cold. He dared not enter its domain, at least not yet. Who knew what ghosts of women walked slowly through the bushlands? There but not wanted, but there so cheap, it was almost stupid not to take the offer. He visualised their taunting bodies opening and closing, lips moving and unable to hear their words. He looked out to the sea and the opening and closing of the clouds.

There had never been a moment in his life he thought, as pointless as it was now. Over the top of the deafening bird cries and the occasional sound of distant thunder, he berated the cruel contradictions of the sea gods, the spirits of the heavens, for keeping him alive. What twist of fate was there in being dumped in a hideous graveyard, this pointless massacre of life? He spoke with arrogance and irritation of his safe arrival, calling it a joke – pure and simple, as though he could talk his way out of the present, remake the past, and order the future.

'Sea! You listening to me at this moment I am speaking to you? You are full of cruelness, you are like women, you sea! Have you finished with me yet or what?'

In reply, the sulky waves barged forward, banged, thumped and dumped their debris further up onto the beach. He jumped out of the way but it was his right to censure the sea. Though he was very weak and feeble from his ordeal, and overcome with emotion from what he had endured, it was his right to say something. So what if he had lost some of his marbles in his screwed up head? 'I know what I am saying,' he hollered. So with a screw loose here and there, he flounced around the rotting carcasses as though he could not smell their sickening stench. His eyes bulged unnaturally from the sockets where his dehydrated skin clung to the crevices of his bones. The wretched shorts and singlet he wore the night he rowed away from Desperance were now torn to shreds. There was no harm in letting off a bit of steam. It felt right to let all the old sea phantoms know that a man like Norm Phantom, even reduced to a mere skeleton, had more important things to do with his life than being dumped ungraciously on a place that might not even exist. He had heard of these places before. Men caught in limbo, who were condemned to live on and on in uncharted, empty patches of the sea.

The mighty sea heaved and sighed. Waves regardless of talk crashed on the beach. The wind whistled past overhead. The sea birds sang their songs here and there in their nooks and crannies late in the afternoon. Surveying the beach like a fugitive searching for a possible escape route, Norm muttered on, convincing nobody but himself of his deeply held convictions about his close relationship with the sea. He was not like other people. Plunderers! Rioters! Tyrants! So the good friend of the sea lamented his misfortune under his breath, of being locked in like a prisoner, of being reduced to a little man.

In this state of mind he started to see signs like neon lights sitting on signposts jutting out from the ocean. Road signs the equivalent of those on the highway south of Desperance – Drive Slow. Slow Down. Cattle crossing. Seasonal flooding to be expected. He read all the signs and tried to interpret them as messages from the spirits. He watched tiny insects devouring rotten fish flesh and he interpreted them as messengers, or disguised spirits. He deferred to a guardian angel looking over his shoulder – an old bearded image of himself that could have been his own shadow. He thought of the clagginess of the clay-pan soil, and was drawn to particular specks of sand on the beach which he thought might have originated from Desperance. Each speck was as insignificant as the other. He aligned the specks into a map for it was his normal way of understanding the world. His eyes darted from one sign to the other, as he tried to link them into a lifeline, a map which would give him reason.

The bush was still with the late afternoon lull from the wind, yet it still felt as though it was full of wild women slowly walking back and forth as they watched his progress on the beach. He needed to be heard over the silence. It was as though the sheer marvellous miracle of bringing human speech though silence had overwhelmed him. He talked and talked, telling the most fantastic of stories about himself. When the wind returned at half past ten at night, it was surprised to find him still talking after six hours, and it jumped at the chance of revenge. Sand flew up from the beach like little dust storms and wrapped around his fallen words as though it was picking up the rubbish. The sand cut into his face like attacking ants, forcing him to close his eyes, yet this did not stop him. On and on he continued, talking to the Gods, who had stopped ordering fate just to listen about the strange town called

Desperance. Sea mist poured in from the ocean to salt his wounds. The taunted waves threw themselves higher up onto the beach as though they were the bottom lip of a mouth sulking, trying to reach out to him. The bush line trembled in anticipation. Plying the sea with words was a strange game but wiser men have done the same. Men tend to judge nature's efforts to save them.

The industrious guardian angel of good sense strenuously urged Norm to move away into the bushland. In its catlike mimic of a bowerbird, it cited the industry of ants, as well as the clever beetles turning over the putrid sand, the crabs darting from hole to hole – 'Go,' it said, uselessly urging him to retreat to the bush. He refused to listen to a shadow, for he believed he had formed his own map of the signposts forecasting his future. Finally, he collapsed on the beach, where he sat with his strangely protruding eyes watching the waves roll through the night, too afraid to turn his back for one minute from the ocean, least the rough wave, hiding in the black night, leap out and take him.

Or had he become possessed by the sea's mesmerising monotony of endless waves rising and falling, slap like they did, onto the beach? A fearful scene was unfolding under the roll. Just metres away in the murky grey waters, rolling with dead fish and their relatives, the sand, and slime-coated shells, he saw a city of faces which belonged to dead people staring at him through the undertow. Where even over the din of the waves crashing, and the intermittent raucous cries of squabbling birds trying to sleep, he heard windy voices seducing him into the trap for which he had been waiting.

Out yonder, in the deeper waters, the sea woman was lurking around, waiting for him in the seagrass meadows swaying backwards and forwards under the water. This was what happened; sea men knew she could be the size of an ordinary woman or she could make herself as big as the sea itself. When he was a boy long ago he had dreamt what she looked like. He saw her running about in the ocean of Desperance with hair longer than her body reaching out around her like the poisonous tentacles of the box jellyfish. And her grey skin, coarse and hard was similar to the texture of a shark, although not clean like a shark. She was covered with sheer green-blue slime that clung and hung from her body like the lace which she had collected from her jaunts, in the slime-filled caves along the ocean floor.

So the night passed into day with Norm Phantom still ensconced on the beach as though he had settled there perma-nently to live. His first decision was to stay on the beach to guard the boat. He neither ate nor drank as he guarded the only piece of insurance he had of leaving the land he had been thrown on. His mind hung onto limbo, a delicate branch, as leafless as it was devoid of trust.

That night, a mist crept over him while he slept on the beach. This was when he heard the devil woman Gardajala singing out from the bush. If he had been awoken by her lewd song he did not know, but he had seen her eyes shining like two golden coins – *like dollars* – as she stared at him through the grass on top of the rise. She kept crying how much she wanted him to come up there to her, but he was stalwart, steadfastly maintaining his repugnance as he eschewed her enticements. She was like no other woman he had ever heard, calling her sexual innuendo without shame. 'You don't want me, old woman prostituting yourself, I am crippled up, dried up like a prune,' he called back, in a mocking voice, speaking back at the bush like one of the old senile men of Desperance's Fisherman's Hotel.

But she kept on crying out loud for him, saying he was going to crack, saying maybe he wanted to go up there and keep her warm. 'Quiet woman!' Come on, just one night, just until dawn. 'You got no shame. Quiet or you will stir up herself over there in the sea watching.' The bartering for her desires to quench his, and his to quench hers, went on until he could stand it no longer. He could almost feel his hands touching her body covered in yellow grass where she lay waiting for him. Miserable in his physical needs of lust, hunger and thirst, he strapped his hands over his ears, as he forced himself to recite over and over, 'Don't go thinking of her, don't go thinking of her.' Faster and faster he sang his little lines, at such an exciting pace, while pressing his hands hard onto his ears, and she in return begged faster, and he cried singing faster and thinking of her, wanting her, and she cried, until their ecstasy was consummated. Then, they both curled up in foetal positions on their earth beds, hers of grass, his of sand, and went to sleep.

Chapter 9
Bala, the child of hope

Oh! Magic big time. A land full of tricks. The sea full of spirits. Poor land woman devil Gardajala. The sea woman, whose name must not be mentioned because she might be listening, far out at sea, was spinning herself into a jealous rage. She was almost cyclonic, if you could believe in the power of her magic. She canvassed and corralled her armies. Her movement was slow. The low cloud band radiated out a sea of mist that had already touched her old enemy Gardajala by the time Norm woke from his sleep. And all the while, all poor old Gardajala could do was to raise herself up into a *wirriwidji* whirly wind to throw her spiteful hand full of dirt at the sea.

Everyone in the Pricklebush knew of the poisonous countries out at sea, places where it was too dangerous for a man to go, where the spirits dwelt, like the Gundugundu men who were even more dangerous than Kadajala, the white-man devil, and those of the unhappy warring spirit warriors of the old wars. Gundugundu spirits, if riled up enough, could kill a man straight out in the middle of their stormy wars – not just leave him halfway crashing into the ocean like what happened to Norm Phantom. The movement of Gundugundu was always swift. Faster than a fish or bird. No living person would be capable of seeing them with their eyes.

Only the old people blind in the eye watched them flying

through the air inside of cyclones. Those old people used to tell stories to their families when the cyclones were about. Perhaps their stories were an invention of their imagination whenever they got a funny feeling under their skin, but whatever it was, it was uncanny how they always knew when someone was going to die in mysterious circumstances by a bolt of lightning. One would never know if it was the will of God, or whatever was out there in those waters of the oceans, but everyone in the Pricklebush expected to hear the news before someone died of mysterious circumstances during a cyclone. So say: *Oh! No! They never walked to pick up souls. They got legs alright, and feet too, but funny thing that, because they do not use them, maybe they can't but just fly about instead.* Once a child asked if they had any shoes. Some did. Some wore something on their feet. Sometimes these spirits had to travel over land, travelling many hundreds of kilometres to carry out their ghastly business, but still, they never used their legs and feet to walk. Whenever they came to kill, it all happened in a split second. Afterwards, utter calm was restored.

The boat was stuck fast in the sand where the ocean had dumped it on the previous day. Now, as another king tide built deepening trenches over the sand, Norm failed to notice the water encroaching around the sides of the boat and those watery arms cunningly drawing back enough sand to steal it. Norm heard a small voice telling him to save the boat, but he refused to listen to voices, just as he had refused to listen to the sound of his stomach telling him to eat. Instead, he prayed for matches. 'God help me to make a fire. I got to have a fire tonight to keep those devils away.' The small voice said he would make the fire if Norm would help to move the boat up onto higher ground. But Norm refused to acknowledge the voice. 'You got to light a fire first before moving the boat,' Norm said, puckering up one side of his lips that indicated he wanted the fire lit back up towards the bush, without turning his head around to look at it.

Suddenly – Norm thought he was becoming even more delirious – the aluminium boat was moving. 'Hold up,' Norm grunted, but his movement was slow and weak. As he struggled to get to his feet, he saw that the boat was not being moved by the incoming tide, but through the efforts of a small five- or six-year-old boy with his head bent to the back of the boat, struggling to push it higher up the beach. 'Hold up, Will,' Norm said, instantly recognising the boy as his own son, but the child ignored him. Norm looked at the boy who was knee-deep in water, desperately pushing with all his might. Norm could not believe it, for there was Will, as though all those intervening years had not passed. Now, on his feet, somehow with the restored strength of a man half his age, Norm was able to help the boy until the boat was lugged higher onto the beach.

Once again, the old man's weakness forced him to sit down on the sand, where he slipped into the luxury of his wandering thoughts which were more alive than the busy boy. Yet, undeniably, he could see for himself that the boy was real live flesh and blood. 'You are a good boy, Will, always a good boy,' he said, but the boy was not listening. The boy, with his brown skin, covered in sand and dried sea salt, and wind-swept brown hair, had leapt into the boat, and was rummaging around through the plastic containers.

'Can I use these?' he asked Norm, while holding out some fishing line and hooks.

'Sure, Will,' Norm smiled, 'run off quick smart and get the rest of them kids to help you.'

The boy looked at Norm for a moment and said, 'Alright, I'll get us some fish.' Then without hesitation he was off, running up the beach, leaving Norm looking at the waves and saying half-heartedly, 'And tell your Mother I am here too.'

The afternoon passed by as the sun receded lower in the horizon, until finally the clouds became blood red, and the water looked as though it was on fire. Norm thought Will ought to be coming back any minute now. It would not be easy to have to find him in the dark. His old impatience of his children returned, and triggered his grumbling about how they never listened to what they had been told. 'Well! I have told him. Told him many times about how much those devil-devils were looking for good-looking kids like him in the night.' He began to hear the devil woman's voice crying and singing as she moved through the bushes behind the sand bank. She complained about how her family would just turn up whenever it suited them: *But you are not like proper family. You don't know what love is.*

'He's a good boy. Always listens to me,' Norm tried to reassure himself, ignoring the bush woman. He looked up the beach where the boy had gone, half expecting to see the rest of the family coming back. The expectation of seeing his little children rollicking around as they always did gave him pleasure. He held the joyful memory and took greater pleasure wiping aside all the whispering doubts in the back of his mind, questioning what was real: saying the boy was false. Not Norm though, he chose the best times as his parable. Sand, sun, happy family. It freed him from the impossible future that showed no easy path to the home he had left.

Life was good waiting for the children to come down to the beach, and he found himself promising this and promising that. Everything would be good from now on. Everything. It was so good to start again, to be given one's time over – another chance. The waves kept roaring in, and old Gardajala started up in her windy song, singing, *There was nothing as foolish as a silly old fool who lost his boat, lost his wife and lost his house, his children too, and what is he going to do, sitting by himself, lonely by himself, and coming by himself, to me*. She could make a singsong all night out of nothing. He knew other women like that.

Over his head, she blew treacherously taunting words in her wind. He had ducked for cover behind the boat, when all at once, he saw her long hair blow out of the bush in a gigantic whorly wind, carrying a solemn haze of red dust, large flocks of sea birds, and seagulls, in among clouds of white down feathers from the rookeries in the swamps over the sand rise.

When she disappeared out to sea to find her opponent, he was again surprised when he looked down the beach for the boy. What came instead of children after the dust, feathers and birds, was the screeching of a lone cockatoo flying up the beach towards him. It reminded Norm of his bird Pirate. 'Where's your flock, boy?' the bird hollered out its question, like so, whenever he clapped eyes on Norm walking out of the house in Desperance. The bird fell out of the wind like a little spirit. The little black eyes peered at Norm. It looked and looked, until suddenly it announced matter-of-factly, in a flat voice, 'What are you doing?' Less feathered than Norm remembered him, the bird's remaining feathers, enough for flight, were covered with filth and oil.

'Hello old boy, how did you get here?' Norm said, putting out his hand for the bird to come to him.

A spray of sand went flying through the air as the boy landed smack bang between them. The bird jumped back in fright.

'What the hell you go and done that for?' Norm asked as he retreated his hand with its twiddling fingers.

'You leave him alone,' said the boy running to swoop up the bird in his arms.

'You are handling him too much with your filthy hands. No wonder his feathers are falling out,' Norm said, chastising the child's dirty fish-oil-stained shorts and fish-smelling body.

'No it aren't.'

'Yes, it is.'

'No it aren't.'

The boy ploughed back up through the sand towards the bush where the whirlwind had passed with the bird perched on his head. The sea wind blew down over the top of them. Funny sort of kid, Norm thought, briefly watching the boy, reasoning it was not like Will at all to start behaving like that. A half an hour would have passed before the boy came back down the beach, bird still sitting on his head, carrying a blue plastic bucket. When he reached Norm, the boy plonked the bucket down in front of him, then he took his own place in the sand some distance away.

'Nice fish,' Norm said, looking at four charred-baked barra covered in fire ash stuffed into the bucket. 'You want some Will?'

The boy looked at Norm, shook his head with the bird on top, and sat waiting for him to eat.

'Where's Mum?' Norm asked eventually, after he had eaten one of the fish. He felt nauseous from eating too fast.

'None of your business,' the boy replied.

'Course it's my business, your Mum's my business, that bird on your head is my business too. And, you are my business.'

'Bird aren't yours.'

'Look Will.'

'And I aren't Will either.'

'Oh! Then who am I if you are not Will.'

'*Malbu*, I don't know who you are, and my name is not Will either.'

'Old man am I? What's your name then if you are not Will either?'

The boy points to the sky and says, 'Bala.'

'Since when did that happen?'

'That's my name Malbu – my Mum and Dad called it to me.'

'Your Mum and Dad eh! And their name?'

'My Mum,' whispered Bala. 'Well! Her name was Hope and me Dad is Will Phantom.'

Norm stopped eating. He placed the fish back into the bucket. He looked hard at the boy. He did not know Will had a child but then, why would he know anything? Who told him a thing anymore? Of all the things Will had to go and do to the family. 'I am going to kill that bastard when I see him.' Yes, Norm decided on the spot, Will had gone too far this time. The old hostilities jumped from his heart into his head. Instantly, there was no sign of Will in the child anymore. Only the family resemblances from the other side stood out, as clear as day, he was surprised he had not seen it straightaway. 'I must have been mad,' he mumbled, unable to stop the words coming out of his mouth. He was staring at the child as though he was looking Old Midnight in the face.

The boy moved back out of reach, sensing the poison pouring out of the heart of the old man for whom he had cooked the fish. He thought the fish might have been one of the poisonous fish, like the puffer fish. He glanced in the bucket just to make sure he had not made a mistake. He edged further away just in case the old Malbu grabbed him because he might be a Gundugundu man, or some other devil-devil from the sea. He might have been the one who killed all of the fish along the beach. The small boy was reminded of his Mother's voice: 'Stay away from all strangers here Bala.' He knew he had to be careful and he should not have fed the old man. She said they had to hide from the bad people because they might be devil-devils in disguise. He had asked her to explain what was *disguise*. She said anyone he did not know. But he thought the old Malbu looked very sick. That was why he fed him. He contemplated how he was going to take the bucket away from Malbu because he needed to keep it.

He knew his Mum would be mad if he lost the bucket. She had said they could not afford to lose anything. He did not want to make her angry. It was only that he was lonely that he helped the old man, old Malbu, because he sat on the beach and did not move. He had watched him all day and when he did not move, he had been convinced he could not walk. It would be alright he thought to make a friend of Malbu. Even if they were friends just long enough to see what he could use from the boat, because they needed things like fishing line and hooks. Then the old man could go back to the sea.

Norm saw how frightened the boy was by the way he had become withdrawn. He was the living image of his father – Will the capable: 'Will the fucking stupid who went off with that stupid slut Hope from the other side. Living *dandaayana*.' The thought of mixing their blood with his, was like a hex. His face twisted up into a knot. But the truth, terrible in its reality, was that any *dandaayana* people could produce a child that looked like the pride of the Phantom breed, which was what everyone thought of Will, until he went stupid. Norm considered how his own flesh and blood was the worst kind of mongrel who went around looking for trouble, until he caught the *dandaayana* people's disease which he claimed must make you stupid. Now, way out in the bloody woop woop of Christ knows where, sorry Lord but it was true, Norm told himself, 'I finds some kid who happens to be my grandchild.'

'Give me the bucket Malbu,' Bala demanded, standing up in the sand, with his hand out ready to snatch the bucket and run off with it. Norm gave him the bucket and thanked him for the fish.

'I will bring you more tomorrow,' Bala says, relieved it did not require a fight.

'Alright little fellow, you do that. You can take some more hooks and line from the boat if you want too.'

'Maybe tomorrow then.'

Norm watched the boy hurry away up along the beach where the wet sand was firm and hard, and turn over the sand dune before disappearing into the dark bush of pandanus palms and mangroves dotting the coast.

Norm brushed away the proud feelings. What was the use of it? he thought, when he knew that mixing up with the other side was what causes problems, like all their rotten luck, ever since the families started mixing up together. He knew who to blame for that. Angel. No, not the seagulls or any other kind of angel doing good deeds like saving lost fishermen. Norm meant that woman, Angel. For years he had watched her bringing trouble into their home. Saw with his own eyes how she established her kind of lazy example. He knew how kids watched the Mother. They knew. He remembered telling her many times this would happen but she ruined her kids anyway, before walking off without even saying goodbye to anybody because she could not be bothered. Her choice, and he cried wishing he could bring her to this place for a minute to actually show her how she had ruined their lives. Life was just full of bad luck, bad luck, bad luck. If she could see this child, she would know straightaway that it was her fault.

Norm rose to his feet. He wanted to fight somebody. He wanted to fight her. She must have heard him because she came back to fight. Norm started throwing his weight around the beach while Angel was throwing her weight around in his mind, swinging her hips in his face, a blade of sweet buffel grass hanging from her lips. The green stem stuck through her teeth bobbed up and down while she cursed him. Diseased salt fish she called him. Doors slammed around her. It reminded him how she loved slamming doors. He noticed he had even conjured up his frightened-eyed children onto the beach too, to watch.

Doors opened in the transparency of images while others slammed shut as the couple pursued each other throughout a house that now consisted entirely of doors. In one of these doors, Will blocked the entrance. Norm had momentarily frozen when he saw the anger in Will's eyes before he turned his back and walked away. The door slammed behind him with an earth-shattering din. Another door flew open. He looked to see Will again. The anger perplexed him. He needed to see it again to make sure he had really seen it at all.

The doors were as if they had been strung inside a mal-functioning weather clock with the fairweather lady and the rainy man. In and out. One went in while the other came out. Nobody knew how the weather would turn out. Norm was amazed with the revelation. It was just like life. Here he was. He would have to start again. This he would do by building himself a new home.

He started to pull everything he had left to his name out of the boat: plastic containers, oars, rope, some fishing tackle and hooks, a knife. Together he stacked them neatly on the beach in one spot. Not satisfied, the stack was shifted and restacked several times. He struggled to roll the dinghy over on its back. Next, he pulled it around side on to the sea to create a windbreak. He looked at the oars, but with the thought of something happening to them – snapping unexpectedly under the weight of the boat – he decided they were too precious to use. A sudden flash of pain flew through his chest. It reminded him of how he could die just from thinking about what could go wrong. What was wrong with devouring life like a big meal? 'People did it,' he thought, while deciding what to use instead of the oars, 'people like Will for instance. I suppose he never got a bellyache from eating too much bad apple.'

Old rope, old rope, he decided. He glanced at the various shapes and sizes of logs and bits of driftwood scattered over the beach from the storm. There were trunks of magnificent trees, uprooted pandanus palms, mangled mangrove trees. The discovery was just beginning. There were whole rainforest trees that had the soil eroded from their root systems by excavating floodwaters and tidal surges. Norm estimated that these had floated down mighty rivers from countries halfway across the world. They had been thrown out alive into the seas, and now, had washed up on scores of foreign beaches like exiles. Finally, all trees landed on this shoreline where the spirits waged their gloomy wars.

There were plenty of strong limbs from branches to be found, to rig up a prop to lean against the side of the upside-down dinghy. He eventually lay down and went to sleep and dreamt of the Milky Way. In his dreams, he began sorting out the star patterns, viewing one then the next, after which he jumbled them up and waited, while some tumbled back into place, others slightly realigned themselves, and he travelled along the new settings, memorising his route, then way into the heart of his sleep, the way home.

This was a dream full of rich thoughts of spectacular places. The sea he saw was full of depressing wars, heavy with dark shadows of things he was unable to determine. There were no broken lines. Each place had its own star, and he knew the only safe route as he travelled, had to be full of brightness which would only be revealed in dreams. No broken-down man, one who had lost the belief in his own strength, should follow any route until he saw the stars illuminated in his dreams like streetlights, safely showing him the direction to travel.

His dream died as soon as he started to follow the track. He had passed the lit road, and into the darkness, he became fearful of what lay beyond the first corner. The what-ifs. Hell if he went forward or backwards panicked him into wakeful vigilance of the sea. Although the night was not waiting for him, his thoughts of dying in his sleep from the fear of his own dreams kept him awake. When he finally fell into a deeper sleep, thoughts lingered of distant storms circling him as though they were strapped over his back. He saw the warriors of the spiritual wars using their mighty lightning weapons to jump across the skies and bolt into the earth where the dead people raced up so they might grow into waves as high as towers. The towers became barricades in his seaward journey. Constantly, he saw himself thrown into paths of diversion chosen by these barricades, forcing him to float around in the life of an exile in a sea maze, who knows where.

In the morning, he was woken in a startled state by his own coughing and the horrible, familiar sound drilling into his brain. Listening to the rain and the waves crashing, he recognised the screeching of the cockatoo. The bird was sitting on top of the dinghy just above him with its white angelic wings stretched wide and flapping wildly in the breeze. 'So you must be my bird after all,' Norm said, although he wished it was otherwise. The bird poured life back into the soul but made you forget your dreams. When the bird spotted Norm's interest, it broke into the loud-mouthed lingua franca it had learnt in the Pricklebush. For a moment Norm thought he was home, until he realised tears were falling from his eyes, and the cause of his coughing was dense smoke. He had almost cried, for on the sand in front of him he saw the remains of a fire, and in the ashes of a log that had burnt all night, the unburnt bits were still smouldering.

For a long time he sat looking at the fire, throwing bits of dry sticks in to get it started again. If he could keep the fire going, he would be able to look after himself forever. Or at least, for as long as it takes either to die or survive. There would be no need to go running to the no-good son to save him, wherever he was, who could have at least checked on his own father's health. 'I could be dying you idiot.' Never mind about giving the likes of him any thought. Now, with the fire, Norm reasoned, while rubbing his hands together, he would be able to catch whatever he wanted: fish, crab, prawn, plant and animal from the bush, and cook it. He reassured himself as he surveyed his surroundings that from what he could determine, a man could get real strong in this place.

He felt certain that it must have been the boy. Norm guessed the little fellow had come back in the night and made the fire to keep the devils away. This was good. He was a good boy. Where was he? Norm looked up to the bush but saw nothing except the pandanus palms now laden with red nuts which he had failed to notice before, and further down the beach, closer up to the water mark, thick mangrove swamps stretched into the sea. It was low tide over the mudflat. The view was empty and lonely. Surveying the broad stretch of its circumference, Norm looked out for the boy; so long as he did not show up with his Mother. Even the blessing of a night's sleep was insufficient to soften his resolve never to set eyes on the parents as long as he was able to breathe air. The plan was short-lived. Norm strolled off down the beach in search of the boy.

'Bala,' he called several times up to the bush, but received no answer except a lonely silence. The copycat bird called, 'Bala,' and Norm watched it fluff its chest feathers. It occurred to him that if he followed the bird, he might be able to find their camp. He would not go into the camp itself. It would be the last thing he wanted to do, to go about inviting himself to his son's place. He decided if he found the camp, he might go nearby, stand off in the bush where he could have a bit of a look. See what sort of turnout they got themselves, these invisible people.

Norm knew that Will could look like a pandanus tree if he wanted to hide. He knew how to melt away into countryside. In a flat stretch of claypan, Will could flatten himself out behind the clumps of yellowing grasses and become caked mud all afternoon while a search party walked all over him. Norm knew there were police searching for Will, *shame of the family*. The government were after him too and you do not go around playing with the government – mucking them up. 'It was not dangerous,' Norm thundered, pushing Will out of the yard. 'It was plain stupid because nobody can change the government.' Norm had often heard some government politician talking about Will on the radio. He remembered listening to all the talking voices describing Will Phantom as a curse to the Gulf who had to be stopped, and Norm agreed. He empathised with the tone of the voices he heard over the radio talking about the trouble Will was causing to everyone in the Gulf, and in the State of Queensland, and the nation, by stopping business at the mine. 'They sound the same as me,' he said happily. 'We all want to kill the bugger.'

Always trying to save the world, well, look where it got him. Norm turned and surveyed the emptiness of his surroundings and the cloud-filled sky. This was where you end up from trying to stop the mine and ordinary people from doing their work. He wished the people from the radio station had come around and interviewed him about Will because he would have told them everything they wanted to know. He would have told them it was not only the white people who wanted to kill him. There were Aboriginal people who wanted to kill the bugger too, including his own father. Go ahead police. Go and find him and lock him up.

'I made you somewhere to stay old man,' Bala said when he arrived.

'Ah! Bala! I am alright here, I got to stay here and mind the boat.'

'No Malbu, it is too dangerous here. We got to get off the beach and hide the boat now,' Bala said firmly.

The boy started to kick sand over the fire but Norm tried to stop him by reaching out and pushing him away. The little boy was too quick, ducking and weaving himself from Norm, keeping on the other side of the fire, kicking more sand over the fireplace until he had smothered the smoke. Then he went around the back of the boat and knocked it down flat.

'What did you do that for?' Norm yelled at him in an angry voice.

'Shh! Listen! Be quiet. This is a quiet place. Always quiet. Always hide.'

The boy pointed out to sea, then pointed up to the sky out at sea, and brought his arm down and around until his hand slapped down on the boat. He gave Norm the serious look of Will Phantom, who spoke with the gravity of the final word on any matter. 'Shh! And pack up, Malbu, cause I got to take you away from here.'

'You put that boat back up you little bugger, go on,' Norm demanded.

The boy ignored him and started to pick up a plastic container but Norm pulled it back and placed it in the neatly paraded belongings of all he had left in the world.

'Where's that father of yours anyway? He should have come down to see me. When I see him I got words to say to him. You tell him to get his black arse down here and tell me what he is doing here, because I am waiting and I am sick of waiting. I don't know what they are going to say the world is coming too, when I tell them a little boy is going around telling his old grand-daddy what to do.'

'You are an old man but you are not my grand daddy because my daddy said he is one smart man, even if he is not talking to us, and sometimes he only talked rubbish anyway. I know one thing for sure, you not smart, Malbu,' the boy did not mind arguing back as he snatched for the plastic containers. He was talking his head off just like his father: diverting while trying to make a grab at any of the old man's precious belongings. He was determined to make off with the pieces he snaffled, until there was nothing left for Norm to stay around for.

'What you say about you Daddy? Him saying what? If his name is Will Phantom then I am his Daddy. You tell him to come down here at once because I want to talk to him.'

'You prove it first.'

'How am I going to prove it? You just do what I tell you, that's what,' demanded Norm, feeling hungry. He had not eaten yet and the situation was becoming annoying, and he would be telling Will straight out as soon as he clapped eyes on him just what kind of Mother he had given his son. 'Fancy yourself now stuck with one of those *Wangabiya dandaayana* kind. Where's their manners?' The boy was like an animal. This was what you get when you do things against your family. He would tell him that.

To search for their daily food…

Squadrons of sea birds from rookeries in the swamps flew low over the beach, then gradually ascended into the cloudy skies across the low tide mudflats towards the darkened sea. Simulating his grievances with the world, Norm Phantom lay prostrate in the sand in a statuesquely comic pose, wishing he were dead. Bala was thinking of leaving the old man lie there with his battered dinghy forever. The birds flew around performing single loops before dropping down like projectiles onto the mudflat. Slightly distracted by their performance, the child reminded himself to scan the skies for the bad men. The old man had created a dangerous situation for them. Whatever interest he originally had of befriending the old man was fading. Even the possessions he had snatched seemed useless. Each would only have a limited life. Fishhooks break. Fishing lines end up snagged. He was not interested in lugging around the plastic containers or the Pepsi bottles. He was tired of carrying things around.

With a little scratch under his salt-laden hair which was forever itchy, Bala estimated that his own gear would last awhile, and all he had to decide to do was to run away. The old skeleton man? Well! He would leave him. He could live or he could die. Most probably he would die soon. The child thought the man would probably die when the next high tide came rushing in with a storm. Either today, he thought, or tomorrow. It did not matter, for he would die. And if not by the sea plucking him right off the beach; well, he would die when the bad men returned. Bala felt cold. He could already feel the presence of the other men sneaking along the bush line when it became dark. If the old man was just sitting out on the beach like a sitting duck; well! they would sneak up until they captured him. He thought of his Mother again and he felt scared and wanted to run. She had warned him to leave no signs for the bad men, and here was old Malbu with his boat tilted on its side, like a big shiny beacon. Its storm-scoured underbelly would be seen from the sea, and if they came flying in a helicopter again, Bala knew they would see it easily from the air.

'You want some duck?' Bala finally asked.

'What duck?'

'I've got a duck if you want it.'

'Well! Alright, you get it then and we can cook it together if you like.'

'I'll get the duck if you promise to help me make you another camp.'

'And what about your Father, will he come there too?'

'Maybe, I'll have to ask him and see what he thinks.'

'Did he tell you I take fish from the ocean and make them dance in thin air? I bet he didn't tell you I am the best fisherman that ever breathed, or that I can talk to the birds for company, and I follow the tracks made by the stars so I never get lost, and some-times, I go away fishing and never come back until people forget my name?'

'He told me you make your family cry and if you know all of those things then how come you got lost?'

'You go and get the duck.'

Bala stalked off, straight back up over the sand dune, and disappeared into the bush. On his way, the child thought about the possibility of finding a wondrous old man in someone like Malbu. Was it true he could follow tracks made by stars? He must have lost his power to make people cry.

Malbu reminded Bala of a lot of things. One night, when he was out in the boat fishing, his father told him, if you know the stars you can always find your way home. Since that time he always looked at the vast network of stars at night. He was already teaching himself so that by the time he grew up he would know how to travel in the skies. But as for mixed-up Malbu, who got washed up in the bad storm that carried off half the beach, threw up dead fish, and stranded dugongs to dry out and die on the sand, Bala believed he was lucky to be alive.

Of course he did not know what he was going to do about Malbu, since he thought Malbu was an idiot. If he knew his way by the stars like a magic person, he should have been able to drive storms away too, shouldn't he? At least the old man was too stupid to be one of the bad men. If he had been sent by the bad people he would not have mentioned his Mother because he would have known she was dead. All of his questions came with quick answers. If Malbu was his grandfather it did not matter because his Dad said they had to be alone, and his grandfather made his family cry.

All he wanted was for his father to come back so he could tell him what had happened. He wished he never found the old man who made him think too much. He wished the old man had not come at all, because up to now, he had been alright just looking after himself. It had been pretty easy because all he had to do was what his Mother had told him – keep out of the way of anyone. Now, angry with himself, he located and tried to frighten as many roosting birds as he could find, while lamenting how he now had to get food and water not only for himself, but carry it all back for the old Malbu too.

The pandanus bulalula palms and she-oak trees closed in

behind the boy with a swish, as though the bush wished to conceal him as he walked through the yellow green grasses that stood a metre tall. His feet were hardened like any bush animal's to tolerate the scorching ground littered with burrs, and he passed on, upsetting nothing, completely unnoticed by the peewee birds and crows resting in the silent melaleuca trees and paper-bark woodland, decorated for Christmas with bouquets of red mistletoe flowers and the sleepy olive vines of wild medicine and maloga beans.

As Norm watched the boy tramp over the rise, he considered following him into the hinterlands of the island. The moment passed. He had no courage to explore its unfamiliar territory. Instead, listening to the crows culk and chuckle to each other, he understood they were talking to each other over vast distances. Perhaps they had the whole island under surveillance. Their sounds only emphasised how much he did not know. How to interpret his feeling of the presence of the many spirits which belonged to this place? The crowding over the sand dune made him feel as though he had arrived on the outskirts of a town, full of anxiety and anticipation. Yet, in reality, the landscape gave the impression of being a dead country. Something that belonged to no countrymen. He felt incapable of deciphering between authentic vision and what he had falsely created for his own benefit.

He sensed that only the sea claimed this land. Inside the bush, whatever powers – dangerous, malevolent – were crowding on the other side of the sand dune, he believed had originated from the sea. Terrible truths tumbled from his mind. The night sounds of souls divesting themselves, were possessed, without shame, with a yearning for the roar of the ocean. Underneath him he felt the sand was full of the sea's malevolent powers. A poisonous country sapping his strength. More and more he dreaded its hinterland. Things had to be different. This was not his destiny.

Norm thought it was just like Will to have made a pact with the devil spirits so as to settle his family on such a place. Nobody else would have thought of such a haven. With no other logical explanation for his being dumped by the sea in the same place, Norm assumed he was being punished for Will's dalliance. In his imagination, a man thrown off course in a storm that should have killed him, should have at least been allowed to end up anywhere. There was the whole world for goodness' sake. Why the same place as Will? Well! So far, with his son Bala, so far.

Thinking about Bala, Norm grew more positive about his own circumstances. How could he explain Bala? It occurred to him that Bala was in the realm of God's providence. And he suddenly realised why. Of course. His fingers snapped automatically: an action of forgotten years which even surprised him at his age. He knew it. He would have to look after the boy, because the boy was alone, there was no Will and no Mother either. He now understood why the child kept coming by himself and avoided answering any requests to bring his father. He saw the child's face looking out to sea, something of Will in his face, something unexplainable, the look of fortitude which only belonged in the faces and eyes of seasoned soldiers.

So, where were his parents? Why was the child alone? He wished he could be wrong even though he knew differently. He felt the truth in his bones. Anxious again with the disturbance of thunder, he half expected something terrible was going to happen to them. In a flash, Norm saw a large hawk swooping down, talons, hooks, before these snapped through his back. Through sickening eyes he saw the sea underneath spin by until his release: a fall into a bloodied nest. The vision vanished.

Norm surveyed the seascape, closely examining every bump in the ocean, out past the birds wading in the distance of the outgoing tide, to the breakers and beyond: anything that showed signs of moving. His eyes scoured from one end of the beach to the other. The skies were growing fuller with thick clouds quickly passing over the coastline, punctured by flights of birds returning to the rookeries. It would not be too long before it started to rain again. Norm was in two minds whether to wait on the beach for the boy to return, or to start moving the boat up over the sand dune before the storm arrived.

Bird squalls calling up the rain could be heard coming out of the clouds, as well as the occasional throaty sound similar to an old man clearing his throat. It was the channel-billed cuckoo heralding its arrival from its long flight overseas: *And people died useless deaths. People who were fishing people, people who grew crops, people who had families and told each other stories.* Norm shook his head. He had heard the stories a thousand times. He had to concentrate on the bird squalls warning of the drop of pressure in the atmosphere. Somewhere out at sea a swell was building and might turn into a tidal surge. Norm expected the incoming tide would be affected by the winds and the power of the storm. It would bring in the surge and it was going to be high.

Still, the wise weather birds hovered stationary in the air like beacons out over the tidal flat. Their heads turned in the direction of the oncoming storm. All he could do was wait for their judgement. One by one, the birds dropped from their hovering positions, noisily signalling squalls to the others below, and took flight. This meant one hell of a storm was heading directly towards the coastline. Anxiously, Norm scanned the rise hoping the boy would appear. 'Why did he not see the clouds running inland?' The skinny-legged foraging birds were lifting off the tidal flats and quickly returning inland. Soon, they were joined by other birds flying back from places further offshore.

From far out at sea, the big, black frigate birds flew in, travelling at great speed. He estimated they were flying at one hundred miles an hour. They were getting out of the way. The low clouds of densely-packed white birds flying towards him as they made their way inland had assumed the supernatural appearance of the spirits. Norm had never seen anything so spectacular or beautiful as this flight of the ancestral beings of the sea. Their flight was so low, each time one of these clouds came towards him, Norm had to bend over to avoid a collision.

Weighing up demons, Norm was convinced that the spirits lording over the sea were a much worse fate to relive again, than the devil woman and her cronies living in the bush. So, placing a length of rope around the top end of the empty boat, he dragged it up over the sand dune. He knew the last straw, a moaning wind, or even a lesser howling wind, would be sufficient to pick up the boat like a toy and throw it around the beach.

With the boat settled amongst the pandanus, he returned to the beach to collect the remainder of his fishing gear and the oars. He looked for the boy. The clouds were even more ominous with lightning shooting spears that exploded back and forth across the skies. Norm dragged the boat further inland where the bush was denser, and its hanging branches closed like doors behind him. He tied the boat against a large eucalyptus and stacked all of the containers inside. He made a place for himself and the boy to shelter out of the winds behind the secured boat. Every now and then he went back down to the beach to wait for the boy to come, but still there was no sign of him. Perhaps the boy had decided not to come back. It was hard to tell. The wind was now howling in from the sea and the flying sand was cutting into his body. Norm knew he had to take cover. Maybe his father was around after all, and took the kid off some place else. As long as he was safe, thought Norm. He headed for cover, struggling over the sand dune, until he reached the boat.

Bala was in the swamp when the storm struck the coastline. He had heard the birds coming back to the rookeries, but having made spears from the spearwood trees in the swamp, he was intent on stalking a group of ducks. At first, the wind made the waters ripple, and then it blew faster until the slender trees were bending to ground level. Water poured down the sides of every rise, down from the low hills, through the gullies and into the swamp, and very quickly the knee-deep water was up to the level of his neck. The boy struggled to keep his head above water and stay afloat in the deeper waters that were pouring through the swamp in a flood. The swamp soon became a wide river roaring though the bush as it found its ancient path down to the coast to join the sea.

Meanwhile, the tidal surge had overtaken the mudflats, as its grey waters moved in faster and deeper to drown the mangroves and slap itself against the sand dune. When it could go no further, the waters poured back to the sea, forming a wave that grew as it came rushing back to force itself against the sandbank, and again reaching its pinnacle, retreated. Each time this happened, millions of tons of sand were carried back in the roll. As Norm listened to the deafening roar of the sea stripping into the sand dune, he knew the sea would eat its way through the sandbank and tear into the bush.

The boy had quickly lost his foothold in the flooding, and the *dumularra* floodwaters hurried him swiftly away through the bush. Rushed along with everything else, he saw branches, trees, hollow logs – the boa constrictor snake hanging off the top of a platform of leaf litter. He had lost the duck he had caught. He reached out for tree branches, but no sooner had he gripped a hand full of leaves or a branch his weight and the speed of the flooding waters pulled him away.

The jackhammer waves tore further into the sandbank. Norm, forcing his way through slapping branches bent over by the sheer force of the oncoming wind and rain beating into his face, unable to see further than a few metres ahead, struggled to crawl up to the top of the sand dune. He looked down at the clawing waters and saw nothing else. He knew that the other side of the wall had been torn down and at any moment, if he did not move fast, the rest would topple. He rolled down the dune and ran.

The lashing rain tore at his hands as he worked as quick as he could to untie the boat. Panicking, he roped the plastic water containers, while pouring out enough of the stored water to decrease the weight inside the dinghy. He hauled the loaded boat through the wet eucalyptus and melaleuca bush, in his desperate bid to find higher ground.

Soon, he realised he was struggling to stay in front of the little boat as it slid easily over the wet leaves. Hurried by the gale force of the tailwind, both he and the dinghy flew through the flattened bush side by side. Broken branches and snapped trees bustled past, sometimes crashing over them, before stumbling on. Each of these flying objects resembled the *yinbirras*. These were fairy-like people the good storytellers told about the strange Yanngunyi tribe whose true home was beyond the sea.

The *yinbirras*, they said, were related to all of the tribes. These Yanngunyi were people who lived beside other real people, and even though you could hear them going about their daily business, shouting at each other to listen, they would not let anyone see them because they 'did not want to be found', or 'made civilised'. Or something else could have happened to these half-deaf fairy creatures. The old people hotly debated the fate of the Yanngunyi. Envoys were dispatched to debate theories throughout the Gulf of Carpentaria. They even went back and forth between East and Westside camps to talk about the latest 'so-called' glimpses of the *yinbirras*. The old people of Westside remained resolute however, that sometime, no one remembered when, *because no one was keeping a look at the clock*, those people simply disappeared into the wilderness of life. Why? Because they did not want their histories contaminated with oppression under the white man's thumb.

They were pure people and the storytellers said they were black angels. It amazed him to see them running past him through the bush. Some were quick runners, faster than any kind of ordinary person he had ever seen before in his life. He kept moving as quickly as he could to save himself, but all the same the *yinbirras* sent cold shivers running right up and down his spine. Not that he was frightened of them, or the bush woman Gardajala, he was far too preoccupied for her. What kept screaming through his head was the fact that he was on the land, beyond the sea. The *yinbirras* too kept running, but tried to distract him by calling out to him in their strange tongue. He looked behind and saw others running along in the same direction as him, normal people, women and men carrying their children, and old people being helped along by the younger people.

There was something even stranger in the way that they ran, it was as though they glided through the bush, but perhaps he was doing the same because he felt light and the boat felt even lighter. People appeared on both sides of him, and when he looked behind because the boat felt as light as paper, he saw some young men were actually pushing the boat from behind. A fish-faced old woman with eucalyptus leaves strewn through her wildly flowing, wet white hair, sat in the boat. She gave him a toothless smile although he could see she had a look of sheer terror written as plain as day, all over her face. While shielding his own face from the rain, he tried to call out to her over the thunderous sea slamming all of the world's rubbish into the sand dune.

'*Wanyingkanyi ninji nanagkurru jila?*' What are you doing there? And she, like a queen, said grandiloquently, '*Wawaru*. Nothing,' she said. 'Nothing.' Her voice had a guttural sound as though a tree had spoken. Then she said things to him in a language he did not understand. She looked as though she was quarrelling with him, and when he kept looking at her and not understanding a word she was saying, she gave up. Instead, still scowling, she wiggled her fingers at him to look ahead if he did not want to fall over. Her action excited Norm's curiosity even further, for when she wiggled her fingers, he believed he saw fresh green eucalypt leaves spring from their tips. The leaves immediately flew through the wind and several hit him in the face. He smelt her astringent aroma, and when he was stung in the eye, he instantly turned his head back to the direction he, they, she, the wind and rain were heading.

Now fully focusing his attention ahead of him, and following the others running through the bush, and believing that they must know where they were going, since he knew he had no clue at all where he was, he hoped to reach the high ground. Then, through the sound of waves crashing in the distance, a chorus of voices was calling him, something like *malirriminji wadara Malbu*, old prickly bush humpy man. They knew where he was from. He felt he was in the middle of another nightmare. He had to turn around, just once, to see his tormenters. Now the boat was crowded with old fish women who bared their open mouths at him. He guessed that there had to be at least twenty crammed together like sardines, hissing him on. To his disbelief and incomprehension, for he knew that together, they could not have weighed a kilo, because it cost him nothing to carry them. These women were also dressed in muddy clothes scattered with leaves and foliage fallen from trees, as though they had just risen from the wet ground where they had been sleeping.

He turned briefly to check how clear his path was ahead, to be sure there were no trees to smash against, and when he looked back, he yelled, '*Wanyimba?*' They did not change their expression or respond, and he screamed at them again, '*Wanyimba?*' What's wrong? '*Wanyimba?*' Finally, their gaping mouths found voice, which was the sound of total fear: an ear-piercing primordial roar that pierced him to the core of his bones. Again, the finger wiggling began, '*Kurrkamarra*,' many mob, with the leaves springing out of their fingertips, and as he was about to shield his eyes, he saw that this time they were pointing directly to the ground, *Looking out for safetyness*, they seemed to be saying, and when he too looked down, he saw the bad *bari* waters creeping along the sides of the boat. Now, he knew he had to travel faster, run faster from the *bari* waters, run in the direction the others were going even though he felt as though he was breathing in the rain, running out of breath, and to keep ahead of the boat, which was moving faster again with the young men with heads bent, pushing from behind.

The sea waters had overtaken the bush, and in every direction he looked, water was running across the land. He tried to see ahead, to see if they were coming to higher ground but visibility was limited because of the rain. It was hard to tell, perhaps the ground was rising slowly above sea level. They seemed to be reaching nowhere. He thought that his guardian angels, this ghostly tribe, would run forever. Perhaps this was the only way to escape the tidal surge. Perhaps they were taking him to the Gardajala woman of the bush. He almost felt if he turned around, he would actually see her sitting in his dinghy, a finger resting on her cheek, ironically contemplating his fate. He was so convinced that she was staring at his back with her icy eyes, he heard his heart thump over the thunderous roaring of the sea, until he almost collided with a tree.

He ran on, not knowing how much longer he could last. The island could not be that large. Or had he underestimated its size? Was reality larger and parable truer? What if all of those old hags back there in the boat were Gardajala women? And what if he had mistaken their look of horror, when in fact what he saw was his own face reflected in theirs, like wet mirrors. His pain chased away the thoughts which strangled his mind. Still, he saw no sign of hilly country ahead, not a single rocky outcrop, nothing but flat country. His throat felt it was on fire and his lungs would explode. He did not have much more left in him to run.

Through the soles of his feet he searched to feel changes in geography, telltale signs of gravel indicating they were moving to higher ground. Nothing changed however from the pacified softness of sand, and his splashing through the rising waters pulsated in rhythm with his heartbeat. He started to feel that there was no hilly country on the island, the ghost people were running nowhere. Was he being run to death? He had joined a dying race. His fear terrorised his legs with numbness. There was nothing he could do to prevent the heaviness of his body slowing his pace.

Finally, Norm caught his first glimpse of something happening up ahead. The bush people were not running anymore. They had come to a slight rise, not large in space, but it seemed to be holding out, just metres above the flowing waters. He saw that there were about thirty or forty of these phantom people huddling and shuffling together, while the rain fell over them, like it does over leaves in the bush.

The little sea of people became quite volatile when they saw Norm trying to pull his boat up to the higher ground with his cargo of old women still sitting there. Several of them began running towards the boat while screaming and gesticulating at the men who pushed the boat from behind to help them. They literally dragged the old women from the boat and Norm watched in stunned silence as he saw that they were dressed in what looked like sodden, inflorescent compost heaps where the rain ran through the crumpled leaves, bush blossoms, tangled strands of grasses and twigs before splashing down onto the muddy ground. It took several people to lift up each of the women, who in return complained bitterly about their undignified treatment, and a fusillade of leaves flew everywhere off their person, while they were half dragged, half carried in an undignified manner to the higher ground, to join their kinfolk.

On the other side of the rise, Norm saw a river overflowing with the incoming king tide, and joined by all of the floodwaters gushing down from the southern foothills. Its incredible flow twisted around a hundred kilometres of stories the prophets had tabled in the scriptures of law, safely locked away in the vaults of their minds. Somewhere along the route the two floodwaters had converged. Norm knew not far north was the coastline, from where he had just escaped, and this was where the river would empty back into the sea.

The phantom men were bare chested and in assorted coloured shorts, much like himself, and it occurred to him, that they must trade with 'real' people somewhere. He tried to argue with them about the boat but they kept yelling at him in their strange language, and raising their hands up, gesturing exasperation to match the looks on their faces because he did not understand. Several of the men kept on rummaging through his belongings throwing things on the ground, until they found what they wanted. This was Norm's anchor rope which was long enough for their liking. While still screaming instructions to each other, one of the men began to secure the loose end of the rope to the stern of the little tin boat. Norm stood watching, until he was lifted up like the old women, and under protest, half dragged to the boat.

Norm did not know what was happening with everyone yelling and screaming, and pointing down the flooding river. He was put into the dinghy, and whenever he tried to get out, hands sprang forth to push him back into a sitting position. He did not know what was expected of him as they launched him into the flood. The boat quickly took up speed as it moved through the metre-high foam gathered near the bank to join the raging torrent of yellow waters. About twelve men who were holding the rope, gradually eased out more of its length, slowly, knowing that if they let it slip too fast, the boat would turn broadside and overturn. Norm, unsure of what was happening, kept looking into the heavy rain falling between him and their serious faces, while his hands worked the oars, while he calculated how much rope he had stored in the coil.

The boat kept making its way down the river heading towards the sea in the storm. The men handling the rope were starting to look a long way away behind him. Soon, Norm saw that they were forming a human chain in the waters, while more and more people were coming down from the rise and joining the men, who were being dragged along with the flood. Norm saw the serious faces of those closest to him, and feared that it would only take one man to be dragged under, and they would all be dragged into the undertow.

He turned to save himself when the boat stopped suddenly, until he saw it had jammed in the branches of a lonely rivergum. He looked back at the men desperately trying to keep the human chain together, then he turned quickly to disentangle the boat from the tree. It was then, through the heavily pouring rain, he was able to see in amongst the branches and leaves piled up together, the boy. 'God have mercy,' he cried. 'Let him be alive.' He pulled the boat in amongst the foliage, but it was useless trying to get any closer. 'Bala! Bala! Wake up.' He called to the boy but there was no response. Norm realised he would have to leave the boat and climb over the rubble of foliage to reach the boy and untangle him.

When he was close enough, he reached out. 'Come on Bala,' he urged, but the child just looked at him and clung tighter to the branches. Norm started to pull him away from the branches, but the frightened boy struggled, saying he was staying with his

Mother. Norm could see that Bala thought he was wrapped in his Mother's arms, and it suddenly occurred to him that the boy believed his Mother was dead. Did this mean that Will was dead too?

'I think your Mum wants me to take you now Bala,' Norm said, speaking gently, while working to pry his little arms out of the wet branches. 'She asked me, she said, "Grandad, would you mind coming to take Bala home now?" and I said, "Of course. I will make a good journey home for me and Bala." I said to her, "We will be waiting for a little while until the stars come back and tell us the right way, and then we will go with the big fish, follow the big fish, straight through the sea, with the right wind coming our way, and we will be going straight home, fishing all the way." And you know what she said, "That's good, take Bala now and I will see you later and tell him that, tell him I will be looking after him."' Norm looked at the boy's weak face with rain pouring over it, but he saw Bala was listening. Finally, he released his grip for a moment, which was enough for Norm to pull him back to the boat. As soon as they were both on board, the dinghy started to move backwards, while Norm rowed to keep it heading straight for the rise in the flooded river. As he looked across the river, he could see the chain of men struggling in the water to bring the boat to safety. One by one, they helped each other out of the water, while pulling the rope towards them.

'The bad men took Mummy,' Bala whimpered, as he sat locked between his grandfather's legs, while Norm rowed towards land.

'Then, I heard her screaming in the sky, and when I looked up, I saw her fall into the sea.'

It was Will's voice Norm heard rushing back into his mind. His face, hard and defiant, snapped, 'One day, Men will kill for this mine, remember that.' Norm only saw the fury of an injured being. Moments before, a helicopter had buzzed over their heads.

Its shadows fell over the house as though casting a bad spell on their relationship. Will had a contemptuous look on his face, full of what? Disappointment, or more: revulsion for a father who thought so little. 'So blind,' he had taunted, shaking his head. 'And so completely satisfied with the status quo.' Everyone knew about the security helicopters patrolling the district at regular intervals. All times of the day and night, the helicopters flew along their grids, throwing shadows across the Pricklebush. The memories passed. Norm looked down at the little boy's head and cried in relief. Rain, tears, rowing the flooded river, he knew this was the solace of Elias: how he used his death to help an ignorant old man find his grandson, to rekindle hope in his own, joyless soul. He rowed.

The ghostly tribe was already leaving by the time Norm pulled the boat back through the foam. One by one, they had started disappearing through the flooding bushlands, most likely following their own familiar roads back to the hilly country further inland. They had tied the end of the rope to a tree. Norm left the boy in the boat and quickly pulled it along through the watery bush, searching in the direction where the strange tribe was vanishing into the rain ahead. In his mind, he had a vague plan to gain the highest ground before nightfall. If he could reach a hill, he would climb the summit and wait for the sea to stop ploughing into the coastline.

A summit had to be found. There would be no point moving after the skies turned dark, because the people he was trying to follow would have dissolved into the bush of night. He knew as soon as night fell he would never see them again and his memory of them too would be gone.

Chapter 10
The giant in the cloak

Even God goes around like one thing, they say...

Too good! Even everyone sitting around nice in the Pricklebush say they knew who the maker was. Phoney talk was often spoken there: *Oh! Yes! We know him personally*. Hmm! Hmm! Just like they knew November over the flat country. Oh! Heavy heart, if you were to see miracles happen, look to the heavens in November. See him properly for yourself in those dark, stormy skies of the Wet season build-up. Look for the giant in a cloak. Brace yourself when he comes rolling through the dust storm, spreading himself red, straight across those ancient dry plains, heading for town. Watch carefully for the evaporation creeping down invisibly, right into the ignorant minds of the people living in Uptown and, you know what? He turned some of them mad too, just like all those people you see living about over there in the Pricklebush.

That's right. The giant sugarbag man of the skies walked from horizon to horizon, carrying storms and hazes of madness, and sweat! Humidity was plain old sticky syrup falling through the atmosphere like a curse. Fools. People went for it. Went mad from it. Uptown called the sugarbag man spirit 'seasonal rains', or their 'silly season', and among them there were fatalities. Statistics rocketed in mortality for both black and white, when the air grew heavy and fat. The perpetual dampness was terrible. It lasted for weeks on end, and how sick and tired of it people became. Every day, grimacing with the glare, they gazed upwards hoping for rain, and chucking their weight around for good measure when none came. You should have heard them. Presumptuous to the core, the way they assumed so much familiarity towards the Almighty maker: Calling out in their cynical voices – *God! You never seem to end*.

Have they gone mad? Secret! Air caused madness. Sanity? Where about? Lost, like respect was, trampled in the sodden ground. The mindless buggers split: ran off to the bush. Very likely careering around dressed as feral fairies or devils, and who knows what else they thought they were, hugging trees, or hiding among spinifex like birds, and some never came back. Others turned killers without cause. Everyone, regardless of colour, had to put up with it along the shores of the Gulf, before the rains came.

Meanwhile, mould of strange-coloured greens invaded every dampened premise, person or thing. The mildew, fed on moisture-laden air steaming up from the earth, spread a magical, sealike world above water, throughout Desperance. This short-lived phenomenon was regarded as something strange, occurring out-side the realm of nature, before the dust storms came to slam doors open and shut. The mould could cloud rational thought, and they (Uptown) said some funny things to each other. When hard put by the weather, they found the words to describe a multitude of flukes, and this year, when Norm never came back from the sea, was no exception.

For years it was believed that the hens of Desperance had become bewitched and purposely covered the eggs they laid in a putrid fowl-yard muck. It was like that when the build-up called into town like an enchantress whose prime motive was to saturate everything and cause creatures of domesticity to become demons. Dogs and cats became covered with infectious sores from head to tail, and sat scratching themselves all day long. The oldest children in the population of Uptown, well on the way to becoming real Aussie battlers up North of the country, were one step ahead in being more suspicious than their parents, and without a word of doubt, cautioned younger siblings at the breakfast table. They sniggered, saying how they knew a real googie-egg when they saw one, or which were imposters used by perverse parents to insult the intelligence of children. 'Them the ones that come out of those ugly, bare bum chooks,' they squirmed, visualising the moulting chooks down the backyard walking around in the mud. 'If nobody moves that egg from the table I am going to vomit.' Whispering about the foetus: 'See, that black thing? That is the faeces of a devil.' A sledgehammer would not have forced one of them little Uptown kids to open their mouth for an egg after that.

See! All summer long it went on like this: What to do with children of Uptown who would not eat egg? Of course nothing but those grimy eggs had to be the main topic of interest when those little Pricklebush boys, the petrol sniffers, were arrested and taken to a shimmering silver, green, gold and red tinsel-decorated jail. Tristrum Fishman. Junior Fishman Luke. Aaron Ho Kum. Three little boys. There was a roar for those three little boys, saying, 'They got their just deserts.' They got their just deserts? You could spend the rest of your life examining those five words, change the sound, bend them, twist them up, even change it into something like: Just deserts! They got theirs. Like eggs. Hey! There was no cause for a speck of glitter, no fortitude of spirit to waste for them three. Why had no one walked right down there to Main Street of Uptown, to bail out of jail any one of the little petrol-sniffer boys who had been accused of viciously killing Gordie, the neighbourhood watch, the night when Norm Phantom had rowed away, taking Elias's body back to sea?

Citizens protected by the net to keep trouble away – secure citizens, living in real houses with nice graded Uptown streets –

needed to talk about ways of producing clean eggs from backyard hens, so they watched their pet fowl very carefully, to add to the conversation. Vogue was what vogue was. Nobody watched for the little boys down in the jail.

The hundreds of inbreds kept strutting about, free ranging, and with the moult, appeared half plucked, while bucketloads of summer downpours rained down on them. Hours went by: beautiful linear hours. The casual prickly bush observer, either East or Westside, knew, with the kids of Uptown, inbred fowl had no brain. The town camp people never ate those eggs. The grocery shop tried to flog cheap, dollar a dozen, dollar fifty for two, in the cartons of proper eggs which came from clean farms, 'Down South'. Same thing, people started to get scared of anything else, foodwise, Uptowners produced to eat, like vegetables, fish cakes, sponge cakes on fête day. You could never be too careful of catching something. There was no point asking for problems.

In this era of modern domesticity, where personal interest smothers the hope and joy of all of mankind, no one in Uptown ventured outside of their louvred homes where windows were tightly shut. So much caution about the colour of skin had been dragged from the past into the new millennium. They said it was to prevent all the goings-on in the street from moving inside their homes with the breeze. Outside, in the backyards, they watched, investigated and took note of fowlry shuffling around in mud-bearing ulcerated chests, and flashing red raw bums of the summer moult.

Day in, day out, nothing seemed to be happening for the boys accused of killing Gordie. They were left there, locked up in the town's little jail, known as Truthful's planetarium, neglected amongst the crowded foliage of the *jarrbikala*'s strappy and viney tropical indoor oasis, feeling like they were starting to rot. Nobody gave a continental that those boys were standing in the same

311

clothes they had been arrested in. Clothes turning mouldy in the damp cell. If they had looked all sweaty-skinned from the humidity building up in the bullyman's jail, nobody noticed. That they waited *sine die* for justice was nobody's concern.

'You are going to get your just deserts for this. You are all going to pay for this, just you wait and see,' the boys were told enough by Truthful, who, not accounting for the initial brief sideshow, when everyone in town wanted to have a look at the accused killers the day they were arrested, had increasingly become their only human contact. It often seemed to the boys, as the hours passed by, that the waiting for justice seemed to be becoming the punishment itself. They watched Truthful cleaning up around the jail building and they could see, and he wanted them to see, that he was really proud to be an active, crime-stopping policeman again.

It was obvious to the boys, watching his every move, that their jailer drove down to the pub himself to get their meals. It was not easy for E'Strange. The hotel cook, his single aide-de-camp, shook her fat permed head of stiff mauve-tinted hair in disgust, when she handed over three disposable plates of meals wrapped with alfoil. 'Lovie, you are wasting you time,' she warned him, as though the food was too good for those boys. The clientele watched the methodical Truthful going past by the glass windows of the public bar carrying the meals at the taxpayer's expense, and grumbled into the bar that it was a bloody waste of taxpayers' money and why don't they shoot the little buggers?

The three boys, Tristrum aged ten, and his brother Luke Fishman aged twelve, and Aaron Ho Kum aged eleven, all Bob Marley look-alikes, had asked no questions, did not expect any favours, and asked for no one. Together, when they had been left alone, when sure no one was listening, they huddled in a corner spinning out in a whirl of raw-felt fear, clawing into each other, believing they were not humans. Often, they spoke about how they thought they were being kept like lizards in a zoo. Sometimes, they would hazard a guess by trying to make heads or tails out of why they were there in the first place, waiting for their 'just deserves'. Spinning on their addiction and sudden withdrawal, they interpreted 'just deserves', as the impending time when Truthful would molest them.

The terrible murder of Gordie during the night of the first seasonal storm left a sour taste over little Götterdämmerung, the twilight of the Gods, some called the ceremony of thunder, on the eve of heralding all the nights of stormy weather. This particular night was the same night, coincidently, that Norm Phantom had cast off into the gloominess of the open sea under the pretext of going off fishing, and never came back. It was surely strange, given that the whole town regarded Norm with suspicion, accusing him of many unsolved crimes in the past, that no one laid a finger of blame on him for Gordie's death. The other murders Norm had been accused of were not like Gordie's murder at all. Those, they agreed, were only black murders. This was different and required the very best one could expect of civil action from the Australian law.

So, this was what happened. Quietly, the town celebrated Norm, the fisherman's fisherman's return to the sea. Years ago, before he stopped fishing, Norm's relationship with the sea had been a beacon of light to others. His understated prowess in maritime adventures had led all nature of mature men to believe that they lived in the good company of a sea wizard in God's own country, and once again, simply from living in close proximity to Norm's prickly bush camp, his good luck would naturally flow onto all the others who went fishing too. The pressure imposed from the weight of seamen's graves lifted. All negative thoughts disappeared. There was no longer an ocean full of bad omens and impending deaths. Norm made it safe for others. Everyone could go to sea now, even if only in fishy dreams of trevally-loaded seas. What other explanation could there be, for the heavy cloak of suspicion reserved for Norm Phantom to have been lifted so swiftly, and without a shadow of doubt? The nights that followed were full with a thousand elaborate dreams of seas so choking with fish, it was easier to walk over them, than take a boat.

All the brave hearts talked fish at the Fisherman's Hotel. In calm conversation building in gentle waves, they said, 'And why should he come back?' It was a time for wishing and great solace was found in it. They wished that they too had no reason to come back. Everyone wished to escape paradise from time to time. Wished to slide away in the middle of the night out to the storms, throwing their fate to the sea.

So this was how it was. Ineluctable, magical moments of light-headedness flowed through town during the humidity. Somebody had been murdered, some boys had been arrested, and somebody had left town. Normal! Although many often complained about 'the dead town with no life to it at all,' and frequently lamented how they wanted to leave one day, it was pretty difficult to unbuckle the notions of permanence. The constricting binds strapped into their lives, strangling them with the fear of possibility. Nobody found it easy to leave their life: home, friends, parents, grand-children. A known place to be buried in when they died.

There were not many who were prepared to take a gamble with leaving a place like Desperance. Yet, the town boasted an above average representation of professional gamblers. The leader by a long shot, was the mayor, Bruiser, regarded by some as possibly being an alien, because he knew how to brush with good luck. He sat about inside his modern lounge room with a couch bigger than anyone else had to sit on, on those stormy nights. With brown Nugget and brush, people spoke about seeing Bruiser polishing up his old bookie's leather money bag, in readiness for the dry winter race day, to set up his bookie box outside of the pub. But Bruiser daydreamed about money traffic, where anyone passing could wager for or against Norm Phantom ever making it back to the melancholy seashores of Desperance.

When Bruiser brought the leather bag into the Fisherman's Hotel hoping to catch what he called the 'night swill', word got around Desperance. *All praise to the sea. Is he our man of absolute sea fidelity? Fifty to one, he's not.* Very quickly, wishing became excitement and entertainment. The gambling fever overtook the town's shock at the murder of Gordie. The pub became so congested with gamblers and arguments about seamanship, that Truthful was called in to see what he could do. The owl-faced barman, who was implicated in the murder case by being the father of one of the boys in jail, although he had never owned up to his paternity, helped Truthful to build a queue of those inside the small crowded bar, jockeying for space.

Yesterday, all of the town was up in arms about the killing. Their usually complacent faces had turned aghast, knowing something so terrible could grab your heart and violently shake you into the quick pulse of the world. It was a pulse that demanded pay-back from your knowledge of having a little bit of secure life. It asks you to deal personally with a world where children kill. Initially, so shocked were these shattered townsfolk, they cried out to each other, *What has the world come to?* It was a difficult thing to deal with, this deception in their little world of Desperance. Their lives were solid, built on generations which had through the decades guarded their net of privacy and minded their own business.

Parents in this world believed in its unique position to the rest of the world. Lives could be lived in the pristine vastness of the quiet mud plains, silent saltpans and still spinifex plains, where children grew up with a sense of nature and the knowledge of how lonely the planet could be. Children in this world belonged to the thinking of fairytales which came out of books, or else, the happy life of children's television. Theirs was the quiet world where murder was not a child's toy.

Initially, when people of Uptown heard of Gordie's murder, they had remained in their houses, examining their souls, never expecting to be confronted by a hideous crime committed by children. This was the sort of thing that only happened elsewhere in the mean, bad world, where the crazy people lived. They knew this because they had seen the lot on television and felt lucky, it was not Australia. Never in their wildest imagination had they expected to see the likes of downtown Desperance splashed across television, like New York, Jerusalem or Kosovo.

So, unlike the rest of the world, it was decided by the Town Council that nobody was ever to see the crying face of Desperance on television. It made a humble request to the citizens to keep their mouths shut: 'We don't want anyone thinking we are not decent people.' The silent word spread the usual way by the invisible net's strictly confidential notification system, through word of mouth. The town's ranks closed. Even a fly found it difficult to penetrate such a closure to lay its maggoty eggs. This was truly the only place on earth where decent, lip-sealed people lived. No one would see Desperance laying its soul bare. No one would see perplexed faces stretched like fawn-coloured lino across the nation's screens. No one would see Desperance as Desperance saw the world – static broken and lacy lines for the seven o'clock news punctured with electrical storms, until a complete blackout was achieved. This was fondly known as nature's censorship. No one would go publicly to the world at large asking, 'How could this happen here?'

So, poor old Gordie. The whole town cried as they rallied together one way or other to help the victim's family. There was praying to do. The burying. They would take their part on the jury to see justice was done when the case finally came to the district court. Everybody thought mightily of their poor old Gordie. 'He never hurt a fly,' they said.

Initially, on that eventual morning, on the eleventh hour of the eleventh day of the month of November, when Gordie did not play the remembrance bugle, everyone thought: *Alright! Something is astray. Something smells mightily funny to me.* Although, at first, everyone had thought very little about it. Perhaps Gordie was sick with the summer flu. Nothing to be done about that. Life went on as usual. Desperance was a normal town where even the bugle player had as much right as anyone else to get sick with influenza and stay home in bed. Normal people knew how to tell the time without depending on a clock, or a signal, and had enough decency, unlike the rest of the country, to stand for one minute's silence in respect of the fallen on the eleventh hour, even without the bugle of the returned, to remind them. However, valiant attempts at normality could not replace the bad smell in the air. The people of Uptown, without realising it, started waiting for the bugle. A wave of uneasiness flowed through the town. They felt as though someone was playing around with their sense of security. Everyone started to look out for Gordie. *When will he come?* they complained. *He should have been by by now.* Fair weather or naught, everyone knew Gordie walked the town, even if he had influenza, doing his job to the hour, but naught had happened and this was not good. The day was ruined because of Gordie.

Ruined more than they thought. After the rain stopped, some poor unsuspecting anyone was whimsically walking along, with thoughts only of ploughing through the mud with a useless pair of thongs on their feet, on that same path now through the bush, and minding their own business, when Gordie was found. The body was steaming like hot bread with the two o'clock sun pouring down. Well! After that, it was Lordy! Lordy! There was nothing abstract about hell breaking loose in Desperance. The town bell would not stop ringing under the flagpole where the bugler used to play the remembrance tune. Every single citizen, first-class, second-class, third-class and any other riffraff after that, had been summoned onto the Council lawns. All ears rung with the talk, talk, talk which followed on for what seemed like hours. The powerful voices of the Town Council were overwhelmed with emotion when they said to the assembled populace, that it was a miracle any of his physical remains were found at all.

The Christian connection on the Council said Gordie must have had a guardian angel, because nobody would have found him at all if he had not been covered with blowflies. *There must have been millions of the buggers*, they said of the wet body. *They were as thick as a black cloud*. They said, those people who were at the site, that if you had moved within a certain closeness, Gordie looked like some kind of disjointed black buzzing devil letting off hot steam.

You could even see various parts of him jumping up here and there, and the rest of him – Well! Let's say, thank God his Mother was in an institution. And two, the Council ought to start doing something about all of those camp dogs. Anybody should be allowed to shoot the bloody lot of them on first sight whenever they go up and down Main Street. Bloody nuisance they are.

The whole town began participating in an uproar about wandering dogs and petrol-sniffing kids. *Find out where they come from and get the damn lazy government in Canberra to ship the whole lot back there. Send them all to Canberra.*

No, the body was not a pretty sight, and the ugly head of all of those wild pig stories resurfaced about the ghost of Abilene. Terrible memories were opened up again. The grisly bush deaths in the past two or three decades, which could be counted on one hand, very quickly became exaggerated into something else. *This sort of thing happens all the time*, chimed some of the more disturbed townsfolk. It was the kind of talk that got everyone revved up and excitable. Volatile language was used.

There were others who had to bring the cemetery into the equation, by making one sour point after another about who was buried there. Anybody. Anything. Sometimes not even a body was even put into a grave. There should be rules about burying things over at the cemetery.

'You want to know the truth about the cemetery?' A loud foghorn of a voice piped up. 'It is chock-a-block full of graves with bags full of the bits and pieces of incomplete bodies.' Everyone knew who was talking because the foghorn man had insisted his son be buried there after he disappeared. Everyone knew he had just run away from Desperance: driven off in his Falcon after half-a-dozen send-off parties. Some day he would return, and find he had already been buried by his father.

The old people from the Pricklebush who had been picked up by Truthful, and forced to attend this meeting, were not very happy at all with this talk about the cemetery. They spat on the ground at each piece of tripe, while Uptown moved sideways in perpetual motion. It was they who saw all the dead people walking off into the afterlife. What Uptown liked to call tritaroon, quadroon, octaroon, full blood, or if speaking about themselves, friends and neighbours. Or, else, those broken parts, looking like a far cry from God's image of a quintessential man. Imagine that. A bizarre soul hovering forever over the district, searching with the eye of an eagle into the guts of an albatross for the rest of their parts. They knew throwing stones dipped in holy water never worked miracles. Or, leaving the gizzards of a cow on the spot of the fallen. Or, throwing into the ocean, a pot of stale urine taken on the night of a full moon six months previously by a sober person from an intoxicated person. Nor any other chic, New-Age spells that people tried, to cast away the evil from invading their homes. If you were dead and still hanging around searching for parts of your body, your soul might choose a better home than the miserable one you had before.

Such was the wisdom of the elders. They said it was to be expected that people who believed only those who helped themselves got along in life, would resort to magic even in this day and age, although they never expected the Uptown mob would own up and say they were involved in it. These were serious-minded people who had escaped wars and famine from all over the world. This was why the elders were quiet at the meeting about Gordie. Anything could happen. Who knows, they whispered, what ideas Uptown would put into their heads from losing their Gordie. 'Remember! Who bloody knows what kind of traditions people have, who say they came from nowhere and don't believe in their own God anymore.'

Sometimes people like Norm Phantom called the community disarray of Uptown the net of irrelevance. It did not take much for ordinary Pricklebush residents, family people, to see what the elders were able to see all along. Deaths like Gordie's gave the townsfolk the heebie-jeebies. They became hooked into a sub-conscious mind which was used to seeing things, particularly in those typical red-tinged cloud-covered skies of the Gulf, the *narwhal*-coloured disembowelled spectre of the supernatural. Half the town claimed, on the gospel truth, they owned extraordinary gifts of perception enabling them to see ghosts, as though it was like the purchase of a new car.

Everyone was blaming the petrol sniffers for killing the neighbour-hood-watch person Gordie. But those little boys were never told why they were in jail. The three little boys did not speak or ask questions because they knew not to listen to anyone in town. They had been told, *Every time you go into that town, close your ears to those white people who might not even be human, who may be, may be not.* Uptown was a world apart, like the spiritual world, which could be imagined by children to have living there white-man spirits like fairies, goblins, elves, imps or leprechauns, or something else more sinister. What else could be true, if they had come from out of nowhere? It was hard not to listen when Uptown talked so persuasively. But little kids want to live, so they closed their ears up good.

When the town had come together on the day they found Gordie dead on the path, not many of the people who lived on the outskirts, whose houses did not qualify for the protection of the net provided by municipal services, bothered coming up to town. 'Who cares what,' the Phantom sisters grumbled. They agreed that they were not going anywhere near the town, if they had to stand within inches of those smelly land-thieving cunts from the other side. 'Talk about your own business yourselves,' Janice Phantom joked, looking towards the town, up the muddy track, as though she had the power to be heard long distance. For good measure, she held out her full left arm, with her index fingers giving her best 'up yours' signal, while her right hand shook the other arm up and down. 'You wanta stop being so stupid,' Patsy told her, and Girlie agreed.

Patsy was trying to feed a bowl of stew to Kevin with a spoon. She was annoyed with her brother because he knew he was an imposition, and by clamping his mouth shut on her, he was creating even more of a nuisance of himself. She knew he was sulking because his father had gone to sea without him, but that did not bother her, so before too long, she put her best effort towards forcing the spoon through his lips.

Girlie had just taken a shower and was feeling better after spending at least thirty minutes watching the alcohol-ridden stench of Truthful wash into the drain. There was no way any of them were going to tramp through a kilometre of muddy road just to go and listen to a bunch of rednecks. Kevin, seeing Girlie come in with just a towel wrapped around her, opened his mouth, and Patsy stuffed it with several tablespoons full of the thick mix of meat, potato and carrots. 'Well! That's that then,' she said, quite satisfied with herself that the meal was finished. 'When is that blasted bell ever going to stop ringing?' she said. She had half the mind to go up there and bloody well kill whoever was ringing it.

The town clerk Valance, with decades of background in municipal service that had never prepared him for the likes of his position in Desperance, could not get the crime off his mind and the more he thought about it, the more he could see himself becoming twisted up in a knot about having to explain what had happened to the assembled people. The way they kept sitting around outside the Council office examining him from a distance with stern-looking faces, he thought they must have thought he had committed the murder. So, not knowing what might happen if he stopped, he kept on ringing the bell.

It looked as though the whole town had arrived to watch his baby blue eyes staring abstractly into space. His tubby body slithered up and down with the rope, pulling and sweating, as though he had been ringing that bell forever. He looked straight through the bewildered assembly who watched him very carefully, while they tried to determine if he had lost his marbles. No one felt anyone had the right to interfere with a man's job, particularly someone they had only known for about eight years, so they sat and watched and waited, determined to let him go on ringing, at least until the law arrived.

Looking past reality, Valance saw another landscape transposed on his mind, a perfect world he had temporarily created, although it did happen. The hinterland people were saying, 'Yes sir, listen to the bell, the angelus bell, Angelus Domini,' and walking like pilgrims, like the holy folk would, coming into town. His efforts were especially for the town camp brethren, calling on the Holy Trinity in the storm clouds above by ringing the bell, hoping his Gods would look down on those poor unfortunates and shower them with the strength to walk to town.

Praise men of ambition who strive for newfangled ideas like reconciliation in old Australia, for Valance with his pricked conscience used every opportunity as town clerk, to make town campers feel like they were a part of the broader community. Even though Gordie was not their neighbourhood watch, Valance considered the community service was available for all folks. Yet, the longer the bell rang, the more people on both sides of the old Pricklebush wars were declaring from their respective sides of town, how they were going to destroy that bell once and for all one day, as soon as they got the chance.

In the end there was great relief to hear Bruiser and Truthful had arrived. They heard Bruiser's mango-green reconditioned Valiant's powerful engine groaning up along the patch of bitumen road outside the Shire Council office like some kind of suffering mud creature, until it gave up the ghost on the footpath outside the Council lawns. Bruiser, Levi's-jeaned and check-shirted, looked hot under the collar when he got out of the car. He surveyed the assembled crowd with a quick glance to see who was missing. It did not take long before the bell was silenced. Bruiser quickly donned the mantle of his Lordship the Mayor, and with a few great strides in his moccasins, went straight across to Valance and squeezed the town clerk's wrists until they cracked. Shocked by the pain, Valance immediately came out of his trance. 'He won't be doing that again for a while, let's hope,' Bruiser said.

'My mate here,' Bruiser said, patting Truthful on the shoulder. 'He knows what to do, and he will be doing it directly, straight after this meeting is finished. There will be no mucking about getting the cops up from down South. We got our own policeman right here, who knows us, knows what we want, and knows this town doesn't want to be mucked about. Not like in the past, about all of them unsolved deaths around the bush here.

'What did those police that they sent up from down South somewhere, know what to do? They don't know us. Did they look like they knew us, or were even bothered to ask us what we think, and we live here all the time? No, they just went around wasting taxpayers' money, made a right monkey of themselves, and whoosh! Where did they go? We looked around and found ourselves sitting here like we always have because? Because we belong here.

'They had gone off, no goodbyes, thanks for the hospitality or anything. They just got back into their chartered planes, and flew off, and that was the last we heard of them. And what did we get out of it? Sleepless nights wondering if we's going to be murdered in our own beds, wondering if we are going to wake up in the morning, or whether we might be dead. You right mate? A penny for them?' Bruiser turned to check on Valance. There were coughs and silly grins in the audience.

'We found the evidence, darn right we did,' Bruiser continued, pausing to slap Truthful on the shoulder again. Truthful nodded. Valance looked up from his seat with interest. The townsfolk sighed relief. 'Poor old Gordie and his wretched soul, parts of which would be being digested by camp dogs but for the strangest coincidence,' Bruiser rattled on as though talking about a normal day, flicking the switch occasionally for good measure, to throw in a bit of the fanciful the locals loved to hear. 'But you know what? There were rainbows appearing across the sky through the clouds.' Something miraculous seemed to have happened, because one of the rainbows actually ended directly over the spot where they had found Gordie. Even Bruiser took on an angelic face when he pointed out the phenomenon. The crowd turned around, craning their necks to look in the direction Bruiser was pointing, looking over the roofs of houses, to the outskirts of town, amongst the ruby saltbush on the side of the muddy track. Multiple rainbows were fairly common in the wide skies of the flat lands.

'See! Gordie was going straight to heaven. God sent him a rainbow to walk on for only God knows where Desperance is. You know where the good folk live, don't you Lord? But for God's sake! What! Listen! There was more to it. God was telling me what to do, God was telling me he will punish the wicked. Thank you Lord, I said, but we already know who did it Lord. We know for sure, and we will make sure they don't get away with it. So after we finish talking, we are going to go straight there and arrest the little buggers. Well! Goodbye then, Gordie ya big long streak, we will always remember you. Pray for us Gordie.'

At this point Bruiser, sticking to his script, shut his mouth. He looked into the crowd with feigned innocence on his face. He searched the eyes for non-believers of the Christian faith. There had to be someone. Where? Where? Who was it going to be this time? Instead, to Valance's astonishment, people started babbling all of their hidden prayers, praying loudly for Gordie. And Bruiser, whose scarred face usually gave him the impression of being a descendant from aliens, now looked different too. Valance was at a loss to understand what he had done to his face. He began to see what others were already seeing; it was like looking at a holy man.

'Hush now folks,' Bruiser finally spoke, repeating his request over and over, until he regained the full attention of the meeting. 'Save your prayers for later folks, we have got a lotta hard work to do here first. First, we need to get organised with putting some men together, because we are going to arrest those little petrol sniffers who did this to Gordie, too right we are. Whose names we got coming now?'

The air bristled. Everyone knew what Bruiser was referring to. It was plain easy to reminisce the kind of yesterday antics of Will Phantom: arsonist, stirrer, troublemaker, cars running up and down the street in the middle of the night. So much trouble, fights and what have you, all because one person kept telling the world he did not want the mine to be built. The very building they were sitting in front of, the beautiful new Council offices, had replaced the one they all reckoned he burnt down. Someone had to have done it. It could not have burnt down by itself. Happily for everyone, the good neighbour mine came to the rescue. It honoured its word: said it was going to donate a brand-new building when it got the green light on Native title problems. They had Will Phantom to blame for that too. Well! It looked as though something like that was stirring its ugly head about race relations again.

'Ya gotta nip it in the bud this time, ya hear me, ya honour?'

'We aren't gonna put up with that same trouble. Turning everyone inside out.'

'No,' Bruiser was the first to agree. 'Just like I said. We will do it differently this time, won't we?'

Everyone knew of those little petrol sniffers living in fortresses of abandoned car bodies. The window smashers. There was a whole group of them moving from one car body to another. Just recently, some had moved to a car abandoned by the Fishman mob lying right next to the path that Gordie used. It had been stripped down to nothing. They were the ones who spray-painted graffiti on tin fences around town, *Petrol Sniffers Don't Die*. You just had to read it and say – *Who were they kidding?* Everybody knew who they were. They knew because the boys had broken into their properties and stolen things and nothing happened to stop it. They knew because petrol had been taken out of their cars on such a regular basis, big, fat padlocks had to be welded onto the petrol tanks, because nothing was done to stop it. The whole town had to become fastidious about locking up: car doors, doors to their houses, everything of value locked up for security against petrol sniffers, and still nothing was done about it.

Everyone had seen these boys walking about town, speeded up on petrol fumes and looking like zombies, walking straight past people as though they did not exist, sometimes with their little girls in tow, initiated by older boys on petrol as well. Disgusting skin and bone creatures who looked like nobody fed them. Or was it right like Valance kept saying: petrol was the only thing that kept the hunger away?

'How did you know it was them?' Valance asked, still nursing his wrists, wading against the tide.

Bruiser, whose motto had always been *Hit first, talk later*, glared at Valance, hoping he would get the message to shut his bloody mouth up. If only Valance had been a drinking man, Bruiser had always thought, once again regretting the Council's choice of recruiting another Southerner to the job. Two minutes in town and he had something to say about everything. The man had been driving him crazy ever since. Down the pub it would have been different. He would have settled the matter of a man like Valance wanting to be a control freak, quick smart, and afterwards, he would be broken in about how to get things done in the Gulf. He regretted not having broken his bloody hand or bashed his teeth in: one thing or the other. He reminded himself to do the latter first opportunity, but not now. This was a delicate matter, except, if Valance pushed too far, Bruiser wondered whether he would be able to stop himself.

'How come we know? What are you saying Valance? How do you think we go about making accusations? I'll tell you something Valance, and listen good because I am not going to repeat myself about this stuff. This is not a Council meeting Valance, where we are sitting around on our arses pushing paper about like we got nothing better to do with our time.

'This is about real people who get out there and they get the job done. Maybe some people need to get out of their air-conditioned offices once in a while. Like the rest of us in the heat of the day. But hey! Wait a minute. Valance, are you trying to tell me something like I think you are thinking: that I am making little fibs to tell people? You think people are stupid or something? If you are accusing me, you better get out with it Valance. Let's stop beating around the bush because I will tell you something, I haven't got time for frigging around. You know what I should be doing right now? Getting a thousand head of cattle to ship to Asia by Tuesday. I've got no time on my hands I can tell you, to sit around pondering, who bloody did it.'

The townsfolk were in awe about the enormity of Bruiser's life. 'Man! A thousand head of cattle. Those cattle on the road now, Bruiser?'

Valance interrupted: a nervous response which had momentarily overtaken him. 'No! How do you know it was them? That's all I am asking.'

'Tell him, Bruiser. He's got a right to know, I suppose,' another voice strung out of the meeting. The silence of consensus followed, and chastened Bruiser who continued directing his speech to Valance, in a tone which suggested he was talking to an idiot.

'One of them little black bastards left his red thong behind right there on the spot, that's what, and whoever it fits, or whoever we find walking around with only one thong on his feet – Well! You work it out. Number two. Another one left his cap behind. He was in such a hurry, rushing off, and it don't belong to anyone either because it belongs to one of Mozzie's boys. It's got the kid's name written on it. What a shame the father don't stay around town and be a real father for a change. That's the proof of it and we found another thong left behind as well. Well! We not going to wait around for the CIB, or any other Southern copper to come up here and fail his duty to this town, like last time when that smart-arse Will Phantom ran amok, remember that? Burnt down half the bloody town and got away with it. Lack of evidence still makes my blood boil: Lack of evidence. Bullshit.'

Trailing off his speech by making a fist into his open palm, Bruiser felt he had said everything that needed to be said, and looked across at Truthful standing beside him for support.

The crowd grew noisier. Neighbours spoke to one another across the rows of plastic chairs in approving terms of Bruiser's no-nonsense course of action. All of the men and their big boys volunteered to spend the rest of the day hunting down every petrol sniffer in sight. Bruiser was quick to rein in the stampede for the man-hunt. 'Whoa, hold on boys. We got to get a grip on this thing first, hold your horses, hang tight to your seats there for a minute. The Constable here has to do some checking first off. Go for it Constable E'Strange.'

'Alright! Alright! Settle down everybody,' Truthful took over. 'We all know a very serious crime has been committed and we have to make sure we follow the letter of the law because I don't want to fill the jail up with the wrong people, and I don't want to be arresting you folk because you are upset neither. We, you and I: it is our responsibility to see justice is done and done correctly. So, let's be calm now.

'First off, we are only after three boys at the moment, there could have been more, but we got to go by the evidence, and we got the evidence like the Mayor just told you. We know who we got to go and find, young Tristrum Fishman and his brother Luke.'

Voices in the crowd interrupted Truthful, calling out that these kids should have been hung, drawn and quartered a long time ago.

For two little boys, they certainly had a bad reputation in Uptown. Someone speaking loudly, told Truthful to fix the little bastards this time. One woman added her voice to civic duty: 'This time lock the little mongrels up so they can never get out, and throw away the key while you are at it.'

All that said, Truthful continued. This part troubled him. 'The other boy we have to find is,' stopping mid-sentence to take a deep breath, before he said the name, 'Aaron Ho Kum.' That raised a few eyebrows, and complete silence. Nobody wanted to call out about the parents now, like they were doing a minute ago.

A penny for your thoughts now, big, righteous Uptown. Every person sitting there knew who these boys were, even if they were not considered the property of the town itself. Hinterland, edge people was where the petrol sniffers came from. From the camps somewhere where the blackfellas lived, because you do not get this kind of trouble from the sons of Uptown, except…Except there was a question mark on Aaron Ho Kum. Those two Fishman boys belonged to Mrs Angel Day. She goes and has them one after the other, after she leaves her real family high and dry to fend for themselves in the Pricklebush. Oh! Yes, she was the one, everyone knew her: a real tart. And where was she today? *I say she's lying flat on her back hmm! hmm! legs spread doing you know what. Too busy to spare a few minutes to come down to the Council lawns like everybody else and get involved with civic duty.*

'She don't look after them boys does she?' the white lady folk were whispering loudly to one another, 'No, she can't be bothered. She just lets them run loose.'

No one looked in the direction of the barman, Lloydie Smith. Everyone knew he was the so-called father of Aaron Ho Kum, even though he had never publicly acknowledged the mother. Well! Radar was what radar was. There had been talk when that child was born. Everyone had been dead keen to have a gander at it, to see if it was white, and she had only been half a kid herself at the time. The scandal of it, no one thought having a baby to the barman would mean she was destined to live Uptown. When that turned out to be the case, she just wrapped that kid up, summer time and all, so nobody could see it.

Nevertheless, black was black. No living person could change the colour of skin. When the white father had never even bothered claiming his coloured child, even though everyone else was saying it was his, she made a horrific vow. Just as she said, she never ever went to Uptown again. Some say, it was because of the vicious rumours, that the poor woman decided to live cooped up in a little dark room with the door shut and locked. Her brother claimed she made her stand, her skin eventually turned white, just like a white woman's. Now, he claimed, she was scared of what people would say. She was too proud to come out and face the music after all these years, and why should she, the wise brother said, explaining: 'The world goes round and round, and it was not going to change one little bit for one moment in her lifetime, or anyone else's who's black around Desperance as a matter of fact.'

Never a flash man, he spoke plain about what other people only liked to think. Miscegenation was the word, he said, for inter-breeding: 'was treated as though good white sperm had been falsely procured by a lesser kind and produced a snake.' The woman's brother looked after everything the best he knew how, including being a father and a mother, right from birth, to the little trouble-maker Aaron. Everyone knew he did everything, while trying to mind a herd of goats he kept on a high block, south of town. He now had two hundred goats, all kinds and colours interbred from building on fifty years of goats, living on the very same spot. Whenever the wind turned, and ran from the south, the pungent stench vaporising out of that piece of ground stank the town out. The goats' wind it was called. The wind with no wife. The Uncle worked hard because of the goats, fed his family, fed the goats, milked the goats, made the town's cheese, and bought freezers to store his product when the Town Council provided him with a power line. It prided Uptown to see Aaron Ho Kum's Uncle do well with a hard life. It pleased them to watch the goat shepherd walking on foot, in weather fair or fraught, tending his flock. Only thing though, and it troubled Uptown, for they could not help thinking that Aaron was funny sort of material to be mixing up in the gene pool and all.

There were a lot of theories, but no answer.

All the country mob in the Pricklebush were shaking their heads disbelievingly, when they heard about what happened. Up and down the Pricklebush, you could see people going along to each other's place, and asking: 'You know why those three little petrol sniffers would want to kill Gordie in the middle of the night?' It was a million-dollar question.

The three boys were asleep when Truthful and Bruiser found them. They were lying side by side, just like they were sardines squashed in a rusty shell, and this was what they might have looked like, when they were found inside the upside-down Holden sedan they called home. The car body was jammed into a camouflage of dense thickets of pricklebush. The dehydrated boys, awoken when dragged out of the car body by the neck, were vaguely aware in a déjà vu kind of way, that something bad was happening to them. Had they escaped one net and fallen straight into another? Only yesterday, members of the Fishman's convoy had unsuccessfully scoured the whole countryside around Desperance searching for those naughty boys.

Angel Day told Mozzie the boys did not live with her, they moved around with relatives. She hardly saw them and that was true.

Those up-to-no-good boys hid here and hid there, even though they knew their old Daddy was looking for them. They knew how to dissolve into thin air, being nothing more than skin and bone kids. One minute they were seen, and the next minute they were gone. Each could have been a blade of grass, or a little prickly bush, they knew how to do it.

When the convoy left town, those cheeky boys came out from hiding, jubilant smiles running across their faces. 'You are in charge Tristram.' 'You the power.' 'No you the destroyer man Aaron.' 'You are.' 'You are.' Tumbling through fairyland, their voices rang through the grasslands, and this was young hope, the place where optimism should dwell. Finally, sitting on the roof of the old car body, feeling safe, they watched the exodus of dust heading down the south road. The last thing they wanted was discipline. Being on the road for months and months with Mozzie Fishman's convoy was not likely to be any picnic. He had warned them: 'Break ya leg first with a bit of wood if I ever catch ya sniffing petrol.' They had heard all about the Fishman's reform agenda for petrol sniffers.

It was unfortunate for them that they were incoherently high on petrol, glue, metho, or whatever cocktail had been their last meal, when Truthful and Bruiser found them. Neither of the three had any idea what was happening to them when the two men threw them into the back seat of the lime-green car and sped over to the jail building. They were dragged inside the premises of the lockup, through to the back, into the walled exercise yard, and thrown around the walled space as though they were sacks of potatoes. Like potatoes, the boys just hit the floor and stayed where they fell.

Manhandling was proving to be a pretty fruitless exercise, as Truthful was quick to discover. He suddenly stopped throwing the boys around. A cop had to remember his duty. Truthful noticed how abstract their blood looked, as it dripped down from the clean walls and onto the clean concrete floor. A sickening image of cattle being slaughtered flashed across his mind, and the first thing he understood was, he would have to clean up. With a mind trained for recording detail, he remembered the detainees were semi-comatose when apprehended. This fact would be written into his formal report. Now, he finds, they are starting to look as though they had been put through a mincing machine.

Even Truthful knew this was a dumb move. 'Hey! Come on Bruse, this is not getting us anywhere.' He noticed the panic in his voice. If! If! imprinted on his consciousness like a highway poster. If there was a Death in Custody. He knew the sucker who would take the rap for it. But not if he could help it, he was not going to be the fall guy. It would be Bruiser's word against his. Quickly the pennies fell, all saying, someone needs to be smart. He realised there wouldn't be one politician, or bureaucrat connected with the State government, who would be game enough to challenge the influential Bruiser, Mayor of Desperance in the woop woop, and get away with it. 'Constable,' he told himself smartly, 'you are on your own.'

The policeman watched helplessly as Bruiser hauled up one of the boys, holding him at face level, while his spit sprayed into the boy's face as he spoke.

'Where were you last night, you little piece of shit?' Bruiser demanded, his scarred face set like concrete, sweat running down from his hairy skull, over his lumpy forehead, and onto his exposed brown teeth, baring now like those of a savage dog. The boy looked dully at the man through his hooded eyelids, incapable, it crossed Truthful's mind, of even opening his eyes in fright. The lack of response from the boy did not lessen the sport, because Bruiser read the situation as meaning only one thing, contempt.

'You don't want to tell me, and if you don't tell me, you make me mad, and you know what's going to happen if you make me mad?' He looked into the boy's face, which was only inches away from his own, and found it was blank. So, with his other hand rolled into a fist, he rammed it into the boy's stomach and sent him flying. Truthful saw the boy land, slammed into the far wall, where he fell into a crumpled heap.

'Shit! Bruiser. Enough, before you go too far.'

The big man was lost in a frenzy. His huge frame stomped from one end of the small exercise yard to the other, while kicking and dragging up one limp sack and throwing it against the wall, then picking up another and throwing it, and another. This struck Truthful in an oblique kind of way as overwhelming reverence towards the search for truth, to the point that it meant killing everyone in the increasingly bloodied yard to find it.

Truthful tried to drag Bruiser outside, but the older man was bigger, and stronger in his new-found strength. 'Let's go mate and see if we can round up the parents. Who knows? Maybe they can give us a clue about what happened,' he said, trying in a last ditch vain attempt to place himself in front of Bruiser who was ducking and weaving to get past. 'Stop it! Stop it! You want to be up on a murder charge?' Truthful yelled at him.

Bruiser could scarcely believe his ears. Was he hearing things? Who was going to be on the murder charge around here?' Thump! Crash! Another kid went flying past the cop. At this point, Truthful lost his temper. The idyllic country cop was dismissed with a click of the fingers, and the Valley cop re-emerged like a circus trick. Here was the set face of law and justice in a city alley after midnight. It belonged to a cop who did whatever it took to survive rort and corruption. He drew his gun. A shot went into the sky. The whole town must have heard it. The clouds paid back with thunder. He pointed the gun straight at Bruiser's face, stood firm, following Bruiser's movements. 'Fucking stop fuckhead, or I'll fucking use it.' Bruiser looked at him for a moment, noticing the finger firmly over the trigger, and laughed. 'Bloody Mafia,' Bruiser blurted out over his laughter, having been reminded of scenes from *The Godfather I* or *II*, it did not matter, it was what he thought. 'Has anyone ever told you you look like the son of a Sicilian Mafia leader?' Truthful kept his aim with his eye fixed on the target.

'Well! Okay. If you want to shoot me, then, come on, shoot me here,' Bruiser pointed to his forehead. 'Then look at them murdering scum and shoot them, put them out of their misery the dogs, you idiot!'

The moment passed and the cop put his gun away. He felt defeated. He was angry with himself now. Only a junior cop would go around pulling his gun like a cowboy. One stupid decision and he knew he had lost all the credibility he had earned, cultivated over years, to become Bruiser's mate. Now, except for the sound of rain falling and thunder from a nearby storm, there was silence in the human corral. The cop dragged each of the boys inside to the cell and locked them in. Bruiser dusted dirt off himself, and washed his hands at the wash basin in the office, then stalked outside to wait in the car.

They drove around town through heavy rain and mud, wheels spinning in the wet clay, engine smoking, skirting the mud larks. Bruiser did not seem to care anymore about the condition of the car: forgetting how he had considered it was sacrilegious if anyone laid a finger on the shiny new paint work. To the passing stares, he sneered, 'Wave. Captains of society wave. So wave and show some respect, even if they didn't teach you those things where you come from.'

They arrived at Angel Day's Uptown house first. Her house was a little grey fibro job. Nondescript really, with cracked and broken fibro louvres, sad and sorry walls. The lot thrown together sometime in the sixties on a cement slab in a big empty yard. It had one saving grace. An address that somehow stoked the fires of passion in even the hardiest of hearts, as they passed by. A house which showered cupid's arrows on sweethearts it was thought, by those who believed it had happened to them, because of the house. A house infectious with burning lust which inspired forbidden imaginings in passing lovers. Dogs and cats on heat stopped by each evening to mate in the yard. Which goes to show, that love knoweth no obstacle, and does not discriminate.

This was the house of the long hot summer night. Mozzie Fishman had bought it for a song, when Angel had abandoned her plain old life for another; 'simply,' she explained, 'to lose myself and come alive again in hot, humid caresses, for love's sake, for the last third of my life at least.' The wish was granted. With the lights out, it could have been a shrine of love from another time or another place, equal to the greatest loves of all times, even the Valley of the Nile, for sometimes after the devil's dancing hour, it became so inflamed, it floated, and he could have been the Mark Antony of men, and she, the Cleopatra of women.

So far from the truth. In this house, Angel Day spent numerous months alone with her two new sons, to sing the lonely person's lullaby, *Send me the pillow that you dream on, so, darling, I can dream on it too.* During Mozzie's many flights of absence, she claimed to any audience whatsoever, the loneliness had caused her to collapse into temporary insanity. If the imagination could stretch the truth, then, it was just as Angel Day claimed, when she said: 'It was the house that sullied the mind of all who looked at it.' This was why she too thought it was a house of miracles. For goodness' sake, from it materialised the birth of two boys at her age, and he, an old man. This twice lucky phenomenon, the whole town marvelled at, as though it had been lust that did these things, but Angel Day said sadly, as far as she knew, it was both times an immaculate conception. That Angel Day, she had no shame, and she gave those two boys the Fishman's name, even though they were not even married.

As a matter of fact, in that very house it was rumoured she had loosened herself, by lying about in others' arms during her lonely moments. With bated breath, the town hung in suspense for Mozzie's return whispering, *Well! The truth will come out now*. But the miracle of Mozzie Fishman was that he forgave her from the bottom of his heart, every time.

From across the road, people heard Bruiser's car pull up. Dolly Parton was singing loudly on the radio, *God doesn't make honky tonk women*. Along the rooftop sat a line of seagulls looking down, staring at Bruiser and Truthful with beady eyes. Both men walked through the gap where the gate had been, in readiness to accost Angel Day, and arrest her too. What for? Neglect. The birds flew off, swooping low over the yard, just as they had done earlier, when they had flown over the exercise yard at the jail.

Of course Angel Day was not at home. The big statue of the Aboriginal Virgin Mary had been left in charge. It stood in the sparse lounge room amidst a mass of plastic flowers, as if to watch over the birds that pecked each other on the roof, and the house's proportion of the Gulf country's croaking frogs that sprung into silence in the grass outside as soon as they heard noise.

Truthful said he thought the house looked like a shrine or a grotto, which was very strange, because he did not think she was a religious person. Statues were the kind of thing his Mother had in her house. If they had come when she was home, they would have known she had left behind in those silent walls, a barrage of abuse to the petrol-sniffing sons who hid themselves from her, every time she wanted them to do something. The statue dominated the house, and the eeriness for them felt too serene in its total silence. It was as though someone had died.

The atmosphere of religious piety felt disconcerting, so, being thorough, in case of some deception, some trick of the eye, they broke the house. Nothing would be preserved of the quaint architecture for the town's posterity. In the shadowy walls, the ghosts of rosaries watched, while the two men worked desperately hard to destroy its incomprehensible meaning, its contents, its beliefs. The ramshackle house remained silently serene as the yard frogs approached, when the two men left. One by one the green creatures came inside, and so did the birds, hopping up to the open front door, deciding to move in, rebuilding the life of the love nest.

'Nothing doing,' that was the size of the thing, the two men agreed. Again, they walked around the rusty Holden car body, searching for clues. The day was almost over, and there was nothing left of it with the disappearing daylight, except to go down to the pub at sunset, where the usual group of men hung about. There was not much that they did not know about the politics of the State, thanks to Bruiser. He swung around on his revolving bar stool, giving the very latest news about the legislation going through Parliament, the particular failings of the legislation, and how, yet again, nobody ever took any notice of his advice.

The men talked about the mine down the road. They discussed how the ore body was shaping up in the latest chemical analysis. They talked about which part of the huge open cut was being operated on, how low the underground shaft would go before the mineral vein petered out. The extraction methods tailor-designed for the vein. The never-ending problems of pumping surface water from the pit, and the ground water tests. Could the aquifers be drying up? The talk could go into hours of general analysis, right through to the functioning of hundreds of kilometres of pipeline, the dewatering of the ore on the flood-prone coastline, and the barges operating with near mishaps while transferring the ore onto the big foreign tankers, which were a sight to see off the coastline.

This was the talk of work. This, and talk about herds of cattle and the slump in prices, other people's horses, whose broken fences were needing a blow by blow description of repairs and maintenance. Then, once a man was talking about his outdoor work, he got around to speaking about the mysteries of the min-min light and who saw it where. How long it followed the car. How spooky was that? Or, in October, the morning glories crossing the skies.

Money and wives were two subjects of discussion that made the dozen beady-eyed men look depressively at the comfortable pub decor of stuffed baby crocodiles crawling up the wall, and the tanned skin of the biggest croc ever caught. These were two of Norm's special works of local fish mounted and displayed proudly on the walls. Elsewhere, the walls were stuffed with autographed stubby holders, or pinned with nude pictures of women. From the ceiling hung dusty flytraps that flew about in the breeze of the overhead fans in front of the glass-fronted fridges holding fine wines and red, green, white and yellow cans of beer.

On the jukebox, droning country and western music occasionally seduced eyes to look yonder, through the little window slot that separated the Barramundi bar from the ugly, stained, mustard-coloured walls of the snake pit next door, which was crowded to overflowing with 'the darkies'. As they talked, the Barramundi bar drinkers observed the young men from the Pricklebush around the snooker table in a play-off. They had a good squiz at the dressy black women sitting around the plastic tables laughing as if there was no tomorrow. They placed bets on the frequent drunken fights that went on and on until the defeated ended up lying motionless on the ground outside. Silences led to the usual daydreams of fish, then the talk resumed of fishing and boats, and all kinds of roads, rivers and ocean tracks which led them to fish.

Young Kevin Phantom was not welcome at the snooker table as he swung in and out through the lads standing around playing the game. All the bigger and stronger boys in T-shirts and jeans took appearance and life seriously, while standing beside the snooker table. They said to Kevin, 'This is a serious game.' Kevin had had more than enough to drink simply by persuading people to pity him because he had no money. A few of the lads gave him their own half-drunk cans, and went and bought themselves a fresh one. He was given sips, as he worked his way around the room, just through speaking loudly into anyone's ear, and pestering until someone gave him some. After a few hours, nobody wanted him around, and someone went over to the bar to ask Lloydie Smith, the barman, to get him out of the place.

'Hey! Lloydie, come over here. I want to talk to you,' the woman called out, but the barman had his back to her.

All eyes from around the plastic tables were looking towards the window where the woman kept calling, and waiting for Lloydie to hear her. The more she got into the rhythm, she made a game of calling out 'Lloydie', then standing aside to wink back to the tables, motioning with her lips 'have a look', and rubbing her backside with one hand. Everyone started looking. Their eyes, drawn through the window slot, peered across the bar to where Lloydie was standing, then the nudging began, eyes lighting up in merriment, 'Oh! Look! He is doing it again.'

They saw Lloydie Smith wiping down the bar that was made from grey-brown planks salvaged locally from an ancient ship-wreck. He worked with a wet cloth that was impregnated with spilt beer, and he worked on the wood carefully, in rhythmical motions, as though he were caressing a woman's skin. Truthful watched his hands at work, fastidiously cleaning, smoothing, fussing as he always did. Already he felt in the mood to see Girlie. He left Bruiser, who noticed nothing, to do the talking.

'Well! Lloyd, what about it then, that son of yours?' Bruiser never cut corners with his bluntness.

'I burnt my bridges there years ago and you know it, so it's got nothing to do with me,' Lloydie replied in his short tone of voice.

'You want to come down and help us ask him what happened, you might be able to get it out of the little bugger?'

'Nope! Nothing to do with me.'

'We'll ask his mother then, if we can get her to talk.'

Lloydie happened to know her brother, the goat man, had had it up to the eyeballs with Aaron, and had said he would kill the little bugger the next time he saw him. And she, if you looked in the cupboard with a torch, all you would see was a black woman with white skin, who spoke even less than the spirit of the beautiful fish woman, locked inside the timber planks of the bar. He felt her body responding to the soft touch of his hand. Moving her silvery body further towards him with every movement he made. When he looked at the wood he saw the outline of her body luxuriously posed and hungry for touching. It was fascinating to him that nobody else saw her moving her body around at him through the wood. He could hardly believe that she only had eyes for him, as though they were always alone. She was the she-fish, who had come alive from his erotic dreams, that had seemed so lifelike that he had now taken up the habit of sleeping on the top of the bar at night.

'Go ahead,' Lloydie said, more or less oblivious to Bruiser's enticing. 'Talk to the brother, maybe he can help you.'

By the time Lloydie had finished talking to Bruiser, and responded to the inebriated woman screaming out to him from the bar next door, Kevin Phantom had disappeared.

'Where are you going?' a male voice wafted out of the car window on the passenger side, as a vehicle slowed down next to Kevin walking along the footpath in the rain.

'Yu wanta lift Kevin?' the voice continued, but Kevin kept on walking, hardly aware of the car. He was thinking, wondering where his father had gone and when he was coming back.

'He should'na left me,' Kevin said, continuing to walk, as the car purred, moving slowly along beside him.

'We would'na leave you, come on, and we'll have some fun without him,' the voice hummed in tune to the car's motor turning over.

'You got a party going then?' Kevin asked, opening the door of the car and jumping in.

'Yeah! You're the party coon boy,' the voice snapped, and the car roared off along the sealed road, did a wheelie down the end, roared back past the pub, turning there at high speed, tyres screeching. But it bothered no one. Truthful and Lloydie were outside the pub armed with batons, fighting some of the men who had been attacking each other with broken beer bottles in the mustard bar.

'Clear the whole place out, I have had enough of the buggers,' Lloydie ordered Truthful, as the car swung around the corner. It was action night, the whole place, except the main bar where the dozen men drank, was to be cleared. The car headed off along the bitumen stretch going south of town. All Kevin could see were the white hoods each of the people in the car had placed over their heads. Then he felt the hands of someone in the back seat pushing something over his head. He reached up and felt the rough thread of the material, like a sack, and he could smell wheat or flour, like poultry feed. He knew the smell, recognising it from when he had passed Uptown people's backyard fowl coops. You could smell it from the street if you were passing by some houses.

Kevin knew he had to get out of the car, but he feared the consequences of jumping out, as it headed along the bitumen at high speed. Struggling, he twisted around in his seat until he felt the handle of the car door but realised it was locked. He reached for the lock but felt the knife gliding along his neck being pressed deeply into his flesh. There were several voices in the car, all talking to him at the same time. 'Take this for Gordie,' fists flew at him from the front and from the back. He started to panic, and in his panic, felt spasms running through him. Kevin had moved into another world, when suddenly the car stopped, and he was tipped out onto the ground.

Someone said, 'Great.' He had found the cricket bats in the boot. Kevin slipped in and out of believing it was not happening to him, hearing war cries, laughter, and smelling beer and rum. He tried to rip the sack off his head because he couldn't breathe but the knife dug deeper, cutting him. Then the knife was released by the attacker who had been holding him from behind, breathing alcoholic fumes into his ear. When he started to struggle with the sack again, he felt the knife swung about as if it was being used to slash at his hands.

Whenever he regained consciousness, it was to feel the thud of being struck with something heavy. He heard his bones break with a pain that forced him to open his shock-sealed lips, and call out through the muffling bag to his father. This was when, through the white light of pain, he witnessed his childhood, always moving back into the arms of his father. A little boy safe with his father: telling his father to run, run faster, and he felt himself sinking into water. He was wet and hurt, and his arms, stretched out in front of him, they were being dragged off his body. His skin was burning, he was being skinned alive, pulled behind the car, its exhaust fumes choking his breath.

It was during the night sometime when Truthful was driving towards the Phantom place, and in the headlights, he saw Girlie sitting out there on the road. When he stopped, he saw in the light from the car, the body of Kevin lying on the road beside her.

'We got to get him out of here now,' he said quickly, but she did not move as she sat crying beside her brother, his head on her lap. She continued explaining to Kevin that she had no idea how to bring him back to life. 'Where do I start Kevin?' Truthful saw what had happened. She had only untied his hands and removed the sack from his head.

'I don't know what to do, it will be alright,' she kept talking, rocking him and talking.

'Where's Janice and Patsy,' Truthful asked, picking Kevin up.

'Nobody's here,' Girlie said, barely able to speak coherently as she rambled on to her brother.

They drove Kevin straight up to the hospital. The sister in charge, with no one else to support her, led the way inside the fibro building. It was clear she reigned in this isolated outpost south of town. Within minutes, she had Kevin on a drip with an oxygen mask over his face, pumping air into faint lungs. Then she was on the phone in front of the computer records, 'Is that you Doctor? This is the situation.'

Girlie stayed next to Kevin watching his bleeding chest moving rapidly as he breathed through the mask. She could hear the sister's voice, repeating instructions from the main district hospital six hundred kilometres away, and heard her telling Truthful that the flying doctor was already in the sky, was being diverted to land at Desperance.

By the time the doctor landed on the bonfire-lit airstrip, Truthful and the sister had Kevin set for an emergency evacuation. Girlie watched helplessly as he was transferred onto a stretcher and taken into the plane, then rehooked to the oxygen cylinder and drip. The sister told her there was no room for her to go. Then the door was closed, and the plane was gone.

So, things went on as they do when the bad things happen, with everyone talking about it like they knew everything. So many private eyes. No one owned up to knowing anything in an official capacity. Didn't see it. Truthful should have looked. He heard the car go past. The car sounded like a rally car when it ripped up and down the main road. They said, who was going to get up in the middle of the night to look at town louts trying to kill themselves? There were dozens of people involved in the brawl outside the pub, but they all said they were too out of it to notice what was going on really. *I was too busy fighting man, but I should've seen that car and if I had then I would have killed the bastards.* Some people were kind enough to say that.

Others said it was Kevin's own fault because he was always looking for trouble. And Kevin, any moment he regained consciousness, his eyes looked as though he was looking at a white-fired hell. Sometimes word came back on the grapevine to the family about Kevin's condition. An old tribal lady, a traditional doctor, went down to see the girls, and she said she had seen him. She said she went to the big hospital, all the time pretending to visit sick relatives from out of town.

They knew she had never left Desperance in her life, but they believed everything she told them. As a gifted ventriloquist she spoke with the voice of a spirit, a guardian angel, who had sat alongside of Kevin's bed and waited. 'He tries to scream the word "fire" but he is still running away, still unable to fight the souls of the people who did this to him.' Girlie, Janice and Patsy existed just to get word from the old woman. They sat in the kitchen, or outside in front of the house waiting to see who would come next to tell them something, and waiting for their two big brothers to come home.

Inso and Donny had left their mine jobs and driven all night over the slippery road in the rain, to get down to the hospital to see Kevin. It was just heartbreaking to sit there and look at him. The brothers sat uncomfortably on either side of the bed in side chairs, in the white painted room. There was not much talking, except about going home, and to offer words of support, just to let Kevin know the big brothers were there. They talked normal, not mucking around talking, but strong talk, nothing's changed kind of feeling, because they were the big brothers, to let Kevin know, and let him know when nobody else was in the white room checking every five minutes, he would be avenged, total, and sure, to the end.

They tried to avoid looking directly at him, staring instead at the starched white hospital linen, unnerved by the sight of all of the medical equipment which had become a part of him. The machines had dials scratching jagged lines on graph paper. Others had dials which shook while trying to stay in one position, while regulating tubes going in and out of Kevin's body, wrapped from head to foot in bandages or plaster.

They found they could not communicate anything of how they felt after a few words, so they sat there in silence, pondering who did this to him. Then, Inso or Donny looked at each other and gave the nod to go, so they could talk, and they left. A few hours later, down at the pub, they would use the payphone to call Truthful and ask him, 'What the bloody hell was going on up there?' There was no way, they told Truthful, that they believed he was doing everything he could to catch the buggers, 'Are you?' Each took the phone in turn to accuse him of protecting the bastards who picked on Kevin. 'Aren't you? You moron.'

'Give me a break,' Truthful demanded, and told them to keep away because he was pretty close to catching the culprits and he did not want them frightened off and leaving town. 'Ah! Yeah!' Donny and Inso replied before hanging up on him, while Truthful was trying to remind them about their jobs at the mine. Truthful was moved to the top of their list of how they were going to deal with everything, once they got home.

'They've still got him on the respirator,' Truthful told Girlie, the first, second and third day. He kept coming down to the Phantom place expecting sympathy for the huge load on his plate. He still didn't have a clue who had beaten up Kevin. He and Bruiser were already busy enough investigating Gordie's death.

'There can't be that many hoon cars to look at,' Girlie clipped in the icy voice she reserved for the world of the incompetent. She was sitting at the kitchen table, arms folded, staring straight into Truthful's face. The other two sisters sat around the kitchen table as well, their big arms folded, waiting to hear what he had to say.

'There is no need for the hostilities,' he replied. 'You already know I've asked everybody in this useless town.'

'Oh! Yeah!' Girlie glared, her arms and legs crossed tighter. 'Well! I don't think that is good enough. What do you think Janice? Do you think that is good enough? Hey! And what about you Patsy? Don't you think someone should have been arrested by now? Someone taken in for questioning?' And she looked straight back at Truthful. Her words were like fired bullets. 'You were quick smart about finding a few little black boys to arrest for that stupid Gordie. The pimp. He deserved what he got. But what did our Kevin do? What harm did he do to anyone?'

Truthful was fuming, said he thought they were a mob of hypocrites, 'I seen the way you looked after your brother.' He dared not mention that two of the little black boys Girlie referred to were her stepbrothers. Not in this house if anyone had any sense.

'Oh! Really. And how's that?' Girlie challenged.

'Forget it,' Truthful said, feeling the last thing he needed was to create an enemy out of Girlie right now. He tried to touch her on the arm but she moved away. 'I don't know what I am saying half the time. I have had hardly any sleep for days. I got to get some sleep soon or I am going to go mad thinking about what has happened to everybody.'

There was silence in the room. They knew that he was blaming his lack of sleep on Girlie for not letting him stay with her. They kept their mouths shut for a change, because they knew the truth of the matter was otherwise, it was Truthful himself who did not want to stay. Girlie had hissed at her sisters days ago, 'Said he was too busy. Said he had to guard the prison until he could get some help. Said he had to keep an eye on those boys. Well! That suits me fine, the big ugly bastard, stinking of grog and who knows what. I bet he is molesting those little boys because nobody cares what happens to them.'

The two other sisters had heard rumours many times previously about Truthful, Shh! being bisexual. The boys at the pub talked about it around the pool table in a flippant kind of way. In terms of what they heard had happened to other boys after hours, being picked up on the road by Truthful, or what they thought would happen to them if they ended up locked up for the night. Neither Janice nor Patsy discussed any of these revelations with Girlie, since she was sleeping with him, and maybe she did not want to know, because, surely, she would know. A woman knows.

It was really peculiar how an ordinary house could evoke strange pictures in the loose minds of people. It was really just a simple house. A house built with the hopes of raising a family, Norm Phantom had always claimed, when he talked about his home.

Yet, there are houses, so removed, they have no call for the high moral ground. Such houses are regarded as being so strange, like the Phantom house with its twisty corridor of corrugated iron, it bestowed significant powers in the minds of Uptown. They claimed it would conquer those it conjured into its grasp. Just as Angel's house exuded lust, Norm Phantom's evoked terrible fearings of loathing from the great minds, who, like the black cockatoos in flight overhead, only saw it from a distance.

People who never came to visit. It made your heart jump. They complained it sent the cold shivers running up and down their spines, just from looking at that sinister fortress of corrugated iron flanked by closed thickets of prickly bush. But they looked from a long way off, at the other end of that long muddy road from town. Crows flew around it at night they claimed. The greatest of all Uptown desires was to have the house and all the prickly bush flattened by a grader. Once and for all.

Everybody watched that black sympathiser Truthful with a close eye, while asking, 'I wonder what he's up to now?' Each morning they saw him drive out of town. Slip sliding like a bat out of hell, *there he goes*, in broad daylight mind you, driving down to the Phantom's place, worrying for that young Phantom kid Kevin, even after what happened to Gordie.

'He should stay away from that place.' Yes! This was right, people talk. But it seemed the man did not have a thread of respect for himself, for he went straight to the home of the most hated and fearful man in the Gulf, Will Phantom – *Wherever he was running amok again, who knows where* – and did not care who was watching him. All without a care in the world, even though he knew Will Phantom had dragged the whole town down, when he tried to stop the mine from going ahead. That whole business had caused people to go stark raving mad. A lot of important people in the government said he had no right to do what he had done. Now, the whole world stared at infamous Desperance, and all because Will Phantom could not cop it sweet, his bad luck.

This was the reason why Desperance needed an active police-man, an ideas man, someone like Truthful, who felt this was the big breakthrough in his years in the town. It required a lot of guesswork to know what was going on about the place now. So, since supposition was the prerogative of the police station, it was part of Truthful's occupation to be Will's second-guesser. Once

Will Phantom heard about Kevin that would be it. He would come there as large as life, reeking for revenge. Truthful secretly surmised in his acts of seducing Girlie, that Will Phantom would not expect anyone to think he would turn up at his father's house. Truthful thought he possessed a brave idea. He would be waiting when Will arrived. Ideas were very fashionable in Uptown at the moment, and he felt he had his ideas down pat. He was betting his last dollar on it.

The days passed full of cringe for Uptown, winding themselves up by watching Truthful's mad driving to Norm Phantom's house. The whole town rested on their fearful beliefs, pondering and waiting for a showdown of sorts. Would Will Phantom pick and choose what goose among them was going to cop it – a house fire, a fight, intimidation, terrorism?

Everyone in town knew the story, that Norm would not have a bar of Will, and so far, he had been the only person who could crush him. He had told the big-head off. He wanted nothing to do with him. Called him a no-good mongrel breed, talking about land rights and all of that crap. Yes! Norm told him what Uptown wanted to say, 'We don't want any of that Southern black rights activism stuff up here.' Would Will Phantom return? Nothing would stop him now his father was away. Truthful did not rate a mention, for nobody would be able to defend themselves against the stash of guns and ammunition everyone knew Will had hidden somewhere in that monstrous tin castle they could see down the road. The great speculation about the explosives and equipment he had in his possession was dragged out of memories, and talked about again with interest bordering on paranoia, with new links to terrorism. There were things missing down at the mine every time there was a stocktake.

Word grew that Will Phantom even knew how to assemble an atomic weapon. He had stolen uranium in the area, from the locked-up mine at Mary Kathleen. He had just slipped over the fence and helped himself. It was idiotic thinking, for it was not possible. The uranium mine of Mary Kathleen, some few hundred kilometres away, was sealed, fenced, locked, and guarded. But who knows? Who knows these things anymore when people are living in such a complex world, and people do not talk, do not negotiate a fair deal, do not live by the rules, and will do anything to get what they want?

Blah! Blah! Blah! So on and so forth. People talked of the many foreign boats mixed up with the mining. They surmised a lot. For who knew what shipload of stuff Will had smuggled from black rights sympathisers, from pirate ships bobbing up and down in the moonlight, just kilometres off the coast? Anything! Anything! *Moored there while the stuff was rowed ashore probably.* Anyone could see for themselves what was really going on, they claimed. *He was going to create his own race war up in the Gulf.* Everyone knew that. Knew one had to be very careful with surface appearances, especially with a place like Norm Phantom's, which could be mighty misleading looked at from the other end of the road.

'Idiot! Bloody idiot!' Girlie could churn Truthful around, like wringing him fingers-first through her old Simpson washing machine, while dragging him out at the other end, smack flat and drained. The sisters could tell that she was plain itching to stir him up. Ever since what happened to Kevin, she had become obsessed about old man Joseph Midnight knowing everything. 'He sees everything! Doesn't he see everything?' The hundredth time. Every passing night, for half the night, the two older sisters had listened to her talking about old man Joseph Midnight.

Now, sitting in the kitchen, Janice and Patsy, both with great bags under their eyes and barely mobile because of Girlie's pacing around during the night, wondered why Girlie, who was so quick to see everything, had not noticed the colour draining from Truthful's face as she yelled his inadequacies at him, straight across the kitchen table.

Initially, all she wanted to know was whether he was getting any closer to catching those mongrels and when he never answered her, Well! that was that. It was they who had to eventually serve him some food because she refused. 'Yer can go hungry,' she claimed, eating in front of him, filling her own big mouth with a half piece of toast at a time. The moon sisters watched his olive-skinned face fade from red, to storm-sea grey. They thought it uncanny how the colour perfectly matched the corrugated-iron walls of the cramped kitchen. 'Old man Joseph Midnight will be able to tell you, I am telling you,' Girlie prattled on with a full mouth.

'Then why don't you ask him?' Truthful finally barked at her like a dog breaking into her cruel world. The sweat running down his face sprayed over the table. Girlie jumped out of the way with her plate. She grabbed her cup, grinning now from ear to ear. She had at last found the crack, exposed the wound, forced him to feel her pain. There was no room for little boys around her world. 'Go, Truthful.' Thinking he could just suffocate himself with his own tongue which was already swollen up with bundles of lies stuffed inside his mouth. No wonder he could not talk. But Girlie could grab someone's tongue and shake it around just by using her bare words.

Then, with the bigger sisters sitting and eating, trying to pretend nothing was happening, she noticed he was clamming up again. *Anyone hear anything?*' He put his finger to his lips, indicating to Girlie, she should do the same. Truthful looked as though he had seen a ghost. He had seen old man Joseph Midnight coming out of the mud along the side of the road outside of the Phantom place this morning, as he drove down the road. He had been seeing Joseph Midnight sneaking about just about everywhere he looked lately. This morning, the old fella just stood there staring, mud dripping everywhere, and when Truthful looked at him, he told Truthful he was a bloody idiot.

The dismayed sisters sat quietly like little mice sipping tea, and again, were suddenly surprised to notice how his thick lips were trembling, as though he had just come out of a fridge, or was seeing ghosts, or both, and thought, perhaps he had lost his marbles. They kicked polite circumspection reserved for visiting white people out the door, and Patsy and Janice stared straight into his face, to observe his radically changed personality more closely. Only Girlie, continuing on regardless, seemed to be reaching his lost state of mind. Who wouldn't, with her screaming abuse at them from across the table? The bigger sisters lent in to take an even closer look at his face. His heavy hooded eyelids were twitching uncontrollably as he stared into space past Girlie.

Again, Truthful saw the images which had overtaken his car at dawn. It happened when he had started driving out on their road, and at first, he thought he was losing his eyesight as he stared ahead at the fuzzy, lighter, paler-coloured road and countryside ahead. It looked as though there was a fog ahead, but soon, he discovered it was not a fog at all, only by then, it was too late to turn around. He could clearly see he had driven deep into spider webs as high as the vehicle. A thick sheet of white surrounded him. Perhaps Truthful had never seen such a thing before, but it was an old story that sometimes happens overnight when a cloud of travelling spiders drop onto land from the sea wind, and start building their webs the height of house walls. Ingeniously, the spiders work at night, flying through the air as they attach their silver webs to anything with height: electricity poles, fences, long grass, prickly bush trees. The fat-bellied creatures sat in the middle of their webs, while their long, sinister legs spread like lethal weapons, and looked like stars as big as saucers. He drove on, slowly, foolishly he thought. A multitude of spiders crawled through his brain. He did not know what to do. He could not go back: he did not want to go back. He was locked in: he had to drive forward for there was nowhere else to go, nowhere to turn around.

Without anyone to tell him what to expect, Truthful could never have realised how densely packed together those webs were. The car became thickly coated with layer after layer of the silky, film-like threads. Soon, he saw nothing in the whiteness, except the webs stuck on the windscreen with the angry spiders caught between their nests. There were spiders crawling all over the car and he quickly wound up the windows. He killed those that had got inside with the local telephone book, and within minutes, locked in the airless car and loaded down with humidity, the perspiration started to pour off his body.

He found it difficult to breathe. He panicked, inside his brain he saw millions and zillions of cellular neurons popping around like white baby spiders. The creatures raced into each other, creating old man Joseph Midnight's face, twisted with anger, staring at him and calling him an idiot, then pulsating away into a void the size of a pin hole, only to be recreated speeding towards him again, even quicker than before.

Another crazy thing happened to Truthful. His body became weightless, and with all his might forcing his fingers which felt like rubber, he held on to the steering wheel, to stop himself from floating away. A lulling voice, whispering inside his head, kept telling his body he was going to die. But dying by asphyxiation was not what his body wanted to do. He struggled against the weightlessness blowing him towards the dead relatives assembled in a little huddle in the flowing white distance.

Remarkably, at this point, fate had a little something to give Truthful. His body repulsed the ailing brain. The energy must have come out of his soul, for his hands locked like clamps around the steering wheel, and his feet turned into flattened lead on the floor of the car. His left foot was still planted on the accelerator, and he literally flew out of that road.

Normally, Truthful would have agreed with Girlie. If you ever want to find out about anything in your vicinity, you have to talk to the mad people. She had always said this, although more often in the previous days: 'They know the deepest and darkest secrets of this place.' But nobody knew what Joseph Midnight knew, and everyone knew what Girlie would never know. It was an eye for an eye. A black for a white. It was just starting. The fathers of those louts who bashed Kevin were openly boasting to Uptown about putting a nigger down for Gordie. Kevin was paying for the memories, for being smart once, from a family with airs about themselves, for Will Phantom. *Open slather, open slather*, came the whispered words which kept repeating themselves when he picked up the phone in the middle of the night, while another voice gave the warning, *Stay out of it Truthful, it's open slather now.*

Truthful knew that after the attack on Kevin, no one was really interested in harming the three petrol sniffers accused of killing Gordie. Why would they bother with kids who had cooked their brains so badly they felt nothing? Truthful knew most of the town did not even think the petrol sniffers had it in them to go and kill Gordie. But! It did not stop there. The phone at the police station rang all hours of the night and day, a different whispering voice most of the time, with more warnings, *You come near our boys and we will hang you.* A chill ran down his spine every time the phone rang. At night, he lay in the darkness thinking how the town had managed to mould him into the shape they needed, so he had nothing to fall back on when something like this happened. Nothing could happen: that was the dilemma. This was it. End of story now.

On one of the nights following the arrest of the boys and the incident with Kevin, Truthful had just started to settle down again after the phone had stopped ringing for the last time. Sleep drifted in and he started to dream. In the dream he heard someone knocking on the door, but he decided not to answer, until the knocking grew so loud, he went to the door to see who it was.

He turned the lights on and stood at the doorway looking at the rose garden, deep red roses were blooming, but to his surprise, there was nobody there. When he looked past the darkness to the streetlights on the other side of the road, he saw stray dogs sniffing the rubbish bins. He glanced over the town, just to check whose lights were still on, to pin down where the nuisance phone callers could be coming from. He made a mental note of those houses where lights were shining. He was half asleep, yet he walked around the yard, checked his car was locked, and went back inside, closed the door, flicked the light switch, and turned around.

The only reason he was able to see in the darkened office was because there was moonlight shining through the windows. The police station was full with Aboriginal people crowding through the building. He became very frightened. Their skin was grey. Whenever he blinked, the place seemed to become more crowded. He stayed pressed against the door. He thought if he were to move, the people might see him. There were so many jostling bodies, jammed up against him, that he could feel the closeness of grey shoulders under his nose, and see that the shiny greenish substance covering their skin was a sea slime that felt cold and sticky whenever the jostle accidentally bumped into his face and arms.

The smell of the sea was never far away in Desperance. Except during the Dry, when the sea returned to its normal shoreline some twenty-five kilometres away. Even then, the breeze carted its fish smells back to town. Now, Truthful smelt it like old dead fish guts.

He remembered his Italian Mama's stories about the ghosts of dead people coming to haunt you.

Moments later, in panic and with a racing heart, Truthful thought, *What of his prisoners, the three boys?* 'Excuse me! Excuse me!' He found himself speaking as though he was a ghost himself. He pushed, shoved, inched his way through the throng, thinking faster and faster, if the boys could see them too, then maybe, he was not dreaming. It felt like an eternity to reach the back of the building to the cells. 'Excuse me! Excuse me!' Slowly, like a cloud moving, the grey spirits drifted aside.

'What say they are not alright?' Truthful started to become worried about the boys. He could not move fast enough now. Tristrum and Luke Fishman, aged ten and twelve. Aaron Ho Kum, aged eleven. When the flogging stopped, they had scooted under the table away from Bruiser, and huddled against the back wall, petrified, waiting, for the screaming might come back and take them again. Truthful felt his thoughts thrown through the air by a huge force, crushing back at him through a million possibilities he kept rejecting, saying: 'They are alright.'

Luke was the oldest, and he tore the T-shirts into strips, tied the knots, and carefully examined whether each length would be long enough. The other two boys watched his hands work in the moonlight and said nothing, and then he had everything prepared. They just followed Luke into the darkness and into the light beyond, up on the blue sea, swimming under a cloudless summer sky. Truthful believed he could have reached them in seconds but his body was lead, his head was like the sedentary oleander beside the jail, betrayed by his mind. It was betrayal all round. The boys were dead. Their shredded T-shirts were the first thing he saw. Three strands hanging taut from the cross bar at the top of the bars across the front of their cell. 'Say it's not true,' Truthful said, speaking to the spirits, and just as suddenly as he had been alone before, he was alone again. There was nothing in the building but emptiness and silence.

The only sound was the high tide lapping on the beach. It did not seem possible that they could have hung themselves. The cell was not high enough and when he saw their feet slumped on the floor, he could not imagine how they could have done this to themselves. Yet nobody had come into the building. He would have known. They were sleeping on the floor when he checked before going to bed. Now they were dead, and he preferred to believe the opposite, and cried out to them: 'You are tricking me.' He checked each of their wrists for a pulse, and in resignation, closed their vacant eyes. Still, he was hopeful, he thought they were children. Children playing a game, 'Come on,' he said, and there was the usual, useless shaking for life to come back.

Now, he could not remember if he had checked the cells before going to bed. Of course he had. Didn't he always make the last check on the cells, even when they were empty? He was not sure anymore. Perhaps it had been the day before. Or the day before that. He ran to his desk to check his records. Thank God, he thought, the records were there. He had been checking, but still, he doubted himself. This time he had trouble pushing away the thought that he had falsified the records. He told himself he was only creating misunderstandings. Very much on duty, he went back to the cells and took the boys down. One by one he placed them back on the floor where they had been sleeping the last time he saw them. It had only been an hour ago. He would have known. Three people living under the same roof cannot die without you knowing it. Things were going to be better in the morning, he promised. 'What a breakfast.' A feast he would prepare for his boys with his own two hands.

'There's his car now,' the gossipy people were gathered in a kind of protest on the corner next to the Fisherman's Hotel, and were looking across the street at the police station. There were big-bodied people standing in the hot morning, with skins becoming redder, and every now and again, another would announce that for no reason, he had felt the cold shivers. Then others would announce how they felt faint. It was hard waiting when there was an awful stench coming from the police station, drifting down the street and all over town.

'He mustn't have a sense of smell,' said Carmen, the middle-aged, tightly permed blonde proprietor of the fish and chip shop situated right next to the police station. 'And did you hear the dogs howling?' Who hadn't heard the dogs howling all night! They never stopped howling. Carmen had been complaining of the stench of something dead coming from the police station for days. She felt vindicated now that other people felt the same way she did. It was Carmen who started the street-corner protest when she came across the street to the pub and told Bruiser to tell that Truthful to clean the place up, before she made a formal complaint to the Council.

Inside the police station, Truthful was in another world. It looked like he could flip in any direction. Old man Joseph Midnight came along, and said he had looked through the window across the road, and seen that idiot cleaning around his jail all fastidiously, looking after the three little petrol sniffers, who were already dead. Nobody heard what Midnight said, since nobody ever paid him any attention. Midnight said he had seen four hot dinners sitting on the policeman's special table, which he had moved into the cell for them. Their food was still steaming on the plates.

When Bruiser finished his last glass of beer for the morning, he went outside the pub, stretched himself, and yawned as though he were a bear coming out of its den. He told Carmen and her street-corner gang that he was going over to the station to check on the situation. Three times he knocked on the door and everyone could hear him as plain as day, but Truthful did not answer. Undeterred, Bruiser walked back across the street, said nothing, got into his car, and completed a mud spraying wheelie right across to the police station. This time he did not knock. He just walked straight in after his rifle blew the lock clean off the door.

'What the fuck are you doing?' he asked Truthful, after he walked in and saw what the cop was doing. Truthful did not answer, he was in a daze. Bruiser very quickly understood that the man was off with the pixies – tending dead bodies like that. He stood well back, sickened with the overpowering smell of death. Trying to stay calm, he watched Truthful moving each stiffened body. He was moving the boys from their upright position, leaning against the front part of the chairs where they had been arranged around the dinner table, and carrying them, one by one, back to their bunks, where he gently placed a blanket over each.

'They are dead man. How come they are dead?' Bruiser knew he had made a mistake as soon as he had spoken.

Truthful just stared blankly at the floor with a smile on his face.

Bruiser smiled weakly too, in case Truthful noticed him before he had a chance to get out of the building. He tried to be quiet, like a mouse, without making any sudden noise to upset him. He could hear his heart thumping like a drum. Relieved he had reached the door in one piece, he closed it quietly behind him. He got back into his car and completed a second wheelie back to the pub, and went straight inside, without saying a word to Carmen and the gang who had followed him.

'They are all dead. All of them. 'Cept Truthful. He's gone stark raving mad. Give us a drink will ya?'

'Can't be.' Someone whispered.

'The smell inside, man, it was that strong I am telling you, I thought I was going to pass out. Hurry up with that drink Lloydie.' Bruiser began telling everyone crowding around him what he had seen. They watched him spitting out his words as though he wanted to be rid of the shock as quickly as possible. Lloydie Smith, with detached face, placed a large glass of beer down on the bar. Bruiser swallowed it with a single gulp.

'Can't be,' someone kept whispering. All of the people gathered in the bar had anxiously cushioned themselves around Bruiser, not wanting to miss a word of the terrible things he had seen. Ignoring them, and speaking directly to Lloydie, Bruiser said his head felt like a merry-go-round. It seemed life was not spinning fast enough, for with resignation and loss in his voice, he claimed, 'They were catching me.' This was the best way to explain what he preferred to have kept to himself. The fact that as he was backing out of the police station, he saw the three boys running after him. 'Watch out,' Bruiser whimpered. The words escaping from his mouth surprised everyone listening, including himself. A tighter circle formed around him and he thought he was going to faint. The cool draughty breeze hit everyone in the face. A loud thumping noise filled the bar room, the sound of all their hearts beating loudly.

'You are going to die for this,' Bruiser whispered, dragging Lloydie closer by his T-shirt, so he could speak softly into his ear. Lloydie looked shocked, for what he had heard was the thin voice of a boy coming out of Bruiser's mouth. Everyone heard Bruiser speak like a boy and thought it was a horrible miracle. 'How could this be happening?' Carmen nudged someone close beside her. Those boys were working like angels – it was the only way of explaining it in the white man's tongue. But it was nothing to be frightened about, because their poor little spirits had gone to the sea and you would see them down there playing in the surf, juggling fish above their heads, if you caught them on a lucky day. Nothing was going to touch them now.

'Stop it mate. Pull yourself together because this is going to get very, very bad. If we don't deal with it quickly,' Lloydie spoke to Bruiser, his voice low. 'Ignore it,' he encouraged, for he had done this at times himself to shake off the spirits. Bruiser started shaking his own head as though this would free him from whatever it was that was bothering him. Lloydie stared at the bar, startled, then Bruiser decided to beat it with his fists, as if this would help too. It soon came to the point where Lloydie must have cracked too, for he did a most unusual thing. He hit Bruiser in the mouth with his bony fist. The impact shocked everyone. Lloydie was shocked himself.

Just when Lloydie thought he was going to be paid back, the mayor turned around and said with a grin, he needed it. 'Thank God he's normal again,' piped Carmen. 'Get on the phone, and get Valance to come over here,' Bruiser ordered Lloydie. The first time, Lloydie dialled nervously, and had trouble dialling the right number. He tried again, while everyone waited to hear the phone ringing in the Council office, on the other side of the street.

It seemed like an eternity before Valance arrived, after being watched by the entire pub as he ambled across the road. 'Valance! Truthful's gone stark raving mad. You know that?' Bruiser hollered at Valance as soon as he appeared in the pub. 'He has locked himself inside the police station, with the dead petrol sniffers. The three boys are dead.' Valance did not bat an eyelid at the news. He had heard the flogging from the Council office. 'Now,' Bruiser continued haltingly, trying to think, while waving his hand from side to side, to brush off Valance's attempts to speak, 'we got to be darn clever about this. The cop is likely to kill some-one the way he is, I am telling you.'

Again, Valance tried to speak, but Bruiser, pausing to think, waved his hand between them. Soon, he detailed the plan to capture Truthful. 'What you have to do, use the phone here and get someone to round up all the workers, and tell them to get here and bring their rifles, or whatever they got. Tell them, don't worry about the gun laws. We know they've still got their rifles. We got to sort out what's happening over at the station there with the cop, before there is any more bloodshed.' Valance responded indifferently, taking his time. His soul was nothing now but deep hatred. It walked with hate towards Bruiser but not with Valance alongside, because the shame of it was that Valance knew he could not kill Bruiser.

Chapter 11
The mine

The Fishman had decided to leave town about the same time Norm had taken to the sea. The convoy, with its noisy exhaust pipes spewing black fumes, drove like a long black snake through the storm-darkened town. More white crosses had been hand-wiped over the muddied cars.

The Fishman told Angel he was leaving. He said he wanted to beat the clouds gathering, before the Wet had properly settled itself over the plains again. He drove around the outskirts of Desperance, signalling his convoy to set forth, with a bony arm swinging assuredly, as each car drove off. Then, using a finger sign and a face of total concentration, he instructed, 'Head south.'

Fishman still tried to understand the foreboding that refused to leave his mind since he had arrived in Desperance, but the more he thought it over, the answer kept escaping him. 'Time to move on,' he told Angel again. 'Before the devils catch up.' He hated the illusionary world particularly in Desperance, which was tied to his childhood. He felt as frightened as anyone else of seeing spirits wherever he looked. Where others saw their shadow, Mozzie saw dark spirits following people around. They were inside every house, listening to conversations, remarking like gossips if they believed this or that was right. He watched them putting words into the mouths of the living. He knew out on the road, it was hard for spirits to keep up when vehicles travelled faster than a person could run, and in the convoy, there were too many people around talking among themselves, and drowning out the little voices of their consciences playing around with peoples lives. In any case, Mozzie preferred to dwell in the mystery of people, even if he got them wrong occasionally.

In the end, he drew strength from a narrow point of view, where, even if it were possible, there was nothing to be gained from penetrating the cloudy wall into his depressed state of mind to find hidden messages. There would be no time to catch up with old friends like Norm Phantom, Mozzie smiled as his mind captured the maker of silver fish, labouring over his work bench. 'Oh! He is the real fisherman.' He sat back in the car travelling down the south road, thinking of Norm travelling the seas of oceans.

Ah! The good life. Mozzie worried more for Will Phantom. He had fretted for Will. What was he up to? After he had disappeared at the lagoon, he had not seen him again in Desperance. He thought Will must have heard about the mine men, the ones from the big powerful mining company, Gurfurritt International. Everyone knew they were out searching the area for the body his convoy had seen on their way up to Desperance. Angel said that Will would be around. She heard from the girls, that they had to keep Truthful from finding Elias's body in the fishroom.

This was all becoming too close, Fishman thought, and he told Angel this. He knew if he stayed the feeling pricking his heart so deeply would not leave until something went wrong. He remembered how on the road, he had begged Will to stay away. Knowing that it would be at least two years before the convoy's return was why Mozzie had taken him away in the first place. At the time, Will was lucky to get out of the place.

The whole world had turned upside down two years ago when Will Phantom had blocked Gurfurritt's pipeline in a dozen different places along the 150-kilometre stretch, when it was being built to carry the ore from the mine to the coastline. Rest on your head Desperance! There were insinuators. It had taken some investigation on the state of the art pipeline to establish the method of sabotage. At first it appeared that the pipe was self-exploding across the plains of spinifex. It seemed the pressure of ore travelling down the pipe to the coast needed to be adjusted, then readjusted.

Sweating engineers cursed each other's incompetence each time the thing burst, and they were sent out in the hostile mid-summer heatwaves, to do the backbreaking work to fix the darn thing. It was a nightmare to suspect that a thirty million dollar pipeline had been constructed of the wrong material. What went wrong with the *grando plano*? It was a good question with no answer. Oh! Yes! The Fishman convoy had been lucky to get Will Phantom out of town alive. Security was running mad. No one had seen the likes of it before. Every exit point had been heavily guarded.

When the big miner threatened to withdraw, halting further building of the mine, the town watched as its population increased by one hundred per cent. The State Premier ordered a squadron of police to be flown in from the state's capital down South to help search for Will Phantom. There were dozens of pot-bellied police stationed in plastic chairs at all of the river crossings. When the religious convoy had reached the crossing of the wide, tide-surging Normal river on the edge of town, Mozzie Fishman saw what they would have to confront to cross the bridge.

He studied the rifles first, and behind the rifles, the set faces of dozens of police officers, uniformed and plain-dressed, lined up on the other side of the bridge. Further back, police cars were swung across the road as a roadblock, ready and waiting. When the convoy started to cross the bridge, for it was already too late to turn around, the uniformed police came forward with the German shepherds. Mozzie saw the dogs panting for a drink of water, and very quietly, sent word back through the cars: 'It is nothing. Be brave. The dogs are just a threat. Everything will be searched. Pretend it's nothing.'

It did not pay to protest when the police made the occupants of the unregistered cars push their vehicles over the side into the flooding river. The ones who did, if they had been observant, would have just been fast enough to see the slight tug of the handler's lead, a signal, before the dog lunged. Then, knocked to the ground and savaged, they crawled on their stomachs to slip over the side of the bridge. Well! When they clung onto the wooden planks – as thick as railway sleepers, simply hanging there, suspended over the swollen body of the brown snake ripping along at a tremendous speed below on its way to the sea, they might have heard laughter, and for brief moments felt the sensation of shock at the incongruous misplacement of mirth with fear. Then, with the sounds of savage snarling dogs ringing through their heads, the dogs thrashing about above, ripping at their ears and the backs of their clinging knuckles, their bloodied hands were slippery like black eels. If there were moments to spare, they retained their last hold by dragging their hands through the long splinters of that old bridge which became impaled in the palms of their hands. Finally, they would let go. They fell through the brown depths of the raging waters, surfacing metres down river, looking back to the sea of blank faces on the bridge, watching them disappear to kingdom only come.

But with all of that, it was some kind of comic relief when the convoy got through, and the police missed Will. Still, Mozzie thought, Will was never going to be the picture of anyone's stereotypical black rebel, guerilla, activist, stirrer. He was too familiar, like an invisible man, who walked through his whole life in a town without anyone batting an eyelid to notice what he looked like. The chief detective thought the whole town was brain dead when every person with civic responsibilities responded likewise – 'Ah! They all look the same to me.' 'Can't tell them apart, never could.'

Call it providence! Call it neglect! Call it what you will. There was not a single picture in town of Will Phantom. Both factions gave contradictory descriptions. They used whatever wardrobe full of memories they possessed. Anyone who sprang to mind they gave as their honest opinion of the description of Will. They were more interested in rhetoric. There was more to say about warring factions and community disputes, than the likes of Will Phantom, and his cohorts in crime against others. The senior detective had to say very loudly at least a hundred times in his best attempt at broken English, that he was not into theorising or analysing their brawls. He did not want to think about it. He was a very hard man.

The police hurried away to ring up the regional newspapers, but somehow, even they did not have a picture of Will Phantom. Not a single snapshot in all of their records. Unbelievable! Even though he had excelled in all school sports and was once the student of the year. The police went down to the Council office to look at the historical records. Yes, they were sure there was a photo somewhere – Man of the Match on Picnic Day sometime. An Aboriginal boy with a big grin. Caught the biggest fish during the Easter fishing competition. You heard about the fishing comp? It's very popular? No. No picture must have been taken that year. Sorry!

The police had already been through the school. *Where were the class photos? I can't believe you have no class photos of Will Phantom?* The senior detective hissed how he was sick of being in the mongrel town, while he looked incredulously at the unkempt piles of crumpled photos spread over the green pingpong table. There were dozens of photos, but nothing that showed this person had once spent eight years of his life in the building. *Didn't he go to school?* they asked out of interest.

Yes! Yes! He sang 'Sweet Caroline' and 'Come Lately' when he walked home from school. The police learned Will was a charming boy with

369

a melodic voice who sang Neil Diamond songs. The whole town loved listening to him. Often the whole town would be singing the same song in his wake, as he walked past.

The police went straight down to the Phantom's house. At least twelve good men using a fine-tooth comb searched every inch, two times, maybe three, and came up with nothing. Nobody could beat Angel Day's daughters for fastidiousness. Norm had ordered them to destroy anything that would remind them of Will, the day he left home. Norm Phantom did not help the senior detective either, since he insisted that someone called Will Phantom was no relative of theirs, never was, and never would be.

The Phantom family were paraded in a line at the police station in front of all of the out-of-town police. The senior detective spoke to his men: 'This is to help you men to get a bit of a gander at what you are looking for.' He walked up and down in front of the silent family, and in return they glared back, with spite in their eyes. There was no strong family resemblance running through them, anyone could see that, but the senior detective saw smidgens of familiarity, and must be credited for his exceptional detective skills. The four eldest, Inso and Donny, Janice and Patsy, were on the heavy side although each had completely different facial features. The old people called it a testimonial to the strong differences in both their parents. Girlie and Kevin were worlds apart from their older siblings. Both were skinny as rakes, but again, perhaps, looking more like their father.

Angel Day did not help either. Treating what was happening to her like a terrible illusion, La Goddess of Mozzie Fishman was very annoyed to be rudely rejoined to the family she had quit having anything to do with a long time ago. She had a new life, she told the senior detective. Even minding her own business did not seem to be enough these days. 'What a family,' she had scoffed with her words flowing like butterflies. 'Police barging into your home, and even though we have done nothing, I am forced to come down to the police station and parade around like I was nothing but a bullock in the cattle yard.'

Femme fatale almost flew out of her house after she finished complaining about the invasion of privacy. But she absolutely refused to get into the police car when she saw her ex sitting there. 'I am not going to sit next to that bastard,' she had told them flat, but how were the police expected to know she had been avoiding him like the plague for years? She stood her ground out there on the footpath, holding the police cars up in the heat, until another car was sent around to pick her up.

Once inside the police station, Angel Day demanded that Norm tell her what he was looking at. Norm was surprised himself that he had been glaring at the way she was dressed. Too tight, too short. Wanting to correct her behaviour – arms flapping everywhere, eyeing all the men off, showing her legs like a spring chicken. He wanted to pull her together, stop her making a fool of herself in front of the children, but no, he remembered, she was not his property. Then, if that was not enough, she refused to stand in a line with her ex-husband. Norm went up to the desk where the senior detective was leaning and quietly let him know how insulted he was: 'How dare you parade that harlot next to my family.'

She spat at the foot of the senior detective and when he looked down, he saw that it had landed on one of his polished brown shoes. He looked straight back at her and she winked at him, giving him the eye, as she had given many others before. He thought he was going to hit her. Instead, he instructed his officers to make her stand in line, at the other end, as far away from Norm as possible. She said she was quite capable of standing by herself, and with her head facing off to the furthest wall, she did not have to look at anyone. The senior detective looked at the lot of them – six children, two parents – and asked the assembled police, to note the remarkable family resemblance. 'Believe me! this Will Phantom is going to have a similar look about him.' A hick town crook was not going to beat a smart man like him. Satisfied, he clapped his hands. 'So let's go boys, we got a job to do.'

When the mud dried...

Claypans breathed like skin, and you could feel it, right inside the marrow of your bones. The old people said it was the world stirring itself, right down to the sea. Sometimes, in Desperance, everyone heard the drying mud crack in the vast claypans. You could hear the ground groaning, splitting its epidermis into channels of deep cuts all across the ground. It looked like a fisherman's net, except it was red brown, and it trapped whatever was down below from breaking through to the surface. It made you think that whatever it was living down underneath your feet, was much bigger than you, and that gave them old clan folk real power. They said it was a good reason to keep on living right where they were. Keep it right. Everyone had to keep fighting those old spirit wars, on either side of that, *Got nothing, going nowhere neither, Uptown*.

'This is the only safe place left,' old man Joseph Midnight kept repeating to himself, as he wandered in and out of his old bit of a lean-to home. The structure of tin and plastic, in an ongoing state of disarray, stood behind the brand-new house the government had given him free – lock, stock and barrel – for cooperating with the mine, but which he said, 'Was too good to use.' His relatives, resigned to the fact that the old man was beginning to lose his marbles, took no notice. Midnight was an example of what would happen to themselves one day. It was what they would also do for staying alive so long – the last flicker of life was like this.

Old Joseph had stopped walking over to the town. It had been his daily habit for decades and an inspiration to his clan. He refused to look after himself. He had no food. He just left it up to whatever relatives were around to make sure he got something to eat. They scolded, plonking a sandwich or a plate of stew on his lap. 'Well! What's the point of being alive if you are not prepared to look after yourself properly.' Grumbling and moaning about everything, and no thank you, mind you, they finished up saying, 'You are nothing but humbug, old man.' One square meal a day was not worth being spat on he told them, and they hurried away, bloated with complaints, 'Who cares about being loaded down with the old bugger anyway.' He was like lead, that empty seashell, called relative. Yet, they were so morally obligated, conscience could not be unlinked and unravelled from family matters even on Eastside.

Old man Joseph Midnight, heard speaking to his dead relatives as though he too was already dead, said his kinfolk were not worth two bob. 'Look at us – we are just invisible people around here.' Watching him talking to the wind blowing through town back to the sea, the kinfolk said he had lost his soul.

Nobody chewed the fat over there, and no one used a smidgen of brain, to fathom old Midnight's mind. The poison flowed on like contamination into the river. Nothing stopped the talk of poison outside the fish and chip shop either. Such as Fishman's people saying Elias was dead. Found dead in his boat, they said, on top of a dried-up lagoon. What kind of talk was that?

'Man should be horsewhipped until he lay dead,' he growled, waving a hand of dismissal through the air at the imaginary listener following him in and out of his pathetic hovel. He spat towards the new house whenever it caught his eye. He was suffering the unrelenting pain of a wrong decision. For days, he had been unforgiving of himself, for it had been his own snap decision, made without thinking. He never gave himself time to think.

'Why should an old man have been left to make a decision like that. Why couldn't somebody else have made it? Why send his whole world away?' He was speaking about his grand-daughter Hope and her child Bala whom he had sent away to sea with Elias Smith, hiding them during the night in Elias's boat, under a tarpaulin. No one but Elias knew they were there, when Elias had walked away from Desperance at dawn, pulling his boat behind him to sea.

Old man Joseph Midnight had waited, bent low down on the beach, on the night before Norm had set to sea with Elias's body. He looked out for the robot, Gordie, who was still alive then. He was alert for anything moving in the shadows – terns, hermit crabs, and sea snakes all moved along the beach. Occasionally, he would give an affectionate rub of pride over the side of his old, tin boat, only newly painted mangrove green.

Old man Joseph Midnight had one hope. He knew once Will heard about Hope and Bala, he would go looking for them, because if there was still some good in the world, and heavens knows it was rare, it was the love between Will and Hope, and their little boy Bala. Will Phantom had arrived, soundlessly, in a borrowed car. Slipping along the foreshore through the darkness, checking which boat he would take, Joseph caught him by surprise. Speaking in a gruff tone, he was a heavy smoker after all, Joseph's voice came from somewhere close by, 'I knew you'd be wanting a boat, and I owns the only one going to last the distance you be tracking, so just so you didn't go about helping yourself to what's not yours, I told meself – I'd better sit it out here for a while, and wait for when you decide to come down. You make sure you look after this boat properly.' Will nodded, throwing his gear on board, as he began preparing old Joseph's boat in readiness for the sea. 'It's the only decent thing I've got left, you sabie me?'

Old Joseph told Will how he had been listening through the grapevine, people talking – after he had disappeared from the

Fishman's convoy at the lagoon. 'Knew you was coming home. That was good enough news for me when I heard it. Made an old man's heart feel good again knowing you might be coming home soon.' He had waited at night down by the green boat for several hours after darkness had fallen and when Will never arrived, the cloud of doom had resurfaced and he growled at the wind, which was his way of talking to his useless kin, who in all other matters, he preferred to have nothing to do with.

'Stupid buggers – lot of them. No use to a person at all – never have been. Thought they were too good to learn anything from me – Righto then. Not one of them knows one single thing about the sea to go looking for their sister or the little boy. Idiots.'

From a borrowed car, Will unloaded into the boat the gear he needed to take to sea. It was simple fare, several water containers, fishing gear, some canned food, spare clothing. The old man gave him the directions to the safe place in his far-off country – a blow-by-blow description sung in song, unravelling a map to a Dreaming place he had never seen. 'I grew up in the hard times – not that any bugger cares.'

Will knew. The stories of the old people churned in his guts. He responded in the best way he could to show his affinity, 'Inhumane treatment, I know, Pop.' Yet, old man Midnight remembered a ceremony he had never performed in his life before, and now, to his utter astonishment, he passed it on to Will. He went on and on, fully believing he was singing in the right sequence hundreds of places in a journey to a place at least a thousand kilometres away. 'Sing this time. Only that place called such and such. This way, remember. Don't mix it up. Then next place, sing, such and such. Listen to me sing it now and only when the moon is above, like there, bit lower, go on, practice. Remember, don't make mistakes...' The song was so long and complicated and had to be remembered in the right sequence where the sea was alive, waves were alive, currents alive, even the clouds.

'Will, remember, you will only travel where the sea country will let you through.'

It was only then, while old man Joseph Midnight was watching for Gordie, he whispered the story of what happened to Hope after Will had left town, on the run with the Fishman.

It was clear both had the hunter's instinct, a stillness, and compelling eyes that saw through darkness. Both kept an ear listening for any sound, as unconsciously alert as the hunted animal or fish needed to be, while listening for sounds from up to one kilometre away – past the Fisherman's Hotel, past the rubbish tip, past the last moored boat, past the hovering seagull ghosts simmering in the light of the moon. Tonight, they heard the sound of sea water lapping at their feet on the edge of the beach, while in the distance, timber creaked as moored boats rubbed against one another, and there was the constant ringing of a small bell on board of one as it bobbed in the ebbing flow of the tide. Further out, they could hear the engines of the barges travelling to the ships waiting in the deeper waters for the ore from the mine.

Occasionally, they heard the sound of heavy machinery creaking before sailors yelled, then the droning of ore loaded into the bulk holds. Out there in the bay, it was a noisy night with ballast waters ejecting into the still waters. Nature too, splashed from fish jumping out of the shallows. Constantly, dogs barked at the moon. Close by, a barn owl hooted its stanza. The channel-bill cuckoos disturbed one another, up in the skies, shouting in a frenzy of old man's crackle.

'But what happened!' Will whispered, with urgency in his voice. He needed to hear the story once more, pushing old Midnight further, quicker, while knowing in the end he would have to run with the boat for there was little time left to take the tide out. He needed to capture their life, Hope's and Bala's, to see everything he had missed. There had been no outside communications with either the East or Westside camps while he was away. No telephone to pick up. No one to take messages. No way of getting back. Will knew Hope could not have left on her own accord and found him. The separation had been complete. 'Pack it in ice,' Fishman told his crew was the best way to handle the heart. He said his heart was the perfect model they could mould themselves on if they wanted, if they had problems handling separation. Will tried to imagine how Hope managed alone. And old man Joseph Midnight talked, gently telling the story again, but quicker, as though he thought he might be sprung upon any moment by the elusive Gordie, slithering through the grass line behind.

'Well! I got word, that's all. That the police were going to arrest Hope after those fires. They couldn't find you. They found all of those who fell off the bridge when the Fishman's convoy left town. All the others, they were frisked and searched at the crossing. They kept thinking you were still hiding around the place so they started saying that she was involved with you, even that it was your hand involved in burning down the Shire Council, after the big problem with the pipeline.

'And Elias, he was supposed to be guarding, looking after the place, so they said he must have stood by and did nothing when he saw you doing it. They had conducted their own investigation. I heard all about that bloody kangaroo court they had down at the pub. In the end, they told him to get out of town. After, they were still looking for blood, anyone's. That was the reason why they were coming for Hope.

'They had already started to torment her with questions and threats if she never told them where you were. The police never believed you went away. They was always thinking you was close by.

The town was all revved up and harping on, "Nobody knows the trouble we got because of that Will Phantom". Jeez! Here in town, down at the mine; I reckoned they invented half of it. Everyone reckoned it. I reckoned it too. I heard them saying things like, "Oh! Look! Fancy that, broken glass bottle left on the road. Bet Will Phantom did that". Anything.

'Some woman said it was Sunday instead of Monday and that was your fault too. Yo! Who in charge of changing time then? Bet Will Phantom behind it, that's what. They even believed it when you said once that you could hide behind thin air around here. Well? Now you could have been behind every dust storm so they went searching through it, round it. "Where could he be?" Who's going to find you first? So they come after Hope, just so they could flush you out.'

'Well! Somebody killed Elias,' said Will, running his hand through his hair, still unbelieving, but knowing he should have predicted all of this would happen. Life had no meaning in this new war on their country. This was a war that could not be fought on Norm Phantom's and old Joseph Midnight's terms: where your enemy did not go away and live on the other side of town, and knew the rules of how to fight. This war with the mine had no rules. Nothing was sacred. It was a war for money.

'I know he is dead. Finished poor bugger. Fishman mob told me that,' old Joseph's timbre was breaking and becoming barely audible. Will could see how the old man had been worrying himself sick ever since he heard the news about Elias. Joseph went on, saying he did not know what he wanted to believe anymore. 'You can't go around burning things down Will, you should know that. A bloody waste of money that's what that is.'

'Hope was not involved in anything, Jesus Christ. None of us had anything to do with the fires in town,' Will explained, as old Joseph watched him. 'It was that fucking mine did that, and it's their own money they wasted, so don't feel sorry for them. They never worried about us when they were riding roughshod over our rights.' Will kept his more worrying thoughts to himself. He decided not to talk to the old man about how much danger he thought Hope and Bala were in, if they were still alive. He did not say that he believed the mine had murdered Elias and set him up in the lagoon to trap him.

'Would the mine want to kill Elias? He could of just died out there. Maybe.' Old man Joseph Midnight stopped, as though unable to bear the thought of the consequences of Elias not completing his journey, if all three had lost their lives at sea. He turned to the new revelations from Will. 'The mine people don't want to burn down the Shire Council office and start all those other fires? They got nothing to do with the town. They must of had a good reason for doing those kind of things.' His voice tailed off again. He did not want to understand if it all meant that in the end the hope for a better world had perished in the sea.

'You mob,' old Midnight said, following Will in his readiness to cast off, 'talk all the time about some kind of new, contemporary world. New world – Blah! to that. What contemporary world? It's the same world as I live in, and before that, and before that. No such thing as a contemporary world.' Why should someone old like himself comprehend Uptown having reason enough for killing and burning amongst their own jellyfish white people? 'I understand our mob having a go at each other,' he said, referring to the old wars. 'We got to fight each other until one day we might git sick and tired of it.' What he really meant, Will knew, was that one side must give up and go away. It was the ultimate solution that neither side could resolve. Which would be the loser? It was the only way the fighting of the last four hundred years would finish.

'The way I see it, white people treat each other nice way. That's right what I am saying, init? Uptown got something – a good neighbour thing with the mine. No trouble. No need for trouble.'

'It's called a good neighbour policy, old man, and it means nothing. This town is being used, you know that? Used, and they are too stupid to see it.' Will was annoyed and he wanted to set off.

'Well! That's not true. The way I see it, the mine has got no problem with the town and vice versa. I watch them all mingling, talking like they can't get enough of each other. The mine put money into the town too – all the time by the looks of it. So there is no reason and you wrong at this this time, Will.'

'Of course they got a reason…' Will was about to explain how the good neighbour policy worked to kill opposition, but Midnight cut him off.

'You know I sent the boy down to your father with a note one time,' he said.

'What happened?' Will was surprised. The two senior men of the opposite clans never spoke, or acknowledged the other existed. Their language had no word for compromise. Was this a signal of defeat? He looked closely at the old man to see where the trickery lay in the creased features of his face. No, in the lie of the land, nothing good could have been packaged in this gesture. Norm had never forgiven Will for having a relationship with Hope. And Will knew that Bala was old man Joseph Midnight's treasure, so it was a strange thing for him to say he wanted Norm to look after the little boy after the police came looking for Hope.

'Suppose he never wanted a bar of it. That little fella walked down that road over there and all of them frogs over on Westside just stopped croaking on the sides of the road, just to watch what was going to happen. Well! From what we heard, they saw what was going to happen. That old bastard did not have enough guts to recognise his own blood. So I had no choice. Now, I blame him because all of this would not have happened if he could have helped his own flesh and blood.

'You know what the mean old bastard did to his own grand-child? No? Nobody would have told you. Well! He just looked around on the ground, can you believe that? And the next minute, he picked up a stone and threw it, picked up another – threw it, and another. Threw it all at the little fella like he was someone's dog to get rid of. So, good little fella, he just turned around and come on home. All of them frogs on our side were that glad. All along the road! Well! They never even stopped croaking for one split millisecond when he come past. They were that happy to see him they made themselves dizzy with excitement cheering him on.

'Oh! I wish my little baby was here now and all of these things never happened. I am left with the worse life now. I tell you Will, if I wasn't old and decrepit like I am, I'd be coming with you. And I blame Norm Phantom, nobody else, and soon as I am well enough again I will be going over to confront that dog straight to his face. Square up. Everyone will be asking then, "What happened to that big hero Norm Phantom?" And I'll just be saying, "He's gone away. You won't be seeing him anymore".'

Will listened to Joseph's wishful rumbling – so on and so forth. He wished he could offer credence to Midnight's story, even when he could imagine it as being the truth. True, when Bala was born, there had been silence. Not one sound from Westside – no shouting out, no rejoicing, no herald singers singing 'a child is born'. No one said, let bygones be bygones. No one measured the possibility of the child, who could be the adhesive needed to create peace between the two groups. So, instead of joy, Will thought, stones were thrown of the literal kind. This was where the ambiguity lay in Midnight's story. There were no stones to be found on the claypans over Westside. Only sick in the gut people complained about stones. Whitefellas dreamt of stones. And children thought stones were magical.

Will Phantom was soon far away. Alone, on the ocean, he had become a one-man search party to find his wife and child. He sailed impatiently for several days, after having had no difficulty in finding the currents old Midnight had told him to ride, and finally, he had the low, flat isles in sight. The previous night he had felt the changes of movement in the water – the slower flow, the rise of the water, which pleased him. Now, he sighted land ahead. The number of sea birds increased until he felt that every bird in the world was heading towards the same destination. Their piercing calls became louder and deafening until the familiar sound of the ocean had been drowned to a murmur.

Occasionally, Will felt he was becoming disoriented. It was difficult not to be overcome with curiosity, and unconsciously, his eyes would be drawn to look skyward at the low-flying feathered clouds that swarmed noisily through the skies. His stomach lurched and he felt his mind slipping into a state of dizziness from which he could only escape by concentrating on the sea. The low string of islands were just as old Midnight had told him. 'Bit like mangrove forests – same colour as me boat – good place too,' Midnight had explained. By this he meant, there would be good hunting and good camouflage.

The dense grey-green mangrove forests lining the beaches, stuck out of the water, all the way back towards a sandhill. In between the mangroves rose clusters of cycad palms – *Cycas angulata*, like spirit camps, like sentries with their windswept heads staring out to sea. In the shallow waters, the colour became greyer. Will could not remember seeing sea water like this before, but he kept on steering the boat towards the islands. Later, he realised that the islands were composed of clay, and this caused the discolouration of the water similar to how the Gulf waters around Desperance used to be. Before mining. Very soon the blue of the ocean was left far behind him, with his thoughts of what Midnight had foretold. The imminent expectations of land Will had carried across the ocean now became an invasion of optimism, similar to his experience in the desert, burning his body with thirst, hunger and love.

He rode the boat over the breakwater towards one of the dull grey-green islands. With the boat steering quickly towards the shoreline, he started to notice in the shallower waters breaking onto the beach, an unusual amount of rubbish. Glistening in the sun amidst flocks of seagulls, there were dozens of white plastic cordial containers bobbing along the coastline. Will recognised these as an ominous message from the guardian spirits of the place. It was not a sign he had expected. Midnight had not warned him of any of the dangers associated with his old ancestor's land.

Now at the end of his voyage, he felt as though he was holding his breath in melancholy anticipation. The solitude at sea had been a time of reflection, where he had thought about his life, and a future that could be with, or without Hope and Bala. Heading towards land, he thought optimism had evaded their past, and it had eluded his vision of the future. No good had come of any of their lives. It was these thoughts that were abruptly broken when a final wave threw him onto the chaotically crowded beach. The island had been overtaken by nesting pelicans, watching him with angry-looking eyes, and wherever he tried to cut a path through their nests, their necks lunged out and he saw wobbling up to their mouths, little lumps of sound, travelling and stalling, until breaking out of their beaks into a long, deafening screech. Thousands of the white ghostly birds hovered over the islands, moving like noisy clouds as they filled the next part of the air space while abandoning the last. Later in the darkness, he would see the moonbeams illuminating the birds like white lights, and when the breeze shimmered against their wings, the night droned away as though the whole planet was alive with the sound of Indian tabula and clay drums.

Everything he sensed about the place said that he should leave immediately, so he went back to the beach and thought about what he should do. Nobody could inhabit the islands, which were very small, but he had to be sure. He towed the boat further along the beach until he found a thick grove of mangrove trees by the side of a small creek. He secured the boat under the trees and prepared to wait until darkness fell. He caught some mud crabs and cooked them over a small fire.

In mid afternoon a storm moved onto the coastline, with the same sense of impatience as Will, and within seconds, the clouds burst and the rain fell. Relieved, Will quickly took the opportunity to walk, in the rain, through the nesting birds, which were now too drenched to be bothered with him passing by. As he had thought, the island showed no signs of fire, nowhere Hope might have stayed, nothing that showed anyone had ever lived on it.

He went back for the boat and moved to the next island and then the next, collecting nothing but gashes on his legs from the strikes of angry birds. After two days of searching, he rowed across to a larger island. It was still raining heavily through clouds that touched the water as he came in to the beach. The island was the last in the group of five. He secured the boat just before dawn.

There were fewer nesting birds to bother him as he walked through the rain, and the poor wretched birds that remained glued to their nests had their heads buried under their wings trying to keep dry. He saw a lot more of the puzzling plastic bottles bobbing along the shoreline. He thought they might have come off a ship, a loose container from Asia perhaps, fallen into the sea. Once opened, the container had released thousands of bottles which floated to the surface and drifted, until they had been driven onto the islands. It could have happened a long time ago, or it could have been only a few months. It could be that simple, the bottles were caught in the waters running around the islands between the foreshore and the breakwater over the reefs.

Will stopped dead in his tracks when he heard the tenor. A voice, lush, rich, Italian, had suddenly broken into a full operatic song, just a few metres from him. Blast! the bottles, he thought. Someone's trick – Midnight's? Rain, snappy gum foliage and high grass separated the slow, melodic singer, from where Will stood, dripping wet. He was astounded by his own carelessness. Elias, Norm, Midnight, Fishman – all sprung into his mind. Taught by experts. What would they say? How could anyone be so stupid? He had not been paying enough attention. He had been too sure of there being no one else around.

He glanced down, and saw his heart pulsating through the skin of his bare chest. Then, from the corner of his eye, he saw the singer, standing almost beside him, with a face full of expression, expectation, passionately glorifying the perfect day – *Ma per fortuna è una notte di luna, e qui la luna l'abbiamo vicina*. The big Italian was standing alone in the rain, arms open wide like one of his ancestral Gods. Rain dripped over his golden face. Pearl drops of rain rolled down his black beard. He was lost in his song: fortunately, his eyes were concentrating on his fingers directing the accompanying chorus – a family of singing magpies. The black and white pied birds were perched high in the branches of nearby gum trees.

Mine worker! Will recognised the blue uniform. Shit! Where were the others? He moved back behind the singer, and further back until he was safely out of sight, then he circled around to see why the mining company had people working out on the island.

The man was still singing, obviously alone except for the plastic bottles strewn everywhere, on the ground, in the grass, enmeshed in bushes and undergrowth like large, alien fruit. Will watched the bottles moving by, spirited along in the strong, gusty winds of the morning. The wind, cutting across the island, picked up the song and the plastic and carried them tumbling through the bush, finally rolling them down onto the beach and into the sea's arms. Will was amused by his mistaken earlier scenario of a freak accident, where the bottles had bobbed up to the surface from a fallen container.

Whatever happened to vigilance? Will asked himself. The first and only rule he had learnt about the mine was that nothing happened by accident. The importance of being forever vigilant should have applied even way out in the middle of the Gulf, in a sea desert, in the middle of nowhere. Once, when he was a child fishing with Norm and Elias, they had seen roaming armadas of the world's jetsam in flotillas that were like moving islands that you could walk on. As they had passed by, Will had seen thousands of screeching sea birds fishing off these sea-made apparitions which creaked and rattled as they moved along the circling currents of the Gulf. Norm and Elias ended the fishing and headed home to tell of what they had seen.

The mysterious flotillas washed around in the Gulf for months. Stories that knew no boundaries grew into epics of speculation. This really was news. A wise man's moratorium was prescribed. Everyone was prohibited to go on sea journeys until the flotillas disappeared. The old people went around spooking everyone to stay away from them. They claimed they were made by mad seas. And when the sea was mad, dead men's spirits got caught up in these phantom places. 'Don't look at what the sea has done.' No one did, unless they wished to be haunted for the rest of their lives. Looking at the Italian tenor singing the country in a foreign language, making the land and sea sacred to himself, Will knew he was stupid to have thought in the old way, like a normal person of his own background. Mining changed the way people had to think about looking after themselves. If a man was to survive, he had to first think of what the mine was capable of doing to him.

So much for old man Joseph Midnight thinking the island was a safe place. Yet Will realised there was no point blaming an old man whose vision of the place was ancient. He knew his country in its stories, its histories, its sacred places better than the stranger now singing a love song to it. His time stretched over the millennia. How would Midnight know the speed in which everything had been changed at the hands of the mining company? It was far beyond anyone's realisation. Will started to calculate the danger Hope and Bala faced, if they had made it this far, before Elias was murdered and ended up inland in the lagoon with his boat.

Nearer, as he moved through the bush, wet from the mist, he saw the tenor was serenading several rows of steel drums, half buried in the sand, covered with a net made of heavy rope and tangled with vegetation from the surrounding bush. Further back, he saw a canvas tent set up in the bushes next to the drums, and several fishing rods and tackle. He thought that perhaps the island had become a weekend fishing haunt for some of the mine workers. He needed to get closer to the drums. Water drums innocently registered in his mind. A storage site for fishermen.

The mine worker had his satellite phone attached to his belt. A guard, Will reasoned, who fishes. He started to scrutinise the site more carefully. It was small but open, grass flattened, intended to look like a weekend fishing place. The airborne coastal surveillance team flying past would not be interested – if they even had it marked on their flight paths. Wilderness fishing retreats on islands, which were not much more than wrecked reefs covered by sand and light vegetation, were popular with remote miners. You would have to bring water in. How? Boat! Helicopter! Will scanned for flattened vegetation, and looked to the skies. Everything was clear, only patchy clouds and sea birds hovered, but these did not flatten vegetation.

He moved on. The world he viewed shone dimly. Although

his mind was racing through the possibilities, his body felt too heavy to move. It had already decided it did not want to see what lay ahead, to be told that there was a lot of ground to be covered, to establish whether Hope and Bala had come this far, and what had happened to them. He pushed himself. Go on. Leave the drums. He smiled sarcastically as he mulled over the most obvious scenario of the fishing camp. A riproaring black market trade spinning off the mines in the Gulf. Who was involved? Who knows? Who cares? What was the environmental hazard to his traditional country? Some little operation like this could be very lucrative for any of the miners wanting to make their retirement package. Nothing short of an olive plantation back in the home country for the Italian. Palaces in Europe or Asia for the management.

Will scorned the thought of transport ships now frequently moving up and down the northern coastline. The whole oceanic world seemed to be occupied in the Gulf. It was a grey painter's palette of tankers exchanging mining equipment for mined ore that came to the coast, after the flesh of the earth had been shunted there by pipelines, tying up the country with new Dreaming tracks cutting through the old. Big ships, small ships pulled in from all over the world bringing tinkers, tailors, beggar-men, thieves. Anchored off Desperance, the ships waited for the barges to bring the ore out through the dredge tracks cut in the grey shallow waters where there were once lush green flowing seagrass meadows. How easy it would be for a ship to stop by some remote reef to pick up a bit of unofficial cargo. Uranium? Gold in lead? Will was knowledge galore, navigating his own nirvana.

The Italian continued singing to the birds and Will was moving through the bush out of view. Or was he? Yes, he remembered, he was certain, but why had he fallen asleep? His head screamed with pain. The helicopter roared in flight. He tried to remember backwards. What had happened from the moment he started edging himself away from the miner's camp to now? All he could see was an unfathomable darkness. He lay face down on the floor of the moving sound. His legs felt as though they had been stuck together. His arms were pinned to his side. The tape he imagined, was the iridescent yellow the company used to seal the boxes and eskies carrying chemicals. The sound was deafening. Only pain hammered inside his skull. He struggled to keep together a few simple thoughts. He was on a helicopter. The spinning rotor blades and the engine exploding through his head killed any thoughts of trying to understand what had happened.

Instinctively, he moved, struggled to free himself, before realising he was better off pretending to be unconscious, but it was too late. He felt his head dragged back by his hair. At the same time, a boot was pushed into his back. The tape was ripped off his eyes. His head was jerked around to face the light. First he saw white-edged blue. Then the sun at nine o'clock, and he realised it was mid-afternoon. Down below was the ocean. He tried to turn his head to see the person who gripped his hair, but the boot sunk deeper and his head was jerked back again.

The door slammed open and a cold wind smashed against his face. He knew the feel of her body passing and now that feeling crossed over him, and Hope fell. He sees, sees her face calm, her dress blue, she liked the colour blue like the ocean and sky, and he struggled to free himself. He used every muscle in his body to slither out – to fall with her. In those moments, he slides, pushed and shoved against the force of the wind screaming, but Hope falls with her silent dress blue into everything blue, and he is recaptured by those hands gripping his hair more tightly from behind and the boot, square into his back, planting him down on the floor. The only possible moment had passed, and the door was relocked. He listened, but he never heard the ocean, or Hope, only the flying murderers screaming to each other, then he vomits. The mask has been ripped off his mouth so he does not choke. This time, when darkness descends, he feels the blow striking the back of his head.

All moments in time are the mysterious and powerful companions of fate…

The realisation is especially true for those final moments that end life. The ghostly liberators hastily pass by the living to knock your breath away. No time at all before the soul has sped from the body onto a breeze where a moth was flickering by on a day darkened by low passing, kidney-coloured clouds. Time goes on, and one thinks, *What of the living*? You do not want to believe in death. You do not want to feel the strangeness so peculiar when death has occurred suddenly. There is a terrible shock when what was ends.

Eventually, as time trickled by, Will began asking himself if he had really seen her, watched her fall, unable to prevent it from happening. It was so easy, preferable even, to begin doubting yourself. He kept asking himself – was it really Hope? Could this thing of nightmares have happened to her? How could he have been so utterly powerless? In all of his visions of the future, which he believed were in his grasp, there was no place where dreams were snapped off at the base to prevent growth. He wished he had only dreamt what he had seen. But this was not his dream.

The helicopter blades droned on through his head as he lay semi-conscious on the floor of the moving aircraft. He breathed fire from the stench of aviation fuel. He fought against his inconsolable sadness. He wiped away confusion and nausea by imagining it had to have been someone else's limp body he had imagined going through the door a hundred times. But every time, it was Hope who came back, coming back into the open door of the helicopter smiling, then falling out again, over and over. He could not remember the look on her face as she fell, but nothing could take away the fact that it was her.

The very first time he had seen her, she was walking in the rain, and from where he was sitting on the ground, the first thing he noticed was how her bare feet slushed through the mud. Wet yellow grass blew on both sides and he had watched her from a distance, coming his way, with a dirty, sodden, royal blue doona wrapped around her. She looked like a big child amidst the smaller children who walked with her. He knew they had come from the Eastside camps to join the people he was sitting with next to the river. Everyone had been talking for hours about the mining company Gurfurritt. Will was listening, sizing up the mixed reactions to the mine.

Sabotage playfully plagued his mind. He listened to someone saying people were dying while they were talking. 'We are burying people and all we do is talk.' It was true. Even this meeting had been adjourned for a funeral. Will had come hoping to recruit helpers with his fight for land rights. The fires were getting out of hand. Half of the plains were burning. He had to be careful whom he trusted. Allegiances were changing constantly and he knew the reason why. Over many months, he had watched Gurfurritt play the game of innocence with bumbling front men who broke and won the hearts and minds of more and more of his own relatives and members of their communities, both sides of Desperance. Will did not underestimate those innocent friendly meetings where the mining representatives claimed not to know what was required from Native title claims. He believed the company knew government legislation and procedures related to Indigenous rights like the back of its hand. His mildest to wildest dreams were swamped with top silks who provided piece by piece legal advice to the supposedly ignorant Joe Blow, the local mining negotiator, from as far away as New York.

Some people were talking about the jobs they would be getting. *You very, very wrong*. They were arguing against the pro-land-rights brigade. *Whoever heard of it around here before? Land rights kind of talk. Not going to happen here I tell you that right now*. Huuump! Some were called Uptown niggers to their face. Others were saying they wanted the mining company to give the country back. Others were opposed to having any mines on their sacred country. *Full stop*. Some people said how they would kill anybody going against country. *We can make it look like an accident. Get em when they been drinking. Manslaughter kind of fighting*. They claimed murders of *somebodies* could be arranged to look like accidents. *Yah! Yah talkin air*. A nervous vein ran through the meeting whenever the strength of lawlessness was observed in their community.

Talk was always cheap. Cost nothing. And talking like Che Guevara made the huffy people's hair on the top of their heads stand straight up on end. A chill ran right down their backs. So! Without saying a word, because the meek do not speak, they went heave-ho, in favour of chucking out wildness. Everyone who was not talking animal madness like they were hearing, was quiet. Instead, they said, without saying a single word, if it was going to be like that – okay then. No one would bother speaking anymore. Then the moment was broken by the sound of young laughter floating through the air, from this little group from along the track, breaking through the smoke of smouldering fires.

Will knew almost instinctively where the helicopter was descending, flying south, down towards a landing depot, at the mine. The helicopter pad was an isolated plateau where the wind rattled through large warehouses and hangars that had been built by the mine next to the petrol pumps. Light aircraft and survey helicopters were housed in these buildings. The complex was large enough for all repairs and maintenance to be undertaken by the mine's well-supplied workrooms. The precinct was a self-contained entity, enclosed by cyclone fencing. Everyone on earth would agree that it had cost a bomb.

The door to the helicopter opened before the engine had wound down, and Will was thrown out onto the ground. When he landed on his side and felt the dust flying up his nostrils, he rolled over face down into the earth. Through the spiralling red dust, two sets of feet ran out of the way of the moving waves of dust. Each man demonstrated a sharp alertness which meant, Will knew, if they were involved in this kind of activity for the mine, they were most likely in peak physical fitness. He estimated both were about the same age as himself. After the helicopter lifted, he was covered red by the falling dust.

'Are you sure?' The Fishman sought clarity. 'Of course we seen it, we're sure alright.' This was the story of the two thieves, who saw the whole thing happen as they carried out surveillance activities around the hangars, checking on what they called 'that bloody mining operation.' Fishman's men, who had returned empty-handed, waved aside further communications. 'Wait a minute.' Both were bent forward, with hands on the top of their knees, waiting to catch their breath. Not fit men, they had run, stumbling through fifteen kilometres of spinifex. Their legs were covered with bloody cuts. Incredulously they reported the whole darn incident to the Fishman.

'Cut the tape on his legs,' one of the mining men at the helicopter pad ordered the other after the dust had settled. Immediately, Will felt a knife rip between his legs. The two men reached down and dragged him to his feet. When he felt something hard pushed in his back, he had no doubt it was a gun. 'Okay, black arsehole – get walkin.' Fingernails cut roughly cut across his face as the tape was dragged off his eyes and left hanging in his hair. Will looked ahead. No need to capitulate to his captors, not yet. The ground picture was what he needed to know first: deal with the murderers later. He already knew they were dressed in the mine workers' blue. Sight of the landscape confirmed what he had already guessed. He knew this country without sight, even when airborne. Once, when he was much younger and very crude in his methods, he had visited the hangar as silently as an owl one night. He had not believed how easy it was when he had poured industrial detergent into the fuel tanks, and because it was too easy, he created other havoc for the mine, then left unnoticed.

'Get him inside – *over* the left hangar – first one,' the man with long yellow hair, not the Italian, told the stiff red-haired one. He was obviously in charge. He lagged behind, dialling the mobile phone he had detached from his belt. In the grass, families of soft-rasping finches – white-spotted and blue, red, grey wrens, flew out of the grass, settled down ahead, then flew off again. They were quickly joined by hundreds of noisy, virginal white, feathered cockatoos with their plume of golden yellow standing straight up from their heads. Their wild screeching continued to gather momentum as they lifted straight towards the sun.

This was kingfisher country. A lone, deep-sea blue kingfisher dashed across the sky in fright. Will watched its path across to the hills. Its flight was a part of the larger ancestral map which he read fluently. He does not have to speak to ask the spirits to keep the birds away from the mine. *See! Mine waste everywhere*. The grounds were covered in contaminated rubble. *Make them go back to the river*. Will had always been puzzled why the birds flocked to the mine.

Whenever he saw so many birds around the mine, it raised a lot of questions for him. When would they realise the hazards of going there? How many evolutions would it take before the natural environment included mines in its inventory of fear? He and Old Joseph had sat in the hills and watched the water birds flock to the chemical-ridden tailings dams, where the water was highly concentrated with lead. Afterwards, when the birds flew back to the spring-fed river, where the water was so clear it was like looking through crystal, in amongst the water lilies and reeds, and natural waterfalls dropped between ancient towering palms and fig trees: they bred a mutation. The old prophet Joseph predicted mutated birds would drop out of the sky. No one knew what would happen to the migratory flocks anymore. Will surveyed the distant barbed-wire-crowned cyclone fencing. An impenetrable wall three and a half metres high, surrounding the mine complex to at least six kilometres in diameter. And the birds danced over it while wild animals clawed their way underneath.

'You, on the fucking chair,' ordered the big-boned man with the fat face and yellow hair, the mobile phone still to his ear. Will sat on it and waited. He had time.

'Hello? Yeah! We're back. And we got the fucking mother load. We got him. Yeah! Thought you'd be pleased. Told you it was just a matter of time. We've got the bastard.' The man with the yellow hair, eyes covered with expensive sunglasses, looked into Will's face. He casually inhaled from a cigarette in his other hand.

'What does he look like? What do you mean? Don't they all look alike? I don't know. Tall, skinny bugger. Got the kind of mug on him you won't want to see down an alley way in the middle of the night. Remember the cop we had in charge of the crossing that time? '98 or '99? Yeah! Well! He was right. The mongrel looks like the rest of his so-called family...Yeah! It's him alright...What? No, she panicked when we took off. Wasn't any point bringing the bitch back was there? No! Oh! Too late anyway. Alright. We found her camping by herself. Yeah! On the island next to the store. Where we picked up that weirdo that time…Yeah! Elias Smith whatever. So, you were right. It was a good job we gone back and checked…Kid? Wasn't any kid there. Probably didn't make the journey in the dinghy with them in the first place…We found him sniffing around the store. Yeah! The Conte's fine. Singing away to the birds when we last saw him…Alright! We'll wait down here with the bastard.'

Will watched yellow hair put his mobile phone back onto his belt. He walked over to the door, looked out for a few moments, then came back and saw Will was staring at him, straight into his eyes.

'Hey! Shit-head. What are you staring at?' The question was asked with a fist planted straight into his face. 'You wanta have a go, do you? You wanta have a go? Well! Go on.' The cigarette butt burned into Will's lips.

He remained motionless, only his eyes alive. Then he heard the footsteps coming closer from behind him, returning from the kitchenette at the far end of the hangar and with the footsteps came the wafting smells of hot coffee and fried steak. The fried-steak-smelling man with the red hair started winding plastic tape around Will and the chair. 'Just in case you got some fucking funny ideas,' the man snarled, with his stiff red hair standing out on tufted ends.

'Come and eat,' he said, handing the other man his coffee and heading back to the kitchen to deal with his cooking.

'You can see the mongrel's eyes. He can't wait to get his hands on us,' the yellow-haired one replied, drinking the coffee down in a single gulp. He wiped what remained in the cup across the air, in front of Will, and was not hurrying off for food. Whatever was misplaced in his mind was not hungry for food. He found it necessary to torment Will a bit more. He needed some kind of reaction to his achievements for the day. It was as though he could not find enough ways to fill the job description. Inches away from Will's face, he taunted him with his responsibility for the deaths of Elias and Hope, screaming as though the whole world needed to know, not just Will Phantom. Will stared past the man's ravings to observe the blue kingfisher. It surprised him that the bird he had minutes earlier seen flying away with its shrill whistling echoing behind it, had flown into the hangar and was sitting on a rafter, as though it had been sent back to keep him company. You don't kill sea spirits pure of soul, Will instinctively knew in his own mind – like Hope, like Elias. They come amongst the living for a short time, perhaps little Bala was such a spirit too, because he was their child.

The man's voice disappeared. The sickness in his soul swelled inside his body until it burst, looking for company and faded away. His shadow joined in its owner's personal triumph. Both took off their expensive sunglasses. Both mouths pulsating, describing a crusade of killing; describing how it would not be long now, they would be christening the new pipeline.

'It will be a journey an a half you betya! Only fitting boy – after all of the expense the mine had to go to having to build a brand-new pipeline just because of people like you. I tell you what – you got the money to pay what it costs and we'll let you go. No you haven't? Nevermind, once we get you through the mill you'll come out the other end, nothing but a big pile of slurry for the fish to eat. How do fish eat blackfellas like you? Slurp! Slurp!' The yellow-haired man laughed at his own joke until his teeth bared like a wounded dog. Seemingly content, he put his sunglasses back on, and went to get his meal.

Will had not heard the threats. He was thinking about the eyes of the murderer, and how he had looked into those eyes and seen his own reflected back at him. Perfectly matching eyes of despair – a mirror image of the murderer's. The kingfisher was sitting in the rafters preening its turquoise feathers, and as Will watched it, it too returned a steady gaze until, as though hypnotised, it closed its eyes and fell asleep. Will remembered he had not eaten for two days as a sick hunger tugged in his stomach from the smell of meat cooking. Whispering a refrain to himself – *Got to keep the wolves from the door, keeping free of the wolf pack, kill the wolves, keeping the wolves away* – he soon lost interest in food. Searching around the building from where he sat, he began calculating distances and speed in his mind. How long it would take to reach the lagoon, laying out the track through spinifex, until finally, he too fell into an exhausted sleep.

The radio in the kitchenette woke Will to the sound of familiar voices from the ABC, broadcasting across the airwaves, travelling through realms of ancestral spirits over great expanses, to reach into the loneliness of people throughout the Gulf of Carpentaria, the Channel country, and along the Diamantina. Stray rays of sun found their way into openings on the western wall of the hangar. The white beams of light crossed Will to spotlight the dirt and grease on the opposite wall. The radio broadcast only reached this far north about six o'clock in the afternoon. This was after the heat waves had fallen from the sky, and their enormous energies vaporised into a lightness, clinging to the ground. Will listened vaguely to the news bulletin and the weather report. He had to figure out what the two men were doing behind him, but there were no other sounds coming from the kitchenette.

Could they have gone outside? He glanced towards the door. Perhaps their boss had already turned up from the mine, although he thought it was unlikely. He would have been woken up. Inconsiderate! Will cursed the bloke he remembered seeing on TV. After the pipeline was destroyed. Of course that mongrel would keep him waiting, want him to sweat, dreaming up how he was going to carry out his dream to finish off *the little punk*.

Will had watched the bloated red face of someone called Graham Spilling staring from the television screen as though it expected to see someone wanting to destroy his mine jump back at him. Then after an outburst on how the mine was now threatened because the company would fail to meet the timetable of some overseas refinery already threatened with closure, which meant the loss of hundreds of Australian jobs, the face had paused, as if its voice had been crushed, as though a terrible idea had occurred to him, that his own job was on the line. Then, after a few moments, he just as remarkably found the strength to continue: 'I swear, hundreds of jobs, and because we fully support the sunshine State of Queensland, and we want to help the people in this state get ahead and want to see good things happen here like this development, the biggest mine of its type in the world, I am offering a $10,000 reward, no questions asked, for any information leading to the capture of...' He continued, his voice breaking, trying not to be personal about his tormenter, but Will recognised what he was trying to say. For the younger Will Phantom, from the era of destabilising the mine, the sight of the face twisted into mock hyperdrama was a memorable moment, but hardly the result he expected at the time from sabotaging the mine. It had been the day of the terrible hitting back, hit and run, bang! bang! bang! Straight along the pipeline with gelignite.

Will had always half expected that if he had been captured, the mining company bosses would queue up to have a look at the kind of person who would destroy a mine. The very same newsreader had called this kind of person the most feared of the North. But the red-faced Graham Spilling he had once seen on the television was not the kind of man who would be coming posthaste to the hangar in the light of day. The irony was, men like Spilling did not kill other men. Only the person, perhaps inebriated enough to turn into another kind of human being, like Frankenstein, could temporarily find courage to instruct the cold bloodedness of killing. Wasn't it in the dead of night when good people go about their dark deeds?

One becomes more confident when one's not alone, and somehow, this was how Will felt. An odd sensation that made no sense, yet it would not leave him alone. There was no rationale in the stupidity of thinking others – what others? – would come to help him. Even though he had not heard any movement, he was convinced the Fishman and enough men were outside, waiting for his signal. Now he saw a different perspective on his arrival at the hangar when he was thrown from the helicopter. The Fishman's two thieves were lying flat in the grass next to the shed when the helicopter had taken off. Through the dust he had seen them raise their heads from the grass. Hands signalled, questioning what had happened. Then when his eyes followed the flight of the kingfisher, now retracing its movement, taking notice of the whole panorama of spinifex to the foothills, he saw the subtle movement of other men from the convoy stationed in the distant hills on the other side of the fence. They were back-up for the thieves scouting the hangars for an overnight operation. Will knew if they were still around, then the rest of the convoy would be down at the lagoon. What was new? They were short of fuel.

Will looked for the kingfisher but it was now nowhere in sight. He kept an ear on the radio in the background, listened as the weatherman read the weather report. A cyclonic build-up in the Arafura Sea. Will grew interested, remembering an earlier report of a cyclone sitting off the opposite coastline, east of Cape York Peninsula. He could hear the words – *low-pressure system building into a depression heading in a south-easterly direction along the Arafura Sea*. This surprised him. What had happened to the cyclone off the Cape? Nothing. The weather report ended. It must have been in his dreams.

The day he had left old Midnight and taken his boat to sea he had heard the report of a cyclone hanging south-south-east of Cape York, somewhere in the Coral Sea. What happened to that? The weatherman ended with a short statement about a tidal surge due to the cyclone activity in the region. Will closed his eyes and saw the tremendous fury of the winds gathering up the seas, and clouds carrying the enormous bodies of spiritual beings belonging to other worlds. Country people, old people, said it was the sound of the great spiritual ancestors roaring out of the dusty, polluted sea all of the time nowadays. Will believed this. Everyone clearly saw what the spirits saw. The country looked dirty from mining, shipping, barges spilling ore and waste. Something had to run a rake across the lot. 'You really got to watch your step now,' old man Joseph Midnight warned when Will had taken the boat out. His voice had crawled over the water to Will. 'Last couple of years, there was one every few weeks, another cyclone jumping around. Whoever heard of that before?'

Jesus Christ! There was water piling up in the skies. Then nothing. The weather report was over. Stuck in a empty hangar a couple of hundred kilometres from the sea, Will imagined all the satellite activity hovering over the Gulf. Spies of the world zoomed in onto a pimple on your nose, or knew what you were saying in the privacy of your own home. Was anyone looking at Gurfurritt? If someone spied on the weather, why not provide more information about what was going on? Rich men paid for foreign cargo ships from the four corners of the globe to anchor in the Gulf to transport ore.

It was high tide. Will knew how the tides worked simply by look-ing at the movement of a tree, or where the moon crossed the sky, the light of day, or the appearance of the sea. He carried the tide in his body. Even way out in the desert, when he was on the Fishman's convoy, a thousand miles away from the sea, he felt its rhythms.

This feeling for the sea had been inherited from Norm, and

Will began to think of his father on his journey with Elias. *I hope you make it to the old world*. But of course he would make it. Will scowled at his weak sentimentality over his father who never bore his children's burden. A saltwater man who insisted he belonged to the sea like fish. *I'll weather the storm*. So said the veteran of the mother of all storms, invading the hangar out of the blue, to this wasted luxury of his son, reminiscing what was once upon a time: *If the natural forces get me in the end, it will be on the flippen land. Never the sea. I bet my life on it.*

Puzzled, irritated, by the commonsense madness of his father's hick town philosophy, Will twisted about on the chair, muttering to himself: 'If you're dead, you're dead, no need to bet on that.' But the memories of his father were not done with Will's thoughts, even in this moment of crisis. Norm Phantom was keen to show his son whom he had not spoken to in years, something else from the past. The little list. The list boy! Did you remember to bring the list? How a man could come back to collect his winnings, if he did not keep his little list of fools in his back pocket: who owed him money, so forth.

'What's the matter with him?' The Fishman's men had been trying to attract Will's attention.

'Dunno. Throw a stone and see.'

Someone hit Will on the leg with a small stone to bring some sense into his head. Now he saw two men from the convoy standing by the door smiling at him. Then the mobile phone rang.

'Chuck,' the yellow-haired man spat his name into the mobile. He had come out of the kitchenette and was standing somewhere to the back of Will in the hangar.

'What? A fire. You got to be joking…Alright, I'm on my way.'

'What's up?'

'Graham said there's a fire over this way. Stay here, watch him Cookie. I'll look around.'

The next moment Chuck returned, running to grab the fire extinguisher, and ordering his mate to get the other fire extinguisher on the wall next to the doorway. Ignoring Will, both quickly disappeared. The Fishman's men had come prepared. Knives were produced to cut Will free from the chair. Within seconds they were outside the shed again, and looking back, sensed that Will was of two minds about going with them. 'You mad, Will?' They had only moments to get out of the place, and Will was holding them up.

'Give me a knife,' Will ordered, but no one listened to him. 'Fuck you! Give me a knife or I'll kill you. They killed Hope and my boy. I am going nowhere I swear to God, until I kill them. So give me the fucken knife.'

Moving around the benches, Will saw a tyre lever, grabbed it, and headed out the door. The two lads felt blood draining from their faces: this was supposed to be easy. They looked at the fire down at the last hangar. The flames were arching out like waves and black smoke billowed into the atmosphere.

'Look man, I know how you feel! But those arseholes are dead already. They're gone man, I swear it, because as true as God I am standing here, this whole place is going to blow, as soon as the fire reaches the pits. Come on, we got to take you with us, fuck you, or we are going to die in this mongrel place. Look up there and see the friggen fire for yourself man. Come on, man, or we will kill you ourselves.'

The two young men, no more than eighteen apiece, dressed in grey shorts, baseball caps, with Bob Marley staring from their Rasta-coloured T-shirts, worked simply to the letter of the Fishman's orders. They were still wearing workingmen boots supplied by the mine. A lot of the young men in the Fishman's convoy had done their stint in the mine, looked around, seen how it all worked, then walked off with their mining helmets and boots as souvenirs. Both still had their cigarettes hanging from the sides of their mouths, while they used the iron-fisted grit of their fathers to persuade Will to get the hell out of there.

The fire spread quickly across the grasslands, throwing long red tongues down to the south. Will looked at the black smoke billowing into the sky. He tried to see through the wall of smoke to locate the two mine men with their fire extinguishers, but could not penetrate the curtain of blackness. The only thing that was clear, were flames reaching up into the sky at the far hangars. It looked like a giant candle, a millennium flame. A wind of intense heat forced Will and the two Bob Marley faces to flee.

'Come on, Will, get a fucking move on,' one of the lads said, maintaining a firm grip on Will's arm. The second lad did the same on the other side and they ran dragging Will along with them. They kept looking back over their shoulders as they ran, stumbling along through the spinifex and grass and gravel, seeing if anyone was coming from the mine, or if they were seen. Looking ahead at the distance to reach the fence line, each knew, until they were over the fence and into the scrub land and hills, they would be in full view of the mine men when they turned up in their vehicles.

'Let's hope the bloody lot goes up in their bloody faces,' one lad said to the other as they ran, knowing it might be their only chance, if the bloody lot went up. But when they looked back again, the yellow-haired one and his mate were running after them.

'Split up,' Will said. 'Take the left and right, and I will take the centre, go low.'

'Do you know where the opening is Will? Head to the left, one hundred metres. Remember that.'

'Get going. I know where it is, get going.'

The three peeled off in their different directions. The two young lads were looking around. Where was the backup? The whole operation had begun with several dozen men who had slipped in earlier, spreading themselves all over the mine site, to do 'a good job'. It was to have been a pilfering exercise on a grand scale, pure and simple. Then they got word: Fishman had changed his mind. The teams had come in the previous night. They moved on the fuel tanks, syphoning petrol into jerry cans which had to be carried over to the fence line and into the bush on the other side towards a waiting vehicle. They had spread around. *Have yourself a shopping spree, tools and equipment – for the road.* Freezer raid, the Fishman had ordered. Usual thing. Raid everything.

'Man! Where in the fuck are they?' one lad screamed across to his mate. 'Where's the bloody backup, mannn? Jesus!'

Guns were being fired. The two lads heard the strange sound for the first time in their lives as the bullets whistled by, inches past their ear, and both yelled, 'Duck man, they are shooting at us.' Both ran faster, bolting for their lives like jack rabbits, and Will, where was he? They had seen him disappear into the ground like he was made out of thin air. And they did duck, unbelievingly, as they ran, seeking cover behind every clump of spinifex, as though dead spinifex could shield anyone against bullets. But that was what they did, and kept doing, with no backup at all, not even looking back to see that glorious fire tonguing down to the underground storage tanks, nor knowing there were only moments to go, and they would be all feeling what it was like to be blown sky-high, if they did not make it out over the fence and into the hills.

Fate and precious moments are tied up together, and as the saying goes, *What goes around comes around*: the yellow-haired man tripped. Instantly, his head was split open at the temple by a rock that had, up to that moment, lain on the ground, embedded in soil that was thousands of seasons old, untouched by humankind since the ancestor had placed it in this spot, as if it had planned to do this incredible thing.

Rock and roll, it was unbelievable to have seen what happened. Will had been so close, waiting to take what rightfully he claimed, and the man was running straight for him, and only Will saw what was about to happen, saw the rock was ready, waiting for this moment. Instantaneously, it was as natural a reaction as you would expect, but he felt cheated you know. He had even thrown himself towards the man to try to break his fall. It was too late, a snap, how quickly a driven man could be defeated. Will had no idea a rock could rob him of his revenge. He stood, arched over the dead man in a moment of foreboding, watching the blood pouring out of the man's head all over the ground, the glorious yellow hair now tainted red and covered with dust, wishing he had the power to bring the dead man back to life. Where was the justice in this? The murderer struck dead, died instantly without pain, and went on to eternity with the look of peace on his broken face. And there was the stone, still there, unmoved.

'Will! What the fuck are you doing. Keep running,' one of the young blokes yelled back over his shoulder. 'Jesus Christ!' he yelled, 'I never seen so much craziness in you man.' Seeing Will standing there looking at the ground, the young man was certain he would end up going back for him, just to appease the Fishman, and shouted: 'You are going to get us all killed, fuck you.'

Will heard and ran. Out in the open he looked back for the red-haired Cookie, but he was nowhere in sight. Will had missed the moment that the backup men with rifles in the hills had witnessed. In full flight, lifted in midair, Cookie kept running after his prey before he heard the piece of lead explode in his chest. His eyes jumped to the left, then to right, as though undecided which way to go to hell first, before he sunk down into the spinifex.

A dozen convoy men scrambling out of the hills, leaping down rocks, hands cut by spinifex, raced to the fence line to open a hole in the wire. The fence was rolled back for Will and the two lads to run towards. It seemed as though the whole world cheered them, yelling: 'Come on, come on, hurry, you can do it.' Then, the cheering turned into a synchronised ballet of men risking their lives without thought for themselves. They ran out towards the lads, and finally, had the three snatched up by a sea of hands. Their lungs burnt with exhaustion. A human chain passed each of the three along up to the hills, until finally, they were thrown down for shelter behind the boulders, in the fold of the ancestral spirit who governed the land.

The fire burned like hell over there at the hangars and even in the hills, the air was that hot, it burnt your skin. It felt like being in a furnace. Dust-dry hair turned into rust, stuck up straight and waved in the air, charged up to the hilt with electricity. Well! The moment came then, just how the Fishman said it had to be. And it would not have paid anyone to look back if they did not want to have their head blown off in 'the process'. They were the Fishman's favourite two words in those days.

The day, all action-packed like it was, was now all said and done. The men of Mozzie Fishman's dedicated convoy to one major Dreaming track stretching right across their stolen continent, were sitting up there on the side of the hill – like rock wallabies, looking down at what was left of Gurfurritt mine. Just looking, and turning the sunset crimson with their thoughts.

A day at the mine had turned into a modern legend about travelling with the Fishman, and civil morality…

What a turnout. Gee whiz! We were in really serious stuff now. We were burning the white man's very important places and wasting all his money. We must have forgotten our heads. We were really stupid people to just plumb forget like – because the white man was a very important person who was very precious about money. Well! He was the boss. We are not boss. He says he likes to be boss. He says he's got all the money. Well! We haven't got the money neither. And now, all it took was a simple flick. A flick, flick, here and there with a dirt-cheap cigarette lighter, and we could have left the rich white people who owned Gurfurritt mine, destitute and dispossessed of all they owned.

Straight out we should have been asking ourselves – Why are you not hanging your head in shame to the white man? We were supposed to say, Oh! No! You can't do things like that to the, umm, beg your pardon, please and thankyou, to the arrr, em, WHITE MAN.

Somehow though, everyone got carried along the humpteen tide of events, like, we must have swallowed one too many sour pills that morning for breakfast. Now, we were looking at the world like it was something fresh and inviting to jump into and do what you jolly well liked. That was how our dormant emotions sitting down inside our poor old hearts got stirred up by the Fishman when we listened to him talking in that fetching, guru type voice of his, saying we gotta change the world order. Change the world order? Mozzie Fishman! He is sure enough a crazy man. Oh! We said that. But he goes on in his satirical slinging voice about what happened ever since that mine came scraping around our land and our Native title! 'Well!' he says. Us? He wanted us to tell him what that turned out to be! We were a bit cross with Mozzie standing up there, Lord Almighty like on top of that rust bucket of a Falcon station wagon of his. It and all its white crucifixes wiped all over the car through the stains of red mud.

'You know who we all hear about all the time now?' he asked us. 'International mining company. Look how we got to suit international mining people. Rich people. How we going to do that?' Now, even we, any old uneducated buggers, are talking globally. We got to help United Kingdom money. Netherlands lead air problems. Asia shipping. United States of America industry, and we don't even know German people. 'I says,' he says like he is singing, 'we mobs got to start acting locally. Show whose got the Dreaming. The Laaaw.' He liked to empathise 'The Laaaaw' whenever he was heating up around the ears on the subject of globalisation.

We whispered among ourselves. Ignore him. Clap your hands over your ears to put an end to his *blasphemy*. Don't listen to him. Still he was not finished with us. He goes on ignoring our pleas, and in the end demanded, soft as silk, he knew who he was playing with. All satiny voice, he said it was time now to end our cowtailing after the white people. It was finale time. Hands up. Who we got to follow? The white man, or the Fishman? This was the ultimatum. Well! He made us that wild. Of course, we got no choice – we got to go with culture every time. We should have known he was leading up to all of this destruction. But we? We were like following dogs, and we were happy to do it, not think, because we were acting solely and simply on pure rage.

The soundwaves coming off the explosion in the aeroplane hangars at the biggest mine of its type in the world, Gurfurritt, were just about as tremendous a sound you could ever expect to hear on this earth. Like guyfork night. Booom! Booom! Over and over. But one hundred times more louder than that. Ripped the lot. We were thinking, those of us lying on the ground up in the hills smelling ash – what if our ears exploded? What would deafness sound like? We should have thought of that first.

Sometime during our precious time on earth we could have asked a deaf person what it was like to not hear the sounds any-more, before we go around deliberately destroying our own good hearing on wildness. Oh! But there was no going back because no one was going to reverse where the rotten hand of fate was heading. So, even though we were shaking in our old work boots, thinking we got busted eardrums, we watched the fire rage like a monster cut loose from another world. It might even have come from hell. Even the devil himself would have least expected us weak people to have opened the gates of hell. But we watched full of fascination at the fire's life, roaring like a fiery serpent, looking over to us with wild eyes, pausing, looking around, as if deciding what to do next. Then, we could hear it snarl in an ugly voice you would never want to hear again. *Alright, watch while I spread right through those hangars like they were nothing, hungry! hungry! Get out of my way.* It did that roaring along, exploding through walls and rooftops which looked like toadstools bursting open, then once those flames shot outside, going a million miles an hour up into the sky, sparks just landing wherever, like a rain shower, out in the grass somewhere around the back.

The fire spread out the back of the hangars in the dry grass, and then it came burning around to the front again, fanned by a gusting south-easterly wind. Then, the monster smelt the spilt fuel on the ground. It raced through that, quickly spreading itself over the ground weeds, until it found the fuel bowsers, then it paused, maybe the fire had thoughts of its own and could not believe its luck. The fire just sitting there was as awesome a moment you could experience for our men waiting in the hills, sneaking a glance from over the boulders they were hiding behind, peering through the black smoke, thinking maybe their luck had run out and what next.

It looked as though the fire was going to peter out. The fire was just sitting, smouldering, not knowing where to go next because the wind was not blowing strong enough to fan it in the right direction. Our men looking from the hills continued staring at the little flame flickering there, fizzing out. What could they do? It looked like defeat was imminent. And, that same old defeated look, two centuries full of it, began creeping back onto their faces. But, it was too late now, they had a taste of winning, so they projected their own sheer willpower right across that spinifex plain, calling out with no shame, *Come on, come on*, willing the little flame not to fizz, believing magic can happen even to poor buggers like themselves.

Somehow, someone started yelling, 'Look, look, it is starting to move.' The unbelievable miracle came flying by. A whirly wind, mind you nobody had seen one for days, just as a matter of fact sprung up from the hills themselves. It swirled straight through from behind those men, picking up their wish and plucking the baseball caps which came flying off their heads, together with all the loose balls of spinifex flying with the dust and the baseball caps, the whole lot moving towards the fire. When it passed over the open rubbish tipsters the mine had lined up along the side of the hangars, it picked up all the trash. All the cardboard boxes, newspapers lying about and oily rags, spirited the whole lot across the flat towards the line of hangars on fire.

It happened so fast when the fiery whirlwind shot into the bowsers and momentarily, lit them up like candles. Well! It might even have been the old *Pizza Hut* box someone had left on top of one of those bowsers that added that little bit of extra fuel, you never know, for the extra spark, or it would have happened anyway, but the wick was truly lit.

The finale was majestical. Dearo, dearie, the explosion was holy in its glory. All of it was gone. The whole mine, pride of the banana state, ended up looking like a big panorama of burnt chop suey. On a grand scale of course because our country is a very big story. Wonderment, was the ear on the ground listening to the great murmuring ancestor, and the earth shook the bodies of those ones lying flat on the ground in the hills. Then, it was dark with smoke and dust and everything turned silent for a long time.

'You think they heard it in Desperance?' some young lad whispered carefully through the settling dust, because he did not want to frighten anyone by making the first sound of this new beginning. It was so incomprehendingly silent he needed to speak to hear himself talk because he was thinking of his family and the noise of his memories of them was the only sound he could hear.

The sound of this young voice being the first sound was a relief for the others who had been thinking they were listening to the sound of their own deafness. However relieved and pacified they were to hear speech, everyone kept listening, listening for what else remained missing – Ah! It was the noise of the bush breathing, the wind whispering through the trees and flowing through rustling grasses. We needed to hear the birds chirping, the eaglehawk crying out something from the thermals high above, but the eery silence lingered on. The birds were nowhere to be seen or heard, not even a singing willy-wagtail lightly flittering from rock to rock wherever anyone walked, or a mynah bird haggling at your feet. We looked into the dust and smoke-darkened skies and saw no twisting green cloud of budgerigars dancing away in thin air. The wind had dropped. Silent clouds passing overhead cast gloomy shadows over the peaceful trees, while grasses and spinifex stood stock-still as though the world had become something false, almost reminiscent of a theatre setting. We men floated somewhere between the surreal stillness, and the reality of the ants, lizards and beetles and other insects moving through the rocky ground as though nothing had happened. No one spoke or answered the boy, because we guessed the explosion must have been heard on the other side of the world, let alone in Desperance.

One will never know what really happened that day. Fishman, never stopped smiling about it. He said his recipe was top secret. He was regarded with awe whenever he came into anyone's presence because it was a privilege to know the Fishman. He was respected for what he had inside of his head. Too right! Nobody could know the highly confidential material in case someone like Mozzie had to do it all over again some day. Ignorant people would always ask, *How did you stop the mine?* And he would look at them for a long time with his steady eye, like he was making up his mind whether they were worth letting in on the secret. Finally, he would say, *I have decided to give you the truth*, and the truth was the very same words he had always used about what he would do to the mine from the day it got set up on our traditional domain. 'I put broken glass bottles on the road to stop the buggers – that's what I did.' Somehow, this was the truth. Truth just needed to be interpreted by the believers who could find the answers themselves just like the Fishman had done. At the same time he offered another piece of advice, which was, a smiling man would live for a very long time. And he did.

A frenzied media from the bustling world of 'Down South' fuelled up, to fly back and forth over the mine in their helicopters like flies. Unlike any fly, the journalists saw the Gulf through virgin eyes. It was a place few Australians had been too, let alone those of any other country tied up with the Gulf of Carpentaria. It was a world apart from their own. Anything in this new world could be created, moulded, and placed on television like something to dream about, or a nightmare.

What stirred their souls was the pureness of silence and the intriguing sense of loneliness each had discovered on their arrival in single-engine charter planes at the aerodrome of Desperance. There, hours could go by, and the only thing happening was the sound of the weather funnel rattling against a steel pole – Twang, Twang! Twang! Under these circumstances, for the fascinated news people romancing the Gulf, no story became too big or too small, to give to the world.

413

Televised on-the-spot reports of the dead ore body lying across the ground like a fallen hero, filled the TV screens across the nation. Splashed into every news broadcast was a badly composed identikit picture of Will Phantom which bore no resemblance to him. A lot of people in Desperance started asking questions. They wanted to know who that person was that they saw on television every night, who was running around calling himself Will Phantom. It was a good question, because mix-ups and things like that did not help, if Desperance people felt they were complete strangers to one another, and they could not understand the truth of television. For mind you, they were still recovering from the shock of the mine. There was a thin feeling in the air. A tension. It became as though anything could snap at any moment over the very idea of life itself. Anything could fall from a loose hinge into full-blown hysteria.

The multi-million dollar mine, from infancy to its working prime, was probed, described and paraded to network viewers. Interviews and footage of scenery went jig-jogging along in soap opera intensity, before finally shifting to pan, and viewers were encouraged to dissect what had become of this showcase of the nation. They watched forensic scientists fully covered in white protective clothing, risking their lives, hunting through the rubble. Who could even breathe while watching these brave men and women slowly prod through each piece of debris in this solemn post mortem, carried out with the meticulous thoroughness of an ant? It became a televised spectacular, just like the death of an icon, woven with the interactiveness of *Nintendo*. Viewers could call up. They could hear their own voices via satellite and underground cable, coming back to them from the mine itself on television. Ordinary people living thousands of miles away, who had no former interest whatsoever in the mine or its location, joined the growing numbers of bereaved viewers gandering at the still untameable, northern hinterland.

The face of a scientist, speaking behind his glass-fronted mask with a muffled voice which had to be transcribed into English on the bottom of the television set, like the SBS channel, became the anchorman for the task that lay ahead. On the first day he reported that a fire had spread from the main transport hangars to the fuelling bowsers. It was lucky no one was killed. On day two, the wash-up at the end of the day was like at the beginning, this was a major explosion in the remote Gulf of Carpentaria at Gurfurritt, the biggest mine of its type in the world. The scientists viewed viewing what lay on the ground were trying to discover what caused the explosion. There had been no fatal casualties. And so on.

After a week of the hooded scientist, another bald, Mars-faced scientist appeared on the television screen. He was at home with a sad expression on his face which popped out of fawn-coloured clothes. He gave the scientific explanation on the news: 'The fire at Gurfurritt mine initiated from a grassfire. Spinifex exploded and the intensity of the fire it created quickly spread to the bowsers. (Pause.) This caused a major explosion to the underground fuel tanks. I understand that this explosion spread through the underground fuel pipes up to the mine. This action quickly reached the main fuel tanks, which caused another major explosion, causing major damage to the mine and machinery.

'The fuel line to the mine operations connected to the main fuel tanks caused further major damage to occur. The intense heat rising into the atmosphere from the initial explosions generated a chain reaction of explosions throughout the mine. (Footage to air of mass destruction.) An incidental fuel leakage running throughout the 300-kilometre pipeline to the coast caused it to be extensively damaged. (Pause.) This damage was caused by an explosion throughout the buried pipeline which was only running at a third of its capacity at the time of the incident. The force from this simultaneous explosion uncovered the entire pipeline and pieces were found many kilometres from their original site. (Pan shot: bits of pipeline sticking out of the ground and throughout the surrounding bushland like an exhibition of post-modern sculpture outside the Australian National Gallery or Tate Modern in London on the Thames.) At the end of the pipeline, there was extensive damage at the dewatering plant where storage tanks were destroyed.'

When the explosions stopped, the Fishman's men picked themselves up from the ground. They agreed that only the greatness of the mighty ancestor had saved them. It was a miracle they were still alive after the earth shook so violently underneath them, they had thought it would go on forever. A heavy red fog of dust and smoke hung in the air as they moved away, their visibility limited to just a few metres. The fine dust fell slowly, and when it settled on those men who were trying to regain a sense of the enormity of what had happened, they took on the appearance of the earth itself. One by one, camouflaged by dust, they began spiriting themselves away, quickly, carefully, as dust covered their tracks, back to the lagoon of the dancing spirits.

The ancestral trees at the lagoon danced wildly in the ash wind around the Fishman sitting on the ground staring red-eyed from weariness in the direction of the mine. He had been sitting in that position for hours visualising what was happening at the mine, waiting for his men to return. Their return seemed to be taking forever, and those extraordinary followers watching the master, were making other rare discoveries. They were convinced that the Fishman had shrunk in front of their very eyes. They were sure he was growing smaller and smaller with every passing second of precious time. The chances were, if he continued to shrink, there would be nothing left of him by the time they would be compelled to flee. In this perilous locale, they nodded, he would become an obscure beetle left crawling around the edge of the lagoon.

It was true, Mozzie Fishman did seek obscurity. His instinctive trait was to crawl away from adversity, at least metaphorically, into invisibility and nothingness. What caused this peculiarity of his tangled personality was something that went berserk in what he called his stupid brain, whenever he had anything to do with white people. It seemed it was white people who could tug on his conscience, making him degrade himself like this. The truth was, Mozzie Fishman was shrinking, waiting for his men, *Oh! Great spirits of God, let there be no casualties*, he longed, moaning to himself. He was so full of the anxiety and shrinking up into a beetle, he could not see the young men who ran through the bush hoping to evade capture, jumping for cover as skilfully as hares.

Yet, on the other side of his mind, he fought like a rabid dog to maintain an octopus vision of himself, where all arms lead to great glory and success. In this view of the world, there was no room for doubts to interfere with the great spirits of destiny whose permanent home was etched into the land itself, in this place. No one tampered with these arms of destiny which belonged only to Mozzie, as though he had put out a single hand to catch a true stone after it was fired from a shanghai. His general mood was downhearted somewhat and forlorn, yet in spite of the world of calamity he had created, he felt calmly sated as he sat, alone in contemplation.

Chapter 12
About sending letters

The vehicles left the lagoon in the early morning under Mozzie's orders. He had sent Angel Day with them. Several of his men were given strict instructions to take Angel to any large city in the South where she would stay. 'And you must try to be happy,' he told her as a parting gesture of goodwill, although she replied that she had no intention of being told to be happy. After the proverbial dust had settled, he told her, as she finally stepped into a waiting car, he would come by. 'Such is life,' she sighed. With not one tear left to fall on a soaked hankie, only a premonition that her life was to be one squalid mess of moving between overcrowded houses from this point on, she resigned herself to a flicker of hope, because Mozzie solemnly promised as soon as he thought it was safe, he would arrange for her to go home.

The whole convoy was ordered by the Fishman to take a route into a winter of nowhere. 'Break up – as soon as you can,' he ordered. 'Do not go home.' He used many words to describe their new identities. They should become anonymous reformers with the run and mill. Blend. 'Only regroup,' he said, when his word arrived and some day surely, it would. These were his strict instructions. More homilies followed like prayers so the men would never forget that only by following the Fishman's word, letter for absolute letter, did any of them have a chance of invisibility.

'Follow me,' he warned with his one stern eye. 'Or else cop the consequences.'

Well! That was that then. Consequences meant remembering how fish could get caught up in all kinds of nets, and you would know whose plate you were going to land on if you were regarded as being the criminal type of fish. 'Be perfectly assured,' his warnings kept flowing, adding reasons because he liked reasons, in the belief that a leader could not have enough reasons stored up in his brainbox.

'I am not talking about that useless, invisible Desperance kinda net, I am talking about the real ones, just as invisible, thrown out by the police who are wanting to squash people like you, like you is merely a nuisance of a mosquito.' He was still explaining his reasons, while one by one, the men got into their vehicles with whatever gear they owned, and drove off along the slow, difficult curvilinear road out of the valley, to the long, hard, short-cut roads into desert locations, so as to be gone from memory as though they had never existed.

At last, the Fishman caught the first glimpse of the red-dust-covered men with their red watery eyes emerging from the bush after they had travelled by foot over thirty kilometres from the mine site. One after the other they fell on the ground where he was waiting and for a while, they all lay there exhausted, breathing heavily, saying nothing at all until finally, a voice rose from the mass of dust and smoke of panting bodies to say two words, 'Done boss.' The Fishman simply nodded as if there was little satisfaction to be gained from his one big day on earth. He nodded, as he went around solemnly patting each man on the back. Minutes later, the young men moved away and into the ghostly grey and red-streaked lagoon waters, breaking through the thin coating of dust and ash to uncover the fresh, cool water beneath.

'Where's Will?' the Fishman asked, looking around. He knew

he was not there, but he completed a headcount anyway. From the water, the men looked back to the still ash-covered bush on the other side of the lagoon. It looked as though no man had ever walked through there, and it seemed unlikely anyone else would. Yet, the men were certain they had seen the two young blokes setting off to the lagoon with Will. 'We saw the three of them going ahead before any of us, we told them boss, "Take Will up ahead in case of any trouble". But it was useless explaining. There was so little time to lose, and they still had some burying to do.

This was what went wrong. Slowly, the report was given. A map was drawn of the location in the mud at the edge of the lagoon. Two crosses on the ground marked where the two mine men guarding Will had fallen.

'Afterwards, after the explosions, we had to wait see, then we, a few of us, went back to find the bodies of those two.'

It was true; the men had dared to face the scorching heat where the devil had just passed. They had returned to the flat, walking through the burning spinifex, trying to locate the bodies in the heat but had to leave quickly.

'Look boss, there was no way we could find them. We went straight to the places where we saw them go down, the bastards, and they weren't there. They were gone. Abracadabra! Zoom. Disappeared into thin air.'

'How could flesh and blood disappear into thin air?' A sceptical Fishman eyeballed the tall-yarn spinners.

'What we were saying: we thought the ground swallowed them up and they went rolling down to hell. After we heard the explosion, we looked all around the ground with one second, that's all we had, true God. Even in that time I swear to God, we never seen anything like it. The ground started to come at us, like the skin of a wild animal rippling up and down as it is running along, with rocks jumping everywhere. Behind the ground moving, the dirt and rock went flying everywhere. Well! We had to duck for cover after that. We were flat on the ground and all we felt was movement underneath us, like the devil was coming up to the surface.

'And he was accompanied by the sound of the devil's orchestra playing the horrible, sizzling music of hell by thumping their own heads together – Bang! Bash! Bang! We never heard anything like it. The sound was so terrible, we knew it could only be the sound of damnation. The only thing must have happened, the explosion lifted them up first, threw them to kingdom come, and when they fell, the devil took one quick look and said, "Curry them in hell, the buggers". Or, it could have been, they got buried themselves.'

The tellers of tall stories were given a cursory glance by Mozzie as he continued fidgeting with his hands, twiddling his thumbs in circles, as though the action would conjure the simple truth out of a gammon story. But in the scheme of things, it did not really matter who was telling the truth. *Hey! Yo! Why tempt fate? No one here was going back anyway. Wishes were the only thing left.* A simple wish was all anyone could ask: that wherever they fell, nobody would find the bodies until they were well and truly gone. *Whispering again.* Such a truthful mind running nilly-pilly, and so little control over his speech.

Mozzie turned his gaze back through the rustling tree spirits to a spot where it seemed they were beckoning him to look, and he saw another truth in the blackened landscape. It was a truth he had seen earlier, as he looked towards the mine, at what had become of normality, as a spectator of this thing they called hell, and seen the devastation over the hills. Now he saw the real immensity of what had happened in front of him, as if the only purpose of such a miracle was to brand him, small and inferior. Blown bits of rose-coloured human flesh, amidst burnt black cinders, had fallen onto the ground. At that moment, seeing what he had, he wished it undone, but the terrible truth did not yield to the wish of a simple man.

A fortune-teller's time sped fast over the same ground where dingos, prowling in the middle of the night after he and his men had gone, were taking whatever remained of those people, scattered over the plains, before running and snivelling back to their rocky lairs inside the hills of the great spirit. A tragedy kept unfolding, and he, unable to acknowledge his culpability, wished to hide in the smallness of men. He chose. He would not see the extremity of his weakness, nor claim it straightaway: he referred time elsewhere. The Fishman felt a dull pain again, pulling his heart apart. The indecision was breaking him in two. Now, he was uncertain if he should believe in his safe vision of what had really happened. Did he need to know the truth? But the truth was, there would be no going back.

Then, while the dark clouds of the Gulf crawled by, darkening the already hazy atmosphere, and cloud bellies touched the tops of the again windy bush, the attention was drawn of a young turk with the very best eyes, and respect for all religionalities among them, who yelled out in a rasping voice like a Christian crusader, 'In kingdom come, thy will be done. Thank the Lord, here they come!'

The Fishman peered over the rims of his sunglasses, and it was true whether from his good eye or the glass one, for the young followers were running, and others followed through the swaying branches of the spearwood trees. They were coming alright. The Rasta boys, under ash, with Will Phantom stumbling along, half dragged by the sheer willpower of the Rastafarian god men.

Privately to the Fishman, the two young men, still winded by their efforts to return to the camp, explained in his ear what had happened. 'We come along, like you said, and we are saying, "We are bringing the Fishman's gift of life".' They said they believed Will Phantom was just a man wishing to die. 'You better off watching him. He's got a death wish. A date with death. Can't stop him.'

'We should have left him there.' The young blokes complained in a haughty manner, although suffering from smoke inhalation which hampered them from talking more, and burns. Will lay on the ground in front of them. Explaining their difficulties, they said, 'We could have been killed a half-a-dozen times because of him.'

'We want you to know he doesn't listen to a fucking thing.'

Finally, they explained how he went back, they had to chase after him, while he looked for the two dead men from the mine. 'We were nearly half baked alive, crawling on our bellies through a bloody spinifex inferno. You couldn't breathe nothing but fire, all the while, trying to pull him out of there.' Finally, exhausted, the two young men ceased talking. Ignoring the Fishman, and bending over with their hands on their knees, trying to catch their breathe, both cast a hostile glance over at Will.

'Yeah! Yeah!' The Fishman hurried them along, anxious to hear what else they had to say.

'We found the buggers dead of course. We dragged them out of there, with clumps of spinifex exploding into flames everywhere you looked, and the bloody fire, chasing us.'

'And!'

'They are just over there.' One of the lads indicated across the lagoon with a hand he barely lifted from his knee. 'And we aren't touching em again, neither.' Fishman went over to Will and gave him a fatherly pat on the back. 'Good job lad.' He got him some water, then called some of the men to go and bring the bodies back from the bush. Soon enough, the two charred bodies were laid out at the feet of the Fishman.

'I guess we had better bury them,' he decided. 'We better get to work and bury them. Over there in the bush,' he said finally, looking back towards the road.

'No, we are not, we are not burying them at all.' The Fishman looked around on hearing Will speak, and saw him standing, completely covered in ash, dust and congealed blood, but there was no doubt, it was the familiar Will Phantom's easy stance. On first glance the Fishman was reminded of Norm some thirty years ago, standing in front of him with the same ease: calling it quits to their dual leadership on the religious road.

'You remember Elias's boat?' Will spoke quietly into Fishman's ear – lest the wind heard and told the trees.

Fishman nodded, remembering the unpleasant, hot day they had found poor, old Elias, sitting out there in the middle of the lagoon, and thinking he was there fishing, but knowing that dead men don't fish.

'Well! What do you think, hey? If we get that boat from up the hill over there, and we leave those two there for the crows to feed on?' Will talked on. He took no notice of the look of concern growing on the Fishman's face.

The older man had shocked himself, when he unwittingly looked inside the charred skin of the two broken bodies that had been dragged one way or the other through hell. There, their spirits lay, unable to move, as though locked in limbo, and from their heads stared frightened eyes which jumped left and right at every rustle in the bush to which Will wanted to condemn them. Instantly, deep sorrow moved Mozzie to forget his own grievances and to make a sober decision. There was no thirst for revenge. Whatever it was, was quenched. He had no mind left for the callousness of Will. Instead, he replied, 'We going to bury em decent. Decent. You understand me Will?'

'No, I respect you. You are the boss, but I got to do this,' Will replied just as determinedly. 'They killed Elias. Left him here like he was just fish bait, and, yesterday! Yesterday they killed Hope. These bastards threw her out of the helicopter. And now, I don't know for sure, but they might have killed Bala as well. So, I am going up there to get Elias's boat, even if I got to do it myself, and I am going to leave them there to rot, until they are found by the people over there at the mine.'

'Eye for an eye is it Will?'

'Yeah! From now on it is.'

'You know what will happen if you leave them in the boat, don't you? Their ghosts will come haunting you whenever you are in the water. Leave them in a boat and they will come rowing over any sea and throw evil at you until they kill you. So, now I am telling you no more. You listen to me. You got to bury them decently, no matter what they did.'

'I couldn't care less. You will have to kill me first before you bury them in our sacred country. If they got holy country somewhere for killers, well let the mine take them there and bury them themselves. This is our own sanctified country, not theirs. They got no place here.'

'Alright, have it your way, it's your life. But I am warning you. You'd be better off picking your targets. Leave no tracks and biding your time. What can I tell you? I am only an old man. No use listening to me. What can I do? I got my only sons plus one other little fella I didn't even know, to bury.'

Will looked on sympathetically while the Fishman continued talking, now that he was able to tell someone what had happened in Desperance. He recalled how the convoy had arrived at the lagoon, and while they were coming in, he was naming who came in which cars. He had been taking careful note of who was driving, their driving ability, and the condition of the car. Everyone had set up camp at the lagoon, and finally now the spirit trees knew who was there, you could see something was wrong in how they were dancing when the wind started to blow up suddenly like a telephone was ringing.

'It was a bad business what happened next. There was only a wind talking through the trees, that was all, then all of a sudden, everyone was saying, 'What's that? Sounds like engine noise.' Everyone was a bit worried because we know the sound our cars make.

'Anyway, a late car turned up. Seventies model Holden station wagon rode in flat chat, "Look out," reckless driver and all, coming down the road into the lagoon. Did it belong to the convoy everyone was asking, and I said, no it did not. I knew who it belonged to, it belonged to the family of that silly, old troublemaker – Joseph Midnight, same man. So, I said to Midnight's car, when it pulled up in front of everyone and before anyone could get out, "You got no respect coming in here like this. I don't like what you are doing here," I told them.'

Will perfectly understood the significance of this story because everyone knew that old man Joseph Midnight and the Fishman had nothing to do with each other. Both were like his own father Norm Phantom. Stubborn old mules who anchored their respective clans in the sordid history of who really owned different parcels of the local land. Fishman claimed the lagoon, and not just the lagoon either. The old war went right up the coastline to Desperance and out to sea. Will remembered hearing the Fishman explaining that he was the living bible of all times. 'I am pointing to my brain,' he said, pushing his fingers into his head. 'Inside here is the whole history of your government. I can tell you if everything is correct, right back to when time began, before Adam and Eve. I can tell you perfectly for four hundred years, the Midnight people have been doing the wrong thing.' The Fishman had taken Will Phantom out to the spinifex where the mine was to be built. Following the old man's yellow cat eyes, Will watched the warring spirits falling from the skies in the middle of the night to fight on the flat lands until close to dawn, before fading away. 'I see everything,' the old man said with the utmost sincerity in his voice. 'And you come along with me and I will show you because I have been alive forever.'

When the mine was built it exacerbated the situation because it created a window of opportunity for Joseph and his family to start making Native title claims over the area. So, Fishman said, he told Joseph to his face, 'If I see you anywhere around the lagoon I will kill you with a spear.' Old Norm did not get involved in the dispute but Will remembered him still, slinging on about those greedy Midnight pigs, 'trying to justify whatever', in a long-forgotten string of accounts to justify the family feud. The whole lifestyle of old Joseph Midnight's family grew into one sick family joke about pigs slopping around in their sty, waiting for scraps from the mine.

'So, I told them Midnight boys before they had a chance to get out of the car – "You got no ceremony here. You got to go back to your own country. Joseph Midnight's country is a long way off to the West somewhere, salt water and water buffalo where the wild people are living. Go and fight them if you are looking for trouble and you might get lucky enough to get your land back".'

Even in the light of a quarter moon, the Fishman said he was smart enough to see the frightened looks in the eyes of the young men, so, even while thinking he was getting soft in the head, he let them talk. A young voice from inside the car finally spoke. 'Don't get hot under the collar, old man, we will be going. Grandfather sent us to tell you something and we are sorry to have to be the ones that's got to say any bad news to you.'

Will understood when the Fishman paused in this story of his to talk about his premonitions before leaving Desperance. He said he was no angel, but he was listening to the sound of angels singing like when you feel something bad is about to happen. All the way, while driving down to the lagoon, Fishman said he did not know what it was, but his mind was in overdrive, waiting for something to happen. As he became trapped in the quagmire of his imagination, he said he had tried to gasp one single image, but the kaleidoscope refused to come into focus.

'It had to be in one of the cars – it was so close,' he said of the sensation which gripped his mind and was, by now, all over the place. All he could think was that one of the cars in the convoy was about to roll. 'I stopped the cars must of been ten times, got out, and told them off for not driving more carefully.' Every car kept slipping through his mind, while he was trying to figure out who the spook was, not driving his car properly.

'Imagine that!' he spoke quietly. 'But it was too hard, I couldn't see it because I had no faith in my own premonitions. They were the last ones – my own flesh and blood. It was why I could not see them, could not explain, could never picture their future, because they never had one. Poor little boys.

'So, the voice says to me, "The cop killed them, maybe. Maybe, Bruiser, too, because they both flogged them really terrible". Well! I know what Bruiser is like. And you know too that town has gotten worse since the mine came. Killed three little boys, babies really, my kids. Stupid Gordie the reason being, although you can't really blame him can you? Poor thing. I had to think then. Think about what was happening here. Think about why. Why my sons, and not theirs, killed for nothing? I kept thinking it was strange how things were starting to happen around here – all since the mine. Strange, how ordinary people were getting killed, I thought. Innocent people like children. My children. First time I can ever remember, when I did not know what would happen from one day to the next. We always used to know when somebody got killed. Know it. What happened. So, I said to myself, where did it all start? First time, when they got rid of Elias, because he was your friend.'

Will nodded, and listened while the Fishman continued,

reflecting on his story. They walked into the bush and finally, they were standing next to the three small bodies wrapped with blankets. 'Bruiser, it had to be Bruiser,' he said.

'I think Bruiser killed Gordie because he started to be too efficient at his job. Gordie must have had something on Bruiser, so he killed him, then he got the boys to make it look like they did it. I had those Midnight boys out of the car. My blokes dragged them out and made them talk. Well! They knew nothing about anything it seemed. They said nobody knew why anyone wanted to kill Gordie and everyone thought the boys did it. But you know Will, I know they never did it. I wasn't much of a Father, but they couldn't have killed anyone.

'Well! Anyhow, I let those Midnight boys go home. Shouldn't have. They were pleading to join up with the convoy but I wouldn't let them. I told them, "I got no use for any of you so you may as well go back to your grandfather". All I could think of was the amount of trouble they would be on the road. I told them to go back to Desperance, but they said their grandfather had told them to keep going. He said Desperance was no place for young boys anymore. They said they were leaving forever. They were heading South.'

The Fishman said he had selected a dozen young men to stay behind while he had the convoy move out and told them, 'Even if I don't get through, don't survive this, the story has to go on. Nothing must stop our stories, understand?' He turned away from the three bundles lying on the ground, and, as they walked back to the waiting men, Mozzie kept talking.

'I sent men out to the mine with my orders, then two young fellas come flying back with news, "Our Will's over there". That was alright, I sent them back to get you out, same time. The rest of us, we went back to Desperance then, travelling slow and easy, not looking like we were on the warpath with anyone. Silently, like mice, we drove into Desperance, two cars in the middle of the day, driving up the main street.

'The whole place was deserted. No one took any notice what we were doing about the place. They probably are still trying to figure out what happened. We knew where they'd be alright. All Uptown was inside the pub meeting, like they always have a nice meeting together. Having a meeting, when they want to talk about something, like cleaning up all the rubbish in the town – like talking about us mob.

'Well! I said I wanted to be a fly on the wall, and I was, so I heard them. They was all there, jammed in like sardines, and they were trying to figure out what to do about Truthful going mad inside the jail. So, I decided we would take Truthful too. But he was already dead. His rope was still swinging. Sill warm. We take my boys and the other little one as well, and all very quietly, we just slowly drove away and they were still having their meeting.'

Will searched, perhaps half expecting to see the body of Truthful somewhere in the spearwood, or where the crows were perched in the branches breathing in the odours of death, or where the files were buzzing, but he only saw the black cloud of swarming flies hovering around the bodies of the blondie and his mate Cookie. Where was he? Will thought, still shocked at what Mozzie had said. But he could see nothing. Fishman thought he had better explain. 'Don't bother looking around for him. They asked, "You going to bring im too?" Meaning Truthful. And I said, "No way am I going to bring im down here". His type don't belong on our religious ground, anywhere near my boys – let them rest in peace. So, don't go looking because you will never find him here. We left him in Bruiser's house – that's where he is. Sat him up to go cold on Bruiser's personal reclining chair, waiting for Bruiser to come home, singing some old Dean Martin song. Bruiser was going to be hearing that song forever, haunting him, whispering in his ears when he is lying down sleeping in his bed, for the rest of his life. No, I told the men, "Let them look after their own, and we will look after ours".'

Fishman said his last words about what happened in Desperance. 'We never killed Truthful, and he never killed himself either, just like the boys never killed themselves. They were all killed by other hands, just like Gordie, and Elias. The mine made killers Will, and now I've made the mine go away. May the great spirit show us some mercy one day, that is all I say.'

So, so, on Cloud Nine...

The men, signalled with flicking fingers by the Fishman, worked quickly with Will to bring Elias's boat down from the hills. It was not that they wanted to *waste time helping Will Phantom's craziness*. What did they have in common with someone wanting to extract some weird kind of revenge? *The scum of the earth lying flat out on the ground as dead as?* These were nothing more than a couple of charred corpses that should be buried with as much decency as the next person.

Grumbling all the time about being used, *like they were anyone's*, they thought they were something else now; a huge metamorphosis had taken place. In their new grandeur which felt like infinity, it was as plain as day that a special something had been defined out of their 'what for?' kind of half life, in so-called normal society. Their heads swelled with a greatness comparable to the once biggest mine of its type in the world, which they had conquered. It was as though the mine's greatness had been pasted on their identity. It felt like they were on Cloud Nine. Now, revelling in the *Star Wars* theme tune, which they were softly humming as jives to each other, these vigilantes were oscillating on the knife edge of some kind of madness in the 'belly of the big fish', where nothing could be assumed normal, and helping Will! Well! It felt like it was blunting the edge of their mania, and they did not feel this should be happening to them.

So, the men of Cloud Nine worked like a pile of snakes, dragging the only concrete memory of Elias, old *Choice*, through the woodlands and rocks like a piece of Desperance backyard junk. The skip skidded through the unyielding, thick, skin-stabbing twiggy scrub. Their styleless contribution of labour, together with their noisy skylarking full of curses and bad language, had scared the living daylights out of hundreds of scavenger crows perched in the scrub. The birds soared straight up into the red ochre clouds, squawking and carrying on throughout their hurried flight, while others, appearing from out of nowhere, flew in untidy flocks to land. Clouds of birds fought each other for places to perch on the spindly dry branches which in all of the kerfuffle, snapped off close to the ears of the men who became so anxious to leave, they quickened their pace, until they saw the full red sun.

When all is said and done, none of these men had a wish to run about with death. Death had its own air, and in this red haze, that unworldly air sang long, sacred vowels across the land. And while Mozzie's men ran quicker to be away, they heard things they had never heard before. The ghostly poem, summoning the spirit tribes, swept past them as they moved down into the battleground of the spinifex flats. The ode unfolded seasons and months of wind, rain, storm, sun, night owl, swarming flying ants, crows, eagles, dingos, dung beetles, flies, and fish spawning. All came in droves to claim the unprotected spirit until only bare, bleached bones remained.

'Be careful with that boat,' Will demanded.

'What for?' came the reply. 'It aren't that anyone will be using it again.'

'That's not the point,' Will snapped. It was not worth wasting words explaining family sentiment to the Fishman's men.

Once the green boat was moored on the shore again, Fishman came along to have a last glance at the killers. Above, a dark cloud of sentinel flies – dart, dart, darting to and fro – pestered their eternal rest. He looked at the dead men's spirits pleading to be released from inside the decaying bodies. With a deadpan expression on his face, everyone could see for themselves that he had lost interest in pleading clemency for them with Will.

Within seconds, the men had plucked the two dead killers from the ground. 'Okay boss? Heave Ho!' They laid Chuck and Cookie in the boat, side by side, without shedding a tear in mourning. Fishman looked, grunted his disapproval through clenched teeth stained with rolled tobacco, then turned his back and walked away. The men continued the task without thought, and anchored the boat out there, fully exposed, by throwing a rock attached to a rope over the cathead, into the middle of the lagoon.

Fishman led the way with a long stick, pushing along an ancient path invisible to the naked eye, heading through the foothills. Unquestioningly, instinctively, he was following a map etched on his mind from the times of the many fathers' fathers before him. The men followed in his footsteps, each sending off little bubble clouds of thoughts into the wind, thoughts of faraway places, of people and noise, children laughing, and dogs running down the road to see the convoy leaving. They threaded through golden papery grasses rustling with white flower tips, through flowing green-gold spinifex whispering through waving coolabah branches, and silent rock faces of red granite, white quartz, white-grey quartzite, all looking down, watching a funeral procession for the children who marked a full stop in history.

All three boys were wrapped in new, red tartan blankets bound with rope. Inside the blankets, Fishman had covered each of the boys with bunches of a leafy aromatic herb that grew wild in flat clumps over the red land. The strong tangy odour, similar to mint, spilled into the air to drown the smell of death. It was a strange sight of brightness and drab. Most of the men were still wearing Gurfurritt good quality uniforms and boots. Long ago they had ripped off the long sleeves on the shirts, trimmed the long trousers to become shorts, immediately after they had finished up working for the mine. The lads with the smiling Bob Marley T-shirts carried the Fishman's faithful port. The handle of the old brown fifties suitcase had a long stick threaded through it and they carried it ceremoniously, because it was an honour to carry the Fishman's port.

The port contained little. A few rolls of wire, a bit of a canvas, a butcher's knife, a Swiss army pocketknife, spare matches, spare torch batteries, a small radio, a notebook and pen, and a can of Coke he had forgotten to drink. Several men carried black billy-cans containing any personal belongings worth carting around. They walked through one narrow valley after another, and along a spring-fed river lined with dropping paperbark trees. The going was slow in the valleys where the heavy humidity caused them to perspire badly, and it ran off them like water. The men knew what they had been told. They would carry the boys far into the hills to a cave where their journey would end, and the boys would begin their own journey, and when their destination was reached, they would live in a state of harmonious coalescence with their ancestors.

The journey continued for many hours without rest, until at last, the Fishman stopped. He told the men to wait behind, 'Settle yourselves a while,' he said, pointing to a fairytale grove of gidgee trees where the air was so still, you could swear you heard the day-dreams of lazy lizards sunning themselves on the branches. This was the first real break in over eighteen hours of moving west, away from the lagoon. The men watched Mozzie go on alone, until he disappeared into the hills where the only things living were dingoes and marsupials. Down onto the ground, he crawled on his belly into a smelly dingo's lair hidden by grassy tussocks, turpentine scrubs and wild banana vines. From the distance, the men began to hear an echo of bell-like voices wafting down the strange grim faces of the hills.

'How could dingoes make such a sound?' Certainly, it was more than one voice.

'Sounds like cats caterwauling somewhere.' They listened, some asking, expecting more trouble, what could be happening now?

'Listen! Strange words? Listen!'

'Smell that?'

'It's all the dingoes around here.'

'Stop ya cavilling. It's him. Mozzie's speaking a different tongue, a dead language, talking to his passed-away relatives. Tribespeople were shot here.'

For a long time they stood waiting. Time passed. They sat down and waited, and more time passed. They dozed off under a weak shade. They woke up hungry from waiting. These were good men consumed with thoughts of how long they must wait until, one by one, everyone started to relax again. They stretched out long fit arms and legs, comforted by the resounding echoes of Mozzie's voice. Finally, he ended. A long silence emanated from the grim hills, and the men rose to their feet, and craned their necks towards the cave, trying to see if something had happened.

Some of the men threw glances at Will Phantom, seeing what he was going to do, whether he was going to help the Fishman or something. Noise or silence, nothing had bothered Will Phantom. He was still sitting like a sad statue, staring off into space. Small colourful finches bobbed around the ground at his feet, drawing in those who watched them, until, someone who had not been paying attention to the finches, suddenly said, 'Look at that.' Two small green-feathered birds, no bigger than mice, jumped from twig to twig in the nearby grass. Rare birds. Rare find. Night parrots. The reward was discussed, but no one was interested. When Will heard their voices, he raised his head towards the kingfisher he heard flying overhead, and with the other raised eyebrows following his, they watched its flight path, heading north towards the coast.

Soon enough Fishman was heard coming back. He came gently swishing and swashing, pushing aside the twiggy scrub with his stick. It was time to go, he announced in a dignified voice. The boys were carried up, and passed through the dingo's lair into the red-ochre-walled cave. The solemn young men went into the place where only the old people had gone before. Once inside, past the dingo's entrance, the cave opened out to the one large room of towering red walls. On the floor of the cave lay a heavy coating of dust which when moved by their footsteps, flew into the stale air like red powder, revealing its antiquity. They saw small pieces of animal bones, old broken glass, rusted match tins, ancient stone tools – grinding stones, spearheads, axe heads, all perfectly executed in their manufacture. The ceiling left evidence of fires, of those who had come and cooked and slept beside a fire, back, back and further back in time, one hundred thousand years of dreams, ascending in smoke that rose to the ceiling and stayed there in a dense cover of soot.

And the walls, they screamed at you with the cryptic, painted spirits of the Dreamtime. And inside the walls, was the movement of spirits, moving further and further forward, so the surface appeared to be falling into the frightened eyes of the Fishman's men. They all stood there inside, crowded like that. Old Fishman was in another world, crying and talking the dead language, walking around, gently pushing past anyone standing in his way. His staff pounded on the living wall, and the men looked away, down at the dusty floor, before seeing the Fishman moving forward through a narrow opening inside the resting spirit's body. The entrance must have been there already, but it was impossible to have noticed it, because the cave seemed so crowded and occupied with relics from other times. The song cycles' arias of devotion that had droned on in this place for days and days like locusts before rain, which came from forever in the old, musty air inside, were heard now. The men felt the sound lingering inside their heads.

So, it was with astonishment and awe, these men gaped at what they had been shown, and allowed themselves to be taken into the powerful spirituality, which was somehow the same, but much older than the ornate cathedrals made with stone, or the monasteries and places of worship to relics of bones and other bits and pieces of sanctified saints of old Europe and the Holy Land.

Like some old wizard, Fishman turned back, to indicate with a wave of his stick that the men should follow him. The sombre procession continued onwards into the depths of the creature of the underworld's belly, into the people's past. The Fishman kept the march moving, undaunted, and waved his staff left and right, as they proceeded down into the labyrinth of strange corridors in the dimly lit cave, where essential rays of light came tapering down like roots of trees, those of the desert fig tree, or the fat bottle trees, all twisting their roots through cracks in the rocks in search of the cool moisture far, far below. They moved past bones of the deceased laid to rest on rock ledges, or hemmed into crevices. Others leant against the wall in a sitting position, as though they had brought themselves to their final resting place to die.

Using the Eveready torch, kept jammed inside his trouser belt, the Fishman led the way. Behind him, the men followed, carefully watching their steps in the darkness, trying not to slip over the wet rocks in the calcite world of dripping limestone. Inside these chambers, it was a world of cymbals and chimes, children's music reaching further on, deeper into kilometres of underground watercourses feeding the spring-fed paradise far above in the world of sunshine. Finally, their dark, shadowy figures came to a full stop behind the dull light of the torch.

'Well! This is it,' announced Fishman. The men, bunched up behind him, were stunned by what they saw in front of them. On the other side of the small opening, the torch shone across a large underground sea. The open sea was so large rippling waves skimmed across the surface. A breeze filled the darkness. In the ray of torchlight, silvery white seagulls with scotopic eyes that could see in the darkness, were piercing the green water. The birds were feeding on a species of fish the men said they had never seen before.

Shallow shafts glowed intermittently from dim faraway lights which were the stars of this world. The men listened to Mozzie's gravelly, inharmonious voice continuing his nocturne. Perhaps it pleased the spirits that at least somebody had come along to demonstrate his pietism to the old world.

There did not seem to be any other side to this water world. *What's this place?* each had thought. The zealots were simple people, and they found it difficult to adjust to this world which Mozzie had kept from them. Once they had familiarised themselves to the darkness, and explored further, they found a jetty. Glow-worms lit its edge.

All along the stone-carved mooring were well-constructed paperbark canoes resting, it seemed, from antiquity. Each craft was covered in gull droppings and cobwebs. From the bow, a grass rope moored the craft to another cobwebbed rope appearing snakelike up through the water. No one would have been able to guess how long the boats of the dead-language people had been floating there. Many, many centuries, perhaps. The men's recent grand feelings of having saved their traditional domain had now been completely eaten away to a bundle of raw nerves. *What if we invoke the dead being in this place*? someone whispered, and it must have been heard by everyone, for they were all startled, as though the question had been screamed at them. No one uttered a word.

'Where's Will Phantom? Where is he? Land Rights! Is he here?' the Fishman suddenly demanded, as if he had no time left in the world, as if they had to get going, high-tailing it out of the place. Will appeared from the darkness, and moved to the Fishman's side. The old man's face glowed like a peaceful beacon. Will began helping by pulling in a canoe, positioning it beside the flat rock harbour, holding it steady so the Fishman could place his son inside. Others started to help, just enough, so Fishman could perform the ritual of placing the children himself. It was his responsibility. Will joined the three canoes in a line, one behind the other, with the rope. He was surprised to find the rope was still as supple and strong as the day it was made, possibly thousands of years ago. Did it take aunties, grannies, mothers, sisters, sitting together working the reedy grass in a day of clear blue skies with sunlight on their hands as they talked about living things around them? This was what he said to the Fishman as they stood side by side looking at the canoes, rocking steady like cradles, ready to take the journey across the sea into perpetual night.

The old man said he was thinking it was about time to go, to take the boys across, 'I got to make sure they learn the language so they can get on.' Will said that was right, it was time to go, and he gently tossed the rope he was holding, let it fall out in the water, instead of giving it to the hand held out to receive it.

'You did everything, and they are going in peace now,' Will said, with a protective arm steadying the old man, and both watched, as the three canoes moved away from the mooring in the swiftly moving current. Silently, the men stepped forward to pay their respects to the canoes drifting silently into the darkness, before turning to walk away. Up ahead, they heard the cavern echoing with the Fishman's voice bouncing from wall to wall, penetrating their blood, saying his goodbyes to his sons. Wishing them well in their new world. *Be good boys*. He would put his own affairs in order, then he would be coming back to them, very soon. 'Luke Fishman, Tristrum Fishman, and you too, Aaron Ho Kum.' He explained he had adopted this dead boy as his own flesh and blood forever, brother to Luke and Tristrum.

Only Will heard it, while leading the Fishman away, when he looked back over his shoulder. 'Hear it? Listen!' He heard a droning sound, and imagined the sound was converging from many different directions. The sound he heard, was as if someone a long way off was playing a stanza on the didgeridoo, then, others responded with their own version of the melody which went droning on as one long prophetic oratorio. Fishman said he had heard it too. 'Listen!' He dug his elbow into Will's ribs. Will looked back and in the blackness, using his eyes like a cat, he saw the seagulls gathering together like a glittering, silvery cloud over the canoes. He saw how the beating of scores of wings could create its own air currents until the waters rippled and splashed into small groups of white capping waves. In the company of the cloud, the canoes moved away, navigating the routes to the spirit world, across the sea.

'Is it the spirits of the old people? Coming to take them home?' Fishman asked, knowing Will could see far through the darkness.

'Yes,' said Will, while he kept the old man moving along in the direction of the others ahead. Soon, he would have to take the lead and navigate through the maze like a bush animal, retracing its steps.

There was trouble at the entrance. Will cautioned the men to stay back. Through the caverns came the amplified howling of dingoes, resounding from wall to wall, bouncing through them, running down the streams of waters under their feet.

'Wait here, and I will see what's happening. Keep an eye on the old man.'

Will moved ahead. He would be a fool to rush forward, tricked into taking the wrong direction into the maze by the reverberating sound. He judged that the entrance to the first cavern had to be much further away than the sound indicated. After fifteen minutes of navigating by memory alone, he not only heard the plaintive howls, but smelt the overpowering stench of the small den laced with urine markings. He edged his way forwards, as near as he dared to go. He did not want his scent to be picked up by the dingoes, since he knew it would frighten them out of the den.

Then he heard the sound of droning engines. He panicked, believing he was surrounded by men who were not dead, who had known exactly where to find him. He felt suddenly trapped in the catastrophic darkness, and compelled to burst through the lair and run, to rush outside like a savage animal. When they had heard the helicopter coming, the dingoes had taken refuge in the lair. Then, as it started to hover close to the entrance, sending clouds of dust inside, they had backed themselves into a frightened pack against the wall, and started to howl. Their sharp ears were unable to tolerate the vibrating noise of the helicopter at close range. As Will watched them, almost lying on top of one another, he knew very soon they would run.

Moments later the helicopter was gone. When the sound was far enough away, he went through to the dingoes' lair. Straightaway the animals gave him a startled look, stopped whimpering, then shot out the entrance and into the bush. He saw the helicopter heading east, change directions, completing a search grid from north to south, and heading further east to turn, before repeating the pattern.

'Jee-sus! They are onto us already.' Mozzie's men were now assembled on the side of the hill, watching the helicopter making its progress in the distance.

'How did they know we were here?'

'I don't think they knew anything,' Will said thoughtfully. 'I think they just landed for a piss in the bush,' he said, pointing to some turpentine scrub nearby still dripping urine into the wet ground. 'It was just coincidence that's all.'

'They could have been tracking us,' Fishman added, trashing the bush with the stick.

'No, I don't think so. I don't think they would have been able to get anyone local to help them. In any case, I covered our tracks coming here. There's nothing any two-bit tracker from miles around would be able to pick up from us.'

'Are you sure?' There was a persistence in the Fishman's voice. He was thinking about his own tracks, and the trail he had made, swishing with his staff. It was a good sign for Will. Fishman was back on board with the living, thank goodness, covering all corners. Finally, he had pushed back his preoccupations of grief. The men openly smiled their relief.

What remained of Mozzie's convoy stayed in the vicinity of the cave for the rest of the day. They slept soundly. Their dreams proved good. This was how it should be, Mozzie gave his men dreams of youth, good marriages and many children.

Afterwards, when the evening sky was full of storm clouds fiery-blue from the red sun setting low on the horizon, several of the men ventured out into the hills to hunt. The first to return said he had gone through the spinifex ground, and nearly collided with a large female red kangaroo nibbling fresh spinifex shoots. He explained in detail how close he was able to get to the creature, and how he was about to spear it in the heart, when the animal turned and looked at him with eyes like the softest creature on earth, and he felt sorry for it and let it go. Ahhh! Kangaroo meat was good and they were very hungry: but if one must starve for love of an animal, this was understood.

The second hunter returned from the rocky hills and he said he had seen a large red female sitting on a rock ledge, cleaning its paws. Ahhh! No. 'I looked, and this kangaroo was not cleaning itself at all. It had its paws together because it was praying, and on its left shoulder it had a big scar in the shape of a cross.' He said he followed it for a long time because he was hungry, but decided he could not kill a holy creature. He explained, he felt good. He felt like living it up. And let it go.

An ashen-faced Will also returned empty-handed from the hills. Strange, but nobody asked since he offered no story. He sat down. He told Mozzie he had seen Hope playing in the hills with flocks of finches. He believed she was leading him away, always staying far ahead, while looking back to see if he was following, but never letting him come close to her. She was in a hurry, heading back in the direction of the dark purple storm clouds up towards the coast.

'And the finches kept flying towards me, and they kept going south. There, the hills were plentiful with food in the paradise land of the water people. Down in the river, bream, barramundi, grunter, swam through the clear waters, turtles big and small were passing by, floating on top of the water through lotus leaves, and the spear men came home loaded.'

All evening Will went outside to check on the helicopters searching further away to the east, with searchlights, flaring down across the country, from north to south, and back again. He counted at least six helicopters in action and smiled at the cost of modern technology. It was the darnedest thing he thought, 'Who's going to find us? We know this country like the back of our hand.' Fishman came out too. 'I can hide for weeks and nobody is going to find me. I can disappear like a puff of smoke if I want to.'

This was the unofficial search. Highly confidential. The Gurfurritt boss already knew the disaster at the mine was no accident. He knew it, had a hunch, picked it as foul play in minutes, and acted on it. Within hours of the Fishman and his men disappearing into the hills, the bodies were found in Elias's boat on the lagoon. Spilling had a sneaking feeling about this, and went straight to the lagoon. Imagine that. Graham Spilling swore blue murder for Chuck and Cookie. 'Son of a gun if I get my hands on the black bastards,' he thundered all the way back to the helicopter. His words were as solid as bricks. He called the people who paid him.

'No police! No one, hear me, go calling the fucking police up here. Don't talk about this to anyone. Fucking media can piss off. Remember we are mining men and mining men look after their own and mining men keep their bloody mouths shut. We are going to catch these bastards ourselves.' He said this, word for word, after the orders had come all the way from New York, from the very top of a skyscraper, to Graham standing in a muddy lagoon surrounded by a cloud of flies.

The mobile phone screamed instructions into Graham's ear and his face whitened. Strange how a skyscraper in New York could cast spells like magic. It could keep a whole floor of workers occupied with knowing whether every single switch was up or down on every last monitoring device on Gurfurritt operations, in the spinifex mind you, on the other side of the world. It could cast a security net over the whole social reality of Desperance, keeping tabs on how much food was in the fridge, who had just replaced a light bulb in town, or monitor the pulse rate of Kevin Phantom lying in a hospital, while he was trying to figure out whether to live or die. It could rock the town this way or that to make stories. It could burn the Council office down, burn the Queen's picture, to gauge the reaction. Well! As luck would have it, timing was everything this time of year. Fishman and his men were saved by a stroke of nature from early detection by the helicopters. Even the afternoon rainstorms could beat the monitors in New York.

When midnight struck, the convoy prepared to set forth on their long journey west, through the gibber stone desert, following the Dreaming, the Fishman said, as he slowly sniffed the black air outside the cave. In the flashes of lightning from distant northern storms, he looked across at Will Phantom, who was also concentrating on the weather. Both had been thinking about the low-pressure system building up in the Gulf, sensing it in their bones as something different. Seriously different, according to Fishman, twitching his nose in the air to catch the scent of rain coming out of the gidgee trees.

The men were eager to leave, to get moving to avoid the millions of flying ants crawling out of their mounds in the ground. Fishman pointed up to the sky with curled lips, and announced flatly, 'There's going to be floods round here.' Scattered clouds, moving unusually fast, were pouring inland as though they were being pushed from behind by some gigantic monster. Flocks of seagulls had left the coastline and were heading inland. Also screeching, inside these formations, were cockatoos and galahs flying, gliding, south with the coming winds. Fishman looked at all the birds flying overhead, lost in the darkness, bumping against each other, and said matter-of-factly that it would not be long before the helicopters would need to land, 'Or be brought down by the birds.'

'Or the wind,' Will replied.

'Well then! What are we waiting for men? Let's get out of here.' The men were relieved to be finally on their way, even if they were caught in the rains. The faster they moved inland, the further away they would be from the full wrath of the sky spirits, hitting the high country before the floods rushed through the rivers and gibber plains.

'Well! Old man, this is where I leave you for a while,' Will said, tapping Fishman on the shoulder. 'I'm going back up North. You know I got unfinished business to deal with. You got the men here old man, they will look after you. You'll be alright.'

'I am not worried about the men looking after me. The Law is the Law and the Law will be looking after all of us. What about you?'

'I will catch up to you later on, I promise. Or else, I will be here when you come back. Depends on how long it takes. I got to go and find out what happened to Bala. I can't do any more than that right now.'

'Okay lad,' Fishman gave Will one last look. He knew only too well that Will might never return if he went chasing the spirits of his family. He started the departure, 'West, due south-west.' The group of men followed, the pre-storm bush emanating a steamed pungency of bloodwood and herb grasses ahead.

The tracks they followed were the very same as an underground river several kilometres wide, travelling from one side of the continent to the other. And Fishman, traveller of the big Dreaming, countryman and water diviner all in one, sensed the presence of water far underground, and knew exactly where he was headed. By dawn, they had become invisible to the eye of search parties near and far, combing the local bush around the region they had left, for nothing.

Angel Day thought she should have stayed at home. Travelling with the convoy was harder than most people could have imagined. Her longing to return home began almost instantly, once they had crossed the rail bridge, on the road out from Desperance. Even then, it was too late. Mozzie refused to take her back. Her face winced with every bump, as she went on questioning herself for leaving. She never lost the look of somebody who had made a mortal mistake. Now, with nothing else to do but sit in the back seat of the white Falcon heading south, she searched until she belly-ached for a reason why she could not have been happy enough to stay in Desperance.

Invariably, she would be reproached by the same answers. Even Mozzie said that she wanted to leave because she could not stand the place. 'Wasn't that your story?' He had to take her. Oh! No doubt about it: what a mistake that turned out to be. Norm Phantom had always known something that Mozzie had never learned. Angel Day was not a lady, but a queen. Queens make men awkward. Men unaccustomed to waiting on somebody hand and foot were going to come a cropper with Angel.

Abandoned in the white Falcon, driven by crazy boys who looked like they had never driven a car before, Angel was not impressed that Mozzie had not bothered to come up the road himself to say goodbye to her. The whole situation had become intolerable and she told this to the three lads in the front seat. They did their best to ignore her. *Orders were orders, babe.* Hoity-toity bitch, they glanced at each other with raised eyebrows. Although she was flattered with the word 'babe', she found neither of the overgrown boys, or the unbelievable situation Mozzie had placed her in, the least bit engaging.

She remembered sweet-talking Mozzie, right up to the moment they had left Desperance, trying to convince her it was going to be like the holiday she deserved. Now then – where was he and where was she? Little fish come into the dish. Without a word, he had sent the convoy of cars off. She was told by strangers that they were taking her to see Kevin in hospital. She thought about young Kevin, the promising Kevin, then the big boy Kevin who disobeyed her. Kevin who destroyed his life for nothing. She had not seen Kevin in years and she had no idea why he was in hospital, and if he was, it was no concern of hers. Her eyes fumed as she watched the boys in front escaping into the world of reggae. She questioned Mozzie's choice of drivers. Why these three? Were they all like this? Laid-back, the three hummed to the song of 'Buffalo Soldiers' in another people's world. Soon they were in cruising mode, slumped into the front seat in almost subliminal comfort, while Bob Marley's mesmerising voice rose from the dead out of a dust-ingrained cassette player.

Why did he send her with those negligent boys? Talk was talk. *He wanted her out of the way.* Everyone knows talk. *He wanted to get rid of her.* Finally, one day, having put the whole puzzle together on the ground, Fishman mused with self-congratulatory quickening of speech, 'Stand back now and let's look at the picture.' See! them little boys, they took the wrong track. Consequences are what consequences are, and, the white Falcon fell into the hole of a devilish place. Only the shamefaced boys returned eventually to personally explain to the Fishman what had happened to the Falcon. Fishman was correct. Just like he said, they had fallen into the most devilish place on earth.

Let's look at the exact location on the ground where Angel Day's spirit landed. Some say you can still see it there, waiting for her to come by to reclaim it, in order to return home. The white Falcon was speeding all the way to the big mining town where Angel was to go, according to the story. But that never happened. The boys had young minds, not innocent minds, just simple minds flooded with bitter experience.

In the last moments of the journey in the Falcon, heading up towards the main bitumen road, coming off the dirt within the speed limit, the boys explained, 'We were going along all fine like.' Something happened, the dreamy boy driving hit the brakes at the crossroads. But the car did not stop. Instead, the steering wheel spun to the left, and the car crawled along the side of the road that goes through many towns with a pioneer history, until it finally hits the big lights of the eastern seaboard. This was not the road to the right, that led to the mother of all mining towns, and another state border beyond. The boys, excited by the Falcon's powers of persuasion, quickly spun a new version of the Fishman's orders for going to ground.

'Won't be long now and we will be in town,' the driver, a curly-headed boy with hooded eyes, told Angel, while trying not to glance at her as he looked over the back seat. He turned and looked back up the road. The other two pushed each other out of the car, stretched their long, skinny limbs, yawned, and moved off into the bush. From their back-to-front peak caps fish heads with strange eyes stared off into the dry wilderness behind, over the car, and back towards the Gulf. Angel stayed in the car, but watched as the boys casually made their way up a hill overlooking the town. One boy was wearing a navy singlet and work shorts, the other, a rainbow-coloured reggae T-shirt and shorts. Both wore thongs but had no difficulty walking up the gravel hill to the lookout.

The place they headed to, was a sortie for young lovers who drove there in the middle of the night, and accidentally conceived their first children. It was the town's highest point. A summit for broken-hearted people taking a lover's leap. It was a place where myths sprung from nowhere and claimed the deeds of the next-door neighbour who might have or might not have pushed some-body over the top. Modern literary skills adorned the pinna-cle. Curt messages painted over public signs told the story of the town to the whole world passing on the highway. Kill All Coons, or similar, left on the hill for posterity's sake.

Angel told the boy driver she remembered Mozzie calling the racist slur on the top of the hill the white man's title deed. 'He said it was the white people's way of desecrating Native title written underneath. Mozzie said he had seen the real story when the old people showed it to him.'

It was etched deep in her mind how Mozzie hated that town. He never had one good thing to say about it. He said he would never go to that town again and told everyone else, if they had any sense, they would do the same. Her silence made the boy feel tense. He looked up the hill, wishing his mates would hurry up, wondering what was keeping them. It would only take a minute to drive through if it was all clear, and head on towards the coast. They had already decided to head down to a southbound city: Brisbane, Sydney or Melbourne and get lost for a while. It was like the Fishman said.

For the life of me, what was keeping those two? He did not say anything to Angel but he thought of the last time they went up the hill. They had been driven there after the local constabulary had picked them up in the middle of the night. They were kids really! Aboriginal kids who should never be caught in a flash of a torchlight. Caught! It was like roo hunting for whoever looked for young blacks: *Who needed to be taught a lesson.* Understand. *Before they get too big for themselves.* The boys were dumped first. The young girls were dumped miles out of town for a bit of fun. The girls went home and cried rape. *It was only a bit of taunting.* This was a big town and things like that did not happen in there. *We taught them a lesson. Ya can't call that rape. Get out of here.* Their families living black on the edge of town found justice was to send the girls away – it was the only way. They said: *We don't want any more trouble.*

The police let the boys go on top of Lookout Hill. The boy tapped the steering wheel, remembering how they looked down and saw the town lights shining. He and his mates had been left to defend themselves against a party of drunken hoons. The families came in troubled cars and took the three boys home, cut them loose, and sat them down on old newspaper. Then, everyone pitched in and bought bottles of methylated spirits and bottles of kerosene, and bottles of vinegar, but nothing was enough to remove the whole drum of tar stolen from the road works, and the feathers from pillows the white boys found in the back of their 'love vans'. He did not tell Angel Day the story of how their naked bodies burned. His fingers paused on the steering wheel as the lad saw his former self like yesterday, screaming in agony at the burns unit in the local hospital.

The boy did not tell Angel, and she must have thought he had nothing to think about, sitting there, not saying a thing. Nor did he tell her this was the reason why Mozzie took him in the convoy, and the two still on the hill. Bad thoughts should be interrupted, and his were by someone screaming – *Move! Move!* He and Angel both heard it, and their eyes were instantly drawn up the hill. He gripped the steering wheel, ready to drive, all of his instincts telling him to escape. Up the hill, they saw the other two lads running, slipping and falling in the loose gravel, both faces looking wild.

The whole world was screaming – *Move! Move!* It was too late. He could see the police car already, speeding up the road, coming straight towards them. It braked, full stop, beside the Falcon. A swift inspection of the unregistered vehicle determined their fate. *Well! Well! Well! You boys are coming with me.* The three boys were arrested on the spot. Angel watched in silence while the uniformed men dragged them away in the back of the police car.

One policeman came back to the car and casually looked in the window at the back seat. Angel's heartbeat soared, she was certain it was beating against the roof of the car. She looked nervously at the cold eyes that seemed to be looking up and down at her and along the seat of the car. She clutched her handbag on her lap because she expected to be dragged from the car too, and if it was the last thing she was able to do, she needed to take her handbag with her. The policeman said nothing, and went around to the driver's side of the car and pulled the keys out of the ignition and left. The police car drove away.

Angel sat wondering what she should do. Would she wait for the boys to return? She considered the prospect of walking into town by herself. Walk into a town she did not know? Impossible, she answered herself. What an absurd thought. How could she walk into town? White people would stare at her. Who would help her? She did not know anybody. What to do? What not to do? She looked at the bitumen road – left or right. But the more you look at bitumen the more it tells you to move. Move! Move! Just like the boys. She wished she had never left home. There was nothing left for her to do but to wait with all her memories until the future collected her.

She sat in the empty car. She brushed her hair, spending so much time on it like a cat preening and thinking minute thoughts. She cleaned her face with the remains of a bottle of mineral water. She applied new lipstick, the colour of congealed blood, and the sight of it in the mirror made her jolt. She saw blood in the mirror flowing from her two boys, spilling on the floor in the jail. She would never know what happened to them. Mozzie had spared her the pain. After some time reflecting on her image, sitting and waiting, not knowing what to do next, she decided to leave the car. Her plan, now that the heat of the day had passed, was to hitchhike down the western road to the big town where the boys were supposed to take her, and wait for Mozzie. *If he comes. If he comes.* A heroine's plan either way. She would arrive after an hour in a fast car. Who only knows how long it would take by foot.

One kilometre she walked in her high heels, and not one step more. The phantom who had her soul in a bag, came sidling up to her again, *Wanta lift doll?* She thought, *Doll! Well! Precisely.*

That's more like it. She, leg-weary already, never gave it a second thought and she took the lift. Her fate, bizarre and twisted it seemed, had arrived out of hell, in the form of a shiny, black road train, hauled by a Mack truck. Truckies inside, of course. Fishman's men called out her name at the crossroads, having just arrived themselves, noticing her walking up ahead, but it was already too late. The engines of the big truck drowned out their horrified voices like they had been made by little ants. Their lives went off into another story.

Destiny often visited the foot-walkers' convoy during the night in dreams. The men were saying they had seen Angel Day living in the worlds of their dreams. They explained to the Fishman that they saw her whole life ahead of her. She lived for several years – decades if the truth must be told, yes. Yes, it was true, Angel now lived unhappily in a devilish place. She would never see the bright starry nights of the Gulf country again. They were painful dreams encompassing some mysterious, windy world, where dull silver strips of tarnished-looking fish glistened in salt under an overcast sky. Rows and rows of these snakelike fish hung on lines drawn over the land, which swayed to and fro with the breeze as far as the eye could behold. Through this grey country many sad children, some who looked like herself, others who looked like people she had never known, came and went. How did this happen? Praise for Angel Day fell easily from the lips now. She was a sensation who dreamt far above the heads of other people.

People cried and shook their heads in sympathy to the Fishman. They paid their respects. You were never supposed to see the look of a deserted woman in those jarring eyes. They sang her praises to each other. She who looked like a lurid wish come true, who had once walked with hips swinging in Desperance. She was like a trophy for best-kept town, most beautiful, best presented, the biggest fruit of a blessed season. Certainly, certainly, it was the most painful memory. Yet a burning candle for her face stayed in the world of local memories.

She disappeared into another world as simply as looking through a hollow log and having no idea where the porcupine went after just having seen him run through it. Poof! It was unbelievable that a living creature could just disappear into thin air. In the end Angel was lost. Lost on the long road to nowhere. Mozzie Fishman, unable to leave his Dreaming road, never went after her. A spiritual man could not just go galivanting around the world when he had his business to attend to.

It was natural that outside the sphere of their world she became hearsay in their lives. Some strange person amongst the zealots who never dreamed, claimed he received a letter in his mind, and took it at once to Mozzie Fishman. He read what was written. Angel Day, he read, now lives indifferently to her surroundings, alongside a fast-flowing tidal river in a cold country which was a mystery to him. The green-grey foul-smelling river, carried along severed heads of domesticated animals, fruit crates from bustling marketplaces, rotting fruit and vegetables thrown into the river as waste, corpses of white people whose lives had not been considered by anyone to be worth two bob, and the broken-hearted wares of many centuries of a poor civilisation. It was plain to see, Angel Day had gone overseas.

The letter read that Angel shares her home, an abandoned grey warehouse with a moss-covered grey-tiled roof, with others like herself who had lost trust in humankind. Sometimes on dull, grey cloudy days, thousands of grey pigeons assembled from nowhere, and choked for space on the roof. Since it rained all the time, there was rainwater leaking into the building through holes in the roof and gushing along rusty pipes and spilling out onto green slimy floors. In the night, it was no good. The warehouse people went to bed as soon as darkness fell. They slept almost on top of each other for warmth, huddling together under damp stacks of old, rotting clothes.

Every day, Angel Day sneaks away, disappearing through the morning mist like a ghost, leaving very early before the others remove themselves from the tangle of clothes they had crawled into like rats. And in this fashion she goes to work. There, before dawn, she joins numerous others, too many to count, standing in lines like sticks of chalk along the wet marshes of the outgoing tide. Even Fishman acknowledged he could sometimes hear them, flicking their strange-looking lines of plastic rope along the waters. Fishman said he felt that close to Angel, he would turn blue with a cold he had never experienced before in his life. Time and again, he said he tried to ask her what she was doing there but she ignored him. Then, when some complete stranger came along and asked her the same question, she replied, 'Fishing for snakes.' Otherwise, she would have offered nothing.

Words were the enemy of the twilight world where she lived. No one bothered speaking in her world, except to answer a stranger. Every day, Mozzie watched until Angel's line resounded with the twang and thrashing about of waters which others, being more experienced snake catchers, were already making. Then, he watches her smile as the slippery snake, like an eel, starts to wind itself around the line and climb up towards her hand. Stealthily, she flicks the snake off the line into a wicker basket and closes the lid. Again and again, she flicks the line back into the emptying marshes, seemingly, unaware she stood in freezing water.

When the grey tide receded and the waters were still, Angel knew the snakes had gone far out to sea and it was safe for her to move. She wades through deep water to go home. She goes past a man with a transportable aquarium. He drives his truck with the aquarium that is so large it fills the back of the truck and is the height of the driver's cabin. The water is full of grey fish. People pay the tall man to see the fish by throwing money into his upturned grey hat on the ground, but Angel looks for free. Once she reaches the warehouse, she sits in the sun until it fades away, just to put some warmth into her freezing body. Nearby, there are two intertwining trees outside the warehouse and all she thinks about is Fishman or Angel. Eenie, meenie, miney mo, whose dream?

At the first sign of darkness, a hidden old owl hoots from some hole hidden in the branches. Angel runs away to hide while the frightening owl of the plains flies with luminous plumage. No one could even imagine a world with sea snakes flowing in tides, and freezing bodies asleep in damp caverns of clothes where glow-worms lived. But this was how he read the letter.

It felt pretty special to be told any news of a lady like Angel Day although it was hard to imagine her new life. The zealots made up new stories to send to her. She could be like the owl who shone in the night if she slept in a damp place and became covered with phosphorescent larvae. Perhaps her cave in the mountain of clothes was once a palace, glowing with light.

The Fishman exclaimed to anybody in the world that he never knew a woman called Angel Day, whoever she was. 'Don't send letters to Mr Fishman.' Letters were only from whitefellas to other whitefellas. 'And what am I?' He was a blackfella. No one had any business addressing any darn letter to him, he said.

Chapter 13
The wash

Unlike an estuary fish…

The single shrill cry of a wind-swept bird startled Will Phantom and he stopped dead in his tracks just to listen to it. The poor bird cried continuously as it was pushed further and further away in sheets of misty rain. On his journey back to the sea, this was the first time he had stopped walking since he had left the Fishman. Perhaps all it had been was a seagull flying low overhead, adrift from its flock and in shock. Up to this point Will had forgotten to think about anything else. The need to eat or sleep had evaded him as surely as though he was no more than a song sung like an estuary fish: a pelagic salmon, single-mindedly travelling against the flow, or a barramundi being tugged by some invisible thread, to struggle back to the sea.

Will lost his concentration. Nothing but single-mindedness, the only lifeline he could fathom, had let him travel so far and so quickly against all sensible logic. But as he looked for the bird, he was questioning twenty or thirty fathoms deep in the unquestionable: What on earth was he doing heading into the wall of the cyclone? He looked in vain for the bird, for it had been blown away by winds it could no longer fight. There was nothing to see from looking into the skies except a towering blackness of clouds heading across the coast – smack bang over the most improbable of all coastal towns, Desperance.

As he stood on the wet grassy slope, he described the sound. It had been a simple sound. A child could have made a similar sound. In his mind he tossed around many things it could have meant. Could he go so far as to say the bird was pierced with fear? Hesitating, he thought again. Why should anything be so terrible to have pierced a harmless creature with fear? He decided to settle for something more to his liking. He scaled down the underbelly of paranoia. It was not that bad. It was more like the simple sound of incredulity. What did it matter? It was enough to have heard it. He had not heard the likes of it before.

All day and night the wind played ancestor music. The sounds rolled in the skies, gathering up the waters of the ocean in heavy clouds, whistling while they passed through the sodden spinifex grasslands, screaming through rocky ledges of the highlands and through the gorges where the twisting river tracks led. Will would sleep deeply, when he fell. His dreams were fitful and broken by a maddening array of missed opportunities clambering over one another for prominence in his thoughts. He awoke from these dreams in a totally exhausted and depressed state of mind, telling himself he had to move on.

The cry of the bird was the luxury of turning one's back on the roar of churning seas. This was the sound which all species on earth must flee from when they hear it. Now, since he heard the piercing cry, Will grew more conscious of the wave trains in the Gulf basin piling themselves up onto the distant shores ahead of him. He felt his body fighting against the lunacy of his mind's determination to move on.

He swayed forward and bent into the sea winds blowing over the coastline and heading all the way back over the hills from where he had come. He tried to look back through the mist as far as he could, but although his vision was extremely limited, his eyes travelled ten dozen kilometres more through the wet spinifex hills.

The magnificent hand of the wind pushed into his back, and its song whistled into his ears like a devil, and into his mind. It threatened to blow him back into the hills, where in the distance, he clearly saw the Fishman leaving his mind and walking his men into the landscape, as though he was just moments away. Yes, it was so. The old man was safe and leading his men along another path. A windless track heading inland in a westerly direction.

On the Fishman's track, Will heard the sound of a classical Japanese song. It poured into his soul. He could see the song was being performed by a mythmaker fly with operatic voice, creating impromptu notes, as it circled around the Fishman's head. Accompanying the fly, traditional flute music flowed from Fishman's battery radio over the homelands. The landscape of stunted spinifex clumps and gidgee trees mutated through distance, slid from note to note, into mystical patterns of a garden of the Orient under morning dew.

The Fishman's men in broken jeans, shorts and T-shirts faded and holey, followed through the dry riverbeds, gracelike behind the old man with the radio, in a travelling mirage of grey brolgas at one with the universe. Will yearned to rejoin their sense of lightness. Fishman smiled to the world, as though everything was easy. Then, as though he too had caught a glimpse of Will standing alone, close by, he called out: *You can catch us if you are quick, come on Will*.

For a few brief seconds, Will felt his whole body teeming with a desire to give up, *Go on, go back*, urging him to return to the Fishman. He began to calculate how long it would take: 'Possibly five minutes. Less even.' Instantly, time seemed so unessential, any accomplishment could be squeezed into it. Will, realising some things, like this, were easier said than done, knew he was falling victim to his own failings. A crushing sense of defeat stopped him in his tracks. He felt exposed. Sprung by his own carefully hidden deficiencies. Weak. No. He thought he was piss-weak. And the world saw him for what he was: traitor to the family. Here was the crisis point. So arrived the hand of his father, pressing him on the shoulder. Aaah! Breathing a sigh right next to his ear as though saying: 'What do we see son?' Again, invariably, he knew Norm's face was behind him, looking out where he was looking with huntsman's eyes. Will saw his father's presence in his dreams where Norm was always standing behind him like his own shadow, looking searchingly at the back of his head, deciding – *Do you match up?* Locking him into a duel. Will turned, concentrating his attention ahead to Carpentaria. If he was to be a member of his homeland he knew he could never afford a Mozzie Fishman distraction. *There could only be one road.* He wiped the vision of ever wishing to return to the Fishman's haven clean from his mind.

Light rain flew horizontally from the mist hung in clouds hugging the hills against the wind. He saw through all this, navigating the atmosphere, like a fish, where predetermined knowledge dwelled from a world full of memories, told, retold, thousand upon a thousand times from the voices of all times, through his father's voice. 'A homeland,' a great creation site covering these hills, 'this is the story of...' that somehow, Will felt, was creating the tension he felt in the air.

In tiredness, even in dreams, he sensed a mysterious change of great magnitude was taking place in the wetted atmosphere, and in vain his mind swam the depths of the ocean calling for Hope and Bala. Half dreaming of the sea, he saw the water circulating in huge masses hundreds of kilometres wide and as many fathoms deep, become moving columns of water passing over and under each other. Nothing stopped. Not a single drop. He was breathless from the simplicity of all that he saw, and continued, finding his path through the machinery of water.

Somehow he knew he was being prepared for change,

instinctively, like an animal sniffing the air and sensing danger approaching, sensing a quickening in the atmosphere, sensing the future of a place. He wondered if indeed, he did carry a sense of knowing. If he would dare to describe a premonition as akin to that of the thousands of pelicans that had sensed unseasonal change happening to parts of the inland salt-lake country from a place a thousand miles away unaffected by the rains, and took the chance. He and the Fishman had once stood by the flooding desert waters a month after heavy rain and watched the pelicans that had flown inland from so far away to breed, and like themselves, momentarily, had abandoned the ocean waves of their life.

He thought about something else he could not see, a smell perhaps, travelling in the breeze, which might have triggered a single vision in the minds of perhaps a quarter of a million seagulls, who had without doubting, taken flight and headed towards the flooding lakes carrying fish that had fallen like food from the skies. This was the root of ultimate trust he thought, the knowledge of intuition, of understanding the vibrations of subtle movement in the environment. Birds, acting in unison on this slim chance, like a note struck on a piano, and no different to himself, a simple creature after all, were sealing the fate of the next generation.

He continued walking through the dew-covered grasses and the mulurru-turpentine bush, towards a rocky ledge to see whether he could gain a closer view. There, while standing at the highest point before making his descent to the mud plains far below, the mists parted. For several moments the doors were ajar on Desperance and the sun streamed down on the town. From his estimation of the distance he still had to travel, he hoped to be at Desperance by dusk.

Yet, in this simple uncovering, Will Phantom also glimpsed the town's psychosis twinkling in the sunshine. He sighed at the malady of small white-town madness creating another eyesore to feed itself. Irritated he asked himself: Could nothing change down there? He knew his cynicism about Desperance was cruel compared to its naive innocence, but unlike his father, Will deliberately strove not to be caught up in the butterfly net of thoughts which monopolised, hypnotised and tantalised the eyes of the world, especially Pricklebush. He knew one thing and in this, he remained steadfast. He did not want to grow old saying his role in life was to be a watcher in the long grass of Uptown.

The busy, industrious, toiling residents of Desperance had been up like the larks, dressed in woodchopping gear, a brush-stroke image of working Australiana, straight off a Pro Hart canvas, chopping down the remaining few poor, poor old trees. Every man had his chainsaw. Dozens revved. Mango trees – Baaaarrrrrzip! Cedar trees – Raaaarrrrip! Poinsettia trees – Zipped. What would you give for this tree? Such magnificent trees, decades in the making, were once shade in long, bright, burning summers. Poof! No joke. Straight out, lying now, down without a lie, cactus-smacktus, holus-bolus, flat out on the ground. This was called: *The Great Bat Drive*. Will whispered to himself the name the town had given to the annual ritual when tens of thousands of fruit bats, *Pteropus scapulatus – as thick as flies and fleas if you please,* flew up the river towards the coast and, having circumvented the net, descended like a plague onto the town.

When Will Phantom was a boy he saw the dog responsible for this madness. Never had there been a dog alive so consumed by its own stupidity. *So, good job, serves itself right, it died from a bat bite – so say all of us.* Apparently, the dog belonged to old man Joseph Midnight, but when the bat bit it, he said it never belonged to him at all. It was Norm Phantom's dog, he claimed. It was unnatural for a dog to attack a bat but it happened because bats and dogs were both too numerous for a small place like Desperance, so they were bound to collide.

When the dog and bat bit each other, the bat flew away precariously, this way and that, lopsided like a drunk, all crumpled wing, with dog flesh in its teeth. The dog had immediately fallen on the ground, legs up and howling. It looked as though it was having convulsions. The dog suffered immensely, with a fever so great, perspiration was dripping from its skin, froth from its mouth, and its eyes bulged from its head. No one would touch it. By this stage a crowd of people had gathered around to look. Then, when the dog rose from the ground everyone pushed back: *Back, back and give it room.*

So, keeping well out of its way, they watched the dog rage, whilst wobbling with jelly legs, up and down the main street. Then, out of the blue, Will had gone straight up to the dog and killed it right in the middle of the road in front of everyone, by bashing it over the head with a stick. He might have taken it home if it was his father's dog, but it wasn't, it was only old man Midnight's dog, so, what the heck? It didn't matter. Instead, he took the injured bat home and made a juicy barbecue of it on his little campfire down the back. All the Phantom kids ate it.

In town though, the bats had made a reputation for themselves after the incident with the dog. All kinds of legends jumped out of the woodwork about bad bat bites. Elaborate stories circulated on paper from the Council about the effect of falling bat urine on human skin, of inhaling bat spit, or of bodily contact with bat fur, and with so many years passing since Will killed the dog, a little bit of suspicion had gone a long way. Bats were high on the town's list of *things that can go wrong in the world.* Everyone now believed bats carried a deadly disease. A disease which could spread to humans through the treasured fowl pens: *If you looked closely.*

Nobody really saw bats anymore. Showers of bat piss caught the imagination instead. Nobody walked the streets at night during the mango season because nobody had any trouble visualising the deadly virus pissing on the town. Poor Uptown kids crying every night, could be heard right down in the *malirriminji*-Pricklebush camps: *Don't make us go to sleep*. Seven o'clock at night fearing the whole town would be found dead in bed the next morning. It was a sad, sad, self-perpetuating sad town. Nobody had any idea how those kids grew up so fearful of the world and everything.

So that was the origin of the bat and the dog story. Witnessed and assimilated. No one ever bothered to claim the dog, so eventually, it was removed by the Council. That too was one of the local proverbs that lived from the story and Will Phantom gained a reputation as being a violent person. Someone who would strike another as would a virus, was how Will Phantom was interpreted through the bat and dog story. The retelling of Will in Uptown was as vivid and as crystal clear as hearing that original, fatal *Thud!* on the dog's head, through those reliving it all again. And again: *It sounded just like this, Thud!* Will remembered when he was a kid how he responded to the talk of the town. It had made him feel destined to be out of kilter with the neighbours but he loved his persona. For fun he ran up and down Uptown singing 'Dirty Deeds Done Dirt Cheap'. So, whatever he was suspected of, and suspicion fell on him far too easy, it was because he was always seen through eyes tainted by this one significant story.

So, the great bat drive. Shotguns were fired into the air, fire-crackers crackled, more chainsaws kept the noise up, and the occasional explosive let off by Carmen, the fish and chip lady, who sometimes doubled as the pyrotechnic, shook the ground. All of this was reminiscent of previous encounters between the town and the bats. The drive would last a whole day, until either Uptown ran out of Panadol tablets for their headaches, or the bats became tired of flying in circles around the town, trying to land, only to be exploded back into the skies in showers of their own stinking urine, their tiny brown eyes looked longingly back towards the river. Finally, flying away from the destruction of fallen trees, they headed up the river corridor, following the freshly open, pale yellow river-gum blossoms that filled the air with a sweet honey-scented perfume. There, they would eat and expel a foul-smelling, pungent gum-blossom-aroma-like shit, as they moved all the way back up to the freshwater springs and rock caves, several hundred kilometres inland.

It was incongruous that with a clear view of the enormous clouds swinging across the coast, which ought to have been enough warning for anyone on earth that a cyclone was heading their way, with winds that would strip the trees clean of foliage, so that they might end up looking like bones with branches sticking out of the earth forever, the town chose instead to turn a blind eye, and continued with the ceremony of belonging it had created for itself. The sounds of Uptown and the thoughts of watery births clashed into each other in Will's mind, as he started his descent from the hills. The white-flowing curtains of misty rain continued to blow across his path. Frequently, in the flight overhead by flying foxes, seagulls, sea birds large and small flying inland, he saw a cyclone bird, the spiritual messenger of the ancestral creation serpent. This big black bird was the ultimate signal that a big rain was coming.

The noise of the town faded away in the clouds, and the sound of the wind blowing the mist became more prominent, as Will Phantom ploughed on down to the muddy road which he would follow until he reached the town. He still had many kilometres to travel, and walking the straight road to Desperance, he again became absorbed by thoughts of finding the beautiful face and body of Hope swimming under the water, always moving ahead, her long brown hair flowing back. At times, he felt so close to her, he thought if he could reach out, he would be able to touch her hair. So close was this vision he held of her, and always just a moment out of his reach, he was convinced she was urging him on to the place where they would finally be reunited. He spoke to her, reassuring her he would go any place of her choosing. He saw their reunion in the blue of a sea desert, and he was convinced she and he would be alive in this place.

The optimism of this reality felt so near to achievement, he almost fell after it when it disintegrated and disappeared in the wavering of mist closing like light curtains in the flickering of the breeze. He rethought their reunion, trying to capture some un-apparent feature in the flat ocean of the vision he had just seen, to pinpoint a location, a direction to travel. Nothing resurfaced of this broken dream. The images could not be properly remembered or held up for scrutiny like a photo of a place, or a map.

Hours passed while he continued on, fiddling with his day-dreams, until new sounds interrupted his thoughts. The distraction was the rumbling of tyres churning through mud coming towards him along the fog-blanketed road. Realising the cars were coming from the direction of the town, Will stood back, and listened. He heard several drivers doing what they ought to know you cannot do: drive fast over the claypan roads when they are wet.

He knew instantly the town was evacuating. The Bureau of Meteorology had called and translated the message from the ancestral spirits. Drivers were panicking because they could not get out fast enough. The wheels of cars were spinning out of control as they spun sideways in the mud, sending them off into the green slime sludge on the side of the road where their engines roared even louder, as their wheels churned up mud, spat it out behind, and became hopelessly bogged. He could hear people yelling – *Shit on it, AND fucking get that fucking, rust bucket, useless jalopy out of the fucking way or I will fucking run over ya*. It was like that and so forth.

Turpentine bush and spinifex grass growing on the side of the road and spreading across the mudflats with nothing taller in sight, were as good as a tumble weed for camouflage, so, some distance from the road, Will stood like a shadow in the mist. It was too late to move, but he was almost out of view of anyone seeing him, as the sounds of the chaotic exodus from Desperance closed in. Suddenly, the red light on the roof of the police car spun rays that hung lines of red smoke through the mist, then the motorcade burst through the clouds.

An ashen-faced Bruiser drove the police car he had commandeered from the empty police station. Beside him sat the schoolteacher, Danny Real, looking like he was about to die. Will was close enough to notice that Bruiser was carrying a shiny blue-glass rosary, threaded through the hand clutching the steering wheel. The siren screeched, but his glassy blue eyes were firmly fixed on the road ahead. In the deafening racket of the siren, Will could now plainly hear the car horns beeping and honking right back towards Desperance. Blue car after red car, all-colour cars, shapes and condition filed down the south road, all filled with the frightened-face folk of Uptown absorbed by worries of flight. They had left without a single glance back. Their fearful lips recited prayers loudly in closed cars. Nobody looked at the rain-bathed countryside. All eyes were on the road. Cars impatiently honked their horns. Drivers panicked for their car to be ahead of the one in front. Everyone shouted for others to move faster.

Will watched the people, the kindest to the meanest, with heads in and out of their car windows, screaming wildly at the ones in front to get a move on. *We will all end up dead because of you.* The drivers in front yelled back saying how they could not go any faster, and along with a string of abuse claimed: *You will kill us all if you don't shut up.* He saw the people of Desperance who had never in their lives gone down this road before, sitting quietly in their cars, apparently accepting the fate of the mystery road. Other faces, planted with shock by the thought of having their personal dreams and hopes doomed, stared into space. He saw most people had no time to gather anything to take with them except their most valued possessions. The family dog in a Catholic family's car. An old ginger cat. Many carried the prized Desperance roosters and hens. Last, towards the end of the motorcade, came a string of Aboriginal families in Uncles' cars, a red and black Zephyr, a cream and tan Ford Falcon, and sun-bleached Ford Cortinas of dull blue, squatting low and spurting exhaust fumes into the mud. Cattle trucks followed behind. In the back sat all the old people, some younger men, but mostly women with children – all of the Pricklebush mob now – chanting and singing.

Inside the back of the very last truck, Old Joseph Midnight slowly rocked from side to side. The truck was churning along at a snail's pace. Aboriginal driver, Will tried to remember who he was: Chilla! Chilla something or other, Mooch. Moochie. Middle-aged fellow always wearing one of those blue peaked caps. Moochie had been working real hard. You could tell from the mud-stained singlet he was wearing over his fat belly. The main ordeal was over as far as Moochie was concerned. Face like a codfish and casually smoking his cigarette. He looked like he was the only person prepared to accept the conditions of the road.

Moochie was talking about how many times over the years they had been told by the white people – 'Oh! Yaah! Another cyclone coming. We are all going to end up dead one day, you wait and see.' 'You get sick and tired of them telling you that,' he yelled as if he was talking to the whole motorcade, although he was only talking to someone called Fish.

'People Uptown telling you, looking at *wese* living – "Ah! Ha! One of these days you are going to get ripped apart".' He yawned, attempting to pacify his already pacified passengers sitting up in the cab of the truck. Fish chose not to speak, and Moochie continued to offer more highlights from his mind.

'It is going to go around the town like the last time they got us evacuating for nothing and we should have stayed there if you ask me.'

The people in Moochie's truck had experienced false alarms about cyclones many times over in their lifetime, and even though this one seemed to have all the ingredients to cause havoc and the so-called *Wreck and ruin*, they saw no point in hurrying, or being heartbroken about their homes being destroyed. 'Better to get there safe than sorry, I suppose,' Moochie drawled on. He had barely taken any notice of the panic in town. 'Whatever,' he said, replying to the instructions from 'stand-in' policeman Bruiser, who told him that he could drive the truck if he went around and made sure no one was left behind. 'Who's he to go around appointing himself policeman? Where was Truthful anyway? Isn't it his job to organise an evacuation?'

The old man, sitting against the wooden slats on the side of the truck where he was stuck with dozens of others, was the only person who looked at the land. He caught sight of Will standing in the mist. He had almost mistaken him for the trunk of a dead tree, but he looked again, knowing his eyes were not so good anymore, but he had looked at this country hundreds of times, and he knows for darn sure that there was no dead tree of any description along this stretch of road. *Najba ngambalanya nanangkani karrinjana* – There is a man standing there looking at us, he says, before recognising Will, but nobody takes any notice of what he has said.

'What are you doing there?' he asked Will with a flick of his hand.

'Going home,' Will replied with sign language.

'But! Big cyclone coming, boy, everybody *barrba*, *jayi*, *yurrngijbangka* – you better come with us,' old Joseph again indicated with his hands.

'Can't. I am going to find Bala and Hope,' Will replied.

'Better hurry – it won't be long.'

'How long?' Will was starting to judge the distance he still had to get to the town and find shelter.

'*Ngamiri*. Nobody told me. Everyone *kayi*. Big fella coming this time – I heard them, *barraku* talking. Cover the town. Everything will go. Listen to the ocean. Soon. *Warawara yanja ngawu ninya lajib*.'

'Alright, old malbu – until next time,' Will replied.

'Your *damu* Daddy too. Where *ninji Murriba* – who knows? Until next time, *baki*, *yarrbanji*.'

Will was struck by the humility of the old man, and kept looking at him as the truck yawned its way ahead, then disappeared like the end of a fairy story, into the clouds. Will followed the road into Desperance. He became conscious of what the sea ahead was doing once more, and although he knew it was kilometres away, he heard the spirit waves being rolled in by the ancestral sea water creatures of the currents, and conspiring with the spirits of the sky and winds to crash into the land as though it was exploding. The earth murmured, the underground serpent, living in the underground river that was kilometres wide, responded with hostile growls. This was the old war of the ancestors making cyclones grow to use against one another.

So much greater had the winds increased in intensity and speed, Will was struggling to stand upright by the time he made it into Desperance. He lurched from one power pole or concrete marker to another, flying across to grab onto whatever he could, to hold from being swept away. The ground was covered with moving water picked up by the wind and sent flying along with the rain against his legs. Somehow, he avoided the flying missiles of corrugated-iron sheets peeling off the rooftops; pieces of timber, bits large and small of blue or clear-coloured plastic, broken tree branches, and everything else that seemed to have been carried midair: plastic dolls, children's toys, boxes and crates from the Pricklebush camps, and the contents of green garbage bags straight from the rubbish tip through the town. Will passed hundreds of the town's poultry set free in the last precious moments by wise owners who had rushed to the chookyard and set the birds loose to fend for themselves. He dodged, weaved and ducked to avoid what had now become wet deranged bleeding balls of flesh as they were blown and bounced, nilly-pilly along the main road south and out of town.

By the time he reached the door of the pub, the tidal water racing into town from the coastline was up to his knees. He held onto the verandah posts bending sideways, while the wind howled past loaded with rain, and he could see he had no time to lose before the verandah above him would collapse under the strain. Knowing he had to get inside the closed building, he hoped as he threw himself towards the door he would not find it locked. Miraculously, it opened, and he could not believe his luck, that at last, something could be achieved without a great deal of effort.

It was even darker inside than outside where the time of day had become indeterminable from one hour to the next. Water floated around the darkened bar room, and when he saw the red glow of a cigarette, he was amazed to find someone else was using the pub as a refuge.

'Lloydie Smith!'

'Holy smoke! You gave me a shock. A man thought you were a ghost,' Lloydie snapped.

Will collapsed in a chair and said nothing.

'And what the hell's name are you doing here, anyway. There is nobody around so I don't know what you are looking for if you are looking for anyone. If you come to rob the place – go ahead. I won't be stopping you.' Lloydie looked at Will who continued staring at him. 'You look like you've been through a cyclone.' He laughed at this irony and threw towels over to Will to dry himself and clean the blood running from his cuts, particularly on his legs. 'Don't you know the whole town has been evacuated?'

'So how come you're still here?' Will asked, clearly puzzled by the barman's seemingly clear-minded decision to stay, then, seeing the ropes tied to the bar, he understood. It was actually true, Will thought, remembering the women who told love stories about Lloydie worshipping a mermaid locked in wood. They said it was true romance and he thought they were joking. Of course, he was staying with his mermaid. Will looked at the wooden planks, then he had to look away. Had the wind affected his vision? For some strange reason, he saw movement inside the wood. There was a full-grown woman inside the wood, moving like a trapped fish, as though she were trying to swim free.

He looked again to make sure, then turned away again because he could see Lloydie was watching, and could sense the man was becoming suspicious of him. Theirs was a private reunion and besides, he could see the water level inside the building was getting higher. Will moved behind the bar, ignoring Lloydie's silence as he sipped his glass of beer.

Very quickly Will grabbed whatever food he could salvage and threw everything into an empty green garbage bag – sandwiches wrapped in gladwrap plastic from the glass cooler, cellophaned pies from the heater, drinks from the fridge, packets of chips and peanuts. He saw a mailbag floating in the water which he emptied, then threw the green bag inside it and slung the lot over his back.

'Alright! I am going upstairs. You coming, or you going to stay here?' Will asked, looking at Lloydie, who he could see had no intention of going anywhere. The water was now shooting through whatever cracks it was able to penetrate to get inside the closed bar. It crossed Will's mind just how easy it was for water to find its way inside a concrete building. He knew the glass windows would burst soon with the weight of the water but it did not seem to make a difference to Lloydie. He was set to stay.

Will was on his way out of the bar when he looked back and saw that Lloydie was starting to tie the rope around himself as he lay on top of the bar. It would not take much to tighten the ropes and he would be stuck there, even if he had a change of heart about where his mermaid would take him, it would take too long to untie the ropes again.

Will tried to open the back door but it refused to open with the weight of the water banked up against the walls and shooting through the cracks. Will felt a cold flush of perspiration run down his body. For a moment, he thought of the door bursting open with the strain and the water pouring into the bar. He had to get out quickly and he shouted back to Lloydie, if there was another way to get upstairs.

'Get the ladder in the store room.'

'Where's that?'

'Over at the back of the bar, there is a little folding ladder, get it, and look up to the ceiling in the corridor just near the door here. There is a trapdoor. Force it open.'

In no time Will had the trapdoor unbolted and the food bag upstairs. 'You coming?' he hollered through the noise back down to Lloydie. When he got no response, he shouted, 'The whole place will be flooded once the water breaks through.'

When Lloydie did not respond, Will had to decide whether he should go straight back down and free Lloydie of his ropes, or let the man be. He realised that even if he could get the ropes off him, he was unlikely to leave. So he brought up the ladder.

The top floor of the building had been constructed of timber decades before Will had seen the light of day. The ageing wood that creaked with the sound of dryness as the temperature rose in the summertime, now groaned with the 180-kilometre winds and rain lashing the building. The galvanised roof whined, and wind roared across the north-facing verandah, and through the north door to the coast. Like an open-mouthed animal in pain, the wind roared through, and the noise shot down the corridor to the door it had forced open on the south-facing verandah.

Will slipped over the wet linoleum, holding on to the door of each bedroom, until he reached the north door and forced it closed. He went about closing windows left open, or closing the doors to rooms where the windows had been broken. He went back to the trapdoor once he felt he had secured the building sufficiently and called down to Lloydie. Repeatedly, he shouted down to the ground floor until his echo jumped back at him. He could see little into the darkness but he heard the water and realised that it had broken into the building and the whole of the bottom floor would now be under water. The water would be covering the bar. Lloydie had stayed until the end. He listened and heard nothing, so he closed the hatch. The signs of darkness were increasing in the building, and he waited, chewing quietly on whatever he pulled out of the bag.

He knew he had to eat, although he never felt hunger, and he tried not to notice that he was not alone on the top floor of the building. He remembered the strange sounds of his childhood, when his family had joined the rest of the town inside the hotel while a cyclone passed over the coastline in the vicinity of Desperance. Everyone had waited out the storm crowded together in the humidity of the closed building, and he shuffled around uncomfortably, looking for the place where the ghosts came in, until he found a pocket of fresh air jetting its way through a crack.

Sitting at the end of the hallway, he listened to the roar of the water rushing by outside. He heard it lapping the floorboards. He waited. It was still high when the wind dropped. He did not move.

It was pitch-black and he could not see a thing, but he felt other presences in every creak and slamming of objects in the building. He was certain there were others nearby. In his mind, he saw the drowned seafarers of the town coming down to the pub, walking around the building, visiting. He felt the fear of being a child again, hiding behind the wall of the fishroom, listening to his father talking to other men about what happened to all those dead fishermen lost in the sea when a cyclone came. The coolness of the wall touched his ear as he pressed against it, anxious to know what had happened to the dead men.

People say when a humble man really listened and looked past the obvious, then he might fly with music into the unknown. Norm's voice rolled on like waves themselves pouring out the tales of what he had seen at sea and his fathers before him. So, Will's ear by the wall heard it was alright to die a lonely death at sea because a cyclone will always show you the way home. Those lost souls lying down there in their lonely watery grave, many fathoms deep, were thrown up from under the sand, like seaweed plucked from the floor of the sea in a giant waterspout of the ancestral serpent. Nowadays, even drowned sailors were sucked out of barges down in the cargo holds in the dead grey waters of poisonous mine ore.

Lord only knows he always kept watch, Norm said, when he saw the waterspout coming before the rain. For his life he headed in from the sea, and sometimes, just managed to come into the river mouth in the nick of time. Tied up in the mangroves, he saved himself many, many times from going up in the waterspout heading up the river. This was no mumbo jumbo either because other fishing men caught in the rain, never saw it coming to save their souls. Their boats were picked up and thrown kilometres away, and those who survived, who landed back in the exact spot – boat intact – said they were lucky to be alive. So, Norm warned, he stayed where the mangrove fish hid, watching those dead fishing men being spun up into the clouds themselves, and Will imagined his father watching them spin around up there, making pacts with the ancestral being over the sea, until the giant vortex of thundering water travelled over towards the shoreline of the beach, and threw them into the walls of water, perhaps twenty metres high, heading like hellfire into Desperance.

Far into the night, Will sat against the wall, waiting, listening to the deafening winds, rain and flooding waters converge, like sheets of powerful energy attacking the building. But he was never alone. The lost seafarers continued tramping about the building through-out the night. Will heard them moving around through the bar below, laughing at their fate, falling over furniture and picking it up and throwing it against the walls and tramping back into the rooms where they used to sleep. He knew when the waters receded, the sea would reclaim its dead folk and they would be gone before daybreak.

When the big God almighty spirit...

In that wild night of deafening madness, where a moment of sleep was exchanged for another moment of wakefulness, Will Phantom thought a devil had made its haven in his mind where it rolled around, like a dog in dirt. He craved to walk outside into the deluge to escape a world that seemed to be falling in on him; he was overcome with a desire to rip off the bare shell of his being so that he could walk away free from thoughts that were so oppressive, he felt like he was going mad. But somehow, in this madness, a plan was hatching. Other ideas emerged from the twisted wreckage of his brain. Something that resembled an escape plan was fighting its way through the catastrophic imagery like a flea. The plan seemed easy, but it too was slippery to hold, for it resembled something of a truth. So, he lingered. He sought justification. Surely, he questioned, there had to be something wrong with somebody searching for a wife and child he practically could not even remember? This was the problem of being a man of constant vigil. They were people he barely even knew.

No answer could be found to the potent question he had posed for himself, but he searched his soul for it and in doing so, a quietness finally came to him. Will Phantom may have had the skills of a wizard from all his thinking, which went inside the land itself, for all of the old passed-away people he had ever remembered had journeyed back to town, and he saw them assembled in the rain outside on the verandah. He saw them through glass louvres – *You have news Will Phantom.*

He could hear them talking among themselves while the rain swept through their image, then once again, startled, awake, he told himself it was only the timber verandah moaning in the wind. Even if drenched to the bone, old people, he knew were too afraid to come into the white man's building. So, still, their voices: *Oh! My boy! Really sacred one. Scared of that one.* The wind blew the rain with such a force it blew in all the cracks: it blew under each pane of glass in the rows of louvres, until finally, the glass exploded. Then in came an old, skinny, mission-educated woman dressed in a floral dress dirtied by her own country anyhow, and plonked upon her head one of those knitted beanie caps. Well! Why not? So, this woman would come skimming along in Will's dreams too, because she had every right to grab her turn in a countryman's dreams.

From faraway places, far off in realm of the Dreamtime, Will had seen her before, cascading along the floods, singing arias in her pluming voice for the nightmare cyclone, snapping fingers, recording the death toll of all living creatures in a ledger book. She cast a spell on his mind, spinning it like a ferris wheel until times and places became one. When he saw her coming he might have offended the old woman because he never called out, 'Hey! Old woman it's good to see you,' or anything like that. He did not want to offend her now, and in a clipping voice, whether she heard or not, he demanded: 'Don't you notice me here old woman because I feel too sick and tired to talk to anyone right at the moment.' Old woman could cast any kind of spell she wanted to, and it was best to have said nothing he realised, when she made a beeline straight for him. Say nothing. So, the baggitty old Queen of the Pricklebush world stood up there in front of him, and she stared down at him for some moments with her black rings around her eyes like weeping mascara. Then she tapped him on his foot with her hunting stick, and announced in a voice that plumbed his guts, 'Countryman, hello.'

She reeked of turtle fat oil, and she said she had just returned from the sea, and it was good. She said her sons were proper, good hunters, unlike some other people because they had caught plenty of turtle to eat. Will knew this was true, listening to her speak the hoitie-toitie Queen's diction better than the Queen herself. Listening to her, you would swear you were listening to the Queen's Christmas message being broadcast from Buckingham Palace. The only difference was that she never looked like a real Queen dressed in pale lime paisley, like the Queen, but it did not matter; she was a queen anyway, and she said this to Will:

'Remember the real people of the Gulf, those poor black souls living on heartbreak and worries in the Pricklebush because they know all about cyclones, unlike those copycat Uptown *dolce vita* type of people sitting in comfortable armchairs expecting to acquire their ancestral ties with the sea by sitting on their posteriors watching television programs, and never going out to sea on any occasion to pay their respects, like the old people who were the backbone of the Pricklebush who did not mind paying their dues, and will tell you cyclones don't come from nowhere, because there is plenty of business going on when cyclones come onto the country out of the rooftop of the world, like what is going on outside now from the most powerful creation spirits, who come down out of the skies like a tempest when they start looking for Law breakers.'

'Jesus Christ,' Will wished her to be gone.

He tried not to sleep, but his mind kept travelling back into memories of the old people like the turtle woman of his childhood. Old wizards with wrinkled faces and kind expressions for children came by to look at Will. Their faces poking out of brightly coloured beanie caps tugged down on their head, with a pompom perched on top which bobbed whenever they talked, which delighted and fascinated all of the running and screaming Pricklebush kids, who got whacked with a stick, proper hard, for not listening. And if you sat long enough, looking closely into their eyes, you saw aglow the amazing world full of stories they told in competition with each other. *No, my boy, listen to me first. It wasn't like that old fool told you. Never listen to him. He is only number one for a pack of lies. It was like what I am telling you because I saw it from the start to finish and he only know what I copied for him.* Old stories circulating around the Pricklebush were full of the utmost intrigues concerning the world. Legends of the sea were told in instalments every time you walked in the door of some old person's house. Stories lasted months on end, and if you did not visit often, you would never know how the story ended. Will knew a lot of half-told stories and the old people looked desperate outside the louvres, competing over each other's voices to end their story to him.

'Hey! Tap! Tap! You inside there? You heard about my story sonny?'

'Call out and say if you know what is good for you from my little story I tried to tell you one time but you never come back to see me.'

This was one old woman in her multi-coloured beanie cap retelling her story. Will recalled seeing her again, clear as day, dragging a Sunshine milk tin across the dirt in the exact map of the river. He remembered how the line in the ground went about its intention, moving slowly, right up the winding river. Her voice snapped: 'Remember that time?' Nobody had seen a cyclone acting like that before. Even Will was old enough, that time, to witness the storm mass moving away down around the bends of the river, searching for a Law breaker she said, that had caused the creation spirit to come after him. As the cyclone moved on it gathered more and more strength from following along the flat surface of the river so it never died out like it should have, once it hit the high country. This particular cyclone, winding through the hills, caused widespread floods and ripped out ancient river-gum trees, and thousand-year-old fig trees from the riverbank, and what was left of those trees was thrown away like bits of grass that landed flat as a tack kilometres away in the spinifex. The poor river looked like it had been bombed. Then, the cyclone found the man it was looking for. He was hiding in a town which had never been hit by a cyclone before because of its being too far inland. He thought he was safe there, but the cyclone went ahead and wrecked that town to smithereens and worse, and in all of the wreckage it left behind, only one person died. It was the Law breaker.

Will felt the cyclone was attacking the building, ramming into it like sledgehammers, trying to tear it apart, as if it was looking for him, or someone else. He was convinced that there was someone else in one of the rooms at the end of the building driving the wind to them. A magic man or cats. He envisaged the back of a man who was bending over, performing a ritual with wreaths of rain grass to bring the storm to them, who in his heart of hearts Will guessed was old Joseph. He kept reminding himself it could not have been old Joseph, because he was in the truck being driven to the hills. Nobody like old Joseph would have made it back through the storm. A tap on the louvres and Will spun around, 'You know they say he is a witchdoctor.'

'Who?' asked Will.

'Old Joseph. Who do you think I was talking about?' some old person with a beanie shouts his Pricklebush truths.

At this point, believing the building was doomed, that the walls were about to fall apart, Will could actually hear a man chanting the storm-making ceremony, and besides, he heard Norm's voice roll through the ceiling, telling his night-time stories to children in his straight forward voice that told no lie. Low and humble. 'Tell it low and humble.' A voice capable of drowning out the storm racket with incantations inciting Will not to fly to where the white lilies bloomed in the swamp, no matter what the orchestra was playing.

Continuously, thinking of his father, remembering him, Will found he was now imitating someone who had condemned all else he had made of his life outside the Phantom household to irrelevancy. He kept remembering a time when he listened and tried to memorise every word Norm had said to him as a child, and wondering why. Was his life irrelevant if he could barely remember it? Will considered the old people's prophecy. What goes around, comes around, the old people always said: *The father calls the son home. Sons sail home in ships of nostalgia.* It made him think of the Fishman, the man he had come to consider as his father, now a fading memory of a handshake. Time and the huge distance of country each had travelled had created its own sense of forgetting. It was as though the older man had released some magic hold he had held over Will and returned him to Norm, whom Will watched while standing on the shore of some unknown beach.

Norm was busy working and Will watched from the distance, too far away, but looking through rows of silver fish hanging from lines erected on poles across the beach with smoke rising through them. Reminded of a scene from his past life, Will thought of himself watching his father from a distance in the dimly lit workshop under rows of silver fish dangling from the ceiling as though they were swimming in air. He called out to Norm as though he had just returned home after a short absence away. 'Hey! Dad it's me Will. What are you doing?' The big man in black singlet and shorts did not look up, but continued working.

Will heard his voice resounding back to him like a slap in the face, which he instantly put down to the fact that his father was still not talking to him. No communication. Will repeated these words to himself as he tried to decide what to do next to catch his father's attention. But as he stood on this foreign beach, his hurting ears listened only to the deafening roar of the cyclone. It was impossible to be heard in the disorientation of eardrums bursting under pressure; where his vocal cords could not form words loud enough to be heard. Nobody would hear him. He could not even hear himself. Norm continued his work, gazing down into a forty-four-gallon drum, stirring it with a big stick. Will assumed he was making his fish tanning potions again.

Waves crushed onto the deserted beach, and eventually, after several minutes had passed, Will saw Norm take his stick from the drum and head towards the surf. As he scanned around he noticed there was other movement on the beach, and turning to get a better view of what was submerged beneath the clouds, he saw Hope. She was alive and dressed in the same black singlet and shorts as Norm, only these were several sizes too large for her thin body. Not believing what he was seeing, he blinked. Could clouds play tricks with his eyes? When he looked again and saw it was her, he called. But it was just as with Norm, she could not hear him, and she continued on her way. She dissolved in the clouds that covered the water where the waves hit the beach.

Then, when he saw her again, she was walking carefully through the clouds, placing one foot in front of the other. He moved through the fish rows to get closer, he did not want to disturb her, in case she slipped, and fell into the water beneath the mist.

He watched her walk out towards the sea, above the water, moving very carefully, and when the cloud cover shifted slightly, he saw the grey sea water. She walked on top of the boiling water through the roll of the incoming waves. He was surprised that he was not shocked, but he was adamant in his resolve which only made him his father's man. He would stay unbelieving of any passing images and realities except his own, sitting against a wall ready to collapse under the tidal surge of the cyclone. With an increasingly heavy heart, he watched her spirit going back into the sea. It was like another nightmare, trying to keep her in his sights, yet the more he tried to get to her, he was unable to find a way through the never-ending rows of fish. 'Hope, wait up,' he yelled, but it was hopeless. She never heard his voice. However gusty the wind, he saw she kept her hands held out from her side, and in each palm she balanced a red glowing ball. Flares. Flares, she had flares, he thought, thinking they were all alive. It was a sign. She. Norm. Bala? Where was Bala? He had to be somewhere and Will looked again, saw clouds surrounding the beach, then he saw her again.

This time, she was moving out into deeper water, yet still walking on top of it, very carefully, she had to be balancing on something like a thick sea rope, used for big boats, held taut, just below the surface. He never saw it at first, but there it was, barely under water, and Hope walking on top of the water splashing against the rope. She was heading towards a boat painted green, and using the big rope securing it to land. This was the safe boat of his childhood rocking in the surf just as it had done before: Norm's boat. Anchor down, staring at it slipping along the sand, through the green seagrass, where a thousand bubbles caught his eye. Under the sea a strange phenomenon heralded Bala's face of all things looking up towards the light from below the surface of the water, where bubbles followed in a procession from his closed lips. His brave little boy's small hands seemed terrifying, drenched of colour, clasping a moving rock covered in slime.

'Hey! Dad. Over there. Look!'

Will waved his arms frantically and Norm continued his work. 'God! He's drowning,' Will tried to yell into the silent wall of this world, when suddenly, the surface of the waves broke through with Bala on the back of a grey sea fish. The boy swung himself from the back of a huge groper onto the ship's rope and ran along it after his mother, and Will watched them, she first, fading from view into the clouds. It was all over in seconds, but Will was still running through rows of fish, and realising, he could run forever and more rows would take the place of the ones he had passed.

With his lungs bursting, he stopped, and returned to the darkness from his dream. He knew he would run through all of the fish nets in the world and never find what he was looking for, as he would always run, but never fast enough, to catch up to his past. He relived the vision and made a pact. He would find them out in the sea somewhere. But doubt still raised its ugly head and compelled him to check the boat. Hunched into the wall he sat studying the vision. He looked underside, side on, from under the water with a stingray's eye, while gliding across the sand. Doubt saw algae in the place of green paint. Algae flowed in long green hair underneath the hull and along the rope, it hung limp to the boat's side, and inside, a garden of green flourished. Norm had waded out to the waist-deep, grey water.

Will waited for the moment and when the clouds parted with the next gust of wind, his eyes surveyed the beach. Out in the water, he saw his father stirring up the mud with his long stick. Very quickly, he realised what Norm was doing. He had been there before and watched his father in exactly the same way. In the same place. Norm and Elias had taken him there fishing. The three of them had spent days fishing on the open sea. Will was told he was going nowhere when he asked repeatedly where they would end up. Normally he would be told what fishing reef or hole to look out for. Norm had sat on the beach doing nothing after they had come into land. He watched the waters. Elias did everything with Will tagging along. Elias hunted, fished, fetched water, cooked so that they could eat. Norm sat on the beach. Will watched his father's bare back, sitting still in the same spot in the morning after he had woken up next to Elias, who slept with his back to the beach, protecting them both from the blowing sand. Will saw that Norm was watching *majinmaja*, the fish hawk, hover, dive and fly off to its nest. Waiting he said, 'See what *majinmaja*'s doing?' Yeah, Will said he would stay and watch too. 'No you go with Elias.' Why? He always watched *majinmaja* at sea. 'Help Elias.'

The fish hawk came back and caught another fish and went away. All day it was the same. Then Norm suddenly got up and went into the waters. He remembered Norm stirring up the water in a corner of the headland. He had waded out in the same way and spent most of the day, and the night, stirring up the clay mud and sand. Elias said nothing when Will asked him what his father was doing. 'None of my business, yours neither. You and me are here for one thing, to fish for fish.'

In the morning, the three of them had watched the trail of discoloured water drifting away. Years later, Fishman had told him in his raspy voice, which he claimed was from singing too much country and western, that Norm was in a storm-making place. 'He was singing up the spirits in the water, boy, to make storms for his enemy.' Even though the Fishman never went to sea, he mentioned an itinerary of site places along the coast for making storms and counter storms powerful enough to wipe out the entire enemy. 'However,' Fishman explained after naming several hundred sites in a geography he had never travelled, 'I don't know all of these places. But some do. Your father knows, because he can fly through storms like an angel.' Fishman sighed. Reluctantly, he had admitted more than he normally would about other people being more powerful than himself. 'Just one or two, you know. You are always going to have some fellas and women who must have swapped their blood for magic. No, it is right. They only got magic running through their veins. Me! I only got a little bit of both. But they can be wherever they choose.'

Will knew how impossible it would be, trying to find any of the locations he had memorised from Mozzie's long list of names. He already knew some of those places were many kilometres inland in the Dry season, but became the beach, when this land joined the sea in the Wet. Other special sites formed part of a sandbank out in the sea. A place only visible certain times in the right season, and if you knew the right tide to choose from at least a half-a-dozen tides and currents all circulating about in the bay of the Gulf. Or, maybe, you would only reach this place at night, if you knew how to navigate by stars. Mozzie said all this travelling at sea was very dangerous activity and this was the reason why he stayed away from salt water. 'You got to be more than traditional. You got to be mad as…a magician. You got to be a fish…a wizard to find any of those places. Me! I am ordinary for dry dirt.'

The discoloured water was drifting, and just briefly, Will saw it clearly enough to distinguish it was heading east – towards Desperance. On seeing the tongue of water, Will knew he had to remember where the place was, he had to see the beach, to become patient, in the hope he would see it again. Yet his attempt to remain calm disappointed him. He felt he was drifting out of the dream, because once again, he heard the chanting in the room at the end of the corridor, and the sound of water running through the bar below was even greater than the winds and flooding outside. He forced the fish hawk to come back to that day, and watched it hover and dive for fish, pushing through take after take, until finally, he could see the bird working along the movement of the current. This time, he remembered something different about the beach he had glimpsed between the clouds while looking for Norm. In that instant he had been surprised to see Norm standing out in the water. Something had been different about the beach. Now it was too difficult to recall what it was.

His memory grew fainter the harder he tried to remember, while the noises of the building seemed to penetrate not only his mind, but to grow toxic inside his body. Downstairs, bar stools, chairs and tables rattled against each other in the flooded hotel. Bottles smashed against the walls. The noise made him think about Lloydie's fate; was he still roped to the bar, or had his dream of being taken away to sea with his mermaid been fulfilled? He knew he would have to go downstairs and check. The roof continued its non-stop rustling. Rain pelted it. The floorboards creaked in every closed bedroom. The roar of the sea showed no mercy. There would be no letting up. No respite for quietness. There was noise in the movement of water flooding back to the sea carting the wreckage with it. All passed over the flooded land groaning with the remains of buildings, boats, cars, trees, rocks, electricity poles, fences, cargo from fallen ships, plastic consignments scrambled like licorice allsorts and dead animals. All this rolled along, slamming together in the water, just like it had on the beach in his dream. A beach plastered with waste, brown stinking froth and foam where a cyclone had struck. Will was too shocked to move from the realisation of his father's payback to the town.

Of course they had survived, Will agreed with himself, yet argued the toss. It seemed unimaginable that all three of them – Hope,

Bala and Norm – were together, and having survived the catastrophic cyclone, were preparing to leave. He jumped to his feet, speaking out loudly in his excitement – 'It was time to leave.' He ran to open the doors of the bedrooms he had closed the night before, to let out the noise, not stopping to see what happened behind him, the escaping pussycats scrambling over the slippery corridor, a flock of swallows flying frantically up and down in the hallway in a futile attempt to exit the building. It was only much later he would realise he had seen the skin and bone person. A real nomad countryman, living like a gipsy. The sort of person who could avoid being seen by dissolving himself into a wall if he had to. They were the people who drifted silently in and out of the bush, never speaking to anyone outside of their group. Somehow, just as silently, this group had drifted for cover to the hotel, climbed upstairs, and each had sequenced their being into rumples of clothing, bundles of nothingness, in a room of its own.

He stalled at the end room, where he imagined he heard the chanting of Midnight. Although the room was now silent he sensed the macabre power of the old man lingering behind the closed door, and a chill ran through him. At first, he did not want to open the door because he thought he might see a ghost masquerading as old Joseph sitting there. Yet, he had to know, so very carefully he turned the handle, and was just about to say, 'Good morning old man,' so sure he had been that he would see old Joseph sitting there frightening the Jesus out of him as he eased the door open. The room was empty. Yet whoever had been in that room, Will felt the malediction of his presence, and knew he was about to faint as the sweet smell of trampled, wet fresh grass overcame him. He slammed the door shut. He ran up the other side of the row of bedrooms, opening doors, without taking a breath until he reached the door to the verandah to the north, and opened it.

The grey cloud of swallows, a thousand pairs, in an instant

of surreal flight flew through, and before he realised what had happened, they had disappeared into the clouds. Will sighed loudly in the space of the damp, feathered air left by the birds. He inhaled the fresh sea wind speeding inland with the clouds, while thousands of sea birds headed out to sea. He watched them while he thought about his dreams until, moments later, he believed he had struck gold. Of course, he had it at last. Out of nothing, he was grasping the eluding pieces of the escaping dream. Now, cried out to the drowning north lands. Over and over his voice spread, sending a shiver down the columns of birds heading overhead.

His eyes recaptured the direction of the beach with the swaying fish left out to dry. He knew Norm was preparing to leave. Hope and Bala were going on board. She carried blue-rimmed fire to show the way for Bala to follow her out into the fog where the boat was moored in the deeper waters at the end of the rope. Everything was fine because they were with Norm, and he would bring them home through the storm.

And all he had to do? All Will believed he had to do was to ride the outgoing tide and find them. Yes! Yes! Yes! Meet them halfway. He would go. 'I am leaving now – I swear I have already left.' First though, he would go down and tell Lloydie what had happened to him. He felt good. He could not remember feeling so good. It was good to be alive and he would go right down and find Lloydie and tell him that. Mermaids do not live in wood he would tell Lloydie. He would say it nearly cost him his life. 'Knock on wood, Lloydie. Get a life,' he yelled down through the open trapdoor. Water answered instead, as it crashed against the walls and sent the spray up into his face.

Will scrambled down into the darkness, lowering himself down, and the waters responded. He became caught in the whirlpool of muddy waters, and to save himself from being swept away, he grabbed around for a grip, holding on to the solid structures of doorways and corners, as he was propelled through the building. He clawed his way to where he assumed the bar once stood, and realised he was looking everywhere for Lloydie's body, and searching for nothing, when he discovered the wooden masthead was gone. She had taken Lloydie away. They had gone in the out-going tide. She had knocked against the door long enough to dis-lodge it from its hinges, and they had floated through, to join the wide wall of water heading back to the sea.

Navigating underwater, Will steered himself back towards the trapdoor. He surfaced for air, swallowed it, and forced his way back down to avoid being thrown into a wall, or knocked unconscious by the objects passing through the building. Swiftly he moved through the chaos of yellow waters. It seemed like an eternity had passed before he reached the doorway between the bar and the corridor, the door now missing, at the back of the hotel, where he surfaced. He pulled himself out of the water. Luckily the level of the water was high enough for him to reach the trapdoor opening, and luckily he was long-limbed and skinny enough, to be able to pull himself back onto the top floor. As he sat up there catching his breadth, he wondered what Lloydie's mermaid looked like. She would look like a ghost swimming through plains of mustard yellow waters with a dead man roped to her back.

From the verandah doorway he saw the roaring water towering towards the horizon of the open sea. Only the hotel rose out of the flood as a bizarre, twisted, island abode of the Gods. On the rooftop, sea birds were packed so tightly under the heavy canopy of dark clouds, it gave the appearance of a giant white flower full of red beaked seeds. The old wooden verandah had collapsed in the winds and now hung like a shirt collar around the building. Listening to it moan and creak, he thought it was a wonder it had not collapsed altogether.

The longer he looked down in the waters the more he felt like letting go; to fall into its universe. He was sure that at any moment he would see the movement in the racing waters of some living creature, someone alive, and he almost allowed himself to fall. So convinced he would find his destiny in the floodwaters, as though the waters were beckoning him, urging him to believe he could simply drift along in the direction of where the waters were moving, until he saw Norm's green boat.

And Will Phantom was right to think he was lucky, leaning his skinny body out of the building, barely holding on to the doorway, and not caring if he fell, because any second he knew he could simply let go, with full certainty of falling straight into the destiny he had prescribed for himself. He had not figured fate, when the top floor under his feet suddenly moved. The floorboards had been shaken so violently, he was sent flying into the floodwaters. He hit the water hard, went under into the billowing yellow waters, where he rolled blindly *in vacuo* with the dead of the deep, before being returned in a frenzy of breathlessness to the surface. Somewhere, in all of that water sweeping him towards the sea, he was able to turn to see what had happened to his little oasis.

He saw not a hotel left far behind but a small castle for the recreation of spirits. This new reality had nothing to do with the order of man. There was no town of Desperance. It was gone. A monster followed him instead. The houses, the loading port, the boats and cars, every bit of every so-and-so's this or that, along with the remains of the pipeline for the ore from the mine, and even the barges and cargo snatched up by the cyclone had travelled inland, and were coming back. Every bit of it had been crushed into a rolling mountainous wall that now included the hotel where only moments ago, Will Phantom had been standing.

It was at this point he realised how history could be obliterated when the Gods move the country. He saw history rolled, reshaped, undone and mauled as the great creators of the natural world engineered the bounty of everything man had ever done in this part of the world into something more of their own making. Was he shocked? Bugger the hotel, he thought, it could go with the rest. The bulwark of the spirits rose from the waters, and he saw nothing monstrous or hideous in this new creation taking shape, moving, rolling, changing appearance, and beauty in its strident crashing back into the water.

The sight of the devastation was nothing short of salubrious as far as he was concerned. The macabre construction resembled a long-held dream of the water world below the ground where the ancient spirits of the creation period rested, while Aboriginal man was supposed to care for the land. He wrestled with thoughts of the future. When the waters receded what man would walk to the salt marsh to scratch the surface? What man digging under the surface, under layers of silt, would announce the discovery of the devil's polluted palace? Then his view was gone.

He went swirling back into the flow of the water and all he could think to save himself, was what would happen if he got caught in a snag. What if he became entangled in the lines of barbed wire fence strung across some boundary? When the monstrous palace following him would catch up, and drag him under, what then? It seemed like ages before he had a chance to look back at the colossal architecture of the storm. But it was gone. Again and again, repeatedly, his eyes searched for the castle but only waters followed in his wake.

Wish whatever…

What a catastrophic requiem took place in those floodwaters racing out to sea. Listening up high, he swore there were hundreds of God's angels singing: *Gloria in excelsis Deo. Et in terra pax hominibus bonae voluntatis*. The waters poured dead fish. Sodden spinifex grasses. Sticks. Green wood. Branches. Plastic. Plastic Malanda bottles. Green bags tied up with rubbish. He drank the stinking air manufactured by the porridge of decaying fish and gladly, the nauseating stench touched him. Blue and orange plastic sheeting formed a never-ending maze through which he was effortlessly poured. In the mayhem of buoyant bodies, bloated animals floating by touched him ever so lightly. Green frogs resting on the dead hailed him: Vale! The herds. Poor nanny-goats from the goat farm. Farewell! Bruiser's cattle and horses. Say goodbye pack of dogs. Pussycats. Chookie fowl. Sad day for the animals of the bush. Kangaroo, wallaby, wild boars. Feral cats. Marsupial mice. Pelicans. He eyed every bit of the ghostly brown froth and bother heading towards him with outstretched arms, purposely wanting to draw him to its huge, smothering body.

Other things touched him too, and the madness went on and on...

On and on the floodwaters raced until receding far out in the ocean waters. It was there, during the night, that Will was washed onto a wet, slippery object. He did not know what he held on to in the darkness but it kept him afloat. Then he flinched. Something alive touched him and the sensation of fear he had felt in the flood-waters, again overcame him. He struggled out of the water, by clawing into the slipperiness, and climbing, not knowing if he was crawling onto the body of a sea serpent. He clawed higher and higher, slithering over the oily surface of whatever lay below him, unable to stop, while wave after wave lashed him, trying to pull him back. The clouds broke, the new moon shone its halo of peace. Relieved for such an absolution of light, he looked down to find he had been dumped onto an extraordinary floating island of rubbish.

While the serpentine flotation rocked in the waves, the sum total of its parts rubbed, grated and clanked together, as it became more tightly enmeshed into a solid mass that squashed every inch of oil and stench out of the dead marine life it had trapped in its guts. Will listened to the embryonic structure's strange whines echoing off into the darkness, then, he realised the enormity of those sounds was familiar to him. He was astonished and then weakened by the feeling of helplessness, that a man feels, hearing the sounds of labour. He felt like he was an intruder to be clinging to a foetus inside the birth canal, listening to it, witnessing the journey of creation in the throes of a watery birth.

Whenever moonlight struck again through the clouds, he saw the moonbeams reflected off a multitude of hovering seagulls. Their bodies shone far away like glints of silver glitter. He imagined the new island stretching for many kilometres. He was full of wonder at its destiny, intertwined now with his own. He pondered how he might live indefinitely on the wreckage beneath which he imagined was a tightly jammed composition of barges, ship's hulls, fishing boats, prawners, plastic containers, timber and whatnot.

Perhaps, he thought, if he became practical, since he was not wise, he could survive if he conserved rainwater in tanks and whatever cavities he might find on the surface. He knew he would have to work hard to find where the waterholes were and secure them from the birds and from contaminating sea water. Next day! In the morning! He decided to build himself shelter from the elements. Of course! Naturally! The cloud cover would eventually lift, and if he did nothing, he would be exposed to the sun. When the 'low' had blown away, he would salvage material to build his own boat to find Hope and the boy. One day? Soon! Soon!

Come hither fish, come sea spirits, demons, marine monsters. He would have to learn about all of them if he were to survive. He would have to chart nautical routes in his mind. He would have to start remembering the journey of the heavens, all of the stars, breezes, just like his father, Norm Phantom. He would have to comprehend the feeling of water beneath the weight of his island

and make its currents his map. In order to know, he would have to become a scholar of the sea, then one day, he would set off to find her. He would take his raft and float away on it, searching, searching, until the moment their eyes met. Or until it sank.

The island home was, give or take, a kilometre in length after the final unhinging of those parts which, after bidding Adios!, violently crashed to the ocean floor. Flocks of birds came and went on their seasonal migrations. They seemed to accept the drifting structure as a new land.

The nests they constructed with the bones of dead fish and droppings eventually covered the entire surface in a thick fertilising habitat, where over time, astonishing plants grew in profusion. Bobbing coconuts took root and grew into magnificent palm trees. Seedlings of mangrove, pandanus and coastal dune grasses came with the tides, other plants blew on board as seed, and none withered away. A swarm of bees arrived, as did other insects, and stayed. All manner of life marooned in this place would sprout to vegetate the wreckage. A peanut that had floated for perhaps a decade landed one day and grew so profusely it became a tangle of vine-like stems reaching out over the surface to find crevices in which to sink.

A single rotting tomato containing an earthworm settled in the newspaper-lined base of a plywood fruit box, and grew. Within a season, tomato plants inhabited the island like weeds. The worm multiplied into hundreds and thousands of worms. The worms spread like wildfire into every pokey hole of rotting rubbish and soon enough, a deep, nutrient-rich humus covered the entire island. Well! What have you? Peach, apricot, almonds, all grew. Guava, figs – fruit that came with the birds, stayed, and grew into beautiful trees. A wasted banana root survived for months in the sea until it settled on the island where it sent up one big fat shoot after another, in between a mango tree and the figs, then drooped with the weight of large bunches of fruit.

So! Did Will notice? Was he happy? Yes, he was. He was a practical man in a practical man's paradise. He had food, shelter, and his catchments of fresh water were always full to the brim. He grew strong and healthy pursuing his numerous daily tasks. His mind grew with the information he stored inside his brain. Unflinchingly, he ordered the patterns of water beneath him. Daily his mind sifted the information. He was able to recall each day he had been at sea, from the time he began living on the island. He developed a keen eye for the movement of the stars, staying awake to sing the Fishman's ceremonial song cycles all night, from the raising of the star across the eastern horizon to the setting of the big *maliwi* star in the west. Then he would sleep. These were the rhythms of his life which he lived through like lines of poetry.

When the rhythm changed with the seasons, he would stop measuring star movements for the current flow, or move through endless days of charting the flight of birds. Then, like these changing rhythms, he would switch the activities of his daily life. Sometimes, he would concentrate solely on the measurements he kept of the many species of trees on board, his vegetable stock and other vegetation, such as grass, flowers, weeds. After he had completed his measurements, he would spend the remaining hours of the day working on the boat he was building, out of found objects, salvaged timber, on top of a raft, the place where he lived.

Inside this roped, nailed and wired structure, he kept his precious possessions which he had accumulated from his salvage operations, tunnelling down into the depths of the pontoon island itself. Inside his shelter, he had stored fishing lines which had taken him hours, and sometimes many days to untangle; little boxes of precious hooks, nails, tools he had made himself; and dried foods under sheets of plastic. His worst nightmare when he spent the first night on the birthing wreck was how to save himself if the pontoon disintegrated. Now he was able to reign safe in the knowledge that the raft he had made himself was ready, in case of any emergency, which would force him to vacate the island.

In his little world he cooked sometimes on bits of salvaged iron while being careful not to use up his precious supply of driftwood, a mountain of it already stored, even while driftwood was plentiful. Everything was bountiful. If he went looking for driftwood, his hand only had to reach down into the shallow water and as though a magical spell had been cast, the treasure would be his to hold. His thoughts were wishes granted to the island. Any fear had a reality too, but Will was too preoccupied with surviving in those early months to become fearful. He lived on hope, little things such as food and water, simply to keep himself alive.

Those were the golden days, when he could visualise himself, almost ready and able, almost setting sail as soon as his boat was ready. He lived on wishes for a very long time. He taught himself through his many routines of measuring how to navigate the seasonal currents, but then it occurred to him, that the movement of the currents was only taking him in a circle far out to sea. The skies had been telling him this for months, but he was stupid after all, because he had refused to see.

He only had himself to blame but who would have thought his faithful patterns could change, and begin to contradict each other. Instead of rationalising the changing reality he was confronted by, he doggedly continued measuring the rise and fall of the stars. Even the moon affirmed his now-monumental suspicion that his island home had been caught in a sphere of oscillating winds and currents. The question now was how would he ever return? He had no certain answer. One day a huge green turtle tried to pull its heavy body onto his island. He killed it while it was still struggling

497

to come aboard and he ate from its body. Afterwards, he thought the only certainly he had in life was the ghost boat mooring at night in his dreams. More and more frequently the green boat invaded his sleep. Eventually, it came by every night and he would be awakened with the ringing of a fog bell, always heralding the arrival of the ghost boat from afar, in familiar and unfamiliar landings.

Alas! In these dreams he saw himself as the eternal watchman, on guard, waiting for the little vessel to materialise through the darkness. He listened to the oars breaking the water and creaking in the oar rings. He waited, even though he knew what to expect, when out of the darkness the empty boat glided in to land. The repetitiveness of the dream frightened him into believing it to be true. There were occasions when he was so sure he had heard the ghost of the green boat calling by, that he went searching the shore-line of his island in the moonlight. His attempts were futile but that did not wipe the elusive vision from his mind, and he longed for its arrival in his dreams as though it was his only reason for living.

Every night it was the same. Dreading sleep, but overcome by deprivation, he would dream again of the green boat, which never landed when he went looking for it. Will grew suspicious of the dream. For the life of him, he could not comprehend why anything could be so close and not close enough. Real! But never real enough? He searched high and low for a malingerer on board his island. Down in the wet cavities of the wreckage he prowled looking for whoever, or whatever sorcery was tricking him to fret for his unreachable goal. The search became his main occupation. He completely forgot the chronicles written in his mind.

Instead, eager to put an end to the mystery of the green boat, he searched everything just in case his dream had misled him. He was a man who needed more prayers than a million Christians could pray. There was a list a mile long of mysteries to be solved now before he could even dream of leaving the island. So, what if the passenger on the green boat had landed and was hiding somewhere on his island? One day, he decided to perform a funeral service for the unconsecrated souls he believed were imprisoned somewhere below in the hope of finally laying them to rest. He improvised on bits and pieces of memory from church services he had been to in Desperance, but that night in his sleep he heard the night bell ring as clear as day and when he searched the darkness, the green boat slid in to land, and when it did not fade away, and he was able to pull it in by hand, he saw the boat was empty.

So, melancholy started to grow in the island's rich fertile atmosphere and competed for life just like any other seed planted on the island. In time, Will's gloom grew increasingly morose with ideas of space. The distances began to multiply into improbable journeys. Travel? How could he travel? His mind ran wild with the question until he got to the stage where it was almost inconceivable to contemplate his journey back to the Gulf of Carpentaria. He felt stranded and claustrophobic. Even though the island shone brightly with happiness and blooming, he never noticed anymore. He shunned its solitude as a prisoner grown old with incarceration. He longed to be in a better place, elsewhere. Days were now spent looking longingly at the sea to the west. Other places grew more fabulous in his mind, while the island became a dungeon.

One day while sitting seaward and looking towards the western horizon, he began to muse over his future. With his happiness destroyed, he now viewed the island as a temporary structure which would break apart in the first storm. He sincerely believed that the total destruction of the island was only a matter of time. Will Phantom's days had turned bleak and his routines became perfunctory efforts performed with little care.

All of his former hard work in building the boat became gaunt, repetitive checks for structural weaknesses. He became possessed with the idea that the boat was unseaworthy. He had already decided the journey was an impossibility. At four o'clock in the morning he would wake up terrified when he saw himself, in a boat full of holes and the water gushing in, as though it had been constructed with straw.

The night on his island turned out to be an extraordinarily masterful playwright, anxious for Will to fall asleep, impatient for the blood red curtains of his mind to burst open. Another grand play, another brand-new scenario of horror. This gifted corner of Will's mind was a wizard. A genius able to conjure up his innermost fears, as quick as a magician could take a rabbit from a hat. In the end, Will believed his nightmares would kill him. He decided he would avoid sleep altogether. He would become a master in undoing any act of sorcery against him. He set to work on his plan. Nail after nail began to fall out of its hole at the slightest touch on his boat. As he held each nail in his fingers and examined it, it would snap into rusted flakes the moment the least bit of pressure was applied to it. Looking at the pile of rust he had gathered, he realised he was doomed to a hermit's life on the island. He confirmed his fate when he started checking the joinery. The wire binding he had so meticulously woven at the joins, now also disintegrated, and all that was left underneath were trace-mark stains of rust.

He strove on until he eventually found what he feared would most stop him from ever leaving the island. The timber, piece by piece of his beautiful, almost seaworthy creation was crumbling apart with white ants. Could you believe it? Where did these mongrels come from? Will Phantom plundered the island for white ants. He dug like a ferret with his bare hands until blood poured from his fingers: Until he proved the island itself would crumble with termites. A dream come true! More or less a nightmare. This nightmare saw the island fall to the bottom of the ocean at four o'clock in the morning. He sat around relying on the idea of being saved. Others would save him he believed. There was a relentlessness in his belief in salvation. Of all the bits and pieces of uncharted land or floating objects that nobody cared about in the world's ocean, he wished his would be found.

He sat forever scanning the horizons for ships passing on the high seas. Sure enough, in days and months, many ships and boats appeared. He saw passing container ships laden with ballast and others returning heavy with ore. Each ploughed through the high seas on its own charted highway, all equally oblivious to his floating piece of rubbish. His dim, life-wearied eyes saw passing pirate ships and boats trading in human traffic. Desperate boat people crowded these nightmarish vessels but they were not interested in looking at wreckage as they passed by so close he could see their eyes scanning. They only had eyes for a safer place from wherever they had come.

He saw faces scarred by the knives carried in the hands of pirates who stood in front of the half-clothed and naked, slashed wretchedness of victims they had imprisoned. Wherever they were to be jettisoned, no one in all likelihood regarded his island of wreckage as a place for them to go. Watching them pass by he felt asphyxiated, as though there was not enough air in the atmosphere for all of them to share. Through their vacant eyes he saw a kaleidoscope of nightmares. Could he, or could they, believe all nightmares belonged to him?

On these occasions, the spirits of the people returned in dreams, breaking waves in their ghostly boats, through images which grew more distorted, as though the island was surrounded by the mirrors of a travelling sideshow, and it was not until these victims of catastrophe were falling upon him that he recognised their fate. He was told they were dead people on their way to hell. Was this hell? Was this hell? He screamed out in such dreadful fright when he woke up from these dreams, longing and crying for the eyes without hope to disappear forever.

The salvation he awaited was a stranger's voice. A sailor, fisherman, or coastal surveillance officer shouting, 'Ahoy! Land oy.' And he? He saw himself running for what was left of his stockpile of salvaged clothing rotting in the high humidity, and putting something on to make himself decent for his rescue. What could be otherwise? The plan of his rescue had been rehearsed in repetitive, alternating visions of the preferred future. Oh! How he would run up and down the shoreline, waving his arms, shouting, *See me! See me!* And thinking, for it crossed his mind: What would he be? What would the discoverers call the sole inhabitant on his sinking oasis: a native? But the only real discovery being made was by the flocks of seagulls, settling in greater numbers each day, until they reached vast proportions, taking over every nook and cranny on his floating island of junk.

Chapter 14
Coming back

F ar out at sea in gentle swells, a catboat lolled through forty days and nights of good fortune, while the wise man, Norm Phantom, steered the rudder and never slept. He spurned the night's call for men to drift away into the arms of a merciful sleep.

All the lucky countrymen on dry land slept soundly in their whatjamajigs: far away from the old town of Desperance on their bits of dog-chewed foam, which flew them around at night to any place in the world they wanted, cheap – for free. Rain-sodden blankets rolled dirt-poor old people on the ground. In your dreams, if you thought they were going back to Desperance again. They were not like Norm Phantom, losing so much sleep in the process to get there as quick as he could. Lucky dreams leave behind asphyxiation and pneumonic coughs, hunger and the rest of it. They were skidding through twilight along a moonbeam's golden gleam, or a star's silvery reflection, into the dreamworld deep under the black ocean of time to fall home on a fossilised, ancient, primeval lake in the Gulf of Carpentaria. If people thought about things like this all day it might cause one hell of a fight about land and all kinds of things.

Very different indeed for Norm rowing over the shadowy surface where sleeping men sunk into deadly illusions. Not him though. He could last forty days and nights without a wink of sleep. His eyelids were not half hooded as they were during the day when the sun would beat straight down on the little green boat struggling along with a breeze in the sail that might have been blown by a mouse. At night his eyes popped open, becoming wide-awake saucers like a nocturnal owl, if you noticed him sitting out there in the sea, on the cross bench of that bit of a boat, watching the stars, navigating the way home.

The amazing thing was, on the fortieth night at sea, Norm was so close to his stranded son Will Phantom, it was a wonder he had not seen him. Only four kilometres west of Will's sinking flotation. Yet, who could quibble with distance? An inch is an inch on a ruler though it measured forty or four kilometres, whichever way you looked at it.

Norm did not sail merrily along to his prescribed destiny, nor fortunately, feel aghast with being lost. These were waters foreign to him but he felt comfortable, just as if he was at home with the brightly lit stars above him. Quietly, he sailed, because he was a quiet person, routinely occupying himself with whatever he had done every night of many, many years of his life when he communicated with the night sky travelling east to west, across the celestial sphere.

The bright Southern Cross which had long ago abandoned Jerusalem, now sat low above the horizon to the west. Having a mind for the memory of all names, Norm also knew the formation as Crux Australis, whose brightest stars bridged a waterhole where a giant rock cod lives, a dark patch in the sky known as the Coal Sack. He then looked across and saw Delta and Gramma Crucis, the Pointers – Alpha and Beta Centauri. Elias must have been close by, because Norm felt as though he was up in these heavens, travelling with them. He looked at *Kudawedangire* – Pleiades, or the Seven Sisters. Yes, Orion – the hunter was there, already starting to appear in the eastern horizon. He also instantly recognised the slant in the line of three stars of the Saucepan which he knew spills the rain in January. Earlier, he watched Orion's killer Scorpio prowling around in the western sky. Soon, soon, he said to himself, knowing when he could clearly see the hunter's two dogs, the big canine and the little Canis Minor, he would know he should have reached Desperance a long time ago. But, it was visible crossing inside of Sagittarius, where he saw the planet Mars, and he talked to the constellation about how pleased he had been with the mild-flowing currents.

Occasionally, he would look down at Hope who was sleeping on the deck boards. Although she slept fitfully, she had not moved since the planet Venus rose in the evening sky. With her head down, looking in the bowels of the boat lest there were reflections on the water, she said she could not look at *Yidimil*. Norm believed she must have told a different version of this same story a million times to Bala. He could not look at the evening star or any *jinkiji*. Rubbish! What a load of bullshit. Where did you hear that from girl? Ah! Cock and bull story. Every word she spoke could have come out of old Joseph's lying mouth. Ever heard that old imposter say a truthful word? Oh! How Norm Phantom wished he could glue that mouth shut. Who would believe anything Joseph Midnight had to tell anybody? Eh! Good job! Save the peace. Let her sleep.

If she was afraid of the evening star, Norm quickly discovered, she was afraid of the morning star as well. When she woke up before dawn, without fail, she looked east until the star set in the west. 'Hey! Look at that over there,' he would exclaim, pretending to see something in the direction of the star, but she would appear not to hear him.

She again told him she only talked of truths, such as there being a death in the marriage if someone looked at this star. 'J'sus! Well! I'll be,' he teased, encouraging her to argue some more with him. What had occurred to Norm was how her beliefs, so different to his own, were so tied into cause and effect. In her defence she listed every death of a spouse she had ever known. People die. It was not unusual. 'Yeah, what about so and so, didn't he die?' And another, so on and so forth. 'So, how can you tell someone looked at the stars?' he would ask out of interest. The script was important to Norm Phantom. While he sought change he wanted her answer not to change. She would say of course you could tell because she had been told that was what happened. 'I suppose ya old grandfather told you that, eh?' Yes, that's right. Good! Norm Phantom loved the wall.

Even so, he was surprised to discover how afraid of the sea she was. He had never seen a person so frightened of sea water. On the first night after they had left the island, from the moment the air grew cooler on the skin with the onset of dusk, she had become more and more silent. She said the coolness in the night air was like dead people touching her. He watched each night while she would try to cover herself and Bala with a piece of canvas that she used for shade in the day. The little boy twisted and turned restlessly all night long while she continued reorganising their cover. Her nocturnal hiding ended when finally, the morning star went down to the sea in the western horizon.

No heart and no patience with any of her imaginings, Norm told her to keep her wild thoughts to herself. She said she would. It was her problem. She said she knew it was her problem. Did anyone ask him to interfere in her problem? They needed to save themselves first. 'We are not fish, you know.' She said she knew they were not fish. 'I am not a simpleton.' Norm said nothing. He had no need to speculate about the genes of the Midnight clan. 'You are a good boy Bala,' he called.

Throughout those mild nights on their journey back to Desperance, while all Hope dreamt of was to be reunited with

Will, Norm used the advantage of clear skies to practice his astronomical calculations. Sitting in the quietness of the night, he would use his fingers at arms-length level with the horizon in front of his eyes to calculate fractions of movement in the daily change of his guiding stars. This was the only way he was able to affirm his calculations for the distance of their journey. But she refused to look up to the night sky, saying she was frightened, in case someone might die. He had drawn many maps of the skies in the sand for Bala and tested him with questions every day before their departure. Whenever he looked at Hope he felt annoyed at her pig-headed beliefs. He knew if anything should happen to him, Hope would not be able to finish their journey. She would change course and head for the wilderness in the ocean looking for Will. He only hoped one thing. When she killed herself with her father's stories, and if Bala had not perished along with her, the boy would remember what to do to survive.

Quite often in the night at sea she cried in her sleep. Distracted, he would look down at his daughter-in-law, sigh, and say – 'Quiet now.' Then, before continuing his nocturnal preoccupation with measurements, he checked the child had not been woken. She huddled the child like a frightened pup from nightfall. Her face vulnerable. She was the first person from the other side Norm Phantom had a chance to look at this close since his eyeballing days with her grandfather, Joseph Midnight. Vulnerability, the delicate, girlish face of the enemy. Never singular. Plural. And all he had left. The weak enemy was no explanation of how this girl who could cry all day long had somehow survived the sea. Alas! Norm, do not search your mind again, for however she had come to be alive at all comes to naught against your parallels. Stay blinded. She possessed a razor-sharp mind for others to see. Sandstorms blew inside his head, to which she was oblivious. Unfettered by old men's thoughts, she huddled her son. The boy who too did not look into the sky. Who would if he saw his mother fall from the sky and disappear into the sea.

When they found her after the cyclone, walking through a mountain of rubble and bubble of foam that lined the beach, she claimed nothing of the sort of falling from the sky had ever happened to her. She said she was just out, having a bit of a walk. She said she had no memory of ever falling anywhere and on that first encounter, she had even turned around, and started accusing Norm of coming onto the island uninvited as soon as she had turned her back for five minutes.

Nevermind that she could not discount five days of absence because she said, she knew what she was doing. 'What was that?' he asked, wondering what on earth was wrong with her. She eyed him with Joseph Midnight's eyes. She said that he was trying to steal her son away right under her nose. 'I know you are playing around with his mind with all that mumbo jumbo stuff.' *Nobody would survive if they fell out of the sky?* He laughed and called her an idiot.

She laughed at Norm's questioning like any normal person would, with a perplexed look naturally spread on her face, and because he was Norm Phantom, used to getting his own way, the more he questioned her, the more she tried to act normal. He became even more suspicious of her. So! A monster. This was what a low-life like Midnight produced. She raised her shoulders at him then hunched them together. Having thought of a new line of attack, she said she knew what was happening: he was trying to demonise her by connecting her to the spirit world of the sea. She said she felt frightened of him. So, she went away, camping in the rubble at night along the beach, where she stayed, sulking until things settled between them. Gradually, as the king tides began eroding the rubble that contained the pieces to fit the jigsaw of their salvation, she started to help Norm to salvage whatever he required to rebuild the green boat.

No great conversation of how, why, and so forth flowed between them since neither needed to speak to the other while they worked. The grey shale, granite calcite, embedded in the island energised them to toil like demons on Norm's wrecked green boat. But questions sprung out of the natural geology. Would they sail back to Desperance so that each could return to their respective sides of town? The more Norm slapped and banged the boat into shape, the more his mind became possessed by the mystery of how Hope did not die at sea. Even if she had fallen from the sky, no normal person (which she was) could survive in the dangerous Gulf waters for very long. 'Wasn't that true, Dad?' she mused, childlike to the core. Did anyone hear that? Liberties found new meaning outside of Desperance. The more they became acquainted, the more carefully he posed his questions to her, and the more her words danced back, with a lot of liberties too. Finally, one day, Norm could not stand it anymore. His nostrils flared with hot air and he snapped at her: 'How would I know anything? Me! I only got my education from reading the Christian Bible.' Had he heard anyone giving her permission to step inside his family? Eh!

Well! For all it mattered, he thought the girl was stupid. He had tried to awaken her earlier in the night to show her the phosphorescence lighting the water. Another good sign to be in the presence of the ancestral serpent. What did you do that for? She clung to the inside of the boat believing any minute that the boat would be overturned and they would drown. He had to tell her it had gone away and eventually she became calm. He told himself he had to acknowledge that the girl was petrified of water and would very likely make his grandson afraid of water. So, without much contemplation over the matter, or bothering to consult her, he decided he would take Bala and look after him. The boy would not be left to live with simpletons. Other people could live alongside their chitchat if they wanted to and be blinded forever with stuff like that. He glanced past Hope and realised he still felt mighty angry all the same with whatnot now, with a child involved. 'Whatnot got a mad wife because he can't see straight.' He hissed under his breath at the expanse of ocean, as though he was talking to his son. 'Whatnot while I am alive I own my blood.'

One time, weeks before the sea journey, while they worked on the all-consuming, energy-draining reconstruction of the boat, he told her finally, 'You'd be flat out remembering what happened yesterday let alone what happened days before.' Again, she taunted, parroting his own words: *If you please how could anyone come walking out of the sea?* He never mentioned it again, because suddenly he thought of Elias watching him and it dawned on him, there and then on that strange beach of rubbish that rattled when the water rushed through it at high tide, that possibly a guiding hand was manipulating the strings, and they were nothing more than puppets. Someone blew the words out of their mouths. Some hand coalescing his mind created this unwanted episode in his life. He stared into that moving mouth, squinting with the glare of the sun, staring at that grotesque, talking doll who had words that flowed like a river.

But he knew if they were to leave the island, work must continue and they had to do it together. First he ignored her when she claimed that the boat was hers since she found it on her island. Then, just to break the monotonous chatter, he asked her if she believed in the Bible. She said: 'No, naturally, I don't believe in all of that whitefella stuff.' He told her he believed in the Bible because the white people had prospered by believing in what the Bible had told them. 'You remember the story about the sea parting for the people to walk through it? No? Of course you people wouldn't know that story either, I suppose, because you people talk, talk, talk and you learn nothing.

'The sea could part and a man could walk on water.' What was more, he told her before she was even born, his own two good eyes actually saw the phenomenon explained in the white man's Bible.

'I was walking if you please, straight out of a world that belonged to marine creatures and what have you swimming about in sea water, who had made enemies of men in the history of the Dreamtime. But, that wouldn't happen to you because you do not know these stories. God don't make miracles happen for people with bad blood filtering through their veins.'

She asked why he thought that, and he said it was because he knew blood like anything, just like a forensic scientist. She had certain behaviour which was from having bad blood. The truth of the matter was that Norm believed someone like Joseph Midnight did not have real blood. It was gammon blood. Thin blood. The kind of weak blood which could not tell fortunes, or make predictions about the future, and could not have premonitions such as if someone was dead or alive, calling out for people to go and find them. So, all that was not thick blood. Thin blood was uncomfortable on the sea. Having had all the time in the world to study what he was talking about, he told her he was thankful to God for this opportunity to justify his beliefs. He said he reckoned the Almighty had only put bad blood in a mangy dog to handicap it in life so it could not do anything to save itself from living worse than a dog. Fuming, she said nothing. She just chucked a few things around instead. He said if it was God's will, he would have to listen to her talk her mad talk until the cows came home, and he reckoned it was the devil's lingo that goes on talking shit, non-stop. Under the circumstances Norm Phantom thought he ignored her the best he could, but understand: he had a predicament to overcome and needed her help.

Mad talk, was what Norm called her while he worked. Listening to her hurrying him along all day long so she could go and find Will: 'Whatever happened to Will, we's got to go quickly and find him.' He was sick and tired of hearing her. He had to think about his own sanity too or he would go mad, so he pretended she did not exist. She begged him to listen to her and she began to have illusions – claiming to be possessed of dreams where she saw Will standing in the distance, trying to reach them. Then she would retell the dream, every detail caressed and described, until hours would slip by and the dream would still be there scraping at nothing and shooting up through the old man's nostrils like sand, suffocating him, flowing through him like boiling water, until he, unable to stand it any longer, dropped his tools and hurried away. She would cry all day long that she had seen the white wash of Will's junk pile island floating further away. Norm said he had not heard of anything like it and he believed he had heard a lot of things in his lifetime about things you find on the sea. Things a girl like her would never even be able to dream up. 'No,' he said, 'I never seen a thing like that before and I don't suppose I am ever going to either.'

What surprised him even more was how she could describe the floating island in every last detail as though she had been involved in its construction. Piece by piece, she was able to describe the angle, position and degree of measurement in the pile of junk, like a carpenter. She told him of the pieces that came from buildings in Desperance which were wedged into the island. Even bits from his own home she described and he became annoyed with her crazy ideas that the town was gone. When did that happen? She said she saw dead people trapped inside the island as well. It was a strange story which mystified Norm. Sometimes the waves rolling onto the beach spill their stories right at your feet. But she did not have one dream to explain whether she had fallen from the sky or not. He could not let her fool his judgement. This strange dream was to entice him to go looking for Will. She was off her head. He would not let himself be enticed by her. Intrigue will not get you anywhere and Norm knew he had the boat to finish working on. He doggedly worked on regardless, so they could be where they were now.

So on and so forth. It ended with Norm, Hope and the grandchild well inside their voyage, journeying with lee tides, on a route plotted through the Milky Way sky. Since she was constantly in his face, it felt different to travelling alone for Norm Phantom, who never cared for company at sea, except one or two he claimed, but he was blowed if he could trust other people. How she niggled him but what choice did he have? He was no stranger to vigilance and with so much ample time to spare with this extra burden to bear, he immersed himself in a ridiculous-looking search for any clue whatsoever that would prove there and then, that there was a clandestine presence on board trying to do away with him. Remember you do not always see what you seek.

In many ways it was a terrible journey. After the ninety-ninth time he had torn the boat and its contents apart in his mind in the course of a day, he told himself to be patient. Never give up! That was the spirit of the man. While it was not clear as day, Norm truly believed there was someone else on board who could possibly be Joseph Midnight chasing his own blood; stranger things were known to happen. He told her how somebody could downsize to the tiniest reminder of himself, as any enemy worth his salt would: Oh! Yes! Laughing his head off inside a matchbox or whatever. He had heard about these things, but she said it was news to her.

'What did you bring on board with you?' he would ask Hope a hundred times a day, and receive the same answer if she was in the mood to speak.

'I told you I brought nothing with me and I aren't going to tell you again,' she would snap at him in her rediscovered vicious sharp tongue when it suited her.

She told him to stop talking to her. She said she could not be bothered listening to his silly stories anymore. Well! He did shut his mouth but it did not mean he let the feeling he had in his guts go to rot. His mind raced around like a fast car and it was telling him one, two, three: they might never reach Desperance if he was not careful. So, he watched her sleep on her secrets and hoped his God would hand him a key. But miracles did not automatically happen to anyone unless they already had the key. Elias was a miracle. He had walked out of the sea. But how could she have fallen out of the sky? He could tell she was no miracle and he would tell that to anyone. Someone had given her a key.

Ah! Bala! Mellowing at the thought, he looked down at his sleeping grandson with his skinny limbs tucked around him like a ball. There, he only saw the country of sea people, yet he realised that as the reality of biology would have it, the otherside was flowing side by side with Westside in that child. Disadvantage and advantage: what could this bring? Very special care would be needed to keep an eye on this child.

He looked through the darkness of the sea and, saw very clearly that Will was not going to be easy to find, no matter what Hope tried in her bag of tricks to lure him on in her search. In his heart of hearts he knew she could not guide him to Will because she did not come from the sea. He knew they could not sail on forever. There was no trust between them. The currents were changing and soon, the Wet season would bring the cyclones again and he felt certain, if this happened, who knows where they would end up. Back where they started? On the other side of the world? Would they become Elias in reverse, condemned to live the remainder of their lives in a purgatory of revisiting, duplicating the wars of all the peoples through the ages of time?

For many days he had felt a jingling of hot blood running through his veins, and he recognised a sensation he knew already, of the sea dragging him towards home. He knew they were close now, and he felt it as though he was nearly there. Soon, soon, he kept telling himself, riding out the curse in his gut. And, he waited, watching for the moment when the star of the giant fish would disappear low over the sky, directly above Desperance. This was the star that Elias had been following for years until one fearful night, he lost his boat in a storm. The old mariner had called the star *Fomalhaut*, the brightest in the constellation of Piscis Austrini which followed the water carrier's jug of Aquarius. Norm knew it too as the star of navigators, or the Southern Fish. It was the groper who swam from the sea at certain times of the year to the sky and down again, falling back into the shallows of its groper's hole.

This was it. Ahead, just to the south...the fish sank. On seeing the star sink into the sea, he pinpointed the location. Now he knew he was very close to land. He would navigate the coastline back to Desperance in the morning. He dropped the sail, and relaxing for once, he waited until dawn. In this utter quietness of becalmed waters, he heard the distant sounds of frogs all calling together from the land. He listened more intently and was surprised how these amphibians could be heard so far out at sea. Even though he remembered how densely the frogs populated Desperance, it seemed to him as he listened more carefully, that there must have been an extraordinary explosion in their numbers in town this year. Ah! The good rains, he thought. It seemed logical on that still night, sitting there at sea, that the breeze should carry their song to him. He wondered if Sinbad the Sailor had returned home voyage after voyage to such joy. So! Sweet was the song of frogs, he could not believe it was this sound he had missed most of all in the time he had been away.

When he saw the first faint light silently rising at dawn, Norm scanned the sea to sight land to the south. What he finally saw was not what he was looking for. There was no sandbar. There were no mangroves. Yonder no tree country. Through the red light of dawn, he saw the shores of a flattened landscape which the cyclone had left in its wake. Hope and Bala were now awake, and the three of them stared at the low, flat mark along the southern horizon. Bala said it was a big, yellow snake. Hope said nothing. Norm told them they were very close to Desperance.

Hours later, after sailing further along the coastline, he was ready to bring the boat into land. The little tattered sail made of dried, salted shark skin caught a light breeze and quickly, the boat glided through the water towards land. Hope and Bala stared ahead at a landscape which meant nothing to them. Being used to the stoical silence of the salt-hardened face of Norm, they did not expect him to say anything about the wilderness they were approaching. Behind them, they did not see the look of caution on Norm's face as he exercised great care with his right hand, steering the rudder.

The surface of the water was so smooth, it felt as though the boat was sliding over silk. Bala looked into the flowing seagrasses in the waters under the boat and when suddenly he saw the giant fish, he screamed with excitement. Norm looked over the side and both of them saw perhaps a hundred gropers swimming under the boat. The fish followed the boat through the deeper waters, until it hit the sand. Norm jumped over the side and towed the boat through the mud towards the high-tide mark, still more than a kilometre away.

With the boat secured on the wet land, Norm stared ahead, trying to survey the landscape for familiar landmarks. In every direction he looked he could not discover one familiar feature of Desperance. He turned to Hope and said absentmindedly, 'Perhaps we will see something soon.' For one moment, he had thought Hope might be questioning his judgement by her silence.

Could he be wrong? 'No! No! This is right. I was right,' he mumbled, still confident that he had navigated correctly. They were home.

They began walking on the empty land. Ahead, there was nothing. Norm watched the excitement on the small boy's face as he ran wild, pleased to be safe on land, and shouting for all he was worth at all the frogs jumping out of his way. Hope looked at the flattened moonscape but did not show that she had one skerrick of interest in what had happened to the town. Norm instinctively called Bala to him and he hoisted him on his shoulders, then walked ahead, tramping through the watery clay mud, towards the invisible town.

Somewhere, as he walked, Norm realised he could only hear his own feet slurping through the mud, and he knew that she was gone. He almost paused, almost stopped to look around, but he walked on. He wanted to call after her – demand she come back. Tell her she was stupid. He nearly let his temper fly. Every muscle in his body ordered him to go after her and drag her back. But each time he turned to go back, he was blinded by the sun. The intensity of its white light hitting the water, reflected back in his eyes as though a shield had been put up between him and Hope, forced him to turn back towards the land.

Unable to see anything except a blinding darkness, he held Bala tightly on his shoulders and stumbled on away from the sea, until the moment passed, and he opened his eyes into a reddish haze. He knew he could not interfere with other people's dreams. He said nothing, not to upset Bala yet, and let her go. But he heard her fear, gasping for breath, running back to the boat. He heard the boat dragging through sand towards the outgoing tide.

It was at this point he started to believe in her and even how a woebegotten people like the other side could rise above themselves with audacity to discover hope in their big empty souls. He smiled, knowing she was going to find Will before it was too late with that crazy map she had inside her head. She could go. The journey was hers to chart. 'Good luck to you girl,' he said silently. 'You bring him home.'

The red glowing waters around the boat began to swarm until the boat looked as though it was being propelled on the back of something solid through the water: the groper fish circling the boat, building up speed, crossing each other under the boat, picking the boat up and moving it back to sea through the surging flow of the changing tide. Hope rowed with all of her might with the outgoing tide. She was so blinded by her mission she did not see the gropers helping her.

In his heart, Norm knew he had no more journeys to make. Well! Not for the moment. He continued walking ahead, down his memory of the main street of Desperance. He was met by the bony, hollow-ribbed, abandoned dogs of the town that had run to the hills and back again after the cyclone. Now, having appeared from nowhere, they roamed along streets that no longer existed, searching for their owners. They did not bark or howl. The shock of the cyclone had left them like this: speechless, dumbfounded, unable to crack a bark. Unable to emit a sound out of their wide-opened mouths. Hurling a string of abuse, Norm sent them back to their invisible yards where they sat miserably, waiting for him to go away. He put Bala down on the ground and they walked towards Westside.

'One day,' he said to the boy, 'your Mum and Dad are going to come and get you after the grass grows green, and when the clouds of grasshoppers have come and eaten the grass down and died in the wintertime, and when you have caught one big, fat barramundi in the lagoon. Can you wait until then?'

The boy thought about all of these eventualities, where the enigma of time sidestepped desire and ran away from dreams. His face lit into a smile as he looked up at the big man surveying the flood plains. All dreams come true somehow, Norm murmured, sizing up the flattened landscape, already planning the home he would rebuild on the same piece of land where his old house had been, among the spirits in the remains of the ghost town, where the snake slept underneath.

'I reckon we will go home then,' he said. So, they walked in mud away from the town left to the dogs that tried to howl for their owners. Neither spoke, because neither would have heard the other. It was much better to listen to the mass choir of frogs – green, grey, speckled, striped, big and small, dozens of species all assembled around the two seafarers, as they walked.

It was a mystery, but there was so much song wafting off the watery land, singing the country afresh as they walked hand in hand out of town, down the road, Westside, to home.

Acknowledgements

I would like to thank my good friends in Central Australia and the Gulf of Carpentaria, particularly David Ross and Tracker Tilmouth for their support, and Paul Memmott who gave valuable advice whenever I called.

I am deeply grateful to Nicholas Jose, and to my agent Rose Creswell, who was the first person to read the manuscript and whose enthusiasm and professional advice gave me strength and confidence to continue my work.

I am also blessed to have worked with two of the finest editors in Australia – Bruce Sims and Ivor Indyk – who at different stages in the development of the book contributed their insight, understanding and impeccable judgement.

Gavan Breen's valuable work with the Waanyi language was a great resource for me to draw upon in bringing the words of our language into the novel.

I am also grateful to the Aboriginal and Torres Strait Islander Arts Board of the Australia Council for their generous support.

This project has been assisted by the Australian Government through the Australia Council, its arts funding and advisory body.

Australian Government

Australia Council
for the Arts